ROOMMATES

OLA TUNDUN

Storm
PUBLISHING

Ebook ISBN: 978-1-80508-080-0
Paperback ISBN: 978-1-80508-081-7

Cover design: Leah Jacobs-Gordon
Cover images: Leah Jacobs-Gordon

Published by Storm Publishing.
For further information, visit:
www.stormpublishing.co

To all the women that carried, dragged, encouraged, humoured, challenged, accompanied and led me to this place – I love you.

PROLOGUE

Please. No. Not Again.

My eyes fly open in my soaked bed. I feel the heavy weight on my chest before my windpipe starts to restrict. I lie, frozen on my back, unable to move or make a sound.

Let it be over soon, please.

Slow trickles of tears make their way from my eyes and pool in my ears before dripping slowly into my ear canal, where the ringing is getting louder.

I know what I'm supposed to do, but I can't think past my pounding heart.

I will myself to breathe, but I can't.

I just want it to be over, but I know that it will get worse before it gets better.

'Help.'

My silent cry disappears as a forced exhale through the open windows into the dark night.

I attempt to stretch my trembling fingers to reach for him but I can't move.

'Jas?'

Nothing but restricted air escapes my throat.
As soon as the room starts to spin, I force my eyes shut.
Let it be over soon, please.

ONE

ARIELLA

I wake up before the sun and the first thing I see is him, like I have every morning for the last couple of years. I scan his sleeping boyish profile, his short, sandy-blond hair, rough from a good night's sleep; and then his face, from his thick eyelashes to his slightly parted mouth. My stomach still flutters at the sight of him. Careful not to disturb his peace, I leave our bed to turn on the shower. As I wait for the spray to warm up, I study the exhausted creature reflected back at me. I cannot let my nerves get the better of me. I made up my mind in the small hours of this morning that I am going to have to hurt the person I love the most today.

Drenched by the heavy rain outside, I walk into the expansive glass and steel lobby of my office building, and order a hibiscus tea in the café. While I wait, I look at the noticeboard and take down a little note advertising a room in a shared flat. I fold it neatly and put it in my bag, along with the others I've liberated over the last three weeks.

Large en-suite bedroom to rent in Hampstead. Caleb ext. 5645. Do Not Remove!!!

'He's going to lose his shit when he finds out who it is. He was here last Friday, accusing us of taking it down,' says the café manager.

I smile apologetically.

'Don't worry, we didn't say anything.' She winks and gives me my tea. 'Why do you keep taking it down? Did he piss you off? Because apparently, there's a growing line.'

'No, nothing like that. I've been thinking of going for the apartment. I'll sort it out today, I promise.'

'That's a shame. We've had an entertaining couple of weeks, watching him replace it.' She giggles.

I thank her for the tea and make my way to the bank of elevators that services the building's forty floors.

I've always loved the way the lights flicker on as I step out onto the twenty-second floor; home to Ivory Bow, the international marketing and communications agency I work for. It's a busy, fun office, so the silence that greets me when I am the first person at work is the highlight of my day. No small talk, no distractions and, most importantly, I have space to think.

I get to my desk and switch on my Mac. My diary, event projects and task alerts present themselves and I scan for any urgent items before I settle down to prepare for our daily 10 a.m. meeting. My department is responsible for creating luxurious brand experiences for our global clients, and 'The 10 a.m.' is our often stressful, daily company update meeting.

'Ariella Mason! I swear one of these days we're going to find out that you're secretly living here!' comes a loud Scottish voice, followed by laughter.

Lara is in. She announces her arrival by shaking the bun on the top of my head, then sits on my desk. She places one Louboutin'd foot on the floor, leaving the other swinging in the air.

Lara is what most people would call a bombshell. She stands at five-eight at least, with wild, curly red hair, green doe eyes and full lips. Today, those lips are blood red; I can tell she's had a good weekend. While Lara fits the Ivory Bow employee visual perfectly, she also breaks all the generic beauty rules. Most of the employees here are worryingly slim, extremely manicured and perfectly polite. Lara is beautifully feral-looking, confidently curvy, with a vocabulary that makes sailors sound like choirboys.

'Babe, you're really going to need to start making an effort. What's going on with this bun? Also, a bit of make-up isn't going to kill you, you know,' she teases, giving my hair one last poke with her index finger.

I know where this is going. Lara has been trying to give me a makeover for as long as I have known her.

'Someone's got to break the mould around here.' I smirk.

'I thought that was *my* job!'

Lara is my best friend at work and always manages to make me laugh at the beginning of the day. She is popular in the office, although scary to some, and I admire that she is always unapologetically herself – usually up to some kind of mischief, armed with her delightfully dirty laugh. We are total opposites.

I'd hoped joining the company would make me more outgoing, but found the permanently upbeat, unwaveringly enthusiastic 'work hard, play hard' culture intimidating; so I retreated instead. Lara and I started at the same time and, while she took to the company like a duck to water, I found myself drowning. If Lara hadn't basically forced a friendship on me by stalking me into submission and dragging me everywhere with her in those first few months, it would have ended up being an isolating place to work.

What I lacked in social status, however, I made up for in hard work. In my twenty months at the company, I've had three promotions, with increasing project and team responsibility each time. The last promotion was the most uncomfortable, effectively making me Lara's boss. Not that you could tell. I went through a full week of vomit-inducing worry before I told her, convinced that I'd lose the only friend I had. When I eventually did, I waited for our relationship to deteriorate. Instead, it brought us closer together.

She pokes my arm. 'Good weekend?'

'Yes, thanks. You?'

I know that the next ten minutes are going to belong to Lara, so I settle in. Lara works with the music accounts and is always at a festival, gig, concert or party. She works hard, long and late but recovers incredibly quickly from challenging events, usually involving high volumes of alcohol.

'The festival was awesome! I wish you could've come. The music was amazing, the clients were on their best behaviour, VIP and backstage were packed. I barely did any work!'

'Sounds fantastic.' I flick my eyes at the digital clock at the bottom of my screen. Yeah, that document is going to remain unfinished.

'Don't lie, it would've been your worst nightmare!' She laughs and rolls her eyes.

She's not wrong. This is what I love about Lara. She knows, loves and accepts me for who I am.

'...And I assume you were on your best behaviour, Lara Scott?'

Lara looks around, moves closer and drops her voice to a whisper. 'Define best behaviour...'

'What did you do?' I cover my eyes with my hands.

Lara always treads a very fine line. It is another of the things I admire about her, but it also makes me very nervous.

'I may have been seduced...'

'Nothing new there.'

'CrimeSpree may have—'

'Lara. Please tell me you didn't cross the only line you're not meant to cross, with a client you are responsible for, while you were working with them. You're supposed to be keeping *him* out of trouble. And he's engaged! And he's creepy. And you're gay. And... goodness, I can't...!'

Lara starts laughing.

'You're joking?'

'I didn't sleep with CrimeSpree.'

'Phew. He's always sniffing around you. That "sexy body" song he sang at your desk when you became his account manager was ghastly. Especially when he grabbed his crotch.' I chuckle, recalling the performance. We get them all here.

'Yeah. Yuck!'

Lara and I burst out laughing and relief floods through me.

'So, don't freak out. I slept with his fiancée,' Lara says, biting the edge of her bottom lip guiltily.

'That's it, Lara. You need to leave my desk.'

I start to pat the side of her perfectly round bottom lodged on my desk, to shoo her off. She can't keep doing this to me. I keep enough of her secrets. This one is too much.

'I know... but Aari, she's beautiful. And clever. She's tough, angry and sexy. She's just...' Lara sighs, and I'm not buying it.

'Different? Haven't met anyone like her? You'll be bored and screening her calls in a week!'

'I'm thinking of handing the CrimeSpree account to someone else.'

This is new.

'Lara, she's engaged to your client. One who chooses to call himself CrimeSpree and makes his living churning out chart-middling hits glorifying his felonious life.'

Lara inspects a long, red nail and waves my concerns away.

'Oh please. His real name is Cyril Sparks and his middle name, by the by, is Bertrand. He lived at home with his mother until last year, and that tattoo? Custom stick-on. He's scared of needles.'

'You're unbelievable, Lara.' I cross my arms.

'I have no plans to run away into the sunset together, but I like her enough to see if this might go somewhere. Let's face it, this shit could get me fired. It was stressful enough hiding from CrimeSpree all weekend. We almost got found out yesterday morning. Nightmare!'

I stare open-mouthed at Lara. She has outdone herself this time.

'So, I was wondering...'

'No, Lara. I'm not babysitting CrimeSpree.'

'It's only for—'

'Break a leg. Get hit by a bus. Have a killer hangover. I'd happily cover. This, no.'

'Go on, please?'

She pouts and I ignore her. 'Pout all you like. I'm immune.' I wave her off. Her little tricks don't work on me, but it doesn't stop her from trying. Every single time.

'Fine. I'll figure it out. What did you do this weekend?'

By comparison, I live a pretty dull life. This weekend, however, like the last six, was painful to get through, but I don't know how to tell her what's been on my mind.

'Jasper was working, so...'

'*Again?!* Ugh. He may be the last of the absolute decent ones left, but a work-free weekend won't kill him.'

'It's fine. I went riding on Saturday morning and spent the afternoon working out some recipes. It was too late to do anything on Saturday night when he got back home, but we had Sunday lunch with his mom and went for a walk afterwards. It was nice.' I force a smile.

'He's so lucky to have locked you down. If it was someone else— shit! It's almost ten! I haven't done my report!' Lara gets up abruptly, taking my pen pot with her. She scrambles to pick the mess up. 'Lunch at one?'

'Oh yes!' I smile. I can't help it.

'I'll have a solution by then, naturally concocted behind your back, so you can have plausible deniability, don't you worry.'

After navigating the 10 a.m., I spend the morning swallowing my anxiety and keeping it together as I stare obsessively at one of three glass domes in the office, trying to figure out how to approach the conversation with its resident. I only realise that it's lunchtime when Lara reappears.

'Are you pregnant?' she says, sneaking up on me and making me jump.

'No! Goodness! Why would you say that?'

'You've been in and out of the loo all morning, and it was the politest question compared to the alternatives.'

I try to force a smile.

'Seriously, Aari, what's up?'

I feel tears welling up and try to blink them away.

'Come.'

Lara grabs my hand and drags me into the bathroom. As soon as we are in, she pulls me into a warm hug and I let my tears fall.

'I know you're a secretive cow, but are you okay?'

'Yes. Just facing the fear and doing it anyway.'

Lara attempts to lighten the mood. 'Look at you, plagiarising self-help authors! You'd be a perfect fit for CrimeSpree. He's always nicking other people's lyrics. Did I mention he gives out free merchandise? I'll even buy you lunch.'

'I might skip coming down today, if that's okay?'

'Sure. I'll bring up some crisps and chocolate, so you don't starve,' she suggests.

'Seriously, you have the diet of a malnourished six-year-old.'

'I'll take that as a compliment. Now, wipe your eyes and stand tall.' Lara gives me a tissue and straightens my shirt. 'Bit of advice. Don't be afraid to look whatever is scaring you in the eye and stare it down. You'll find that once you confront it, it becomes really easy to conquer.'

I nod, keeping my emotions in.

'Little catch-up later?'

'Okay.'

With that, she gives me a kiss on the cheek and leaves. Fortified by Lara's courage, I step out of the bathroom onto the half-empty work floor and make my way to the glass dome.

TWO

CALEB

'Come in!' I respond to the knock, glancing at my computer screen to make sure that nothing incriminating or inappropriate is open.

When I joined Ivory Bow as a brand experience sales manager and moved into my glass cubicle, or 'Bow Dome' as we call it, I took great care to select one that allowed me to obscure my screen from prying eyes. Initially, I'd taken the job out of desperation, so the plan was to keep sending out my CV until something better came along. Then, I hit a lucky streak and couldn't leave. Now, I have a little idea brewing, so every once in a while, I'll work on that when it's quiet.

I am relieved when the girl walks in quietly. She shuts the door but holds on to the handle, like she has no intention of letting go. I relax a bit. She is a little fidgety, but clearly understands boundaries. She's obviously new and very junior, judging by the way she is dressed. Working in this building will soon take care of that. Before long, she'll join the tribe and find herself in clothes she can't afford, make-up her skin can't breathe through and heels she can't walk in. I smile to myself. The monster gets its way every bloody time.

'Is the room still available?'

Well, hello, straight shooter! No flirty smile, no introductions – just down to business. I like that she has just cut through all the crap, but I have absolutely no plans to rent my spare room to a girl. Even if I did, it most definitely isn't going to be her. I appraise her riding boots, ironed jeans, sky-blue button-down shirt and the tweed jacket hanging on her. Her accent suggests public school, probably bolstered with an Oxbridge degree.

She seems almost annoyed to be speaking to me; I can smell entitlement like this a mile off. Her unwavering stare and the slight tilt of her nose confirm my assessment. She must be an intern with a loaded, well-connected daddy. She expects the room to be hers already, but there's no way I am living with her. Some rejection will be good for her, so I decide to entertain myself a little.

'How did you hear about the room?'

'The staff noticeboard downstairs?'

She doesn't look like she has earned the right to be called 'staff' just yet. She looks like she volunteers at a horse stable. That jacket is very odd. Maybe she is from the countryside living magazine a few floors below.

'Sorry. The advert was for Ivory Bow employees only.'

'Advertised in the building's café?'

'Yes, sorry.'

'It's no problem. I work at Ivory Bow.'

'Also, no interns.'

'I'm not an intern.'

'Really? Where do you sit?'

She turns round and gestures to the events team. 'Over there.'

'How long have you worked here?'

'Just under two years... Can't I just send you the paperwork you need?'

She looks impatient, but stays glued to the closed door.

'How come I've never seen you?'

'I don't know, but I see you and the sales team when you give your updates every Friday at the ten a.m. So, is the room available?'

'Yes. I mean, no. The room isn't available.'

'Which is it?'

'It is, but I'm not really looking to share with a chick. You're cute and all, it's nothing personal.' I know I am being terribly blunt, but I smile and give her a wink to soften the blow.

'Please don't call me cute, and I'm not poultry. Why won't you share with a woman?'

Someone clearly didn't plan on charming their way into the apartment.

'It's more of a guys' apartment.'

'How? There are two bedrooms. The only guy in there is you.'

She's a feisty one. I find myself starting to like her as she stands there, seemingly with no intention of moving. In fact, she finally releases the handle, crosses her arms, plants her feet and shifts her hips to one side.

'I don't think having a female as a housemate is going to work for me and I really don't have to explain.'

'Listen. I need this room. I'll pay twenty per cent above whatever you're asking. I can send you three months' deposit and six months' rent in advance, within the next two hours, if we can agree to this right now. You can have priority over the living room for whatever *guys' activities* you have planned, and I'll stay out of your way in my bedroom. I am going to need the kitchen though. If I decide to cook, I'll cook for two; and, aside from staying away from any serious allergies you might have, I don't take meal requests.

'We each have our own bathrooms, so no issues there. The rest of the bills, we split down the middle. I won't be your maid, but I will do my fair share of communal cleaning. I'm giving you one minute, and if you don't take me up on my offer I'm walking out. I won't negotiate and won't make the offer again. Let's hope the hypothetical guy you'd prefer to move in with doesn't make excuses about why the apartment is always messy, or why he can't quite make the rent again this month.'

She sets the timer on her little gold and silver watch. Wait... is that a Rolex?

We look at each other and silence sits between us. When she checks her watch, I glance at the ticking second hand on my desktop's digital clock. I wait until five seconds to time.

'Fine. Deal. You're a tough one.' I laugh.

She doesn't. In fact, she looks like she is about to cry. Oh no. What have I done?

'Great. I'll use the original rent figure as a base and pop twenty per cent on top. Can I have your bank details and home address?'

She steps forward purposefully with an outstretched hand. I scribble the details down and hand the paper over. As she scans it, I deal with some additional points.

'I'll get some keys cut and the tenancy agreement over to you this week. When do you plan on moving in?'

'Today, after work, at about six thirty? It'd be great to do keys tonight, but I don't mind waiting for the agreement. Is that all right?' She allows herself to smile a little. Finally.

'I'm out tonight.'

'No problem. I'll sit outside and wait for you.'

She's not being sarcastic; she means it. This girl is running from something. I've been there, so I try not to be an arsehole.

'I can be a little late. I'll meet you at six thirty.'

'Thank you.' She exhales, backing away from me.

'You should've been on the sales team... You didn't tell me your name?'

'Ariella.'

She doesn't extend her hand for a second time. If anything, she inches closer to the door.

'You should've been on the sales team, Ariella.'

'Maybe,' she whispers.

Just before she leaves, it hits me.

'How did you know about the base rent figure? Have you been taking the advert down?'

Her embarrassment is unmistakable when she faces me. She nods slowly. 'Yes. I'm sorry.'

'Seriously?! I could've rented the room three weeks ago!'

'I know. And I'm making up for that with the twenty per cent surplus. I really am sorry.'

I don't need to end our truce with a fight, so I let it go. 'Thanks for being honest.'

She nods and leaves as quietly as she arrived. I watch her cross the office floor quickly, clutching my address to her chest.

I already know that I am definitely not going to enjoy living with her, but I have to respect the angle she came at this from. This is a business transaction and I am getting a great deal more than I was expecting. I'd already padded the rental price, expecting to be negotiated down, not offered more, so I really can't complain.

I learned, earlier than most, to focus on the result you want when it comes to getting what you need. Growing up on the wrong side of the tracks, at the tough end of the street in the beautifully jagged city that is Liverpool, will do that to you. You learn very quickly to put personal feelings aside and do whatever is needed to survive. Emotions don't pay the bills and they sure as hell won't fund a business. I'd have let Hannibal Lecter move in for twenty per cent over asking—

'*Qu'est-ce qui s'est passé?*'

Nicole. Shit. This is not going to be good. Nicole is best categorised as one of my 'friends with benefits', but the last thing anyone would class her as is friendly. Watching her stand at my office door, wearing that tight little black leather dress I like, paired with red heels, makes me think of her many benefits. Her platinum-blond hair is scraped up, with her glasses perched at the end of her nose. She has done this on purpose. She knows that I have a thing for hot teachers. I have to blink myself to the present.

'What was what?' I try to sound casually distracted and, for extra effect, look harder at my computer screen, pretending to focus on something important.

'Her.' She points to the events area, looking disgusted. 'The one with the frizzy hair that dresses like a jockey and acts like she's too important to talk to the rest of us. What was she doing in here?'

She closes the door firmly behind her and fixes me with one of her stares. I am instantly turned on. Damn.

I know I should have run from Nicole at the Christmas party. I'd been warned. Repeatedly. That night, I had every intention of staying away, but too much booze and what the guys call 'The Nicole Factor' depleted my resistance. Before I knew what was going on, I was waking up next to her.

The great thing about friends with benefits is that we know the score and enjoy each other's company. When we are alone together we have a great time, but we don't acknowledge each other outside of that neat bubble. Unfortunately, that's not the case when it comes to Nicole.

'I thought you said no contact at work,' she spits, angrily pointing a long black talon as she sits opposite me.

'And yet, here you are, Nicole,' I say, exasperated.

'Are you sleeping with her?'

'Of course not!' She's having a laugh. If I had a type, Ariella would be the opposite.

'Please don't play the "of course not" card with me. I know I'm not the only one.' Nicole is actually serious.

'Bloody hell! I'm not sleeping with her.'

'Good. You better not be, or planning to either. Not that I can imagine why you would want to.' She shivers, as if repulsed. She catches me watching her, shifts her body and quickly transforms back to vixen. 'So, are you free tonight?'

This girl is killing me.

'No, I'm not. And for the hundredth time, can we not do this at work?' I ask, frustrated, handing her a sheet of paper.

She takes it and scans it, confused.

'We're meant to be working?'

Finally, she gets it. She throws her head back, laughing. I wasn't going for hilarity.

'Caleb, everyone knows we're *good friends*. Let me know if you change your mind about meeting later. There might be a little surprise waiting for you.' She gets up, winks and leaves.

I immediately regret my hasty rejection. Her little surprises are always immensely good fun.

Yup, Nicole is trouble.

THREE

ARIELLA

I have to move fast. The minute the clock on my computer flashes 17:00, I grab my jacket, wave goodbye in Lara's general direction and make my way into a waiting black cab.

I can't stop fidgeting as we whizz through London's West End, joining bus lanes wherever possible. We turn off Tottenham Court Road and I wait impatiently for the car to stop in front of the beautiful three-storey townhouse in Fitzroy Square. I jump out, ask if the driver is happy to wait for the third time in as many minutes, and run up the steps to the front door. My hands are trembling so much, it takes four tries to get the key into the lock.

I run up two flights of the large, winding staircase until I reach the master bedroom. I dart across it, straight into the walk-in closet, and yank out my suitcase. I have been thinking about this day for a while and it dawns on me that I've been subconsciously planning my exit. All my shirts are neatly folded on one shelf and my trousers and skirts are hanging together, ready to be lifted into the case.

My underwear tips easily from the single drawer it resides in, and in the bathroom all I have to do is put my toothbrush in my washbag and zip it up. I toss my shoes into a jute bag and grab both my handbags. Seven minutes – good. I rush down the stairs, out of the door and into the cab. Just as the driver pulls off, I beg him to stop. I run back into the house and find our little noteboard. I grab the Sharpie from the fridge door and a Post-it, and scribble quickly.

I love you, I'm sorry, but I just can't. Aari x

I remove my engagement ring, placing it next to the keys I've left on the counter, before hurrying back to the waiting taxi. I am burning in hell for this.

Walking out on Jasper, my best friend, soulmate and fiancé, is devastating. Aside from my parents and brother, Jasper is the only other permanent fixture in my life. We lived next door to each other all our lives and for as long as I can remember he was always at our home, running around, pretending to be Indiana Jones.

My mother referred to him as her third child, regularly telling the story of how Jasper, at three, would insist on sleeping over to guard the baby. I still remember being five and biting him so hard he cried. I'd lost my two front teeth and had a point to prove. Even during the extended session on the naughty step imposed on me as punishment, he sat with me most of the time, and snuck me cookies from the kitchen under his Indiana Jones hat.

Jasper was supposed to be my brother's best friend, but I always felt that he belonged to me. It was difficult to fit in with the chatty, relaxed children at school and I felt much more secure hanging out with Jasper and my brother, Zachary, who regularly and actively pretended I didn't exist. Zachary would behead my dolls and hide my toys, but Jasper was always kind to me.

So, when Jasper invited me to their boarding school leaving

ball because he didn't have a date, it was no surprise. My parents were concerned – I was only fifteen – but Jasper just explained that he could hardly take my brother. I had to endure extended birds, bees, crown jewels, milk- and cow-purchasing metaphors for what seemed like hours from my mom; but I was eventually given the green light.

At the ball, Jasper stayed at a distance, but kept a watchful eye in my direction and, every once in a while, came over to check that I was okay. Zachary disappeared five minutes into the evening after a quick and distracted, 'Don't get pregnant. Stick close to Jasper.'

At the end of the night, Jasper pulled up at my home, helped me out of the car and walked me in. With the house lights off, we walked clumsily into the dark hallway. When my eyes adjusted to the darkness, I discovered that my face was merely inches away from his.

After what seemed like for ever, he leaned in, gave me a hug and whispered, 'I'm glad you came with me tonight, Aari,' into my hair. He pulled away smiling, asked me to lock the door behind him, then walked out of the front door quickly without looking back.

Jasper was hardly around that summer. After their results came through he went to Bristol to study archaeology, while Zachary went to UCL to study law. While he was at university, Jasper was more of a constant in our home than Zachary, never missing birthdays and visiting during the holidays. Two years later, I got early admission into Bristol. It was the exact course I wanted, and I knew Jasper could show me around while the other freshers were finding their feet.

Jasper was in his final year, so we didn't get to see much of each other, but we promised to have dinner once a month. When Jasper cancelled the third dinner in a row, I stopped trying and so did he.

The distance between us grew and neither of us tried to do

anything to stop it. When his twenty-first birthday came around, I attended the mandatory family dinner and binned the invitation to the unsupervised party for his friends at his house the week after. By the time Jasper graduated, we barely saw or spoke to each other. In the graduation picture we were forced to take, we stood side by side, trying not to look at each other; we both wore cold, toothless smiles with a gap as wide as the Grand Canyon between us.

The very next day, Jasper packed his bags and went travelling for two years. He just left. He sent a group email to everyone once a week and a postcard once a month, filling us in on his adventures, but I very quickly learned to read between the lines. He filled the screen and card with words, but told us nothing.

I buried myself in work at university, took a receptionist job at a local hotel and avoided people who knew him like the plague. For the next two years, I stuck to a routine that kept me busy. After my final exams, I went home for the weekend and found out that Jasper was back. He'd decided to give up on archaeology and had found a job in London at an investment bank. The last bit of Jasper that I could hold on to had gone.

The first time I saw Jasper after his graduation was at mine. He remained at a noticeable distance, gave me a graduation gift that I never bothered to open and kept his congratulations short. He didn't bother to stay for my graduation lunch.

The isolation I kept myself in at university reared its ugly head the following spring, when it was my turn to celebrate my twenty-first. We had the usual, mandatory family dinner with everyone present. I thought about having my own house party, but realised that the friends I had made at university were either work or class buddies, who I spent no time with outside of those two environments. By the time I admitted that I had no friends to myself, my parents already had a trip booked, so they left me home alone that weekend. I decided to celebrate with a food and film weekend.

I'd been expecting a quiet Friday night; so the sudden interruption of the doorbell ringing frightened me. I grabbed Zachary's cricket bat and put it next to the door before I opened it, just in case.

It was Jasper, suited, straight from work, carrying a crate of gin bottles. We'd obviously neglected to tell him there was no party; he looked surprised when I opened the door in my pyjamas, with a shower cap on my head protecting my hair treatment.

'No party then?' he asked cautiously.

'No.' I offered a small apologetic smile.

'Okay, happy birthday, Ariella.'

With that, he turned to retreat with the crate to his car. I wanted to shut the door and return to my film but it didn't feel right. I went after him barefoot.

'Jasper!' I yelled as I ran.

He was putting on his seatbelt. He looked up.

'Do you want to have a drink with me?'

'I'm sorry, Aari...' He shook his head as he began.

'It's okay,' I said and walked as quickly as I could back towards the house.

'Aari!'

I ignored his call. I heard his car door shut and his feet hitting the gravel as he ran up to me.

'Aari!' He grabbed my hand. 'Wait, please let me finish. I was going to say I'm sorry I can't join you for a drink, because I'll have to drive back to London later, but I'll have some tea while you get going on this.'

He offered a small smile and shook a bottle of an artisanal gin I had never seen before.

'Yeah, I can do tea.'

We walked to the house, heading straight into the kitchen. I opened the glass sliding door that extended the entire width of the kitchen to our pool and garden, letting the breeze outside rush in. Having Jasper so close after so long made me feel a little boxed in.

He sat at the breakfast table, watching me as I grabbed some tonic for myself and filled the kettle.

'Get anything good for your birthday?' he began.

'I haven't opened any presents yet,' I replied. 'How's work?' I scrambled for acceptable conversation topics.

'Busy, but good. Lots of numbers.'

I looked in his direction, which prompted him to inspect the corners of the kitchen. I put everything down and stood opposite him at the breakfast bar.

'Jasper, when did chatting become so difficult?' I said, staring directly at him.

'I don't know.'

'Can we figure it out? Please? I miss my best friend.'

Unexpectedly, little pools welled up in my eyes and, as I tried to blink them away, big fat ones rolled down my cheeks. Jasper sat, frozen where he was.

'Please don't cry, Aari. I can't handle it.'

'I feel like I don't know who you are any more,' I managed between shallow breaths.

Jasper immediately got up and walked out, slamming the front door. My tears fell freely. I heard his car start up and drive away and, after I'd calmed down, I finished making the G and T and gave myself permission to drink 'just this one' alone.

As I was leaving the kitchen with my drink I spotted Jasper, changed into old, faded, soft navy-blue jogging bottoms and an old T-shirt, walking towards our pool. He had obviously crossed over from his parents' adjoining garden. He was carrying the crate he'd tried to deliver earlier.

'Let's talk,' he said as he walked in, dropping the crate on the kitchen island and wiping my tear-streaked cheeks with his fingers. 'However long it takes, Aari, we'll fix it.'

After I'd made him wash the treatment out of my hair as punishment for making me cry, we built a makeshift den in the middle of the living room like we used to and stayed up all night, working our way through the gin and just talking. We covered work, his travel and my course; all safe territory – but then I had to ask, 'Jasper, why were you avoiding me in Bristol?'

I heard him sigh before he put his drink down.

'I'm sorry. I was pissed off at you for something that wasn't even your fault.'

'You were pissed at me? What did I do?'

'You came to Bristol.'

'I don't understand.'

'Have you ever wanted the freedom to just rediscover and maybe even reinvent yourself?'

I shook my head.

'I did. University helped me test my boundaries in an environment where there was no one to let down. I didn't always have to do the right thing and I didn't always have to be "good".'

'Oh. I wish you'd told me. I would've played along.' I nudged him with my elbow.

'That's the thing. It wasn't a game, it was me. It turns out that I'm generally a decent person, but there were other things about me that weren't so decent, and I enjoyed exploring that.' He threw me a sly smile and continued. 'Anyway, when you showed up I felt like you brought everything I was trying to get away from with you. You could've gone to any university you wanted, but you followed me to Bristol. So, I was a little annoyed.'

'Why didn't you say anything?'

'I did. We all did. You didn't listen.' He patted my hand softly.

'I'm sorry. I had no idea.'

'I know. I'm sorry too. I was a dick.' He drained the last of his gin.

'I'm a little envious. I wish I'd seen university like that. I returned pretty much the same person.' I laughed.

'Surely you dated, got a boyfriend, had your heart broken...'

'Nope. I went on a total of two dates. They both started out fine and ended weirdly. Who asks you who you live with on the first date? I had to get campus security involved on both occasions. After those, I was done. Too stressful.'

Jasper burst out laughing. I laughed along.

'What was your big discovery? Get your heart broken?' I teased.

'A little bit. It was preferable to hurting someone I really liked, though. That sucked. I'd promise myself I wouldn't do it again, but always found myself at the same point, having to break up with someone amazing. It was horrible.'

'That was the big revelation? I could've told you not to break up with amazing people. For free!'

'That, and realising that I didn't want to come back home,' he added solemnly.

'Why?'

'Too many reasons, and not enough.'

The heaviness of his response made me let that one go. I looked at the time: almost three. I was hungry and tired, but I didn't want us to stop. I lay on my side.

'What is Cambodia like?' I asked, partly to distract him from the time.

He re-energised. 'It's beautiful!'

As he launched into sharing his road trip, I felt my eyes getting heavy. It was the happiest I had been in a very long time.

The next day I woke up just before noon, and watched my sleeping friend's chest rise and fall. I was happy to finally see the warm man that replaced little boy running around the house, chasing me and my brother, pretending to be Indiana Jones again. He may have been taller and his hair darker, with a more professional cut, but it was just as messy, with his eyelids hiding those green eyes with the brown flecks I had known all my life. His mouth still curved up at the edges, even while he was sleeping. I got up gently, so that I didn't wake him, for a shower. By the time I returned, he was tussling with the coffee machine.

'Morning, Mr Grumpy,' I teased. 'You still love Mommy's pancakes?'

'Yes! Dahlia has ruined pancakes everywhere else for me.' He laughed.

'Mommy's pancakes it is. After you've had a shower. I bet you're stinky,' I said, eyeing him suspiciously.

'Deal. Want to do something fun today?'

'You don't have to get back?'

'Not till tomorrow night.'

'Yes!' I jumped for joy inside.

'I'll be back in twenty.'

'I'll have pancakes!'

'Done!' He jogged away.

It really was the best birthday weekend. After Jasper had eaten five pancakes, leaving me with one, we jumped in a taxi. We spent the whole day in the bowling and arcade centre we'd practically lived in when we were kids.

Afterwards, we left to have dinner at the massive American diner we used to love as kids, and very quickly realised our love for the place was fuelled by ignorance, balloons, sugar and the free shiny little toys.

'Sleepover!' I announced when the cab dropped us off at

home that evening. 'Put your pyjamas on and meet me back at mine. Ten minutes!'

'Fine!' he agreed, laughing.

By the time he arrived, I had changed into my warmest onesie and was making some strong coffee, so I asked him to close his eyes and led him to the living room.

'Surprise! Movie marathon!'

I pointed to our old VHS player, hooked up to our television, with three Indiana Jones tapes, in Jasper's specific viewing order, next to it. He laughed so hard he bent over, holding his tummy. I smiled to myself. He liked it.

'Goodness, Aari, you're so dramatic! Why didn't you just download it?'

'Meh. It isn't the same!' I knelt by the cassettes. '*Temple of Doom*?'

He nodded as he pulled two cushions to the floor, opposite the TV.

'Before you get comfy, there's vanilla in the freezer – that's your job. I'll bring in the coffee. Affogato time.'

We made our desserts and settled in.

I fell asleep somewhere at the beginning of *The Last Crusade* and finally woke up to the final credits of *Raiders of the Lost Ark*, with a dull ache on my side.

'Hey.' Jasper had felt me move.

'Hey. Good, wasn't it?' I pretended I'd been awake for it all.

'You were snoring and drooling before the first film finished.'

'That's not true. I made it to Sean Connery!'

'Only because I was poking you awake!' He burst out laughing.

'I try to do something nice and this is the thanks I get.'

'True. Thank you.' He half-bowed mockingly.

'We should do this again! Next time, let's do a *Mummy* marathon. I can come to you.' I poked his chest.

'Maybe. It's just that work is busy and I don't have a lot of down time.' Jasper started getting to his feet.

'Maybe? Definitely! You've got to eat, right? Food? Rachel Weisz? Hmmm?' I raised my eyebrows twice at him. I remembered his crush.

He considered me for a while, like he was thinking of what to say. Then he stopped looking at me altogether. It dawned on me. He was making excuses.

'What's going on, Jasper?'

'What? Nothing.'

'You're not doing this to me again.'

I felt the tears spring to my eyes, so I went straight to the sliding door and yanked it open. He didn't want me anywhere near him in Bristol, and he clearly didn't want me anywhere near whatever personality he was experimenting with in London now.

'Hold on. Can we just dial things back a bit?'

'I'm so stupid. I thought we fixed it. I almost broke my neck coming down that death trap of a loft ladder, with that stupid VHS player for you. Why did you come over last night? Did my parents ask you to babysit?'

'Of course not.'

'I'm such a fool. I was so happy to see you, I didn't think.'

'Zachary texted and told me he'd meet me here,' he defended himself.

'Yeah. Sure. Please leave.' I stretched our garden torch towards him.

'You're serious.'

'Goodbye, Jasper. Reinvent yourself in London all you want.'

Jasper approached and pushed the sliding door shut, sealing both of us in the kitchen. I yanked it open again.

'Goodbye, Jas—'

'Please shut up, Aari, and sit down.'

It was shocking to hear Jasper raise his voice, but I wasn't giving in. I crossed my arms and stood firmly by the sliding door. He placed both his palms on the kitchen counter, dropped his head and sighed.

'It's not your fault we fell out.'

'Of course not. I did absolutely nothing wrong, and you—'

'For goodness' sake let me finish, Ariella!' he snapped. He deflated immediately. 'Sorry, I just need you to listen, okay? We fell out because I didn't want to be friends any more. Remember the Leavers' Ball? Just before that, something changed.

'I got really territorial at the ball even though I knew all I could be was a friend. I thought what I was feeling would eventually pass. You know, hormones.' He laughed lightly.

'It took everything in me not to kiss you in your hallway that night, so I decided that maybe it was best to just get away from you.'

Silence fell between us.

'You should've said something.'

'I did. Just not to you.' He rubbed his palm on his forehead and continued. 'I spoke to Zach. He was literally zero help. He still childishly elbows me and winks whenever you're around or your name comes up. Then, I spoke to Dahlia. She asked me to give it a few years and suggested there was a world out there that I hadn't seen, filled with people I hadn't met.'

'Mommy knew?!'

'Everyone knew.' He sighed. 'I thought about you a lot that first year at uni, but it was slowly ebbing. I finally managed to move on by the middle of the second year, but you showed up six months later and slammed me back to square one. Remember Sophia?

'We'd been on and off since the first year, and finally something solid was happening. We were planning to travel together after graduation. That died less than two months after you arrived. My feelings for her just stopped. I did everything I could to revive them, but you were my kryptonite. After that, I couldn't wait to graduate and get on a plane.'

Without realising it, I'd walked over, and was standing next to him at the kitchen counter.

'Jas, I felt something too the night of your ball, and maybe I was a little clingy at university, and I'm sorry. It's just really hard making new friends and not being friends with you makes me feel really alone. Can we find a way to stay friends? Please? You can't just take it away. It's cruel.' I felt the tears brimming again.

'Aari, you're not listening. I don't want to be friends. It's been over six years since the Leavers' Ball and nothing has changed. I've been in love with you since before that night, and it never stopped. It just hibernates when I don't see you. Even yesterday in that ugly old dressing gown, covered in biscuit crumbs and looking ridiculous with your treatment cap on... It just came rushing back. I've tried everything to stay away from you. Nothing works.'

I could feel his exasperation.

'Maybe you shouldn't.' I loved Jasper. Maybe I felt the same way. I felt something that night, and it stayed with me. I wasn't sure what it was, but I didn't want to lose him.

'Don't be ridiculous. Dahlia will adorn her ears with my testicles. You wanted to know, so I told you.' He got up to leave. 'I'm going to need that torch now.'

'Don't leave, Jas. Hold on.' He grabbed the torch and I panicked. He couldn't leave like this. 'What if I told you I felt the same?'

He shook his head. 'It doesn't work like that. You can't just summon it, Aari.'

I grabbed his hand, lifted as high as my toes took me and readied myself. 'Okay. Kiss me.'

'No, Aari. We can't take it back if we cross that line.'

'You're such a chicken!'

I leaned forward, tilted my head up, closed my eyes and kissed him quickly, but gently, on his lips, to gauge his reaction. He didn't kiss me back and, instead, looked at me like I was being obtuse. I persevered and leaned in again, leaving my lips on his. This time, I felt more confident when he kissed me back softly. When I retreated to look at him, his eyes refused to meet mine. I went in once more and felt him exhale into the kiss as his tongue gently found mine; and we settled, as if synchronised, into the kiss together. He pulled away slowly.

'I feel like I pressured you into this.' He searched my face.

'No,' I replied breathlessly, suddenly feeling shy.

'Good, because I need you to be sure. Are you sure?'

I nodded, and his lips found mine once again. The joy that erupted from inside me enveloped us. I loved him.

After a while he stepped back to separate us. 'I should go. Want to have lunch tomorrow? Like, on a date?'

'Stay.' I put my hand in his.

'I can't. Things have changed a bit.' He smiled, put his hand through his hair and playfully pulled my onesie's hood over my head.

I nodded as my tummy fluttered. 'Did Zachary really tell you that he'd meet you here?'

He pulled his phone out of his pocket, opened up his text from Zachary and handed it to me.

> Mate, god knows which weirdos Aari's invited to this bash. Will be late, so swing round with some booze and stop her from cowering in the corner and ignoring her guests, would you? She'll probably still be rolling around in her dressing gown. We can't let her down.

'I didn't lie to you, Aari. I never have,' he whispered. He put the phone back in his pocket, gave me a quick kiss and left.

I couldn't stop smiling. I ran up to bed and tried to get to sleep, but my eyes wouldn't shut. I'd spent my whole life around

Jasper, and now I was jittery just thinking about him. I touched my lips. He kissed me back. The way I'd felt, kissing Jasper, was indescribable. I wanted to kiss him again. And again.

I sent a text to Zachary.

I know what you did.

You're welcome.

That night, I went to sleep replaying our kiss; feeling wanted, beautiful, and his. I'd finally found somewhere I fitted.

Memories of that want, that excitement and that night four years ago fill my head and belly as the black cab turns onto the street in Hampstead. As the cab rolls to a stop, I hope I am doing the right thing, walking away from the only person I have ever been in love with, and been building a home with, for the last two years.

FOUR

CALEB

When I see Ariella get up from her corner of the office, I take it as a cue to grab my messenger bag and head home. I take the brisk walk to Bond Street and ride the Jubilee line to West Hampstead. There are very few things I am attached to but my home is one of them. From the very first time I saw the space, I knew I had to buy it, so I've sunk every penny I have into turning it from the unloved disaster it was to the minimalist pad it is now.

The transformation has been painfully slow, but worth it. It would have been nice to continue to have it all to myself, but I have bills to pay and, potentially, a new business to fund. I keep it spotless anyway, but I do a quick visual sweep to make sure nothing inappropriate has been left out. I check the guest room. The sheets remain clean and unused since I put them on two weeks ago, and the bathroom is shiny. It's a little stuffy, so I open the large bedroom windows to let some air in. It crosses my mind to get flowers from the corner shop, but I abandon that idea. A welcome drink at some point after she has settled in will do the trick. If she drinks. Probably not. I scrap that idea too.

When the buzzer goes, I look around the apartment one last time and remind myself that this is only temporary.

'Hi, top floor.'

I buzz the communal door open. It doesn't take long for the doorbell to go.

'Hello! Welcome to Casa Caleb!' I whack up the charm, trying to start off in a good place.

'Hi, thanks,' she whispers, dragging a suitcase and carrying a small jute bag.

She looks completely different to the confident silver-spooner who held me hostage in my office earlier. She has clearly been crying. She flinches timidly when I try to help her with a bag, so I back off.

'I'll come down and help you with the rest of your stuff?' I offer.

'Thank you, but this is it.'

It doesn't look like very much.

'Shall I give you the tour?' I take the handle of the suitcase beside her. I'm not a total prick.

'Please.'

The living room is a vast, square space with charcoal-grey floors and a wall of glass overlooking the city, and leads on to the kitchen with its central island and cooking hub, six chrome chairs lined up in front of it. The front and sides of the island extend out to create a flat surface that functions as a dining table. The place formerly had five bedrooms, but these have been knocked into the two huge en-suite bedrooms and a home office. I beam with pride as I walk her into her room.

'This is your room, here are your keys and let's just figure the house rules out as we go along.'

'Thank you.'

Disappointingly, she looks unimpressed as she reaches into her bag and extracts an envelope.

'The confirmation of the advance and deposit.'

'No need, I got a text from the bank. Make yourself comfortable. I've got to go, but call me if you have any questions. See you later.'

She's a big girl. She'll be fine; plus I figure the less we see of each other the better. So I leave as fast as I can.

I meet the boys at the Bell, the pub down the road from my flat and unofficially my second home. Tim and Jack already have a pint for me at our usual table, next to the fireplace.

'What took you so long? Your pint is warm,' Jack says.

'Hello, boys. New flatmate, landlord duties.'

'Bloody hell, that was quick. The only reason I'd move that quickly is if Em kicked me out indefinitely,' Tim says, genuinely concerned.

I'm not ready for the crap they're going to give me when I tell them that my new housemate is female.

'I'm starving! I fancy ham, egg and chips.' I put my hand up for Bev the waitress but can't get her attention.

'Maybe leave it for a bit,' Jack advises.

Tim gives me a questioning look and puts his hand up and she immediately walks over.

'Caleb, you fucking arsehole!' he growls quietly as she approaches.

'Hi, boys, what can I get you?' she chirps at Tim with her back to me.

'Steak and chips please, Bev.'

She nods, scribbling happily.

'Please can I have—' I start.

'Jack?' She smiles at him, cutting me off.

'I'll have the bangers and mash please, Bev.'

'Bev, please can I—'

'So, one bangers and mash and one steak and chips.' She closes the pad and walks away.

'Caleb, you didn't,' Jack whispers, casting an eye at the bar, where the landlord – and incidentally, Bev's father – is jovially pouring pints for the customers.

'You slept with her, didn't you?' Tim accuses.

'I didn't touch her!'

'What happened? She was fine on Friday night!'

'Nothing! I helped her close but she missed her tube home so I said she could crash. We had a couple of beers back at mine and, just as I was about to go to sleep, Nicole turned up starkers in a trench coat and these insane heels. That chick is crazy. We're going to have to change the door code, because she shouldn't be letting herself into the building like that—'

'Caleb! What happened with Bev?!?' Tim demands.

'Nothing. I let Nicole in – because, who wouldn't – then asked her to wait in my bedroom. Next thing I know, Bev is demanding, quite rudely actually, that I put her in a cab, so I did. Maybe she caught a glimpse of Nicole half-naked from the couch, I don't know. But I definitely did *not* touch Bev.'

Jack and Tim look at each other.

'What? You said don't touch the landlord's daughter, and I didn't touch the landlord's daughter. I can't get barred again, guys,' I plead.

'Jack, you tell him.' Tim puts his face in his palms.

'He's not going to get it,' Jack responds.

'Forget it, Caleb.' Tim gets up. 'I'll order your ham, eggs and chips.' He sighs.

This is the problem with having friends in relationships. Tim is a couple of years older and owns the local building company that converted my flat. He is married to the very maternal Emelia, with three kids to boot. He's a straight, honest, decent bloke and the first person I met in London who I actually liked. He introduced me to Jack and they sort of adopted me. Jack and I are the same age and he has just proposed to his girlfriend, Louisa. Out of respect for Jack, I'd never call her a bitch. The guys have become like brothers to me so, if Lou comes with that, then I have no choice.

'So, Tim, how are the plans for Jack's stag coming on?' I ask when he returns.

Tim groans. 'The only reason I'm stuck organising the bloody thing is because Em and Lou don't trust you. I work seventy hours a week, have three kids, and a wife who can shove my nuts in a vice whenever she feels like it. I have to pretend I'm in some pub quiz league to see you guys on a Monday night. How the hell am I supposed to organise a stag?'

'... And that's what you have to look forward to, Jack. If you want, I'll get someone at work to organise the stag,' I offer.

'Nice!' Jack whispers, looking excited, while Tim shakes his head.

'Don't do it. It's going to end badly. The girls are going to find out when it's not curry and beer at the local Indian.'

We both shoot Tim threatening looks.

'You can't do curry and beer for a stag!' I complain.

'Just so we're clear, I'm not going to some Eastern European country where people I don't know try to convince me to cheat on my wife and potentially get arrested, Caleb.'

'I would never!' I make a point of looking offended, and quickly drop Prague and Tallinn from the location list in my head.

'Actually, Tim, I was thinking maybe the South of France. We could hire a boat, hit the casinos, eat all the steak you want... That sort of thing.' The mention of steak has got Tim's attention.

'Tim's got a point. Lou's still fuming at *me* for the way *you* treated her sister during her birthday trip. It was one weekend, Caleb. Three bloody days. Would it have killed you to keep it in your pants?'

'And her best friend. The same weekend,' Tim adds, enjoying himself.

Louisa's birthday weekend retreat to Italy had put twenty, mostly single people, with few inhibitions in her parents' opulent, fully staffed and catered mansion; complete with booze, a pool, hot tub, and lots of places to hide from sight. A recipe for disaster.

'In his defence, Jack, we were miles from anywhere, and you know how he gets. I'm the last person to defend him because he's a dick – sorry, mate, it's true – but they didn't give him a chance. He wasn't the only one those two cracked on to that weekend, trying to outdo each other.'

'Thank you!' I shoot Tim a grateful look. 'It wasn't like we had name badges. I had no idea who anyone was until Lou started screaming at me.'

'I get that, but the last thing she needed at her birthday was her sister and best friend scratching each other's eyes out.'

'If we think about it, I'm the victim here. They knew each other. I was the one without a bloody clue.' The fact that I'd enjoyed myself immensely was irrelevant.

'Can you punch him in the face please?' Jack asks Tim, seriously.

'For the millionth time, I'm sorry, okay? How long are you going to be shirty for?'

'Depends on how long *she's* going to be shirty.' Jack is being unfair.

'If it's not this, it'll be something else. It's always something with Lou.' I glance at the fingernail scratches on the side of Jack's neck.

'You know, if I didn't have Em and the kids, I may have made the same mistake.'

Jack and I stare at Tim in shock, then burst out laughing. Tim is as dedicated to his family as it gets.

'Yes. Sure, you would've. Anyway, I'll ask one of the project managers at work for a few pointers on the stag do. How does that sound?'

'Yup,' they both agree.

We finish dinner, get some beers in and, as always, come last in the pub quiz. The perfect start to the week.

FIVE

ARIELLA

I wake up startled, unsure of where I am; until yesterday's memories start seeping through the haze of the bottle of red wine I drank alone last night. After I unpacked, I went out for a small bouquet of flowers from the corner shop to cheer myself up and returned with a couple of bottles of wine. Sitting on my new bed, surrounded by silence, I gazed out of the huge bedroom window, looking over the rooftops and night skyline, as I slowly drained the bottle. I might have opened the next, but thankfully a solitary text from my brother interrupted my catatonia at about ten thirty.

Seriously?

I didn't know how to respond, so I didn't. My mother wasn't calling me, so the news had only made it to Zachary and his girlfriend, Isszy. For now. I took a long, hot shower to wash the day away, and crawled into bed, only to lie awake for what seemed like half of the night.

I was just drifting off to sleep when my new flatmate came crashing into the apartment singing, 'You'll Never Walk Alone' at the top of his voice. When Jasper came in late, he was always quiet and considerate; kissing my forehead before getting undressed; and then, when under the covers, he would pull me in to his body and curl over me for warmth. Lying in my vast new bed, I'd never felt lonelier, but I knew it had to be my reality for now.

Thankfully, I'd also picked up my breakfast staples yesterday, and put them in the predictably empty fridge. It's bound to be a beautiful morning in the living room. It has large windows eager to flood the space with sunlight, which is exactly what I'll need this morning to chase this hangover away. That, some grapefruit and tea should do the trick.

Coming into the living room, I see a half-naked girl wearing little more than a Liverpool FC shirt, sitting at the central kitchen island drinking coffee. Caleb has a girlfriend?

'Good morning, I'm Ariella. Lovely to meet you.' I stretch out my palm to shake her hand.

'Hi,' she croaks, ignoring my palm as she puts her forearm on the counter to rest her head.

'Rough night?' I soften my voice.

All she does is grunt. I quickly deduce that is all the communication I am going to get. I grab my grapefruit from the fridge and split it in two, putting the other half back. I silently make some tea and escape to my room, giving her the pleasure of solitude. I'm hardly shining company either. I sit at the small desk in my room, looking out of my window as I eat.

Even though I was petrified of what would happen, I expected Jasper to call last night – but he didn't. I'm not sure what that means, but I force the thought aside and hit the shower. When I return to the kitchen with my bowl and cup, the girl is gone, and in her place, eating cereal and watching cartoons, fresh from a run, is my flatmate; the picture of health and vitality.

'Morning. Sleep well? Those beds are amazing. They cost a fortune, but they're worth it, aren't they?' he asks brightly.

'Yes, thanks.'

'Great! I aim to please.' He laughs, pointing his spoon at the TV.

'Your girlfriend didn't look too well. Is she okay?'

'She's not my girlfriend.' He smiles, keeping his gaze on the TV.

'Is she all right?'

'Oh yeah. She left when I got back from my run. Tequila is no one's friend. Time for a shower, then work,' he announces brightly, slapping his hands together.

'I'm heading in now.'

'It's a bit early, isn't it?'

'I usually get in at about a quarter past seven.'

'Aren't you the office pet?' He laughs. 'Maybe it's a good thing we aren't heading in together. People might talk.'

'About what?' I ask.

'They might get the wrong impression.'

'What impression is that? We share a flat.'

'People tend to jump to conclusions... In fact, maybe don't mention that we live together.' With that, he dashes into his room quickly.

Strange boy.

I struggle through the morning. I've heard nothing from Jasper, but if he was with Zachary yesterday I know that he's fine. My brother is brutally honest and isn't always the warmest guy, but he has a great heart and can motivate anyone into doing anything. His relentless inability to let a task go until it is complete makes him an excellent lawyer. With Zachary by his side, Jasper is going to be okay.

I, on the other hand, feel numb. The 10 a.m. passes in a blur and I keep getting emails from Lara, first with playful insults, then asking if I am okay, then asking if I need anything. At noon, she shows up at my desk and drags me out of the building into a dim sum place nearby. She spends the first part of lunch filling me in on CrimeSpree's girlfriend and other things I don't remember.

'That's it. I've had enough. What's going on with you?'

It's only when she grabs my phone that I realise I have been staring at it the entire time. I inhale deeply. 'Can I have it back please?'

'No. It's rude. If you're not going to talk about you, then at least give me some advice. CrimeSpree's lechy girlfriend might get me fired if she doesn't cool it with the texts and indecent selfies to my work phone.'

'You were so keen on her yesterday,' I said, expecting this.

'Like you said, she's my client's girlfriend!'

'Yeah.' I exhale.

'Why aren't you having a complete meltdown and listing all the different ways I can get fired, while praying loudly that they don't make you do it? What's up with you?'

I should tell her. I am not handling this well on my own. Okay, here goes. 'I moved out of Jasper's last night.'

'No! Really? How did he take it?'

'He wasn't there.'

'Ouch! But, when did you guys break up?'

'We didn't. I just... left.' I shake my head, and a large tear unexpectedly rolls down my cheek.

'I'm not doing anything after work. Wanna key his car and let the air out of his tyres?' Lara suggests sincerely.

I can't help smiling when she puts her hand over mine. 'Let's just save the criminal activity for a bit,' I say. 'He didn't do anything, it's all me.'

'You. Really?'

'Yeah.'

'You have such huge blinkers on when it comes to that boy and I'm willing to bet it isn't all you.' She gives my hand a squeeze as lunch hits the table.

'Can we talk about you?' I ask, wiping another tear away.

'Absolutely, babe. So, she's still at my house.'

'Why is your client's girlfriend at your house, Lara?' I groan.

'It's a bloody nightmare. Look!' Lara shows me a picture on her phone. 'She's taking half-naked selfies in my bed and posting them. Those legs, though...' She starts smiling.

'Lara! Focus!'

'Yes. Of course. Anyway, she's turned things up a notch and I'm fucked if work finds out.'

'Technically, I am "work"! You're supposed to be hiding your shenanigans from *me*.'

'Please can you step in with CrimeSpree until I sort it? I'll do all the work, you just have to go to the meetings.'

'I'll go to your next meeting and only your next meeting; only because I know it's on Thursday.'

'Thank you, thank you, thank you, Aari, you're the best boss!'

'I'm not. I'm terrible. I can't believe I am covering for you. Again. Lara, please give your client's girlfriend back.'

'I will. I stupidly told her to make herself at home and leave whenever she wanted yesterday. When I got back she'd made dinner and was prancing around in next-to-nothing, so I thought, in for a penny...' She shrugs.

I can't help the laughter that escapes. 'You've got until Friday, Lara. After that, you're on your own.'

'It'll be done. Scot's honour.'

'Scout's honour, you mean.'

'Do I look like I've ever been a Scout?'

'If CrimeSpree starts asking uncomfortable questions, I'm sending him to you.'

'Agreed. To repay the favour, I'm taking you to work drinks

tonight. I'm not leaving you miserable in your hotel room. You're obviously hiding from home because Dahlia and Hugh probably love Jasper more than they love you.'

'Er, no thanks.' I don't correct her.

'Why? You're single now, so let's live these ten minutes of freedom up because, let's face it, that boy isn't going to let you go.'

'I only left yesterday. Isn't that a bit insensitive?' I look at her disapprovingly.

'Don't take this the wrong way, but you moved out of your home, without warning, and without telling your fiancé; but you're worried that going for some post-work drinks with your colleagues is insensitive?'

She has a point. 'I want to stay away from the office gossip and politics.'

'They gossip about you anyway. They already think you're stuck-up; however, your limited wardrobe stops them from being too harsh.' Lara chuckles as she waves her fork at my jeans, white Oxford shirt, boots and jacket.

'Wow, I *really* want to come now.'

'Come on. Make them feel like you're a part of the team. Maybe, for once, I won't have to make up more stories about your ugly boyfriend.'

'Jasper isn't ugly!'

'I know that. But they needed a reason to feel superior. Telling them you're engaged to some hot, super-nice, loaded bloke that worships the ground you walk on wasn't going to help.' She pops a steamed parcel in her mouth and licks her fingers.

'I'll come for one drink, for the team.'

'Three drinks minimum, and—' Lara winces.

'What?'

'You're going to need to tone "you" down. Don't ask for their fine wine list, a gin that no one has heard of or a specific tonic water. Think of ice-drowned cosmos, vodka-cranberries, and diluted Tanqueray-tonics as your hazing. You have a lot of human ground to make up.'

'Great, I can't wait.' I clap sarcastically and Lara rolls her eyes.

'Honestly, I don't know why I bother. Saving you from social suicide is thankless and futile. Have you always been this difficult?'

'Absolutely.' I laugh as Lara throws a wooden chopstick at me.

After lunch, I am finally able to focus, push Jasper to the back of my mind and get stuck into work. When a package arrives for me at the end of the day, I unwrap it quickly, expecting it to be one of the many samples we regularly receive. Inside, I find a shoebox and my heart sinks so fast, I feel like I am going to fall through the floor. My Hunter wellies. There is a note inside with Jasper's beautifully scrawled and uneven handwriting.

You left these behind.

That's it. He doesn't want to talk, he doesn't want to see me, he doesn't want to know. We are done. I am on my own, and it's all my fault. I left in the most horrible way possible. He would have come home to silence, discovered that cowardly note and found all my things gone. I deserve this, I really do.

I start an email to him and delete it halfway through. Then I start a text. That doesn't go well either. Then I think maybe I'll call. In the end, like the hideous, awful person I am, I do nothing.

I look around the office and find that it's already half-deserted, so I dial Lara's extension. I have nothing left to lose.

'Shall we?'

'Just wrapping up. I'll get you in five.'

Lara grabs my arm as we enter the busy bar around the corner from work, and tells me to smile. Tensely, through clenched teeth, I do as I am told. She orders us a couple of tequila shots, which we down quickly, and follows them up with two long double vodka and cranberries. Not long after we arrive some girls from our floor, and others I don't recognise, make their way over.

'Hi, Lara.' One of the girls gives Lara a hug.

'Hey, girls, Ariella's joining tonight.'

'Great!' she says, turning to me. 'I'm Ash. It's good to finally see you find the time to come out.'

I ignore the subtle dig. 'Thanks. It's good to be out. Do you work for Ivory Bow?'

'Yes, in PR. We actually share some clients.' She looks a little annoyed.

'Which ones?'

'DigitalFinger and Betabounce.'

'I saw your DF campaign. It was genius. Can I buy you a drink?' I want to get away. This girl doesn't like me.

'Sure. White wine spritzer.'

Strangely, when I return with her drink, her body relaxes and she warms up.

'So, what made you come out tonight?'

I might as well be honest. 'I found out that I'm pretty unpopular.'

'No, you're not. People just don't know you. I actually think you're really nice.'

'I clearly need to keep the drinks coming.'

She laughs. 'I didn't expect you to be funny. Why has—'

'Hi! I'm Nicole.'

A tall, blonde, impossibly beautiful woman who I see

frequently in the office steps between us. She is pretty hard to miss.

'Hi, Nicole. I'm Ariella.' I stretch out my hand and she takes it. 'Do you know Ash?' I try to bring Ash into the conversation, with the hope that they start talking and I can sneak away.

'Yes, I know Ash,' she says dismissively. 'I saw you in Caleb's office yesterday...'

She leaves a pause. I am not sure what she wants, so I don't respond. I just fix my smile on my face.

'Ugh. Caleb. Really?' Ash comments as she rolls her eyes.

'What about Caleb?'

Nicole turns to Ash. I inhale. The mood just changed. I feel the hairs at the back of my neck prickle as Ash squares up to Nicole. I am also a little relieved, because this means I can escape.

'He's a bit of a man-whore, isn't he?' Ash responds.

I drain my drink quickly. 'Can you ladies give me a second? I'm just going to grab another drink. Nicole, what can I get you?'

'Pinot Noir. French, not the South African. Large.'

I nod. 'Ash?'

'No, I'm good with my spritzer, thank you, Ariella.'

I'm watching the barman do his thing when Lara appears.

'How's it going?'

'Okay. I just ordered myself a cosmopolitan, but I think there's tension between Ash and Nicole.'

'Nicole is incapable of having tension-free exchanges.'

Lara takes Nicole's drink to her and they air-kiss, communicating like two alpha females, respectful of each other. I watch Lara dissolve the tension between Nicole and Ash like magic before she returns to me.

'You should know that Nicole doesn't like you very much.'

'She's in the majority, according to you.'

'Not any more, actually. It seems like coming out tonight is swinging opinion.'

'Great.' I make a show of draining my drink. 'I'm going to go.'

'You've been here half an hour. You can't turn up, talk to two people and disappear!'

'I've had my three drinks and I'm starting to feel a little tipsy.'

'You're fine. Let's get you some wine – that'll make you happy. I'll introduce you around. Don't worry about remembering any names.'

With Lara as my anchor, I spend the next couple of hours meeting some of the people on the floor and in the building. Half of the time, I have no idea who or what they are talking about, so I just keep a tight smile on my face. Lara keeps my drinks topped up all evening and, before long, I know I've had too much. When I start to feel light-headed, I take it as my cue to leave.

Outside, partly energised by the fresh air, I jump into the first black cab that rolls up and reel off my address. It isn't long until I am standing at my front door, looking for my keys. I press the bell and keep searching through my bag before it suddenly dawns on me that I don't live here any more. I slowly back away from the door and, just before I turn to take the last step, the door opens and I am confronted by a thunderous-looking Jasper.

'What do you want? It's only been twenty-four hours since you took it upon yourself to move out of our home, Ariella.'

He stands there seething in the doorway, bags under his bloodshot eyes. The initial shock of this is replaced by an appalling realisation – I did this.

'I'm sorry,' is all I can manage. Everything else is wedged in my chest. And I am. I'm sorry for all of it. I attempt to leave and step back, but miss the final step and fall backwards, breaking the fall with my palms and landing on my bottom.

'Are you drunk?'

'No. Maybe a little bit, but I'm okay. I'm fine. Honestly. Sorry.'

His eyes narrow and I see him struggling with himself as he observes me quietly. My hands and knees graze the unforgiving pavement as I begin to stand. There's going to be blood.

'Get in here now.'

He steps outside, grabs me at the top of my arm and pulls me inside, refusing to look me in the eye. He guides me into the kitchen and sits me roughly on one of our stools before he retreats quickly to the opposite side of the room, as far away from me as possible. He crosses his arms, unsure what to do next. I silently fight back tears and do all I can to avoid eye contact.

'I am so, so sorry. You don't deserve any of this, Jasper.' My voice cracks, giving away my heartbreak, and I suddenly feel his anger drain away.

He wets a tea towel and approaches me cautiously. I try not to react as he turns my palms up and starts to wipe the dirt away. It stings a bit, but I sit there quietly as he cleans the tiny cuts, grabs some cotton pads and antiseptic wash to disinfect them, and pops a plaster on the biggest one. He doesn't say anything either. When he finishes, I wait until he has turned his back, then pull out my mobile phone and order a car. Twelve minutes.

Jasper catches me confirming the pickup. 'You're leaving?' he asks, deadpan.

'I really should,' I plead.

He fills a glass of water, places it next to me and starts to make some coffee. I watch him move around our– *his* kitchen carefully, with a longing that is killing me inside. I am grateful when the coffee grinder comes on, filling the silence and relieving the tension in the air. I lovingly watch every move the back of his head makes. I know every parting and ambitious grey strand on that head; and I love every single hair on it.

When the machine stops he brings over a white porcelain cup and saucer. The memory of us picking those cups together on a rainy Sunday afternoon in Fulham comes to me.

'Drink.' It isn't a request.

I take a sip and start. 'Jasper—'

'I don't want to talk, Ariella. You're drunk and the way you left nullifies any conversation.'

'I just want to—'

'Your note said everything I need to know.' This is pushed out through clenched teeth.

'I'm sorry I left the way—'

He cuts me off again. 'How long until your car gets here?'

I look at my app. 'Seven minutes.'

'I'll be in the study.'

'Jasper, it's just that—'

He stops and turns around. '"You love me, you're sorry, but you just can't".'

'It's not that simple.'

I see Jasper lose the restraints on his anger before he explodes.

'Ariella – it *is* that simple! You made it that simple! You left me! You didn't try to have the discussion you're trying to have now. You left, with absolutely no warning. Want to know how I found out you'd gone? I got a fraud alert that someone had spent £27.45 using our credit card at Kazim's News and Booze in Hampstead on the way home. I thought it was hilarious the fraudsters didn't aim higher. Then I came home and called for you...'

He stops and composes himself. I feel what he must have felt in that moment. He shakes his head to clear his thoughts and continues.

'You're not even staying at a hotel or back at home. That would scream that whatever this is, it's fixable. You're actually living somewhere else. I know the dedication it takes to go flat-hunting in London; you've been planning this for weeks if not months.'

'That's not true. It was only that day I—'

'Save it. It hurts, but I have to find a way to let you go. I won't follow you. I won't ask you why. I won't try to get you back. There's nothing to discuss.'

He pauses and looks right into my eyes, repeating it like a mantra.

'You love me, you're sorry, but you just can't.' With that, Jasper turns to walk towards the study.

I stand still, disgusted at the finality of my actions yesterday. This isn't what I want, is it? 'I'll tell my parents this weekend,' I offer.

'Do whatever you like, Ariella.'

My phone beeps. My car is outside.

'That's your cab. See yourself out.'

Jasper opens the door to his study and, without looking back, slams it shut behind him. It takes me a few seconds to decide not to go after him. Shutting the front door behind me now feels much more painful than the first time.

Suddenly, I hear my name. Jasper. As I see him burst through the door, I reach for my phone to cancel the taxi. The driver will be mad, but this is worth it.

'Jas?' I answer, hopeful.

He looks uncomfortable. I understand. We've both said stupid things.

'I love you more than anything else in this world.'

He says it so sincerely, I'm about to burst into tears.

'I lov—'

'But please, don't come back here. Ever again.'

He barely gets the words 'ever again' out as he walks back into the house, shutting the door quietly behind him.

I get in the car and finally let my tears flow, wishing I could relive the last day and a half all over again.

SIX

CALEB

'Hey! Hey!' I call from the couch, sipping on my beer, as the front door opens.

'Hello.'

She sounds croaky, so I look over.

'Bloody hell, what happened to you?' She looks like one of those creepy red-faced dolls. 'You look like you've been in a fight.'

'Rough night,' she whispers.

As she walks closer, I confirm that she has been crying. Hard. This is why sharing with chicks is a problem. I should have said no. It is only day two and I can already feel her sucking all the fun out of the flat. I focus on the extra twenty per cent. Maybe I should make an effort to console her.

Today has been tough and I'm exhausted. My sales have dipped, I might have to head out to Singapore to fix it and Nicole was particularly omnipresent today; complaining as usual. I look at her out of the corner of my eye. Maybe if I stop engaging, she'll keep walking and won't stop. I don't want to get into a discussion about her 'rough night'.

'You'll be all right in the morning,' I say, ending the conversation. I take another swig of my beer and turn up the episode of *The West Wing* I'm watching, hoping she'll take the hint.

She does so, entering her room and closing the door quietly.

Now I feel like a shit. Maybe something really horrible is going on. She's an adult though, and I am her landlord, not her friend. I'm here to put a roof over her head as long as she keeps paying rent, not brush her hair while handing her tissues.

Against my better judgement, I go to her door and knock.

'Yes?' she says softly.

I didn't think this far ahead.

'You know that if you want to have a couple of friends round, you can?' I offer. It is the best I can come up with.

'Thank you.'

'Just the hot single ones, though. And they're more than welcome to stay over.' I laugh. She doesn't.

'Is that all?' she asks.

I feel like a total dick. 'Yes, that's all.'

'Sure, goodnight.'

'Night.'

Well, no one can say that I didn't try. I get back into my show and try to put today's challenges aside.

The next morning, Ariella is about to leave the flat in what looks like the same outfit she's worn since Monday, with only the shirt colours changing daily. Nicole made a big deal pointing out her 'uniform' yesterday and was less than complimentary about her, which seemed a little harsh. Yes, she might be a little dull and may come off as a bit of a snob, but she seems pretty harmless.

'Morning.'

She is more smiley this morning, or at least attempting to be, as she tips her finished grapefruit in the bin.

'I ran past the Tube and there was a queue outside, so you might want to get the bus to Swiss Cottage before you hop on.'

Daily local morning news, delivered in person – one reason not to move out.

'Thanks. Do you mind if I fill up the fridge? The butcher and grocer are meant to be delivering to my old place today. Can they deliver here instead?'

Who has a butcher and a grocer?

'Sure, whatever you want.'

'I think I might make a garlic and rosemary poussin tonight. Will you want some?'

'What's that?'

'Just a small chicken, casseroled, with some root vegetables, herbs and lemon.'

It sounds a little posh for a Wednesday night, but I don't mind. If she's cooking, I'm eating. Bev still isn't talking to me, so it might be good to stay away from the pub for a while.

'Sure. I'm a bangers and mash kind of guy, so I'm sure your poussin will be fine.'

'Would you prefer bangers and mash?'

I thought she didn't take requests. 'I'll eat anything, the choice is yours.'

'What time are you back?'

I am about to take the piss and tell her she isn't my girlfriend, but decide against it because she still seems fragile. 'Why?'

'So your food isn't cold?'

She looks at me like it is the most obvious thing in the world. The last time anyone cooked for me, all it required was buttons being pressed on a microwave. I suddenly feel uncomfortable.

'I'll probably be back at about nine, which might be too late for you.'

'It's fine, I'll just stagger the time I pop yours in. I'm going to the Le Creuset shop today anyway. I'll get a big dish and two small ones.'

I have no idea what she is talking about, so I agree and she picks up her bag and leaves. She is such an odd creature that I consider the possibility that she may be more interesting than she looks.

Nah.

My work day is tough, so I'm thankful it is Wednesday. I've been training in Muay Thai since I was eight and, on Wednesdays, immediately after my own fight training, I run a class for seven, pain in the arse, fourteen-year-olds. I am not a natural teacher, so it's a nightmare. I inherited the knuckleheads from my own Muay Thai instructor and training partner. He went to visit his family in Thailand for two weeks and I grudgingly agreed to fill in. That was over a year ago. Now I am stuck with them and they are painfully hard work. Today is no different, but I take comfort in the fact that the one thing I can count on, every Wednesday evening, is total exhaustion.

By the time I get back home, it is almost ten. Ariella is in the kitchen, filling a glass of water.

'You look exhausted.' Concern floods her face. 'Want some dinner?'

It's surreal, having someone standing in my kitchen, comfortably drinking water in a faded Gonzo and Camilla T-shirt, asking me that. I remember. 'Ah, your baby chicken.'

'I'm sorry... I didn't make the poussin. They delivered to my old address after all. You said you liked bangers and mash. It's not quite right, but would you like to give it a try?'

She's nervous. I don't understand why; I'm the one at her culinary mercy.

'Of course. I'll eat anything.' I drop my bag, ready to sit at the counter.

'I'll get it ready while you shower.'

'I can serve myself, it's okay.'

'I just need to do some last bits to the mash. Go.' She smiles shyly at me as she quickly pulls her long, thick, dark, curly hair into a bun at the top of her head.

Surprisingly, I do as I am told without resistance and head into the shower. This is new. It feels like I've walked into the 1950s. Frankly I don't get the appeal. She had better not start with the whole 'How was your day?' conversations.

I return and find that she has set a place for one at the central island; and by setting a place, I don't mean the food is there – I mean a proper place setting. She has put out what looks like a black slate mat, polished cutlery, an almost blindingly white starched napkin, wine glasses, a water glass, a jug of iced water and the pepper shaker. It looks like a table setting at an expensive restaurant. Oh my god, she's nuts.

'Come, sit.' She beams at me.

I am a little scared, but I take a seat. She retrieves a small orange dish from the oven and places it on the black slate.

'This looks amazing.' *Please don't kill me, you psycho.*

'Thank you. Red, white or beer?'

'Er, beer please?'

She whips away both wine glasses and pops a bottle of beer on the table before she opens it. When it is all set, she removes the lid of the orange dish. The smell that hits me is mouth-watering.

'I've never made bangers and mash before, but I had a lot of fun playing with it tonight.'

She looks unsure. Maybe even a little nervous. I relax. *Okay, this is her thing.*

I spot a couple of tiny black specks in the mash, but decide not to mention it. She looks handy with a knife and she is staring intensely at me. I take my first mouthful. Oh my days, it's *insane.*

'What's in this!?!'

'You don't like it?' She looks anxious.

'It's beautiful. I've never tasted anything like this! It's so good.'

'Thank you. I picked up some Toulouse sausages and cooked them in a red wine and honey reduction, then threw in some root vegetables at the last minute. The mash is truffle, garlic and Camembert. It works?'

'Oh, it seriously works! Did you have the same thing?'

'Yes, but I feel it still needs a little bite. Maybe some pink peppercorns?'

'I don't think it needs anything. You cook like this all the time?'

'Experimentally? I suppose.' She shrugs, embarrassed.

'Wow.'

It doesn't take me long to finish the bowl. As soon as I put my cutlery down, she begins to clear the place she set.

'What are you doing?'

'Clearing.'

'No, you're not. You cooked, I don't expect you to clear up. I can do that.'

'It's okay. It'll only take me—'

I stand up. She needs to relax. 'Ariella, I'm clearing up.'

I reach out to still her hands, but she moves them away a little too quickly.

'Okay.' She backs down and moves out of the kitchen.

'While I've got you, I'm trying to organise a bachelor party in the South of France. A bit of gambling, maybe take a boat out and have some steak?'

'Sounds like you want the Cannes to Monaco stretch.'

'Can you recommend some cool places? It'll just be for three blokes.'

'I can put together an itinerary and some prices too, if you want? We get agents' rates at work, so as long as you're going we can do it fairly inexpensively.'

'You don't mind?'

'I know that part of the world and our partners there really well. I can throw it together and email you in a couple of days.'

'That's fab, thanks.'

'You're welcome.'

'And thanks for dinner.'

'Glad you liked it. Goodnight.'

She goes quietly to her room and closes the door. I dive into the fridge to see if there is any more. None. Damn. I get another beer and I notice five little orange ramekins with the same branding stamped on them, covered with cling film. They are all filled with mashed potatoes, with different stickers on them, ranging from plain butter and Himalayan salt to fennel and spring onion.

I could certainly get used to living with someone who likes to cook, but I can't help but feel that something was off about dinner tonight. There was something a little uncomfortable about the whole experience. I can't put my finger on it, so I let it go.

SEVEN

ARIELLA

The last three weeks have been torturous. Just when I thought the pain was receding, a more intense wave would hit.

I'm not sure what I thought life out of the flat would be like – maybe exciting work days followed by nights having drinks in cool bars, meeting new people and dancing till morning with Lara. In reality, I retreated after the team drinks and haven't been out since. This seemed much easier in my head. I was still waking up often through the night, with panicked pains in my chest, and going into work foggy and unfocused. I'd fallen into the ritual of packing up my stuff and then unpacking every other night, each time intending to go back home to Jasper, which was crazy as I couldn't even bring myself to phone him.

I also completely underestimated what it would be like moving in with Caleb. I heard that he had a bit of a reputation and had dated extensively within the company and the building, but I didn't understand quite how much. If he was so bad, why did they keep giving in? It was a rude awakening to discover that people actually live like this. If I wasn't waking up to him coming in with someone new at the wrong side of midnight, I was usually meeting a new face over coffee the next morning.

Thankfully, his Wednesday evening training means Thursday mornings are guaranteed to be visitor-free. The rest of the week is completely unpredictable. I'm meeting more colleagues at home than I did at my company induction. I've learned very quickly to keep my eyes open but my mouth shut.

When I said hello at work to a girl I recognised, she smiled tightly and rushed off. Caleb came home that night and set me straight, admitting he had similar *arrangements* with a few ladies in the building. He actually congratulated himself for being effectively discreet.

When I accused him of being immoral, he happily explained that he was honest with everyone, they knew the score and signed up willingly. He then claimed to be a feminist, helping women exercise their right to sleep with him, with no judgement and no social constraints, as would have been the case in a more serious relationship.

This is who I am living with.

I'm having a quiet night when the doorbell goes and I open it. I am greeted with the massive chest of a worryingly large man in the doorway. I have to look up to see his face.

'Hi,' I say nervously. 'Can I help you?'

He looks confused. 'Is Rachel here?'

'No, sorry, wrong door.' I smile as I start to close the door.

That's when I spot the long metal pipe by his foot. I panic and try to shut the door, but he wedges his foot in. I quickly turn and put all my weight against it as my heart slams against my chest. 'I'm calling the police!' I scream at him, using my heels to wedge my body against the door.

'I know she's in there! I just want to talk to her.'

I push back harder against the door, reach into my back pocket for my phone and start to dial.

'Rachel!' He sounds like a wounded animal.

'There's no one here called Rachel!' I shout.

How is 999 busy? I don't know if Caleb is home, but I imagine if I drop a guy's name he might take off. 'Caleb! Can you come out here please?'

The man starts to laugh, unexpectedly. 'Yeah, come out here, Caleb!' he shouts. 'And bring my girlfriend with you.' His voice breaks and it hits me. I stop pushing against the door, but stand firmly in front of it.

'I'm sorry, he's not here.'

'Yes, he is. I followed them into the building and your neighbour downstairs sent me straight up here.'

'I still can't let you in, especially not with that,' I say, pointing to the pipe.

He kicks it away. 'Can I come in now?'

I see him holding back tears and my heart breaks for him.

'Sorry, no, you're frightening, but if you move your foot and let me close the door I'll check to see if she's here? I promise I'll be right back.'

He nods and removes his foot, resigned.

I close the door and run to knock on Caleb's door. 'Caleb, do you have a girl in there?' I whisper.

No response. I carefully try the door. It's locked. I know for sure he is in there because our doors can only be locked from the inside.

'Caleb, can I talk to you please?' I whisper a little louder.

No response.

'Please can you send her out?'

Nothing.

'Caleb, I'm going to count to five. Then I'm going to let him in and leave you to it.'

Caleb's door opens when I get to five.

'You wouldn't dare,' he seethes.

'I *so* would. Do you have his girlfriend in there or not?'

A small, stunning blonde with dishevelled hair steps out from behind him, eyes wide with panic. I'd probably feel more sympathy for her if Caleb wasn't topless, with what looks like smudged lipstick on his torso, rolling his eyes and pouting like a small child.

'Rachel?' I ask.

She nods in response.

'Is the man on the other side of that door dangerous? Do I need to call the police?'

She shakes her head.

'Now would be the time to speak up, because I'm kicking you out,' I say.

'He's not dangerous.'

I escort her to the door and take a picture of her and the guy. 'Just in case,' I tell them as I shut the door. I lean against it, close my eyes and allow myself to breathe. My legs feel like they are about to give way.

'What the hell did you just do?' Caleb says, approaching me.

I ignore him and focus on getting to my room. My body is beginning to shake with adrenaline and I need to find somewhere quiet to sit for a minute.

'That was none of your business.'

Still shaking, I stop and face him. I shouldn't be dealing with his rubbish.

'I live here too, okay? I deserve to feel safe. I deserve to open the door and not find a guy with a metal pipe, desperate to put it to use. I get that you're comfortable having a different stranger in this house every night. That's fine – it's your life. However, I'd quite like to have a quiet breakfast from time to time. I shouldn't dread coming out of my room because I don't want to play shrink to, or defend myself from, the array of women that I find here almost every morning. That was absolutely terrifying. We have no idea what that guy is capable of, but I've just handed over a woman I should be protecting, because I was too frightened for myself. This happens again, I'm moving out.'

I'm shaking badly. Caleb notices, reaches out, and I step back. Embarrassed, I escape to my room. I tap into my breathing exercises as I try to stave off a panic attack. This conversation has been brewing for a while. I need a shower. It will make everything okay. By the time I step out of it, I'll feel better.

A knock comes a little later, as I am taming the curls in my hair.

'Hey, Ariella. Can we talk?'

Caleb stands in my doorway in his pyjama bottoms and a T-shirt, with his black hair shiny and damp from a shower. He almost looks human.

'I'm sorry.'

The last thing I expected to hear was an apology.

'Can I make you a cup of tea while we have a chat?'

I'm immediately suspicious. 'Okay.'

I don't want to have an argument, but something's got to give. I grab a hair tie, follow him through the living room and hoist myself to sit on the kitchen countertop. I watch him put on the kettle carefully and quietly. He reaches for my evening lemongrass and ginger tea, dips the bag twice, then lets it steep while he makes his own. He then removes the bag, grabs a lemon from the fridge, cuts a wedge, then squeezes it; exactly as I would before bed. I unexpectedly feel my guard drop and my anger leave as he hands it to me.

'I really am sorry.' He sits on a stool and looks up to face me where I am perched. 'I don't want you to feel unsafe, and I can't imagine how scared you must've been earlier.'

I look at my mug as I take a sip.

'But I had a life before you moved in and that's not going to change, so we need to figure out what works for both of us, because I don't want you to move out. You're a bit depressing but you don't make a lot of noise, you don't complain... well, until tonight. You don't pry and you're pretty considerate. Most importantly, you're paying more than I could ever dream of charging anyone else.' He smiles. 'So, what bothers you?'

He playfully manoeuvres his head to make his gaze connect with mine. I hold that gaze. I am not backing down. If he is trying to be cute, it's not working.

'I get spooked when you come home late at night and I hear voices that I don't recognise. It would be helpful if you just knocked or even called out that it was you. It also freaks me out a bit when there's a stranger in the kitchen at breakfast almost every morning. I know it's to be expected, but it'd be nice if they didn't help themselves to my grapefruit. Perhaps I can add some pastry and breakfast bits to the grocery delivery for your... guests. I also wish you wouldn't leave the front door unlocked when you leave me at home alone at night. I just want to feel safe here.'

He is nodding along.

'...And I know it's your life and you choose how to live it, but can you avoid girls with boyfriends, please? I think you had a lucky escape tonight.'

A smile makes its way across his face. Really?!

'Okay, I have a responsibility to keep you safe. I've got it. Good to know you're not judging.'

'Oh, I am, silently; but if you want to get STDd up to your eyeballs, it's up to you. Thankfully, I don't have to share a bathroom with you.'

He laughs. 'You're a bit uptight, aren't you?'

'I'm not uptight, I just want to feel safe. I have enough to worry about right now.'

He pokes my rib so quickly, I am too slow to stop him.

'Like what?'

'Stuff.'

'What kind of stuff? You're pretty glum all the time.'

'I'm sorry I'm not entertaining enough for you.'

'Oh no, I find you immensely entertaining. I said you were glum. You're obviously hiding from something and it would be good to know what.'

'It's none of your business,' I say, trying to sound casual.

'It actually *is* my business. While we're talking safety, you could be running from a particularly motivated stalker who might find out where you live and turn up. So, I need to know why you're here, because I need to be able to handle it.'

'You just locked yourself in your room and left me to handle someone's weapon-wielding boyfriend by myself. I think I'll be fine.'

'That's not fair. I didn't know he had that. I would've been out here like a shot. I have to say, though, that I'm impressed with the way you handled yourself. You're a lot tougher than you let on. But if you don't want to tell me, that's fine. Just thought you could use someone in your corner.'

I really don't want to tell him, but then I hear the words come out of my mouth. 'I broke up with my boyfriend.'

He looks at me surprised, then his face contorts and, unexpectedly, he bursts out laughing. Great.

'What are you? Twelve years old?'

'You couldn't possibly understand.'

'What's there to understand? You broke up. Big deal. What are you so depressed about? You should be out celebrating your escape!'

I let my irritation show. 'I'm not promiscuous, unlike some.'

He laughs even harder. 'Do you think he's at home, moping about, thinking of you?'

'I don't know—'

He interrupts. 'Definitely not, and now that he's out of the relationship it's no longer cheating.'

'He didn't cheat.'

'Really? So why did he end it?'

'He didn't end it.'

'You did? Plot twist. Why?'

'I wasn't happy.'

'That's a shocker, you're hardly a bundle of joy.'

I shoot him a dirty look.

'The confines of a relationship are enough to make anyone unhappy. Now you're on your own, why don't you give smiling a go?'

'It's not that easy.'

'Yes, it is. Get out of your funk and do something, or maybe even someone.' He winks and it's the grossest thing I have ever seen.

'You're hardly an expert on relationships.'

'Why would anyone want to be that? The key is being completely honest, right from the start, so everyone is heart-break-proof. I make it very clear that I'm not looking for a relationship, and I don't mess with women in relationships. Tonight was a mistake. I had no idea she had a bloke.'

'And this is working out for you?'

'Of course it is, apart from the very occasional hiccup.'

'There has to be more to you than that.'

'Nope. Money, bit of fun, great sex. That's it.'

'Basically, you're telling me you're shallow.'

'That's exactly what I'm telling you. You should try having some fun instead of... whatever this is you're doing.'

He's on a roll.

'Put yourself out there. You're a bright girl – put in the effort and you'll get noticed. Maybe you could leave your hair out like it is now, put on some make-up or buy new clothes or something. You can't live a full urban life in tweed, boots and jeans. I can ask a friend to take you shopping, if you want?'

I find my voice.

'I've just come out of a relationship, so obviously someone found me attractive.'

'Let me guess – you met him at a stable. All I'm saying is that you're young. Get out there, experiment, bring some boys back home. Just don't throw in the towel. I spotted your knitting needles the other day. You're killing the vibe a bit, Grandma!'

He is enjoying this.

'You're so rude. It's crochet!'

'I'm trying to be nice. Someone has to tell you.'

'Thank you for your candour but I like who I am.'

'As long as you're sure that this is who you are, and not who your ex-boyfriend turned you into.'

Those last few words hit home hard.

'I'm sorry you felt unsafe tonight and I'll be less of a selfish bastard going forward. I leave for Singapore in the morning but I'm back on Friday. Are you going to be all right?'

'I'll probably be safer with you away,' I eventually counterpunch.

'Goodnight, Ariella.' Caleb laughs on his way to his bedroom

Long after he has retreated, I sit there on the counter, mulling the conversation over. Is this who I am?

EIGHT

CALEB

I can barely contain my relief as I board the plane. I miss having the house to myself. The money is worth it, but I'm her flatmate, not a babysitter. This trip to Singapore couldn't have come at a better time. It will be great to see Melissa again. Melissa Chang: the only woman I'd gladly give it all up for.

She's the closest thing I have to a girlfriend, which isn't saying much, considering she is engaged to someone else and has been for the last two and a half years that we have been seeing each other. I'm aware that this is beginning to look like a pattern for me.

We met at a technology award evening I charmed my way into, because I was failing sales-wise in Asia. Melissa was the sole female on my table. I immediately noticed her doll-like frame, her jet-black hair with every strand in place, her big brown eyes, her flawless skin, her dangerously red lips. She didn't touch her food but, every now and then, her hand smoothly lifted her water glass to her lips and back down again. She was riveting to watch. I knew it was going to be my last trip before I got fired for making a mess of Asia, so I decided to enjoy myself. As soon as the guests got up to network, I sat next to her, and I leaned in with as much charm as I could muster. If I was going to go down, it was going to be in flames.

'I'm sure you're told how beautiful you are all the time.'

She turned to me with a bored expression. 'Actually, no,' she responded coldly.

'Well, let me. You're indescribably magnificent.'

'Thank you,' she replied, not even bothering to look at me.

'So, who's the poor sod that's left you on your own tonight?'

She pointed to the most obnoxious man at the table.

'That fool?'

That got a smile out of her.

'That "fool" is the COO of the fastest-growing software company in Singapore, and my fiancé.'

I looked at her quizzically. '*Him?* Is it the money?'

'It's definitely not the money,' she said with a chuckle.

'Good, because I have no money, but I can have you feeling much happier than you do right now.'

'Why me?'

'I haven't been able to stop looking at you all night. I suspect you're much more fun if you let me take you off your display shelf and get under all this packaging.'

'I could be.' She raised an encouraging eyebrow at me.

'Think he'll notice if you snuck away?' I winked.

'He hasn't noticed much all night.' She picked up her bag and stood up to leave. Her quick response surprised me and rooted me to my seat. 'You coming?'

I hadn't expected to get this far, and definitely not this quickly. I straightened my jacket and walked out behind her. Outside, I suggested we get a drink somewhere, and she looked at me like I was dense.

'What hotel are you staying at?'

'The Hyatt.'

She got into a waiting car, gave instructions and, before long, we were in my hotel lobby. I lost my train of thought as she stared at me impatiently.

'What room are you in?'

When I told her, she walked to the bank of elevators, and I followed, wondering who had picked who up.

In my room, she carefully placed her bag down, turned her back to me and lifted her hair for me to unzip her dress. To slow things down, I kissed her neck softly. She smacked my head away.

'Zip! Now!'

I stepped back and turned her round. She was behaving very strangely and I wanted to make sure that I hadn't inadvertently picked up a hooker.

'Just hold on a second. You weren't paid to be his "fiancé", were you?'

'You think I'm a prostitute.' She didn't look offended, just curious.

'I don't know, just checking.'

She studied me intensely, turned her back to me and lifted her hair again. 'No, I'm not an escort. Zip.'

I hesitantly unzipped her slowly as she sighed impatiently, moving from foot to foot until I was done. When she dropped her dress, she looked heart-stoppingly gorgeous in matching ivory lingerie that accentuated her bare porcelain skin beautifully.

She pointed to the bed. 'Sit.'

Good. I could use a breather. No sooner had I sat down than she was on me, taking off my jacket and undoing my shirt. I grabbed both her hands.

'Wait. Just wait.'

'Why?'

'Things are moving a little fast. Can we talk?'

For the first time all night, she erupted with laughter.

'You Brits are ridiculous. Did you think I was going to be some submissive, innocent, fetishized local that you were going to have your way with, and I'd be grateful and happy because you were foreign and handsome?'

It was getting weird. 'No, I just want to get to know you, that's all.'

'Now that I'm here in my underwear, in your hotel room, you want to get to know me? Why didn't you want to get to know me at the table? Instead of the cheap and ridiculous shelf and packaging metaphors intended to lead us here?'

'If it was so ridiculous, then why did you fall for it?' I laughed to lighten the tone.

She shrugged. 'I didn't "fall for it". I was bored and I thought this sorry, foreign, broke misogynist might be good for some entertainment. So, are you?'

I remember thinking she was extraordinarily hot at that moment.

'I think I just fell in love with you.'

She put her finger up. 'That's not allowed.' She smiled and eased the tension.

I pulled her towards me. 'I assume this is?'

I placed my lips on hers and she kissed me back provocatively. Neither of us went to sleep that night. She matched me move for move, kiss for kiss, thrust for thrust and climax for climax. She was wonderfully acerbic, challenging and hilarious as we caught our breath between sessions. By the time the sun came up, she knew everything about me and I still knew nothing about her.

At six, she sat up abruptly, made a quick phone call from bed and walked, unabashedly naked, into the shower. After twenty minutes, she emerged from the bathroom and I saw her face without make-up on. I was seized by panic – she looked worryingly young.

'How old are you?'

'I know, it's annoying.' She laughed.

There was a knock on the room door at the same time, so I rushed to get it.

A man dressed as a chauffeur handed over a large brown box. 'Clothes,' he explained.

She yelled at the man in what sounded like Mandarin from behind the door. He answered quietly and left. She grabbed the box, tore it open, tossed her towel on the floor, then put on some fresh underwear, some loose green trousers, a loose green V-neck top and some flats.

'You work in a hospital?'

'Yes.' She smiled as she unceremoniously shoved last night's dress and underwear into the box. This woman was clearly used to people cleaning and picking up after her.

'I don't even know your name.'

She walked towards me with an outstretched hand. 'Doctor Melissa Chang. Nice to meet you, Caleb Black, travelling salesman. I want to see you again. Give me your key. Get another one at reception. I'll be back here by six.'

'I have a client dinner...'

'Cancel it. I'll make it worth your while. My driver is waiting.'

She didn't say goodbye or wait for a kiss; she just left.

When I arrived back at the hotel, late, and dejected from my last meeting, Melissa was already in the room, sipping on some champagne. I dropped my bag, gave her a quick kiss, grabbed her feet and started rubbing them distractedly.

'How was your day?' I enquired.

She narrowed her eyes at me. 'Do you have a girlfriend? You mustn't lie to me and I won't lie to you.'

'Okay.' Her intensity made me chuckle.

'So, do you have a girlfriend?'

'Trust me, I'm not boyfriend material. Besides, why do you care? You're engaged.'

'I want us to be honest. No bullshit.'

'Melissa, I can assure you that before I leave, probably for good, tomorrow, you'll get zero bullshit from me.'

'What if I want to see you again?'

'After this trip, I can't imagine I'll be coming back. I haven't managed to land a single client.'

'You won't visit?'

'No bullshit? No. Upside is, we won't get bored of each other, so we should make this memorable.' I leaned in to kiss her and she climbed on my lap to straddle me.

'I like you,' she whispered. It was the first time she'd seemed to soften.

'I like you too,' I whispered back as I pulled her shirt over her head.

We fell back onto the bed and made every second of our last night together count.

I woke up the next morning to the sound of my phone ringing, with Melissa gone. It was a Singaporean number I didn't recognise.

'Hello?' I greeted groggily.

'Mr Black?'

'Yes.'

'This is Leonard Yu, head of marketing, Pacific Mining and Metals. I understand you're in the country, providing services that may be of use. I was wondering if you have some time at about eleven a.m. to come in and discuss this with us?'

I scrambled out of bed. 'Yes, of course.'

'Fantastic. My PA will email our details over to you. We look forward to meeting you.'

'Yes, thank you.'

He hung up and I punched the air. I'd had Pacific on my hit-list my last three trips, but that place was a fortress. I looked over to Melissa's side of the bed and saw a sheet of hotel notepaper.

Caleb,

I would like to see if we get bored of each other. I've taken your business cards and found your company target list. Clear your day, get the latest flight you can tonight and expect a few phone calls.

I like you.

Mel

My phone didn't stop ringing that day. I filled my diary with appointments, and for what was sure to be my next trip in three months. Every single meeting was successful. That is how Melissa built my career and Ivory Bow's immense success in Asia. If only work knew.

After very little digging, I discovered that Mel was the only child of the owner of one of the largest construction companies in the city. As his bright and exceptionally capable daughter, she had the world and wealth at her disposal, which made pursuing her dream of being a surgeon easily achievable. She, like her father, had a reputation for being a hard nut to crack and a workaholic.

After her father died, she had to assume senior roles in his businesses, in addition to her hospital work. She was engaged to Kevin Wong, a software entrepreneur who she met at university. They'd been engaged for a while and the rumour was that a particularly hefty prenuptial agreement was responsible for delaying the wedding.

Mel confided that she didn't want to get married and kept finding ways to put it off. It worked well in the eyes of society to have a man on her arm, and Kevin Wong wasn't complaining about the benefits of being engaged to Melissa Chang. I wasn't complaining about my benefits either. I was removed from Singaporean culture and fantastic in bed, so I was her escape. It was the perfect relationship.

When I left Singapore, we had no contact, but as soon as I landed back there, she moved into my hotel room and lived in bed with me for the duration. I had no idea where she lived and we never went out in public. It was the way it had to be.

As usual, I am picked up from the airport by her driver, Zheng, the only other person that knows I exist; and find a note waiting for me.

It's time we got somewhere more permanent together. Cancel your hotel. M.

Our own place. That's upping the stakes a bit. Normally I'd be worried; but it's Mel. She's exactly what I'd look for in a woman. Beautiful, powerful, slightly terrifying, knows exactly what she wants and, most importantly, reassuringly unavailable.

Zheng delivers me to a suite at Marina Bay Sands, where a butler relieves me of my bags and puts the contents away carefully. I shower and put on a bathrobe and am on my third glass of champagne when she returns from work, hair up, still in her scrubs. She beams at me as she accepts her champagne from the butler.

'Leave us,' she instructs and he promptly disappears.

'Hello, you.' I stay in my seat with my feet up on a stool, and watch her cross the vast living area.

'What do you think? The Hyatt was getting too familiar.'

'I could definitely get used to this.'

She puts her champagne down and sheds her scrubs to reveal an intricately lacy flesh-coloured thong and brassiere.

'You're so fucking sexy,' I exhale, barely getting the words out.

She grins seductively and slides her hand up my bathrobe. I know what she wants, and I will gladly give it to her.

'Good to know that I still have the same effect on you, Caleb.'

She pulls my bathrobe open, exposing me, and climbs over me and sits slowly and precisely on me, teasing me inside her until I fill her. She begins to move, keeping her body at a distance, but holds my gaze. Her movements become more urgent. She's always like this when we first get together after some time apart. Like she needs to get it out of her system. By the end of my trip, she'll be blissfully relaxed and peacefully exhausted, as always. I watch as Melissa's wave tips her over the edge and she has her first release. I wait a couple of moments after she collapses on top of me to speak.

'Delighted to be back here with you,' I whisper into her hair.

She smiles that slow, feline smile of hers. She eventually climbs off me and hops into the shower. When she returns, she is wrapped in a white bathrobe and is waving the room service menu as she hops into bed.

'I hope you're hungry.' She smiles invitingly.

'Starving!' I confirm, joining her in bed, ready to settle in for the night.

. . .

I wake up late the next morning to Melissa on the phone, instructing someone to consider using Ivory Bow. She finishes the call quickly as she sees me sit up.

'Morning. You slept in late.'

'I was with an incredible woman with an insatiable appetite.'

She hides her eyes as she giggles.

'Was that a new client?'

'Potentially. DMVI. Great company. What does your schedule look like?'

'I have an early-evening meeting tomorrow, then I'm out all of Tuesday, and I have a few new leads to chase down on Wednesday and Thursday.'

'That's a lot. Don't you have enough to keep you busy?' She sticks her bottom lip out.

'I do.' I pull her onto my lap in bed. 'But I should try to win a few of my own.'

'Are you feeling like a kept man?' She smirks.

'A little.' I laugh.

'You are. Get used to it. Cancel your appointments.' She kisses me on my nose.

'I'd quite like to go,' I push back gently.

'Caleb, don't be exhausting. You're only here for five days. Why chase these sales contracts, when I can just give them to you?'

'Because I can't be dependent on you for ever, Mel.'

'Wait until your next trip. I promise I won't stand in your way. I need you this trip... hmmm?' She drapes herself over me. 'We have so many new surfaces to christen, and we should talk about what's going on here.'

She moves her index finger lazily between us. 'I have a wedding date.'

She has got to be joking.

'Melissa. We can't do this if you're married. Even *I* have to draw the line somewhere.' I get up and put a towel around me. I can't believe she is dropping this on me now.

'Relax, Caleb. I'm beginning to think you care.' She chuckles.

'Of course I care,' I spit back.

'We discussed this. No feelings. I know you're not in London alone, crying yourself to sleep over me. I'm very fond of you, but we knew this'd end eventually. When it does, we can't get emotional.'

'Why did you move us here then? It seems pretty significant for something that's going to end.'

'It is significant. I bought it for us. It could be our little hidey-hole when I get married. However, if you insist that this must end, it will become yours.'

'You're trying to turn me into your mistress?' I eye her suspiciously.

She bursts out laughing. 'Would you like to be?' She winks at me. 'Relax, Caleb. The set date isn't until next year and it will probably be moved anyway. Tricky things, prenups.'

'You don't have feelings for this guy. Don't marry him. Don't marry anyone. Maybe I could spend more time out here.'

'And what would that look like?' She lies on the bed. 'Indulge me.'

'Well, I'm killing it at work, thanks to you.'

She raises her eyebrows joyfully. 'You're welcome.'

'We could start up an Ivory Bow Asia...'

'And live happily ever after?'

'I wouldn't go that far... but we could build something together. It could be fun working with you.'

'Us working together? No. You'd have to be my house husband.' She pulls me down over her and kisses me. 'And no offence, but your industry sounds like a nightmare and it doesn't interest me in the slightest.'

'I could be a house husband...' I play along, knowing it would be my worst nightmare.

Mel relieves me of my towel and in my head, I instantly cancel all the meetings I have planned. I'm under no illusions though; I know that I am a distraction, a toy almost, that she enjoys playing with; and that nothing will ever come of this. That doesn't stop me from wanting it to last for as long as possible.

NINE

ARIELLA

This morning was a nightmare.

Caleb left for Singapore the day after the boyfriend incident, and I was still jumpy, which made sleeping almost impossible. Then I couldn't get any hot water through the taps, so I had to call one of the emergency numbers Caleb had left. Letting a strange man I'd never met into the house was frightening. Thankfully, the guy who turned up, Tim, was lovely. Embarrassingly, there was nothing wrong with the heating. He patiently explained the controls, then secured the flat before he gave me a wedge to put behind the door in the absence of a door chain. He declined payment when I offered, and volunteered to suggest a peephole to Caleb.

Only four hours of sleep has made me grouchy, and I'm also a little peeved to have been pulled into CrimeSpree's orbit at work. Though he is as white as they come, he seems especially keen to communicate with me using slang that I suspect would leave Jamaicans unimpressed. I grew up in leafy Surrey with an African-American mother and a father from the north of England. I genuinely don't understand what he is saying. Lara is going to have to claim this one back.

'When were you going to tell me that CrimeSpree's girlfriend is that "Bamidele" girl?' I say at lunch, popping a chip in my mouth.

Bamidele is an artist dedicated to challenging the norms and pushing the conversation. Her last project was a 36-foot installation of the ungroomed female body, rumoured to be an ex-lover, lactating and menstruating, with audio of women during childbirth playing every fifteen minutes.

Lara's perfectly manicured nails wave my question away. 'Any normal person would have asked the internet.'

'I shouldn't have to go on the internet, Lara. Besides, you can't trust Bamidele to keep this under wraps.'

'Why not? Did you know her name means "take me home"?' Lara raises an eyebrow. She is obviously not taking this seriously.

'I'm certain that wasn't the context her ancestors were going for. Give CrimeSpree back his girlfriend, Lara.'

'She isn't a possession. Plus, he hasn't noticed for weeks.'

'Think of your job, Lara – but, more importantly, think of your soul.'

'I gave up on my soul ages ago. Have you not been to a CrimeSpree gig?' She sniggers.

'Glad you mentioned that; he's gone from four concert dates to twelve.'

'I hate you. Why didn't you just lead with that?'

'I was hoping you'd do the right thing.'

Lara reaches across the table with her fork.

'Ow! Don't poke me, it hurts.' I rub my arm.

'That's for trying to force me to occupy the moral high ground with you. It's insulting and way beyond my natural disposition.'

'Lara!'

'Okay, okay. I'll end it. While we are sticking our noses in each other's nightmares, any Jasper news? Is he still holding the butcher and grocer hostage?' she says with a laugh.

'Annoyingly, yes. I know he's not cooking the stuff, he's just being petty.'

'You rich people and your problems. I don't understand why you don't just fight strangers for the last manky cabbage at the supermarket like everyone else. Aside from that, have you heard from him?'

'Don't overreact, okay?'

'I won't. What?' Lara is absolutely going to overreact.

'Mommy called me last night and demanded I bring a date to her fiftieth birthday, because Jasper is coming to dinner with a plus one.'

'Wait, Dahlia has found out? When did that happen?'

'Last night. Apparently, Jasper's mom called her with the news.'

'You haven't told her this whole time?'

'No.'

'Why?'

'Because she's...'

'Dahlia,' Lara finishes.

She knew. I didn't tell my parents, for two reasons. Firstly, they both love Jasper as much as they love Zachary and me, but I knew that they'd immediately take my side, which seemed unfair. Secondly, they'd ask why, and it's not a question I know the answer to. He wasn't guilty of any of the usual offences people in relationships commit. Everyone loved him, he looked after me; he was kind, generous, hard-working and dependable. So, telling them was going to be difficult and I'd been putting it off.

Last night, when my mother called while I was waiting for the handyman, my trepidation had unexpectedly become reality.

'Ariella, why is Jasper bringing someone that isn't you to my birthday dinner?'

This was typical Mommy. She delivered it like she was asking a mundane question. No small talk, no padding and definitely no initial hellos, when she had something on her mind.

'Oh, Mommy. I wanted to tell you and Daddy. I just didn't know how.' I burst into tears.

Her voice softened. 'Are you okay?'

'I don't know.'

'I'm sorry, sweetheart. What happened?'

I felt her love reach through the phone and envelop me.

'Nothing.'

'Honey, if your father finds out before I get the opportunity to talk him down, things aren't going to end well for Jasper.'

'Really, nothing happened, Mommy. I'd been thinking about leaving for a while and, then, I just did it.'

'You kids didn't break up?'

'No, I really just needed some space. I was feeling...'

'Trapped,' my mother completed. 'Did you really leave him nine words on a Post-it?'

I failed to hold back a sob, as fresh tears started to fall.

'I know I was appalling, Mommy. I just couldn't find the words.'

'I knew this would happen, but not like this, Ariella. This is very disappointing. I can't say that I'm proud of the way you handled this.'

'What did you just say, Mommy?'

'I said I'm disappointed.'

'No, before that.'

'That I knew it was going to happen?'

'Did you?'

'You guys did get together pretty quickly.'

'No, we didn't. We waited, and we talked—'

'No. *He* waited. One minute you're graduating after hiding

from everyone at university for three years and you cannot bear to be around each other. Then we go away for one weekend and suddenly he's asking to speak to your father privately? Your father didn't help either; he wouldn't listen. He was so happy, he gave his blessing away like free chopsticks with takeaway. I love Jasper more than I love Zachary most of the time, but your father loves Jasper too much and was too frightened to trust anyone else with you. Meanwhile, we have a more immediate problem.'

'Oh no?'

'He has a date. There's no way you're going to sit there being a victim while some woman we don't know drapes herself all over him. I don't care who it is, but you need a date.'

'Can I think about it? I don't want him to think I left to be with someone else.' I already knew the answer.

'No. You can't. And we both know there is no chance that he'd think that. Get a date, because hiding in your room for this one is not an option. Oh, and I love you. Even though you've been very, very naughty.'

With that, she hung up.

I hate it when she does that. She knows how to make me uncomfortable enough to do something I wouldn't ordinarily do. I love and trust my mother, but she's always the last person I'd confide in. Unfortunately, it makes no difference. She is always able to sniff out any situation I'm in, pry it out of me and make me take action. She's fearless, bold, confident and isn't scared of anything. She just has a hard time believing that I'm not her.

'Aari!' Lara interrupts my thoughts.

'Sorry.'

'Jasper is bringing someone to the family dinner? Not the "Joe Public" party afterwards, to the actual family dinner?' Lara's voice is getting louder and her finger is getting jabbier by the syllable. 'Dahlia is bang on. You do need a date. And they need to be insanely hot, *and* you need a killer dress. Like, SERIOUSLY KILLER. That arsehole is doing this to piss you off. Bringing his date to the party would be the default revenge move, but the family dinner? That's just a fucking insult. I know your mum treats Jasper like Zachary, but she needs to extend that treatment to include a slap every now and then. Who the hell does he think he is? The audacity, the gumption, the—'

'Lara, you said you wouldn't overreact.'

'This is me *under*-reacting. Right. I'm dressing you for the party.'

Dread fills me. The last time we went shopping together, we spent six hours looking at eye-wateringly expensive clothes that neither of us were going to buy while Lara turned me into her personal clothes horse, even though we have different body types. It was a nightmare and I'm not keen to repeat the experience.

'It's okay, I think I have a dress I can wear.'

'Heeeell no. I've seen your wardrobe. You're getting a new dress and it needs to be insane. I'll pick out some for you to try the day before the party. Next, you need a date.'

'I don't want to rub Jasper's face in it by bringing a stranger, Lara. You have to remember that I'm the bad guy here.'

'Maybe, but he has declared outright war by bringing a date to the family dinner. You have to respond. If we set you up on Swipey, you have three weeks to meet someone and "de-stranger" them enough to invite them to the party.'

'Isn't that just for people that want to get laid?'

'Not everyone wants to get laid... straight away. Just have a couple of conversations, meet them for coffee, string it out a bit and get them to the party. They have to be smoking hot, though. I mean it. Gimme your phone.'

'I'm not sure about this...'

Lara shoots me a threatening look. 'You have less than a month, Aari. You need to wade through the sewer. It's much harder than you think.'

'I'll look at it tonight.'

'Aari?' Lara reaches for my hand across the table and holds it in hers. 'I want you to know that I think you're brave. It takes real courage to walk away from a situation that so many people invested in.'

'Are you being nice or insulting?'

'A bit of both. I'm trying to tell you that you can go to this party alone and be fine. You don't need a date. However, my pettiness and desire for you to get one up on Jasper would love you to have one.'

I have to laugh. 'I promise to give pettiness a go.'

'Don't forget to take the Friday afternoon before off. We have a dress to buy.'

After our meal, Lara and I head back to work and, by the end of that week, Bamidele is back in CrimeSpree's house, without him suspecting a thing.

TEN

CALEB

'Hello, losers,' I say, bouncing into the team sales meeting that Friday morning straight from the airport. I'm refreshed because Mel, as always, flew me back first class.

'Thank you for joining us, Caleb,' the director of sales, Mark, groans. Harrison, our co-founder, subtly gives me an encouraging thumbs-up.

'I just landed, so I thought I'd dump the enquiries today rather than wait until Monday.' I grab an available seat and Mark regains control of the room.

'Let's make this quick. Figures and headlines.'

We basically have to declare the value of the contract, the company and location. I volunteer and take the first slot. I pop three-quarters of a million pounds turnover on the table. The room is speechless.

'How the fuck do you do it, mate?' Harrison asks, laughing.

'I play nice and I'm always open to suggestions.' I smirk.

The next closest table drop is sixty grand. At the end of the meeting, I grab my suitcase and head straight out of the building. Jack and Tim will be up for a cheeky lunchtime beer, and I'm in the mood to celebrate.

. . .

'Hello, Bev,' I call out as I walk in.

She ignores me. Nothing's changed there then. Shame. I commandeer a table with my jacket and the boys walk in just in time to claim their pints.

'Who's the knockout living with you?' Jack asks.

'Whoa! I didn't say she was a knockout.' For the first time since I have known him, I see Tim blush bright red.

'Ariella?' I'm stunned.

'I said she was a lovely girl. Sweet. She didn't know how to turn the boiler on. She thought it was broken, so she called on Sunday night.'

'You said she was beautiful,' Jack challenges.

'Really?' I scrunch up my nose. Tim must have had a few before he went over.

'She's nice. She wanted to pay me so you didn't have to. Even offered me something to eat.'

'I wouldn't feel too special about that, she cooks for us every night... Wait. Do you fancy her?'

This is a big deal. Tim has only ever had Em-shaped eyes.

'She cooks for you every night?' Jack interrogates.

'I don't fancy her. I'm married. I have children. I love my wife.'

'Good, because she's weird; she folds the washing strangely and now wants to buy breakfast for people who might spend the night. I don't need them getting comfortable in the morning and not leaving.'

'She folds your laundry, buys your little harem breakfast, Tim wants to shag her and you don't? Wow!'

'I don't want to shag her and that's disgusting. She can't be more than nineteen. She was sweet, that's all. You need to put a chain and a peephole on that door, Caleb, if you're going to keep leaving her on her own. I can fix it for you, if you like,' Tim offers.

I know he is doing it because he is paternal and old-school, but I can't help myself.

'She's only a couple of years younger than me, so you'd be in the clear. And she's already given me the "I don't feel safe when you come home in the middle of the night with different people" speech. I don't come home with *that* many people,' I complain.

'She's right – it's not safe, Caleb. She was terrified when she opened the door to me, even after she made me recite my mobile phone number.'

'That's just overly paranoid,' I dismiss.

'No, it's practical if you don't have a chain and a peephole. I gave her a door wedge as a poor solution. Did you know she's never lived on her own before?'

'Of course she has. She lived with her boyfriend.'

'Who she moved in with directly from her parents' house and, from the sound of it, had his house kitted out like a fortress.'

'She told you all this in the two seconds it took you to turn the boiler on?'

'Yes, and I stayed to show her how to set it. Then I made sure all the windows were locked and the flat was secure.'

'Did you now?' I raise both my eyebrows at him.

'Yes, I did. She seemed scared, Caleb, and she looked pretty sad.'

'That's her default face. Sad. There's no happy setting.'

'That's a nasty thing to say.' Tim takes a swig of his pint. What is up with him today?

'Mate, you don't live with her. She's a pain in the arse.'

'I hear that. She cooks for you, does your washing and tries to be kinder than you are to whoever you drag home.'

When Tim says it like that, I do sound like a bit of a bastard.

'What's up with you today?' I ask.

'You left a young girl that has never lived alone in a flat without a peephole and a chain. You didn't tell anyone she was there. And I saw your pathetic list of emergency contacts. Nine-nine-nine, one-one-one and my phone number. You didn't even bother to put Jack's on there, just in case. You just left her. I turned up for five minutes and I could see she wasn't doing well. You're all right though, because you're in Singapore shagging your—'

'I need to see this girl,' Jack demands.

'Well, it seems Tim here, who apparently doesn't fancy her, will be returning to put a chain and a peephole on my door. You can be his apprentice,' I offer drily.

'I'll slot it in,' Tim adds firmly, before we finish up our drinks.

It's nice to wake up late in my own bed. Being cooped up, surviving on Michelin star-level room service and doing dirty things with Mel is a little bit like Vegas. Loads of fun, but you're done after a few days. It feels great to knock out some miles running in the brisk air on the Heath. It will set me up for a day wandering around a French Impressionist exhibition Nicole wanted me to see with her. I'm about to leave when she texts to cancel.

> Sorry Caleb. I can't come today. I feel quite ill so I'll be in bed all day.

> You can come over and look after me if you like? Bisous N

> Oh no. Sorry to hear that. Feel better. C

I'm not looking after Nicole. It's not that kind of relationship and I don't want to catch anything. Time to make alternative plans. I open my dating app; maybe someone wants to meet for a coffee. That's when I see it.

'Ariella! Is this you on Swipey?' I dissolve into laughter as I skip out of my bedroom into the kitchen. 'What are you doing on there? Good for you.'

'My friend set a profile up for me.' She giggles, joining in to laugh at herself.

'You need to change your pictures. You look like you're being forced at gunpoint to smile in this one. Also, your bio. This is *not* you.'

'Oh no. What does it say?' She looks worried.

"Looking for brains, brawn and a badass body. Be brave, be bold, but don't bother if you're only down for a booty-call. Brace yourself, I could be your future babe."

Ariella is so horrified she actually drops her wooden spoon.

'Wow... I am *totally* swiping right.' And that's exactly what I do. 'Have you had many responses?'

She shrugs. There is no way I am going to pass this up. It's time to check out the competition.

'Gimme your phone.'

I expect resistance. Instead, she picks the phone out of her back pocket and hands it over.

'Fifty-two, seventy-seven, thirty-seven.'

'You don't just hand your phone and code to anyone that asks.'

'Why not?'

'What if someone goes through your pictures?'

'Why wouldn't I want someone to go through my pictures?'

This chick is living in a different century. I don't know where to begin, so I don't bother. She has tons of messages.

'You haven't responded to anyone?'

'It's only been a couple of days. I haven't looked.'

I swipe no to a couple of guys and my profile comes up. I

look good in the photo, even if I do say so myself. I swipe right for fun.

'Shall I select some matches for you?'

'Sure.' She starts sifting some flour into a bowl.

She doesn't seem to mind, so I sit there vetting some good guys by picture and bio. She matches with almost all of them. Is this what it's like for women on here?

'What kind of guys do you like?' I have gone through the obvious ones and am now looking further afield.

'Someone kind.'

She places a cake tin into the oven and starts peeling some sweet potatoes. She didn't just say that.

'Seriously?'

'Seriously. Someone nice, polite and lovely. If things don't work out, they'd want to be friends.'

She's bananas. 'Do you know how Swipey works?'

'Of course.'

'The whole point of this is to go out on dates with people you might like, but don't want to see again, if you catch my drift?'

She stops cooking and looks as if she is contemplating telling me something.

'Go on, out with it.'

'Okay, but you can't judge me.' She looks at me guiltily.

'Don't you know who you're living with? I'm the last person to judge anyone.'

'My ex-boyfriend is invited to my mom's birthday in a couple of weeks and he's bringing a date.' She looks ashamed.

'So you're going to find someone, pretend you like them and make him jealous?' She's more cunning than I gave her credit for.

'No. That's not it. I don't want to show up alone and make my mom's party about me. But I also don't want to make Jasper feel like I ran off with someone else. I need to find someone I can go with, just as friends. Honestly, I'll be using them. Does that make me a horrible person?'

'It makes you human,' I say, going soft on her. Poor girl, she's never going to survive out here in the wild.

'You don't think it's cruel? It might hurt Jasper's feelings.'

There's that name again. Jasper. What a toffy name. Even the way she says it sounds like money.

'What's your family doing inviting this guy to the birthday anyway? Surely if you broke up, then he's automatically disinvited?'

She shuts her eyes and shakes her head slowly. 'Are you hungry?' she asks unexpectedly.

'I could eat.'

'There's a two thousand and three Margaux in that box. Could you decant it?' She points to an empty bottle. I grab the wine, open it and pour it into the empty.

'Slowly, Caleb. You don't want the sediment in the decanter,' she instructs gently, without being patronising.

She grabs a couple of plates from the cupboard and opens the full oven.

'Fish pie okay?'

'Sure. How much have you cooked today?'

'A lot.'

For the first time since she moved in, she laughs wholeheartedly. I find myself laughing along. It's a naughty and infectious laugh, with her eyes crinkling at the corners. She sets two places for us.

'I hope you don't mind. I haven't had a home-cooked meal with company in a while.'

I don't actually, but the ceremony of the place settings is a bit much. Not that I complain. Ariella fills a jug of water for the meal and pours two glasses of wine. She serves some pie and sits next to me. She smells nice. We clink glasses before she begins the story of her and Jasper.

I listen, entertained, surprised and envious. By the time she finishes, I feel like I know her family, and Jasper's. She confirms a few things I suspected. With a massive house in Surrey, it is obvious that her family is loaded, and so is this Jasper character's. Her childhood sounds worlds away from mine.

Part of me resents her for having everything so easy that her biggest problem in life is walking out on some boy because she didn't want to be his wife. She is spoilt and entitled, and the real world is about to hit her in the face.

'Is the small fedora and whip tattooed on your ankle about him?'

'Yes.' She smiles, recalling a fond memory.

Oh shit. She'll be back with him in no time. The first time I spotted it, I thought she was just low-key kinky, which made her a little more interesting. The reality is much worse. I'm going to have to look for someone else to rent to soon. No way is she done with this guy for good.

She starts to clear away our meal and I join in. I feel the urge to help her. It isn't her fault she grew up the way she did, and I do feel a little sorry for her. She is out here alone, about to be eaten alive. I also want to see what her real life is like.

'I'll come with you if you want,' I offer.

'You don't have to. I should just deal with it.'

'Do you want a friend there or not?'

'Really?'

The sweetest smile comes over her face. Surprisingly, it makes me feel good. I imagine that Ariella is the type of girl men enjoy doing things for. Tim is already pissed off with me and on her side after spending seconds with her. I can do this and tell Tim I've been nice. She *is* a good housemate, just a little clueless.

'Yeah. I'll come with you,' I say, returning the smile.

'Thank you, Caleb. It's formal. Is that okay?'

'Black tie?'

'Just a suit and tie will do.'

'Want me at the family dinner?'

'I wouldn't do that to you. If you could come to the party, I'd be very grateful.'

I get it. She's rising above it.

'I have a slightly related question.' I have to ask.

'Yeah?'

'Where are all your friends?' I've been curious.

'We have exactly the same friends and I don't want to make them choose. Also, the time alone is nice.'

'So, no plans for tonight?'

'Aside from running all this to the shelter and doing some laundry, no.'

'They take food from anyone at the shelter?'

'No, but I've been cooking for them for a while and, whenever I'm cooking at the weekend, I run stuff over to add to whatever they have.'

'If you pack up everything you're taking, I'll help wash up and come with you, if you like?'

'Thank you! That'd be great!'

We clean up in the kitchen and grab a taxi for the round trip. It was good to see her smiling – aside from a slight lip-wobble after discovering that Jasper had dropped loads of food off just before we got there. When we get back, she thanks me for helping and immediately starts the escape to her room. I see my chance to reach out.

'Thanks for the itinerary for the bachelor party, by the way.'

'You're welcome. You guys will have a great time. Let me know if you want any more help.'

She continues to her room. Can't she tell I am trying to be nice? I give it one last try.

'So, have you heard of a show called *The Sopranos*?'

'I've heard of it, but Jas and I didn't watch much TV.'

'Want to watch an episode with me? I've only just started

season one. It's about the Italian Mafia in New Jersey and New York. It's violent and there's a lot of nudity but it's bloody good.' I can tell that she appreciates being asked.

'Will you fill me in on what's happened so far?' she asks, approaching the couch.

'Sure, I'll catch you up.'

ELEVEN

ARIELLA

Lara is literally convulsing with delight in the back of the black cab as we head to the shop.

'Thanks for volunteering to help, but it really isn't a big deal.'

'Are you kidding me? It's not a big deal? This is the first time you're going to see Jasper after Post-it-Gate.' She's bouncing up and down in her seat like an excited child.

'He has a date, Lara. He's not going to care.'

'You are *so* wrong. He's about to remember what he passed up.'

'He didn't pass anything up. I'm the awful one here.'

'Trust me, babe. Dahlia wouldn't have bullied you into bringing a plus one if he wasn't serious about this new girl. She's coming to the family dinner. That's a statement. You don't want him back, do you?'

'I don't know. I still love him.'

'Then you really should've spoken to him, rather than pulling a Houdini.'

When we get to Knightsbridge, Lara blows through Harvey Nichols like a force of nature and immediately plies me with champagne to take the edge off. Up to a point, she succeeds, by the fourth glass, I am trying on everything the personal shopper puts in front of me without resistance. Thankfully, though, I am not inebriated enough to take all the outfits seriously.

We eventually agree on a simple floor-length column gown with a daringly low back. She pairs it with some silver sandals. I must admit it looks beautiful, but it isn't until we've paid that the realisation hits me.

'Lara, I'm not going to be able to wear any underwear with this!'

'Nope! Not traditional underwear anyway. We'll have to get you those patch things.' She beams triumphantly. 'You know, if you weren't my best friend and saving me from being fired, I'd hit on you in that dress.'

When I get home, I hear giggling coming from Caleb's bedroom. I pray that he will be on his best behaviour. We've been getting along, but I am still worried. To my delight, he has settled into seeing only Nicole from work, but he still speaks about her in a very casual way. I've decided to quietly celebrate every day that I don't wake up to a stranger in the kitchen. I hope he doesn't hit on someone at the party. The anxiety of all that might happen tomorrow starts to overwhelm me, so I undress quickly, step into my bathroom and stand under the shower to let the water calm my nerves. As I climb into bed, I let the truth sink in. Jasper is going to be there with someone else.

I get up early the next morning, and walk into Nicole making breakfast.

'Morning,' I call as I pull my overnight case to the door.

The shock on her face is unmistakable. It occurs to me that, because I usually disappear before she arrives, she may not know that I live here. And Caleb obviously hasn't shared that little bit of information either. Time to make myself scarce.

'You know Caleb's housemate?' Nicole challenges.

'Erm...'

Caleb has really dropped me in it this time. The woman I am looking at is not giving off warm, loving vibes. She probably thinks something is going on, which is laughable – but equally believable, thanks to his less than pristine reputation. Thankfully, she doesn't wait for an answer.

'I thought you had a boyfriend.'

'We broke up.'

Okay. Nice dodge, Ariella. Be calm, just leave. I return to grab my leather satchel and pop my Converse on. I am almost out of the front door when Caleb comes through to the kitchen half-naked. I fix my eyes on the floor. Whatever I do, I must not look at him, because Nicole looks like she is about to go for anything that moves.

'Bye, guys,' I whisper, scurrying to the door.

'See you later,' he calls after me.

'What's happening later?' I hear Nicole start yelling at him as I shut the door behind me.

I've always loved watching the imposing buildings of London fade away to the English countryside as my train moves closer to Weybridge station. I jump out, wave to our friendly stationmaster and start the twenty-minute walk home through the quiet, narrow roads that branch off into long driveways that lead to beautiful family homes. Unlike most of the houses on our street, we don't have a gate at the end of our driveway, which also happens to be shorter than most.

I finally make it home and wander into the warm kitchen to find my mother, father, Zachary and Isszy having breakfast.

'Baby!' My mother wraps me tightly in her arms.

'Happy birthday, Mommy.'

I feel her love radiate through me, causing tears to spring to my eyes. Being hugged by my mother always makes everything okay. I see Daddy already setting a place for me to join them for breakfast. Mommy lets go just as Daddy comes over.

'Hello, love.'

I give him a kiss on the cheek before I disappear into his huge hug. I miss home. I am really lucky to have the parents I was dealt, with their vastly different personalities. My mom, who doesn't look a day over twenty-five, was a little black girl who grew up in the Deep South. She was raised to be a prim and proper lady and to have exceptionally good manners. Not that you would know it. She is full of mischief and fun; is warm, provocative, fiercely loyal, and would go to war with whoever she needs to in order to protect her family. She stays current and usually knows much more about pop culture than I do. She is my best friend and greatest ally.

My father, on the other hand, is a patient and calm farmer's son from Cumbria. He is a retired member of the SAS, and still works in some capacity with British Special Forces, through his own private security firm. Aside from being tall and broad, nothing about him gives his work life away. At home, he is always soft and sweet, like a big teddy bear.

'Hey.' Zachary waves from the table, not bothering to get up.

'Hey.' I smile back.

Isszy is next. I love Isszy. She is quiet, bold – and adored, because she effortlessly handles Zachary. She's the editor at a fashion magazine, so she always looks beautifully put together. She has the same dark, rich skin tone as my mother and I am often amazed at how every colour and pattern she wears looks alive against her complexion.

'I thought I'd help you get ready, if you like, tonight? I brought some dresses and make-up with me. Dahlia has given me strict instructions to make you look stunning. I promise not to use too much.' She grins.

'Yes please, Isz,' I say, hugging her and rolling my eyes at Mommy.

I sit at the table and spoon some eggs onto my plate.

'Let's have it. What did he do?' Zachary typically cuts to the chase.

'Zachary!' Mommy scolds.

'It's okay. He didn't do anything. I've needed some space for a while.'

'He's terribly cut up about it. He keeps calling to ask if I know what he did. I've told him to talk to you, but he refuses. I'm not meant to be mentioning this really,' Zachary says between bites.

'I know he deserves an explanation, but I don't have one,' I reply, frowning at my plate.

'You better think of one, just in case he asks tonight. He's a decent bloke, Scraps. He needs something to move on. He came home to his perfect life and with no warning, his fiancée, the one person he's had a thing for his whole life, the only person he's ever really loved, is gone. All he gets is one sentence on a piece of paper. I mean, that's pretty brutal.'

Daddy looks at me with surprise. I feel the shame wash over me.

'You kids didn't have a fight?' Daddy asks.

I can't look at him.

'He didn't treat you badly, did he?' Isszy adds, concerned.

Zachary bursts out laughing, losing half of the scrambled eggs in his mouth to the table. I hate him sometimes.

'Jas? If he only had one kidney left, he'd give it to her; even now. He's obsessed. His entire life plan revolved around making Scrappy here happy.'

He points his fork at me. He knows I hate that nickname. It was what I called him before I could say Zachary.

'That's enough, Zachary,' says Mommy firmly. 'She's hardly doing cartwheels. As much as it saddens me, Jasper will move on. He's bringing a date tonight, so maybe he's moving on already.'

'Who? Katherine?' Zachary rolls his eyes. 'His mom invited her. He wasn't going to come, out of respect for you and Dad.'

This is news. I feel the walls closing in. 'Can we not talk about this any more please?' I ask quietly.

'Yes of course, darling.' Daddy reaches out to hold my hand and the subject is immediately closed.

'I have a gift for you, Mommy,' I announce, going to my bag and returning with a wrapped box. 'I hope I've done it justice.'

Mommy carefully unwraps my present and lets out a gasp, before her eyes start to fill with tears.

It took close to a year, but I managed to get Cartier to replicate an intricate pair of diamond earrings that were given to her by her grandmother. She'd worn them at her wedding to represent her absent family, along with a matching necklace. However, Mommy and Daddy had fallen on hard times when Zachary was three and I was a baby, so she sold the set to keep our family going. That jewellery, the way Daddy told it, paid the rent, kept the lights on, put food on the table and kept us all warm for over a year and a half. It was the only thing she had from her family, but she gave it up without being asked. Zachary reaches under his chair and produces a larger box. It's the necklace.

'Mommy, we know. Thank you for always putting us before yourself.'

'Hugh!' she scolds Daddy as she starts to really cry.

And then Isszy puts another little box on the table. Using the same design, she had a brooch created with an intricate DM integrated into the pattern.

'Oh, Isszy, it's beautiful,' Mommy whispers, unable to contain her emotion.

There is one more piece.

'Is it okay?' Daddy whispers to me.

I nod.

Daddy reaches into his pocket. 'Lia? Jasper wanted me to give this to you. He's sorry he couldn't be here this morning, but he will see you tonight.'

Daddy produces a long box. It contains a bracelet of the same design. Jasper had sent his designs back to the jeweller more than the rest of us and had also secretly had my engagement ring made using the exact same design. I hold back the tears. This is not about me.

Mommy checks to see if I am okay. I smile and nod, absentmindedly rubbing my ring finger, yearning for the ring that isn't there.

Jasper's gift contains a note, which Mom begins to read. 'Thank you for giving me a loving home when I so desperately needed one and for helping me to become the man I am today. Whatever the future holds, you will always be a mother to me. Your son, Jasper.'

Mommy can't contain her tears.

I can't help the tears that fall for my mother and Jasper. He is part of our family and always will be. I love him, I know I do. What is wrong with me?

'I know we aren't supposed to talk about it any more, but he really does need an explanation, Aari. He is our best friend and he's in excruciating pain right now because of you. We can't abandon him. Talk to him. Please?' Zachary urges softly.

No one objects this time. Zachary is right.

After breakfast, the caterers and event designers move in. I cover up Mommy's rose bushes to protect them, and help as much as I can. When I go up to my room for a nap, my mother arrives five minutes later and tells me to scooch over. There will be no napping. She gets in, extends her arm under my head and folds me into a cuddle.

'Are you okay?' she asks quietly as she strokes my forehead.

'I miss him.'

'Honey, I love Jasper, but neither of you should be unhappy.'

'Do you think I made the wrong choice? Lara said I threw away "the dream".'

'You can't stay with someone if you're not happy. Maybe you could both use some time apart; there's so much you haven't experienced yet, baby. I'm not suggesting you be "that ho over there"—'

'Mommy!' I am shocked, but I can't help laughing.

'What? I know what a "thot" is.' She laughs with me. 'I'm serious, though. Life has maybe been a little too safe for you, and maybe you could use this time. Discover yourself, make mistakes, find what makes you happy – and if you go back, if you *can* go back, then just make sure it's what you want.'

I arrive in a bathrobe as Daddy is getting kicked out of my parents' bedroom. Isszy is sipping on some champagne and is already helping Mommy into a boat-neck, navy-blue fitted dress. Isszy's own outfit is a flapper-inspired cream dress that looks beautiful against her iridescent chocolate skin.

I try on some of the dresses Isszy brought, but everyone insists that I wear the white column dress Lara and I bought. I complain about the lack of underwear, but am ignored. They eventually take pity on me and I borrow one of Mommy's light shoulder wraps for modesty.

Isszy does our make-up, straightens my hair and makes Mommy look like a goddess, with navy eyes and nude lips. She gently puts some eyeliner and lip balm on me, leaving the rest of my face bare, and does the same for herself. As we come downstairs to Daddy and Zachary looking handsome in their fitted suits, I feel intense regret that Jasper isn't there. The space he usually occupies, to the left of Daddy, is glaringly empty. This is my fault. I deserve this. Daddy extends both his arms and takes Mommy in one and me in the other, then leads us to the waiting limousine without a word.

When we arrive at dinner, the very first face I see is Jasper's. He is standing in a corner, champagne in hand, talking to the girl I presume is his date. She is strikingly beautiful in a little black dress that clings to every curve of her stunning body. Jasper catches me staring and I offer him a small smile. He returns it and carries on speaking with her.

'What's happened there then?' my father's sister, Aunty Kim, says a little too loudly in her broad Cumbrian accent, jabbing her thumb in Jasper's direction.

'It didn't work out.'

'Please tell me you brought a date?'

'No. It wouldn't be acceptable to do that, Aunty Kim.'

'Too right, Aari. Too bloody right.' She shoots him a disapproving look.

During dinner, I try not to look at him, but each time my eye wanders over there he is deep in conversation with Katherine, ignoring my end of the table. She is touching him, a lot. The five sumptuous courses seem to speed past and just before dessert, Mommy gets up to make a speech.

'I'm the luckiest woman alive. I'm the wife to a loving husband and a mother of four. I've been on the receiving end of the kindest, most generous people; and when I left my family and the sunshine all those years ago, I had no idea that love, friendship and a new family could be found in the middle of all this grey and rain.'

Everyone laughs.

'Hugh, there has only ever been, will only ever be, you. You are my soul, my light, my anchor and my love. I would never have become the person I am today without you. You are the centre of my everything.

'Zachary, you have taught me so much about truth and integrity, and, even though it is glaringly obvious we're getting nowhere with teaching you diplomacy and subtlety, I wouldn't change you for the world.

'Isszy, thank you for being born and thank you for being the only person, it seems, that Zachary listens to and is, quite frankly, terrified of. Your spirit, kindness and iron fist is very welcome in this family and I'm so grateful for you.

'My baby Aari. You are my best friend, my confidante, and I'm so thankful that you've given me the privilege of seeing the world through your eyes. My life is more innocent, warmer and richer because of you. Your heart is pure and, even when your soul is troubled, your relentless grip on hope is an astonishing thing to witness. Finally, to my second son, Jasper.'

Everyone turns to him to witness the look of surprise on his face.

'Our family isn't complete without you. Your presence has taught us to love, like we never thought capable. We missed you at breakfast this morning. You must not stay away or remove yourself, because each and every single one of us is less without you. Life deals us many challenges and our paths do sometimes diverge, but what holds us together is being a family. We will always be your home. I love you, my son. We all do.'

Jasper tips his head down and away from the table. I want to go to him, wrap myself around him and tell him I'm sorry there and then, but I fight every urge inside me to do so.

After dinner we return to the house, where we hear the upbeat jazz band playing from our driveway amidst the party guests arriving. As our limo pulls up, a black cab pulls in front of us, and out jumps Caleb. He stands still, taking it all in, with his hands in his pockets. He's tall and crisp in a black suit, white shirt and a skinny black tie, channelling old Hollywood.

His jet-black hair is swept over and flicked to the side, giving him a cool, young Sinatra vibe. His bright eyes shine against the night sky as he looks around. I had no idea he was able to pull handsome and polished out of the bag, which is a relief. As his eyes fall on me, he gives me a quick wink and a sly smile before he starts walking towards the house. I knew he was going to be mischievous.

'Caleb,' I call.

He looks around before his eyes settle on me. 'Ariella? Is that you?' He walks up quickly and turns to my father first. 'Mr Mason?'

My father nods.

'Good to meet you, sir. I'm Caleb Black, Ariella's flatmate.'

My father takes Caleb's outstretched hand.

'Is this your sister?' He turns to my mother with a charming smile.

I expect my mom to see right through his cheap charm, but instead she giggles and slaps his arm away. My mother only hits you if she likes you. This is not good.

'Stop it!' She beams at Caleb.

I catch Daddy turning one side of his mouth down into a frown. I pull Caleb away as he is checking out my mother. I don't think so.

'Caleb, this is Zachary and his girlfriend, Isszy.'

'Great to meet you, guys – Ariella was right, you are a gorgeous couple.'

'Come on, let's go inside,' I say, dragging him away quickly before he hits on Isszy.

'You scrub up all right. I didn't recognise you!'

I take it as a compliment and let it go.

Caleb puts out his arm and I take it as we go up the steps to the house. By the open door, he takes my wrap from my arm and places his hand on the small of my back to guide me in. The warmth of his hand against my cold skin makes me shiver. Caleb then leans in, whispering and laughing into my ear.

'I'm guessing that you're not wearing any knickers, and that if I undo the clasp over your shoulder this thing is going to fall to pieces?'

He strokes my shoulder clasp. I instinctively elbow him in the stomach, making him release a loud 'Oof!'

'Ariella!' Mommy yells my name from behind us.

Everyone has just seen me assault Caleb. Jasper, who has caught up with Daddy, is smiling. Great.

'She's merciless, Mrs Mason. And a nightmare to live with.' Caleb laughs.

Almost everyone joins with laughter and I see the smile abruptly disappear from Jasper's face.

We are soon enveloped by the sights and sounds of Mardi Gras. Ivory Bow has converted the house into New Orleans, with Bourbon Street starting in the kitchen and ending up in our back garden. I can actually smell Louisiana.

'Wow! Is this us?' Caleb asks, astonished.

'Yes. The production guys have done a great job.'

I stand at the bottom of the stairs with Caleb next to me, which is the cue for the music to die down. As soon as my father relieves my mother of her coat, everyone, including the guests outside, burst into a rousing rendition of 'Happy Birthday'.

At the end of the song, Caleb, as I suspected he would, leaves me where I am and disappears into the crowd. I, in turn, sneak up to my room. I don't want to be confronted with any questions for now. As I lie on my back, I tell myself I'll go down and make the effort for Mommy later. A few minutes later, there is a knock on my door and my mom lets herself in.

'I knew you'd be in here.' She smiles as she sits on my bed. 'I know dinner was tough, but I'm proud of you.' She pats my leg lovingly. 'Caleb is a lot of fun.' She raises an eyebrow. 'He looks like he's lots of trouble too.'

'My goodness. You like him?'

'I do. He's very charming and seems like he knows how to have a good time. I just left him hitting on that Katherine girl.' She stands up and smooths down the front of her dress. 'I just came to check in with you. Don't stay up here all night, honey.'

'I won't, I promi—'

There's another knock on the door and Mommy goes to open it. A sheepish-looking Jasper is standing on the other side. My heart leaps to my throat. The love I feel for him seems to reach out for him all on its own.

'I can come back...'

'No, sweetheart. I was just leaving.' My mother reaches up to cup the side of his head. He lowers it for her to kiss his temple like she usually does. 'Go in.'

Jasper walks in and stands at the opposite end of the room as he waits for my mom to close the door behind her. We regard each other in silence.

'I'm sorry, Jasper,' I start.

He looks up in exasperation. 'I'm sorry too,' he says with a sigh.

I am perplexed. 'For what?'

'For behaving the way I did and saying what I said, the night you came over. For Katherine; I should've handled dinner better. She shouldn't have been there.'

'It's okay. I deserved it.' I get up. I need to get out of this room, because all I want to do is reach out, kiss him and make him feel better.

'Wait. Can we talk?' He steps forward, stroking the side of my face as I lean into his hand. I miss being touched by him. This is not going well. 'Tell me what went wrong, Scraps,' he asks softly.

'I don't know. I lay there every night for months having panic attacks while you slept. I love you so much, Jas, but the thought of being with you made me feel safe and also scared at the same time. Life with you was wonderful, but it started to suffocate me. This is going to sound stupid, but I didn't leave you, Jas – I left my life. You just happened to be at the centre of it.' I know I am making no sense.

'I loved our life. It was exactly what I wanted, and it kills me to know you didn't feel the same, Scrappy.'

He takes my hands in his. When Jasper calls me Scrappy, or Scraps for short, it has the opposite effect of when Zachary does it. I love it, especially after he came back from a boys' weekend away with a small tattoo of Scrappy-Doo, the cartoon puppy, with his paws up on the back of his ankle. Zachary had talked him out of getting it on his chest, over his heart. I'd gone out the very next day and got a small outline of Indiana Jones' fedora and whip in the exact same position.

'I'm sorry, Jas. You've done enough to decide what you want. I haven't. I graduated, got a job, freeloaded off my parents for a few years, got another job and freeloaded off you next. I've done nothing.'

'Firstly, you're not freeloading. Secondly, we could do those things together. I'd take a year out to do anything you wanted with you.'

'Jasper, that won't help. Everything I am is defined by you. I like what you like, and feel what you feel. I even dress like you. Since being on my own, I've discovered that I don't know how to exist without you.'

'Not tonight, you aren't. I'll admit to influencing the Oxford shirts and jeans but the tweed jackets and boots are all you.'

Jasper smiles as he slowly drops my hand, steps forward, pulls me towards him and kisses me. I am not prepared for my lips to part and welcome his, but they do, a little too eagerly. He runs his finger from the base of my neck to the bottom of my spine and lets it rest against the naked skin there.

Jasper has never kissed me like this before, and I want to

leave with him right now. But then I get a grip, and eventually pull away slowly.

'Jas, if we continue like this I'll have moved back before the party ends.'

'Come back home, Scraps.'

I really want to. 'I can't. Not yet. I want to challenge myself; maybe live a little differently.'

'And I can't be part of that?'

'I'm sorry.'

'I'm not sure I can cope with waiting for you, Aari. I nearly lost it tonight. I didn't like the way the chap you walked in with looked at you. Hugh had to hold me back when he touched you,' he admits quietly.

He is standing so close, I can feel his breath.

'Caleb? That's his equivalent of a knee-slap – and he's a bit of a perv, he looks at everyone that way.'

'He won't be the last, though, and I don't think I can handle it.'

Suddenly, my bedroom door swings open with a bang.

'Ah! Finally, Ariella! You're missing the party. Chop-chop! Let's go.' Caleb is standing there, clapping his hands, looking impatient.

'You're not supposed to be up here,' Jasper responds coldly.

'Yes I am. I was having a perfectly lovely time before I was dispatched to get her. So here I am. You, come on.' Caleb points at me and starts waving us past him.

'Caleb, can you give us a minute?' I ask politely.

'No. You guys broke up for a reason. Right now, you're standing there half-naked with no knickers on, he's dressed like James Bond, you're both full of champagne and making googly eyes at each other. Let's be having you. I was in the middle of a very promising conversation I need to get back to.'

'Who the hell do you think you are?' Jasper says, rounding on Caleb.

'Caleb. Housemate. Currently saving you from having to deal with this one on a daily basis; which, as you'll know, is pretty exhausting, so you're welcome.'

'Caleb, we'll be down in a minute.' I step between them as I see Jasper getting angrier.

'Sorry, strict orders, narrow timeframe. You need to come with me, but Indiana Jones here can do whatever he likes.'

Oh no.

'What did you just call me?' Jasper's voice rises in anger.

Caleb looks at me. He knows he has messed up. 'I called you Jasper?' he cautiously offers.

Jasper shoots me a 'What else have you told him?' look, then buttons up his jacket and leaves.

'Oh, Caleb...' I sit on my bed.

'Sorry, sorry. It just kind of came out. Listen, your mum is about to cut her cake and I don't want the girl I'm talking to, to leave. Will you just come downstairs please?'

I straighten my dress and follow him down. Caleb hands me to Isszy and Zachary, then shoots off.

'Cake time?' I ask, looking at my watch. It's still a little early.

'No, not yet. Your housemate and Katherine have been all over each other since they arrived, so we sent him to get you because we didn't want an incident. He's a bit overconfident, isn't he?' Zachary asks rhetorically.

'I think he's kind of sexy,' Isszy chips in, smiling, while moving to the music. Zachary rolls his eyes. 'Not as sexy as you, of course, darling,' she says, teasing him.

'I'll leave you girls to it. I'm going after Jasper.' Zachary leaves us.

'You and Jas were up there for a while. Everything okay?' Isszy asks, concerned.

As I fill Isszy in, I watch Zachary join Jasper and Daddy's conversation. Beyond them is Caleb, pulling a laughing Mommy on to the dance floor before dramatically tossing his jacket off and getting down on one knee to twirl her around him. Three of them stop to look at him and, almost at the same time, shake their heads before they continue their conversation. Caleb doesn't notice. At that point, for the very first time, I wish I was a little like Caleb. Shallow, happy and without a care in the world.

I stay with Isszy for the rest of the night, then, the minute my mother has cut her cake, I go back upstairs, wearily take a shower, put on an old T-shirt and fall asleep, surrounded by the music coming from the party.

The next morning, I wake up to Caleb's laughter, mixed with my mother's, coming from the kitchen. I quickly put my hair into two pigtails, jump into the shower and change into a jumper and some leggings, before I make my way down to the smell of sausages and bacon.

'Morning, baby,' my mother chirps as she looks away from Caleb, who is sitting across from her at the table.

'Hey, Aaaaaari!' Caleb childishly drags out the shortened version of my name. 'You look like Pippi Longstocking,' he says, pointing at my pigtails.

'You're still here?'

'I am, and officially invited by the birthday girl, no less,' Caleb declares. 'So that was Jasper, eh? What was all that about in your bedroom?'

'What happened in her bedroom?' Mommy asks with mischief.

Yeah. Caleb has Mommy hooked.

'They were up there looking all lovey-dovey, like nothing had ever happened. I, of course, was the voice of reason and put a stop to it, because you, had a cake to cut. He's a bit intense, isn't he?' Caleb takes a sip of his tea. He doesn't wait for me to answer. 'You Mason girls... I bet men have no idea what they're doing when it comes to you.'

He winks at Mommy and she giggles. How can she be falling for this? He gets up and makes his way to the cooker. He looks handsomely dishevelled, with the top button of his shirt undone and his tie hanging out of his back pocket. I can sort of see how he could have success with women who don't know him.

'Right, birthday girl, how do you like your eggs?' He unbuttons his cuffs and rolls up his sleeves.

'Well-done.'

'Ariella? Full English or grapefruit?'

Mommy looks at me with a knowing smile and raised eyebrows. I have no idea what that look means.

'I'm going to have cereal.'

Caleb grabs the whole milk from the fridge and plonks it down in front of me.

'Two well-done eggs coming up.' He clumsily cracks Mommy's eggs into the pan.

'Were you here all night?' I ask.

'Nope. After Jasper got sozzled—'

'Jasper got drunk?'

'Oh yeah. Zachary and I had to carry him home. Top bloke, your brother. I like him. No bullshit. Anyway, Katherine said I could crash at hers, so I did. Before you start telling me off, nothing happened. She didn't pass the tea test.'

'What's the tea test?' Mommy and I ask at the same time.

'If I go round and we've been drinking, I always offer a cup of tea to chat over first. She didn't want tea, which in itself is a bad sign. By the time I finished my cup, she was asleep. So I put her in the first bedroom I came across and slept on the couch. Nice girl, though. Dropped me off about an hour ago.' He shakes his head as he flips the eggs over.

'What if she'd passed the tea test?' I ask, even though I already know the answer.

'You'd probably be losing your rag at me right now.'

'Morning, all,' says Daddy, coming into the room, and I get up to give him a hug. He walks round and gives my mom a long kiss on her forehead. 'Caleb,' he says curtly as he sits down.

'Eggs, Mr Mason?' Caleb offers.

'No thanks, just coffee.'

'I'll do it, Daddy.'

I like making Daddy breakfast. I get up and put the kettle on, while Caleb gives my mother her breakfast plate.

'Thank you, Caleb. Aren't you having any?'

'Of course, just grabbing mine.' He puts a plate together for himself and sits next to her.

'Caleb, you're Liverpudlian, aren't you?' Daddy enquires.

'Yes, sir!' He smiles as he loads baked beans on his plate.

'What part?' Daddy asks, making an effort.

'Toxteth.'

'Liverpool is where the Beatles come from, right? Is it quite a musical city?' asks my mother.

'Not really, well not any more. When I was growing up, it was the postcard picture of urban degradation, drugs, racism and crime.'

'You've done well to make it out,' Daddy says.

'Thank you, sir.'

'Is your family still back there?' Mommy reaches out to pat the back of his hand.

'They are.'

'How often do you go back to see them?' Daddy probes.

'Never. I don't go back, ever.' Caleb delivers this casually, like it is no big deal, but the shock around the breakfast table is palpable. Our family is everything to us. The idea of never seeing each other again is horrifying.

'How come?' I ask when I get over his statement.

'That's a conversation for another day,' Mommy immediately cuts in as she picks up her plate and stands up, using his shoulder as an anchor.

'I'll do that, Mrs Mason.' Caleb jumps up.

'Dahlia, please,' my mom instructs him warmly.

Caleb takes the plates from her, rinses them and loads them into the dishwasher. When he is done clearing the crockery, he announces his departure.

'I can run you to the station if you like,' Daddy offers generously.

'Oooh, yes please,' I jump in.

'You're not staying?' Daddy asks sadly.

'I'm sorry, I have a bit of work to do before tomorrow. Can I buy you supper in London this week?'

'How about you cook for me? I'd love to see where you live now.' Daddy brightens.

'Deal. Pork belly?'

'No way is he sneaking off with you to break his diet, Ariella,' Mommy complains. 'You can make him a nice salad and some wild salmon.'

'Awww, Dahlia, just this once.'

'No. I need you around, baby.'

I catch Caleb smiling at the affectionate exchange.

'Fine. We'll go out to eat.' Daddy sulks.

'Thank you, and you know I'll be looking at that receipt,' says Mommy with a smile.

'We should've had this conversation in the car. Go on, get your stuff.'

I run upstairs, pack quickly, knock on Zachary's bedroom door to say goodbye to him and Isszy and whizz back down.

As I arrive downstairs Caleb is receiving a standing invitation from Mommy to come back any time. She gives me a kiss on the cheek, while making me promise to call them when I get home.

TWELVE

CALEB

I had a good handle on what to expect before I set off on Saturday night. It was bound to be full of rich snobs. Ariella and I were getting on better than we had previously, but it was obvious that her life and mine were worlds apart. At least it'd be a laugh, I'd thought. I even imagined that I might meet someone who would pique my interest, so I could get rid of Nicole, who'd decided to give me an earful between mouthfuls of freshly baked pain au chocolat that morning. I resented Ariella in that moment. If she hadn't taken it upon herself to keep buying Nicole's favourite breakfast foods and coffee, she would have left much earlier in search of sugar and an adequate caffeine hit.

'I thought you didn't want to live with a woman.'

'I didn't. She's paying enough to make up for that, though.'

'You knew I was looking.'

'I did. And the first thing you did was try to haggle the price down. She haggled her way up.'

'Is something happening with you two?'

'No. She's my flatmate.'

Nicole narrows her hostility-filled eyes at me. That's it. No more breakfast. These cupboards are going back to being bare.

'Why is she seeing you later?'

I've had enough. 'Nicole, it's time for my run. Want me to get you a car?'

'Why aren't you answering?'

I walk back into the bedroom, ending the conversation. I need to end things with Nicole, but she just keeps showing up with creative ideas that have me struggling to say no. Take last night. She turned up wearing nothing but a thong under her coat, with a pack of cards and a bottle of Scotch. Who'd turn that down? At the same time, she is suspicious, jealous and has a frightening temper.

By the time my train pulls into Weybridge station I've committed to ending it this coming week. Stepping out of the black cab at Ariella's house reinforces that decision. A sea of beautifully dressed people, dripping in expensive jewellery, surround me.

I've already spotted a curvy blonde in a sparkling red dress, an immaculately put together Kardashian-like brunette in a tiny black dress, a regal-looking stunner with a dancer's body in white, and a sexy redhead in a vintage corset. Tonight is going to be fun.

Before I start inside, I hear my name. Ariella. The universe has it in for me. I was hoping to lie low for a bit, maybe cause some trouble under the radar, and then eventually find her at some point during the night. I follow my name in the night air and it takes me back to the girl in white. She is waving at me. That is not Ariella. I've been living under the same roof with *that* for months? She is unrecognisable, with waist-length straight hair – and that dress. It skims her body, complementing its elegant curves. Who knew Ariella had breasts this whole time?

I notice the entire outfit is held together by one shoulder strap, and is one motivated wind gust away from being indecently low at the back. There is no way she has any underwear on. I walk towards her with my eyes trained on her face. My eyes mustn't wander. It's Ariella.

The tall, broad man standing next to her looks like he is about to punch me, so I dive right in and introduce myself. It has to be her dad. He has his arm round possibly one of the most beautiful women I have ever seen. She is small next to him, her flawless skin shining under the night sky. The minute she smiles at me, I instantly develop a crush on Ariella's mother.

The party is a riot. The food is delicious, and the array of Cajun cocktails pack a punch. Everyone is happy, friendly and excited to have a good time, which isn't what I expected. I join in like I've been hanging out with them all my life. It's easy to get caught up in the Mardi Gras vibe and, soon enough, I hit the floor with Ariella's mother for the first spin of the evening. Boy, can she move. I pretend that I don't see Ariella's father watching with a face like thunder.

When I am asked to find Ariella, I get distracted by a beautiful girl in a tiny black dress; before I get asked to restart the mission to find Ariella, I'm making great headway. Fortunately, I quickly find her and her ex-boyfriend, making eyes at each other in her bedroom. I break that up as speedily as I can and return to where I left the girl, only to find her gone. I take Ariella's mother for another spin on the dance floor and, by the time I get shooed away by her father, I have found Miss Little Black Dress in the crowd again. I make my approach and we find a spot beside the pool outside to hang out for the rest of the night, playing drinking games and flirting outrageously with each other... until a second interruption.

'Caleb?'

It's Ariella's brother.

'Hey, Zachary.'

'I need you for a couple of minutes.'

He isn't asking. Have I become Ariella's babysitter at this

party? I tell my date to stay put and follow Zachary through the house and out of the front door.

'Am I being kicked out?' I joke as I follow him.

'If my father had his way, yes, and he'd happily do it himself. Jasper has had a bit too much to drink and I need to get him home. Here, take an arm.'

Zachary points at a folded Jasper, sitting on one of the stone steps leading up to the front door. I grab an arm and lift him with Zachary. Jasper stirs, trying to resist being carried.

'I just need to talk to her...'

'No, you don't, Jas. It's over,' Zachary says, matter-of-factly, without malice.

'We were going to get married...'

'I know. None of us saw it coming. I feel for you, man.'

'But why would she...'

'If I knew I'd tell you, brother.'

'She just moved out. No warning, just...'

'Yeah. You didn't deserve that.'

Zachary patiently continues to have a conversation that he knows Jasper probably isn't going to remember as we carry him into what can only be described as a mansion. It makes Ariella's massive home look like a cottage. I watch Zachary carefully undress his friend before pulling the covers up over him. He then disappears, only to come back with two glasses of water and four ibuprofen. He sits Jasper up, makes him take two, then leaves the remaining two on the side table with the second glass of water.

Watching Zachary handle Jasper so gently, with such concern, touches me.

'Thanks, Caleb. Come on,' he says.

'He's lucky he's got you,' I tell him.

'He's my brother and he's having a rough time.' Zachary shrugs as we walk down the seemingly endless drive in front of Jasper's bloody castle.

'Your dad doesn't really want to chuck me out, does he?'

'Of course he does. You put your hands on his daughter without her permission and are flirting with his wife,' Zachary delivers, deadpan.

'I am not.'

'Yes, you are. But my mother can handle herself.'

When we get back to the house, Zachary extends his palm. 'Thanks, Caleb. I'd appreciate it if you didn't mention this to anyone outside of my family.'

'Of course.' I shake his hand and immediately go to find my new friend. She leaps on me as soon as she sees me and demands we leave immediately. Not one to turn down a lady, I escort her outside and jump into a taxi with her. It isn't until we get to her place that I realise, for the second time that evening, that all I am going to be is a sober companion.

When she drops me off back at Ariella's the next morning, I find Ariella's mother in silk pyjamas and a matching dressing gown, in the warm, quiet, sun-bathed kitchen, about to start cooking.

'Morning, Mrs Mason, I just came to...'

'Caleb! Great, come in, I'm making breakfast.'

She walks towards me with that stunning smile and wraps her arms round me. Her hug immediately puts me at ease, making me feel welcome. I instantly want her to like me.

'You looked like you had a good time last night. We might have to pay for the hole you wore in that dance floor,' she accuses jokily.

'I had a pretty fiery dance partner. She made me up my game,' I say with a laugh, referring to her.

She chuckles as she flicks the kettle on and starts rummaging in the fridge.

'You shouldn't be cooking, birthday girl.' I take off my

jacket, remove my tie and move it to my back pocket. 'Just tell me where everything is.'

'You want to cook my family breakfast?'

A disbelieving smile plays on her lips. It makes me want to make her all the breakfasts she wants.

'I'm stepping in so you don't have to. Tea or coffee?'

'Coffee please. The Brazilian in the cafetière is fine.'

I make us coffee and follow her instructions as she guides me through loading sausages and bacon into the oven, while she sets the table. When we are done we sit at the table, sipping our coffees in a comfortable silence with each other.

'So, what's it like living with my daughter?'

'Annoyingly challenging.'

Dahlia Mason tries to hold it together, but can't help herself. She bursts out laughing. 'I love your honesty.'

'She's a nice girl, she's just sad all the time. I know she and that Jasper guy were in love or whatever, but she has to find a way to move on.'

'Did you just say in "love or whatever"?' She chuckles.

'Oh, don't you start. I get called promiscuous at least once a week by your daughter.'

'You've never been in love?'

'Nope. It's too much hard work and not worth the pain or the chains. Unless, of course, like Mr Mason, I'm lucky enough to find the one person that I'd gladly spend every day with.' It's a loaded statement and she catches it.

'You better not be flirting with me, young man.'

'I've seen your husband. I'm doing everything in my power not to.'

She laughs. 'I'd hold that position with Ariella too. She's the true love of his life. He guards her ferociously.'

'There's absolutely no chance of that. Your daughter is lovely, but she lives in fantasyland. She has zero life skills and her way of coping is just to hide or be overly nice. Even when you poke her enough to make her blow her lid, it's back on seconds later, as if nothing has happened. She dangerously radiates that "save me" energy, but when you get close enough you realise she's no pushover.'

'I'm glad she's moved in with you.'

'That's the opposite of what I expected you to say.'

'Unfortunately, real life is hurtling up fast to meet Ariella and she's worryingly unaware; so I was also going to ask you, if it isn't too much bother, to do everything in your power, as her friend, to try to soften the blow wherever you can. Think you can do that for me?'

'I can try. She keeps her cards pretty close to her chest.'

'Yeah. She's not a big sharer.'

'I've got to ask; what's with the showering?'

'She feels safe there. She started having anxiety attacks when she was about ten. She still has them occasionally and showering helps. That's where she thinks, cries, rejuvenates, celebrates and calms herself down. The water drowns out the noise and walls keep everyone out. It's her sacred spot.'

I am surprised Dahlia is sharing this all with me and it feels good. From the moment I saw her, she seemed to wield an inexplicable power over me. I am pretty sure that if she asked me to hide a body, I'd call a guy who knows a guy. It is nice, sitting in the kitchen, flooded with the light from the rising sun, cooking breakfast and getting to know each other. I could stay here for as long as she wants, chatting and laughing. She opens up about herself, about growing up in the American South, and shares funny family stories, while radiating maternal kindness and mischief in equal parts. When she asks about my family I tell her everything. The bad, the ugly and the downright horrific.

'I'm adopting you,' she declares when I am done, and in one sentence I feel wanted. That belief lasts until Hugh Mason comes down to breakfast and the mission to eject me is initiated.

I see his joy when he succeeds and his sorrow when Ariella decides to come with me.

'Your family makes everyone else's look dysfunctional,' I tease Ariella as I flop on the couch in the living room.

She laughs freely and I see Dahlia Mason's features all over her face.

'You should laugh more often, it suits you. You've been walking around here like you're about to throw yourself out of the window. It's time to stop.'

'Thanks. Tea? Maybe you could take a shower while I make it,' she hints from the kitchen.

'Wow, point taken. You're not disappearing, are you?'

She nods. 'Lots of work.'

'Do it in the living room. I have work too, and many questions about last night.'

'Okay...' she agrees, unsure.

When I return, she is sitting cross-legged on the couch typing away on her laptop, surrounded by a stack of paperwork.

'What's all this?' I grab the mug of builder's tea she's made for me.

'Cads, contracts and compliance that should've been finished on Friday. I'll move later if someone is coming over tonight?'

'Nah, I'm too knackered.'

She immediately zeros in on her laptop. I watch her place a pencil between her teeth, type a couple of notes, grab a sheet from her stack, liberate the pencil and start writing. Tea isn't going to see me through the afternoon.

'Want a beer instead?'

'It's three o'clock!'

'...On a Sunday. The entire country started in the pub at noon, so if anything, we're behind.' I see her waver.

She nods, so I grab a couple of beers and plonk myself next to her on the sofa. I pick up some of the paperwork.

'This looks complicated.'

'Words too big for you?' she teases, gently easing the papers out of my hands.

I'm not in the mood to work, so I distract her instead. 'Your mum is ridiculously hot!'

'Maybe you can pop her on your booty-call list.' She smirks.

Look at Little Miss Sassy. Going home and being around her family has clearly relaxed her.

'No way. She's the one you want to drag down the aisle and marry before she changes her mind. I wouldn't want to take your dad on, though. You're him through and through. Neither of you are easily pleased.'

'You're not the first to have made that observation.' She smiles, like any daddy's girl would. 'What's your family like?'

I flinch. I should give her the full story so she understands how easy life is for her. 'Where to begin? Let's go with poor and stupid.'

'Seriously, what are they like?'

I get up to grab another beer; I'll need it. 'I grew up so poor that everyone on our street had rats and cockroaches apart from us, because even the rodents judged us.' I laugh, and she rolls her eyes like she doesn't believe me.

'Do you have siblings?'

'I have a sister, Kayleigh, and a brother, Curtis. They're both older.'

'Are they still in Liverpool?'

'Oh yes.'

'What do they do?'

'Well, Kayleigh's permanently pregnant. She's got about five kids from goodness knows who. The last time we caught up, she was trying to get on a TV show for a paternity test and a nice day out. Curtis is currently serving at the pleasure of His Majesty.'

She blinks rapidly.

'Yes, Ariella. He's in prison. They exist.'

'Oh my goodness. What for?'

'Take your pick. Theft, arson, GBH, assault, drugs... he's a criminal polymath.' I intentionally omit the hate crimes and lifelong National Front membership, just like my father. I don't want to scare her.

'Your parents must be so proud of you.'

She's not getting it.

'They don't give a shit. I'm just the idiot that keeps the lights on and pays the bills. We raised ourselves. Curtis found his family by joining a gang and Kayleigh keeps trying to find love in places where everything *other* than love exists.'

She lets out a gasp. Yes, she understands that.

'How did you manage to...?' She struggles. Bless her. At least she's beginning to ask the right questions.

'By ten, I was amazing at numbers and making quite a bit of money dealing. People that would do anything to score were everywhere. I had the face of a choirboy, I was selling to my whole neighbourhood and keeping the roof over my family's head, because my brother kept getting caught. Instead of trying to stop it, when my parents found out, they set targets.'

'Caleb! At ten?' Ariella picks at her beer label.

'I was exceptional at it. I even had a party trick. I used to be able to weigh a bag of weed in my hands. Impressive, but an ultimately useless talent.'

'How did you stop?'

She reaches out to touch me. I pull away; she notices and retracts her hand quickly.

'Another beer?' I offer so it doesn't get awkward. She nods. I send her a subliminal message as I grab another for both of us and return: *Don't feel sorry for me, Ariella, that's not why I am telling you this.*

'Jerry McCracken. He spent his every waking moment shouting at the kids on the street. We called him Jerry McCrackhead. He shopped me to the police. He didn't just point the finger, he enlightened them as to when, where, how, who – the whole shebang. They threw me in with the really nasty adult offenders for one night and, by the next morning, I was a frightened wreck. I spent the night praying the guard didn't go to sleep.

'Jerry came to get me the very next day. I never went to court, but ended up working on Jerry's market stall every chance I got. The sergeant said if I missed a day of school, or work with Jerry, I'd go right back in the cells.

'It was on Jerry's stall that I realised that I was a good salesperson. He basically became my father. He would banish me from the shop floor to handle stock in the back if I didn't do well at school, and if I passed he'd leave the stall in my care. When I got into university, Jerry cried. I studied for my degree and worked with him in my spare time. When other students were at the student union getting drunk, I'd be down at Jerry's market stall, learning. When I graduated, I got a job and moved to London... Why are you crying?'

'I just can't believe you went through that. Where's Jerry now?' She produces a handkerchief.

'Still in Liverpool, still trading.'

'Are you still in touch?'

'Yes and no. He's not pleased with me at the moment.'

'Why?'

'A while back, I made a ton of money and thought it was going to last for ever. I bought him a high street shop and a flat in a new development. He was insulted and didn't want any of it, so I rent the shop and the flat, and the proceeds go to his wife. Jerry's a proud man but I figure it's only a matter of time.'

Her face brightens a little. She sees a happy ending. 'Have you spoken to your parents about your childhood?'

What did she think this was? One of those American shows where everyone has a therapist and loves to talk about their feelings?

'Too much damage has been done and too much time has passed. It would also be a waste of time. Back when I still thought there was hope, I bought them a four-bedroom house in the same development near the docks, just to get them out of Toxteth. I managed to get them to pack up and move there, debt-free.

'Within two months, my brother had stripped the place clean. After complaining that it wasn't the shithole I grew up in, they moved back to the old house. Now, I rent the house out to my sister and use the money to pay their bills.'

'Wow.'

'Yes, Little Miss Silver Spoon. People actually have to work for a living.'

'Hey, I work for a living.'

'Yes, but you don't have to.'

'Yes, I do. I'm not any less entitled to my independence. Everyone has a right to find their own way.'

I've hit a nerve. It's cute that she believes that. I concede, because I am too tired to argue about the desire to be independent versus the necessity to ensure your survival. Another day, maybe.

'You're right. I suppose I know what it's like to work for every penny.'

'I work for every penny too, Caleb – and, besides, money isn't everything.'

'Obviously not, or you'd be cosying up to good ol' Jasper right now,' I joke.

She looks like I have just slapped her. 'That hurt, Caleb.'

'I'm sorry. I know you have rich people's problems, like

wanting to find yourself et cetera, but was it so bad? He seems like a nice chap, thinks the world of you and, even though he could use more of a sense of humour and a bit less of the booze, he's all right. I only met him for thirty seconds, and even *I* know he adores you and will look after you.'

'I know, I adore him too; but being looked after isn't enough.'

'Maybe, but what more could you possibly need in addition to bags of money and mind-blowing sex?'

'I'm not even sure I was having that...'

She mutters the aborted line under her breath, but I hear it and I try to contain my glee. Did she just say Indiana Jones is crap in bed? This is going to be juicy.

'Mason. Spill. The. Beans. Now!'

'You're such a gossip. I shouldn't be discussing this with you.' She gives me a dirty look, hesitant to share.

'Oh, come on, this place has more satisfied women coming and going than a Christmas sale. You'd be consulting with an expert.' I tug one of her pigtails playfully before I run to the fridge and grab two more bottles.

'I'm going to regret this, aren't I?'

'You probably are, but don't let that stop you.'

She eyes the empty beer bottles piling up before she looks out of the window towards the setting sun, deciding whether or not to spill. I sit still. If I poke her again, she might shut down, so I give her space. She takes a deep breath in, exhaling voluminously.

'I'm just not sure we had great sex. It was nice, but I'm not entirely sure I enjoyed it the way I'm supposed to. Last night, before you found us in my room, he behaved a little differently. Like he couldn't control himself when he touched me. I felt... desired, you know? And I liked feeling that way.'

'You've never felt like that before?'

'No. I know he loves me, but being intimate with Jasper

felt... dutiful. Like brushing your teeth or something. When he kissed me last night, it felt... exciting.'

'I turned up and ruined everything, didn't I?'

'No, he stopped himself before you came up.'

'Jasper has some serious self-control. When I clapped eyes on you yesterday, I had to remind myself not to hit on you.'

She jokily punches me. 'Caleb, you wouldn't have hit on me. I'm not your type.'

'I would've, in that dress. You almost gave me a heart attack when I realised it was you.' It's true – but I don't want to give her the wrong impression. 'But it's worth noting that I want to jump almost anyone in a dress, so you're not in any particular danger. Plus, you're back to normal now, putting the probability of you getting jumped, back down to zero.'

'Thank goodness for that. I don't want to imagine where you've been and with who.' She wrinkles her nose and hides her deep-brown eyes behind her palms. Such a prude.

'Anyway, back to him. You must've had some kind of sexual chemistry when you first got together? Did that just fade?'

'I think it was there, but making love every Sunday night at nine thirty after we'd both showered didn't feel normal.'

No, Ariella, that definitely is not normal, I want to tell her, but I keep it to myself. I wonder if she has actually ever had an orgasm. It would be hardly surprising if she—

'If I'm totally honest, I'm not sure I've ever had an orgasm.'

I immediately start to choke on my beer. She springs into action, patting my back. This is much more than I was expecting. What the hell am I supposed to say to that? I try my best.

'Trust me, if you'd had one, you'd know. What about your other boyfriends?'

'Jasper's the only person I've been intimate with.'

'Really?... Actually, no offence, but that's pretty believable.'

'He's the only person I've trusted enough to make love with.'

'Now I'm really curious as to how that even happened.'

'It was pretty normal really. When he bought his first flat in London, I helped him move his stuff into his new place. There wasn't much, so when we finished he bought me a thank you dinner before I left. At dinner, the waiter basically bathed us both in red wine, so I went back to his to shower and borrow clothes. While I was showering, he asked if he could join me.'

She covers her eyes. Even I can't believe she is telling me all of this.

'That night was lovely. It felt like our own little world. The next morning, I woke up and Jas was gone. It turns out he went to see Mommy and Daddy, had the "moving in" conversation, emptied my wardrobe and brought its contents back to the flat. We've been living together since.'

'You're craftier than you look, Ariella. I respect that. How did you manage to get him to speak to your dad alone?'

'I didn't know he was going to do that. He'd never mentioned moving in before. When he got back with my belongings, he just said it was time that we did the adult thing if we were going to keep doing the *adult* thing; and that was it.'

By the time she finishes, she looks like she is on the verge of tears, so I lighten the mood.

'Everything in your life sounds like a bloody romantic comedy. Hugh Grant's going to turn up next. Wanna know how I lost mine? It'll cheer you up!'

I tug one of her pigtails playfully again. I need to stop doing that. She nods and a smile starts to break across her face.

'Mine was in a car at night, parked near a McDonald's drive-through, because I wanted chicken nuggets. I can still remember how she felt to this day. Clara Durban. Hot, tiny, platinum blond, always wore these barely-there skirts. We did it everywhere, every chance we got. Mostly in her car though, a couple of times at her house. We had some good times, before she had to leave.'

'Did she move away?'

'Yeah. Her husband found out, reported her and she was sacked from my school. Jerry was furious. He did wonder how I managed to completely fail my French GCSE, with all the extra French classes I was having. The only words I could remember were *oui*, *s'il-vous-plait*, *silence*, *merci*, *pantalon* and *je m'appelle Caleb*. Apart from that, nothing.'

Ariella gasps.

'Thankfully, we only got busted four months after I turned sixteen, or she would've been in much more trouble.'

'Caleb, you know she was a predator and took advantage of you, right?'

'I loved every minute of it and got a steady stream of chicken nuggets. And she left a lasting impression. I can't walk past a McDonald's without thinking about her.'

'And you clearly still have a thing for beautiful, French, platinum blondes,' she points out.

'Oh yeah. I hadn't thought of that.'

'She groomed you, Caleb.' She looks concerned.

'Definitely, McJudgy. Doesn't mean I didn't enjoy it, though.' I pull on one of her pigtails again. Bloody hell. 'So, what do you want now you're free and single?'

I see that she wants to continue talking about Clara but abandons the idea.

'I guess I want to have fun. I want to experience things I haven't before. I want to listen to new music, I want to go to places I haven't been, I want to go out on dates with strangers, and just try to figure out who I am.'

'You've got your app...' Watching Ariella navigate Swipey is going to be fun.

'Ugh, no...'

'Why not? You may want all those things, but if you're not willing to give it a go you might as well move back in with

Jasper. Sometimes the best way to get over someone is to get under someone else.'

'You'd believe that, Caleb, because your lifestyle choices are... unique. Not everyone's like you.'

'Gimme your phone.' She hands it over without hesitation and I open the app's messages. 'Look, no one... okay, apart from this guy – I've blocked him – is being unreasonable. Let's get rid of the "How's your day?" and "What's up?" people and get to the guys that actually say something interesting.' I scroll through, skipping past my own message taking the piss.

'Wait!' She stops me. 'Is that you? Open the message!'

> Lol, you're going to fail epically at this, but good luck! 😂

'That's really motivating, Caleb,' she says with a smile, shaking her head at me.

'Come on, I'll help you. What do you want to say to this guy? He's a journalist and he's written that he loves that you're naturally beautiful with a great smile. Ugh! He's a creep, let's delete him.' He is one of those goody-goodies. Ariella would probably like him and end up in another long-term relationship. She should have a little fun instead.

'No. He seems nice. Tell him thank you.'

Really? She definitely has a type – dull. I grudgingly do as she says. This is going to be the most boring session ever. For the next hour, Ariella and I swipe left and right, answer messages and start some conversations.

'This has been fun.' Ariella points to our beer bottle-covered coffee table. 'What's the time?'

'Ten! Ariella! Aren't you going to turn into a broccoli or something if you don't rush to bed?' I tease her.

'I liked you better when you were judging me silently.'

She pokes me in the ribs and I jump. 'I liked me better then too. This was fun, though. I'm starving. Fancy a bit of cheese on toast?'

'Yes please.'

It is hard to believe that I've been on the couch with Ariella, just chatting and drinking, for the whole afternoon. Time has flown by. At least I now have the benefit of context, and she knows a bit more about me too. I look at the pile of work she's failed to get through. When she catches me smiling at it she starts packing up her bag neatly, while I clear the bottles from the table.

'Cheese on toast à la Caleb,' I announce, making my way into the kitchen as she takes her work into her room. When she returns, I place a plate in front of her at the kitchen bar, along with her night-time tea.

'I can't believe you're cooking.'

'I cooked eggs this morning.'

'For my mom, and you were clearly sucking up to her.'

'Ah, Dahlia Mason. She is *fit*.'

'I'll make sure I tell her.'

'You do that – just make sure it's far, faaaar away from your father.'

She takes a bite. 'This is delicious! What's in it?'

I am not sharing. If she wants it again, she's going to have to ask.

'Secret recipe, perfected at uni. When I couldn't afford a meal, I'd go on the pull, and only followed through if I got myself invited round. I'd always offer to make cheese on toast before anything happened. They thought I was the sweetest guy. I was just hungry and knew everyone always had bread and cheese in some quantity to spare. The result is the carefully honed recipe you have before you.'

'That sounds tough.'

She reaches out and pats the back of my hand before I have the chance to move it away.

'It wasn't. It was fun, and it was the easiest way to get fed cheaply without some stranger feeling sorry for you.' I feel her pity settle on me and I can't handle it. 'Eat up, Princess Ariella.' I find something to tidy behind me in the kitchen.

'Thank you for coming last night,' she says, taking another bite.

'I'm glad I came, and I'll definitely be taking up that invitation your mother extended.'

'You should, you know. She makes the most killer Sunday lunches. If you get through it, you won't be able to move for hours afterwards.' Ariella snickers as she finishes her toast and gets up. I swoop in quickly to take her plate and cup. I inexplicably don't want her too close to me at the moment.

'I've got this,' I offer.

'I'm really awake now. Want to watch an episode of *The Sopranos*?' she suggests.

'It's almost eleven and I know what you're like. You're going to get excited, chat through the intro and be asleep, snoring and drooling on me, before the first scene is over.'

'I won't.'

'Oh, you will.' I chuckle. She doesn't snore or drool, but I have her completely convinced that she does. 'I'll do you a deal. We'll get two under our belt tomorrow. I need to sleep off last night's sofa.'

'Deal. Goodnight, Caleb.'

She retreats to her room while I finish tidying. For no particular reason, I listen for the shower in her room to come on. As soon as I hear the pipes, I smile at her predictability. Then I catch myself at my own ridiculousness, waiting to hear her settle in.

THIRTEEN

ARIELLA

Knowing a little more about Caleb makes life in the apartment easier. After the party, I think we may have become friends. He irritatingly makes a point of reminding me to get on Swipey every day and, by the end of the first week, I'm used to checking it every evening. I hide from Caleb when I do. Left to him, I'd be out at every opportunity with the less salubrious matches and ditching the normal-sounding ones. Thankfully Caleb announces during an episode of *The Sopranos* one evening that, in anticipation of my many male visitors, he is going to get a new door with a peephole and chain put in.

'Tim and Jack are coming over to sort it tomorrow. Normally we're in the pub, so it seems as good a time as any.'

'Tim from the emergency list?'

'Yeah.'

'He was really nice to me. I didn't know you were friends. I just thought he was the handyman.'

'Ha. No. Tim, Jack and I are heading to the South of France together.'

'If you guys are giving up your Monday night in the pub, I'll cook to say thank you; especially to Tim.'

'You know Tim is married, right?' Caleb asks with a suspicious tone.

'Of course! His family sounds very sweet.'

'Good, because I don't want you getting any ideas...'

'Your mind resides in the gutter, Caleb.'

'Just checking. I'm sure the guys won't say no to a meal, but maybe keep it simple?'

'Steak and chips?'

'Perfect,' he says, giving me a friendly little shove. His phone starts to vibrate and I see him send a call from Nicole to voicemail. He's been doing that a lot recently.

'How's Nicole? You guys okay?'

'There is no "us guys". Thanks to you, I almost ended up in a relationship with her, but I'm cooling it and pulling back for a bit to make a point.'

'What point is that?'

'That we shouldn't expect anything from each other.'

'Why don't you talk to her, instead of ghosting her?'

'Like you did with Jasper?'

Caleb hits where it hurts.

'I'm going to bed.'

I get up and Caleb gently catches my arm.

'I'm sorry. You didn't deserve that.'

'It's okay. It's the truth.' I continue to walk to my room.

'Come on, Ariella. Don't make me finish the episode on my own because I said something stupid.'

'I'm tired, that's all.'

'No, you're not. When you're tired, you fall asleep on the couch halfway through with your mouth open, catching flies and snoring. It's gross. I've upset you and you're off to pretend I don't exist... don't do that, please? Just tell me I'm an idiot, I'll say sorry and we'll squash it. Look, your boyfriend is coming on. I'll be nice about Bobby.'

He flashes me a smile and extends his arms to present the TV, like he is showing a gift on a game show.

I return to the couch. 'You were horrible,' I whisper at him.

'I know, I'm sorry.' He pats my leg twice apologetically and points at the TV. 'How dreamy is Bobby in this scene?'

I laugh as he nudges me playfully.

'Don't be pissed off at me, okay?' he leans in to whisper, with his eyes still on the TV.

'Okay.'

I like Caleb when he is like this and I forgive him instantly.

Tim, Caleb and a man I assume is Jack are already working on the door when I arrive home from the butcher and craft beer place.

'Hello, gentlemen.' I smile as I step over the toolbag lying across the door.

'Hey,' Caleb calls, holding our door frame as it is being removed.

'Good to see you again, Ariella.'

'Hi, Tim.' I beam back. 'How are Em and the boys? Is little Alfie feeling better?'

'Oh yes, it was just a bug going around the school and he's—'

'Aww, how cute! Can we please get back to work? This door is bloody heavy.' Caleb scowls at us.

Tim and I laugh. I notice that Jack has a large purple bruise on his cheek.

'That looks nasty. Does it hurt?' I say with a friendly smile.

He shakes his head, looking embarrassed, but smiles back. 'You should see the other guy,' he responds under his breath.

'What other guy? It wasn't— Ow!'

'Sorry. Hope I didn't hurt you too much there, Caleb,' Tim says, not looking sorry at all.

I drop the groceries on the kitchen counter and put the beers in the fridge before I grab a quick shower. When I emerge, our old door is off, leaving a gaping hole where it used to be.

'Caleb, I think Ariella's sending you a message,' Tim announces as I walk in.

'The only message I'm getting is that no one her age should still be obsessed with *Sesame Street*,' Caleb retorts.

I look down at my old Oscar the Grouch T-shirt. It makes me smile.

'Why are you so chirpy today anyway?' Caleb asks Tim, with an undertone I don't understand.

'I'm doing something selfless for a lovely person,' Tim says, turning to wink at me playfully. 'You should try it sometime.'

'You've been dropped on your head, mate.'

I get everyone some cold beers from the fridge before I return to the kitchen to prep and listen to them chatting and laughing about the pub, football and politics. When they've finished hanging the door and washing the debris from their hands, they sit at the island. Jack points to the dining setting in front of him.

'This is amazing. I don't know what to touch first.'

Caleb jumps to the rescue and carefully explains the setting. Both Tim and Jack start laughing halfway through and he happily tells them both to eat with their hands like the animals they are. I like their dynamic.

'Would you like your sake hot or cold?' I ask, pointing at their sake cups. 'I also have some Japanese pale ale, if you prefer.'

Caleb looks confused. 'I thought we were having steak and chips?'

'You are,' I reassure him.

I toss four steaks on the four Japanese hot lava stone slabs and watch them sizzle. After about a minute, I flip them over, and then move one stone on its wooden blocks in front of each guy.

'Careful, it's really hot.' I serve the accompanying fries and finally go back for the sake and pale ales. 'Bon appétit, gentlemen. Thank you.' I raise my warm sake cup and three pale ales head skyward.

Jack, who has been extremely quiet up until now, lets out a gasp after his first mouthful.

'Oh. My. God. What is this? This can't be steak. It's incredible.'

I'm thrilled. 'Thank you. They're A5 Grade Ozaki Wagyu beef sirloins, with wasabi chips and ginger miso gravy.'

'This is so much better than the pub,' Jack continues to enthuse. 'Can I try the sake?'

'Of course.' I grab an additional sake cup and pour him one cold and one hot. 'Most people prefer either hot or cold. I have to say, I like both.'

Jack takes a swig of each. 'Oooh – hot!'

We all laugh.

'This is delicious, Ariella. Thank you.' Tim winks at me. 'I'm glad we skipped the pub tonight.'

'I'll happily cook for you on some Mondays if you want to swing by when I'm trying stuff. Caleb can have a break from suffering alone every day.'

They both stop eating and look at Caleb in disbelief.

'You eat like this every day?' Jack asks incredulously.

'Not this exactly – which is amazing, Ariella – but she'll try different recipes and I give her feedback.'

'How generous of you,' Tim says sarcastically before turning to me. 'You don't have to cook for him every night, you know.'

'Oh, I'm used to it. I cooked Jasper whatever he wanted every night.'

'Every night?' Jack clarifies.

'Apart from weekends. Jasper only liked specific dishes and I'd cook them depending on what he was feeling like in the morning.'

'What if you were out?' Tim asks.

'We didn't go out during the week. He worked late most days, so—'

'No, what if you were out alone late and he got home before you?' Tim presses.

'Oh, that never happened. He didn't like me being out on my own. I came straight home from work because I was never really sure when Jasper was going to be back, so I'd cook what he wanted and wait.'

'How long were you together?' Jack asks.

'Four and a half years. We've only lived together for two, though.' I can sense an atmosphere developing. 'Why are you looking at me like that?' I laugh nervously.

The apartment is quiet.

'We're looking at you like this because Jasper's a dick,' Jack answers softly.

'No, he's not. He's really wonderful. Caleb has met him. Caleb, he's lovely, isn't he?' I look to Caleb to tell them.

'Well...' Caleb starts, just as the doorbell starts to ring.

He jumps up to try out the new spyhole, then immediately springs back and puts his finger to his lips while mouthing something. We look at each other, confused.

'Nicole!' he whispers when he gets back. Tim and Jack shake their heads disapprovingly.

'Caleb, you need to talk to her,' I whisper, pleadingly. 'It's not fair.'

'Let's pretend we're not here,' he whispers back.

'I know you're in there,' Nicole shouts from the other side of the door. We hear her kick it.

'Shit.' Caleb gets up and opens the door slightly, puts it on the latch and lets himself out. 'Hey, Nicole...' is all we hear before he shuts the door behind him.

'I'm glad he did that.' I smile at the guys. We resume eating but just as Jack is in the middle of a funny story, we hear the door being flung open loudly.

'Aha!' Nicole barges through the door, startling the three of us. 'This doesn't look like you're nursing a migraine.'

Caleb follows, looking exhausted. 'These are Ariella's friends.' He puts his palms together in prayer behind her, mouthing the word 'Please'. Jack narrows his eyes at him, then sits in front of Caleb's food.

'Hello, Nicole,' I call out.

She grunts at me. Even grunting, she is stunning. She is wearing a plum-coloured fitted dress that stops at the very top of her thighs, matching patent plum heels and a navy trench coat. Her beautiful blond hair falls in loose curls down her back. A sly smile crosses Jack's face.

'Tim, we shouldn't let this go to waste. Ariella's housemate barely touched it; he was in so much pain.'

Jack splits the steak into two and invites Tim over. Tim happily joins him. I try not to laugh at Caleb's face when they start eating his beef.

'Nicole, can I offer you—' I start.

'No,' Caleb answers, ushering Nicole into his room.

'I don't know how he does it.' Jack shakes his head with a mouth full of Caleb's steak.

'I know. She's beautiful, isn't she? And she always looks like that,' I tell them. 'I have an apple and ginger sorbet for dessert. You guys want in?'

'Yes!' they both respond.

After finishing Caleb's steak, they insist that I leave the washing up to them. Poor Caleb. Thankfully, I bought six steaks, intending to play with two. I pull one out of the fridge for him and leave it on the countertop to get to room temperature for later. I can't help chuckling, though. I like his friends. They know how to get at him.

Just as they sit down for sorbet, Nicole's impossibly long legs make their way across the living area in what seems like five strides before she slams the front door behind her. Caleb emerges seconds later.

'You two would've been more convincing if you'd turned up in drag pretending to be my sisters.'

'Didn't buy what you were selling then?' Tim laughs.

'We'll see when she comes round tomorrow night.' Caleb smiles smugly.

'Mate. What are you doing?' Jack asks.

'What? Did you not see her? She's smoking. Avoiding her is the only option I have to end this. She's very, very convincing.' Caleb raises an eyebrow.

Tim shakes his head and looks at me. I shrug.

'Ariella, talk some sense into him,' Jack urges.

'Caleb will get no judgement from me. I don't have to share a bathroom with him, or a wall, so I'm fine.'

I listen to them insult a victorious-looking Caleb playfully as we all have dessert. The three of them clean up after dinner, against my protestations, before Tim playfully fireman-lifts me over one shoulder out of the kitchen and plonks me on a sofa. I leave them relaxed and roaring with laughter in the living room and head to bed happy. I hear them discover that they've gone through all the pale ales; and when they finish all the sake too, Caleb fetches the Guatemalan rum I've introduced him to, warning them to sip slowly.

Swipey was proving to be a more positive experience than I thought. So far, I was keeping the conversations friendly and platonic, which according to Caleb is basically dating suicide, but it left me with four guys I was regularly in touch with. I ended up with a journalist, a science professor, an oil rig worker and a barista.

I would have liked to keep the fifth guy, a property developer, because he was really nice, but Caleb came home one evening and saw me trying to take full-length pictures of myself in my pyjamas to send to him. He immediately grabbed my phone, blocked and deleted him. So, I was stuck with four.

I've met the journalist and the professor a couple of times, and they are both lovely. The journalist is cool, laid-back, and our conversations weaving around the street art of Shoreditch or Brick Lane market are always engaging. He is good fun. The only turn-off is he keeps trying to hold my hand and I don't feel ready for it.

The professor is really sweet. I've only met him twice, but I can relate to him. He prefers formal dining, showing me scientific and historical landmarks around London, and challenging my perception of the future and the impact of technological advancements on the human race. He is always a gentleman, respects my boundaries, and I always leave feeling excited – but also slightly worried about the future.

The subsea hydraulics engineer is based offshore somewhere in the Gulf of Mexico. He's quite secretive about who he works for, but sends lots of pictures of him in his overalls on different parts of the rig, without giving too much away. We started chatting online just before he went offshore, but we have lots of funny conversations.

The barista works in a local coffee shop and is always good for a joke. We met when I was trying to find Nicole's favourite ground coffee. I find myself laughing a lot when I'm with him, though he has a habit of disappearing and then popping up again.

The greatest thing about talking to so many people is that I actually don't have the space to develop any feelings for them. They are all lovely in their own way, but Jasper still holds my heart and they have all been respectful of that. Lara has been keeping up to date with my shenanigans, and basically thinks I have turned into a promiscuous little hussy.

'Let me get this straight, all these guys know about each other and are all aware that they're rebound guys to Jasper?'

It is the end of the day and Lara is reclining in the chair next to mine.

'Yes.'

'How do you get away with it?'

'I just told them I'm getting over a break-up, so I am talking to new people to expand my experiences.'

Lara shakes her head. 'You're unbelievable. So, who are you cooking for tonight?'

'Seth, the journalist.'

'Mr Touchy Feely.' She wrinkles her nose. 'He's lucky. I haven't been to your new flat yet.'

'You should swing by. Caleb is pretty easy-going.'

'I can't wait to meet this Caleb.'

'You know Caleb.' I point to his office dome.

Lara's eyes widen as she almost falls out of her chair. 'You're living with *Caleb Black*?'

'Yes, Lara. I've told you this multiple times. You weren't listening. As usual.'

'You never told me you're living with Caleb Black! Has he tried it on with you? How has Nicole not killed you? Wait... does she know?'

'He has never been inappropriate, and yes, Nicole knows.'

'You know he's slept with most of the building?'

'Yes, but he's only seeing Nicole now.'

'This explains why you're happily Swipey-ing all the men in London. He's rubbing off on you. Yuck. I just threw up in my mouth at the thought of that.'

I shoo Lara away. Seth will be with me at eight, which gives me only two hours.

'Have fun tonight, and maybe let the guy stand closer than twenty feet?'

I grunt my non-answer, making Lara chuckle.

When Seth arrives, I am just checking the lamb shoulder.

'Oh wow, your place is stunning. I brought you some craft gin, one for you and one for your mum. It'll probably kill you, but it's the thought that counts.'

He unexpectedly pulls me into a hug. This is Seth. He has done something exceptionally sweet, but followed it with this, knowing that it makes me uncomfortable. I disengage quickly, letting him in and taking his duffel coat from him. He fixes his plaid shirt and smooths down his jeans, then pushes up his black, thick-rimmed glasses. When I first met him, he had a man bun, which he has since cut off.

'Wine, gin or beer?'

'Wine please. Mind if I have a look around?'

'No, but this is kind of it. The only other rooms to see are the study and my bedroom, and they're the first and second doors on the left. The bathroom is straight ahead if you need it.'

He wanders around while I set our places on the kitchen bar.

'Wu-Tang Clan on vinyl?' I hear him call from my bedroom.

'I love them. I've been expanding my musical horizons.'

'I can see that. You got that Buika album I was telling you about, The Notorious B.I.G, Rodrigo y Gabriela, African folk music and Tina Guo all in one stack?' I hear him laugh 'We're going to have to do some serious work in here later.'

I catch his double entendre. It makes me uncomfortable.

'Scallops are ready,' I announce quickly. 'I bought a lovely Châteauneuf-du-Pape for the starter.'

'Red with scallops?' He emerges from my room to return to the kitchen.

'It's a white. We have a beautiful Ridge Monte Bello for the main.'

'This is lovely. Thank you, Ariella.'

He leans in to kiss my cheek and I let him, so it isn't awkward.

'Eat!'

The Seth I like spending time with shows up during the meal. We talk about photographing the Calais Jungle, digital privacy and whether democracy can truly exist. Before we sat down, I was beginning to regret having him over. Now I am back at ease, though I wish I liked Seth the way he wants to be liked.

We finish our starters slowly.

'That was amazing. I'm talking Michelin quality. Have you ever considered opening up a food truck? I'd pay for that.'

'No, but Jasper tried to buy me a small restaurant once—'

'Ariella, is it okay if we don't talk about Jasper tonight?'

'You're right. I'm sorry. I should be looking forward and not back.'

'Speaking of looking forward, I bought a couple of Buika tickets and I wanted to take you, but on, like, a proper date...'

Just then, I hear the front door close. 'I'm home! I demand you stop having sex on the couch right now, Ariella, you dirty girl!'

Caleb walks in, pretending to cover his eyes with his training bag, and makes me laugh. Phew, perfect timing.

'That smells good – I'm starving. You must be Seth.' Caleb extends his hand. 'Good to meet you, mate, and thanks for keeping this one out of trouble.'

Caleb walks up to me and pokes me in the ribs. I yelp with laughter and smack his hand away.

'You're gross from training, and in general,' I say, laughing. 'Get in the shower. I have food for you.'

Caleb raises an eyebrow at Seth. 'You're sure you want to deal with this?' He turns to me and shakes the bun at the top of my head. 'See you in a few.'

I look back at Seth, who is silently watching us.

'Ready for some lamb? If you don't mind popping the Monte Bello, I'll set up our main courses and finish off Caleb's starter.'

'He's eating with us?'

'I'm not sure. He wasn't supposed to. He usually gets home much later.'

Caleb joins us just as Seth and I start our mains.

'What are we having?'

'Smoked sesame scallop and bacon salad starter and shredded lamb shoulder main.'

Caleb's eyes widen. 'Oooh, is that the one with the grassy root vegetables and the truffle mash?'

'Foraged vegetables, no mash though,' I say with a frown.

'I'm sure it'll be delicious, Aari. I'll be in the study.'

I dish out his starter and main course. Balancing it all a bit precariously on a tray, he makes his way to the study. He returns briefly to grab the half-finished bottle of white wine.

'Are you guys done with this?'

We both nod and, with that, he is gone.

'He seems nice,' Seth observes.

'He takes a bit of getting used to, but he's a decent guy.'

'So, I was asking you to a concert,' Seth says after we have finished our main course, with a slight edge to his voice.

'I'd love to go, but not as your date, Seth. I'm still not there yet.'

'I want to understand, but I don't. We get along, we have loads in common and we have fun together. We should explore if there might be more.'

'There isn't, Seth. Not for me. I'm sorry.'

'Oh come on, Ariella. You invite me round, you cook for me, you give me directions to your bedroom...'

'You asked me to cook you dinner, so I did. I only told you where my bedroom was because I didn't want you entering Caleb's accidentally.'

Seth moves closer and I instinctively shift back.

'Surely you feel something...'

'I don't. I mean, I do, but just as a friend. I like hanging out with you.'

'Really? Not even...'

'She said no, Seth,' Caleb states calmly as he comes out of his study with his empty plates and cutlery. He places them in the dishwasher and walks right back into the study. We both watch him shut the door behind him.

'This is embarrassing, I better leave,' Seth says, getting up to retrieve his coat.

'Seth, wait. I'm sorry. I like spending time with you and I don't want to stop.'

'I'm good on the friends front, Ariella, I don't need any more. Am I stuck in that zone with you?'

'That's all I have to offer at the moment.'

'Then thanks, but no thanks.' He puts his hand in his chest pocket to retrieve the concert tickets. 'You should go and see Buika.'

I walk forward and cover his hand with mine.

'I don't deserve them. I'm sorry.'

'Do you realise that's the first time you've voluntarily touched me?' He sighs. 'Goodbye, Ariella. Keep the gin.'

He grabs his coat and walks out, shutting the door behind him.

'Did he say keep the gin?' Caleb pokes his head out of the study. Seeing that the coast is clear, he comes into the kitchen and pulls a bottle out of the brown paper bag.

'Did you know he had two bottles in here? I suspect young Seth's intentions weren't exactly pure.'

'The other bottle was for my mom.'

'I knew I didn't like him, but that's made me hate him now. Dahlia's mine.'

'You didn't like him?'

'Nah, too lumberjacky. I bet his cupboards are filled with hair gel, beard conditioner and a whole bunch of products, only to make himself look ungroomed. What's the point?'

'I thought he was very handsome.'

'Clearly not handsome enough.' Caleb raises both his eyebrows at me twice, pours a shot of gin in a glass and knocks it back. 'Whoa! This stuff is potent. Try some.'

He hands me a glass. I take a similar swig.

'Ooof.'

We both laugh.

'Get us some of your ginger-snap dessert – I'll help tidy this lot up. Let's get a couple of *Sopranos* episodes in. *Don't* fall asleep.'

We settle on the couch and Caleb selects our next episode.

'I have to go to San Francisco to on-board a new client next Monday, but I should be back on Thursday. Are you going to be okay? Seth isn't going to circle back, is he?'

'I'll be fine. He's harmless. I should've made myself clearer from the start, really.'

'Look at you! We've swapped roles. You're juggling multiple guys and I'm trying, but failing, to avoid Nicole. I miss having different body shapes and personalities between my hands. It keeps life interesting.'

'I have to admit, hanging out with different people does widen one's perspective.'

'Now that Seth's out of the picture, are you going to replace him with a new victim?'

'Seth and I may end up being friends.'

'Don't hold your breath. You're too much effort and Swipey'll have him shagging someone else by midnight. I'd have binned you ages ago.'

Caleb looks at me as he pops a spoonful of sorbet in his mouth, and we burst out laughing.

'I just got dumped.'

'Congratulations. How does it feel?'

'Exciting.'

'That's not how it's meant to feel.'

'Think the other three will do the same?'

'Probably.'

FOURTEEN

CALEB

Faith Novak is a bright, cute free spirit I met over frozen yoghurt just outside our client's San Francisco office, where she works as a developer. She is sharp and funny as hell, and even though she dresses like a Sunday school teacher, underneath that misleading exterior is all porn star – which is why I never leave SF without a little hello. I've been looking forward to tonight since I landed a few days ago. Now she's standing in front of me in nothing but a thong, she's never been sexier. I take my time to appreciate her outfit, or lack thereof.

'I know what you're doing. I give in.' She approaches, climbing over me into a kiss.

'What am I doing?' I chuckle.

'You want me to make the first move. It worked.' Her lips are persistent.

'I didn't, actually.'

'So, what's taking you so long? It's not like you're waiting for an emotional connection.'

Her hands are on my shirt buttons and making quick work of them.

'Maybe I am,' I joke.

'That's Hunter's territory. Yours is to make me shudder... and you're later than usual, Mr Black.'

Her hand slides over my thighs.

'Hunter? Your gardener?'

She stops and explodes with laughter. 'Hunter is my partner, not my gardener. How much do you think I make?'

'Wait, what? You've been cheating on your boyfriend with me?' I move away. She sits up, concerned.

'I'm not cheating. We're polyamorous. He dropped me off tonight.'

She gently kisses my neck and I move further away.

'What's wrong?'

'You have a boyfriend.' I'm aware of my hypocrisy. Mel is hardly single.

'Who doesn't have a problem with this. I'm not getting all sensitive about you fooling around with Lisa in legal.'

She closes her eyes, and takes a deep breath. 'Caleb, nothing's changed. I've been dying to see you.'

'I'm sorry. I can't. I feel like I've been in the middle of a relationship that no one told me about.'

'But I *did* tell you about Hunter. Besides, it changes nothing. You're still...'

'The guy who makes you shudder.'

She shrugs.

'I'm sorry, Faith. I can't do this with you tonight.'

'But you're leaving tomorrow,' she pleads.

'I'm sorry, I'll get you a car home.' I end our evening.

'Polyamorous? Louisa would cut my dick off and hang it in the window just for knowing what that means.' Jack takes a swig of his beer. He looks happy. The swelling on his face has gone.

'I'm just as confused as her, though. What's your problem? If you thought this Hunter bloke was her gardener, she definitely told you. Partner and gardener sound pretty similar, mate,' Tim chips in.

'I don't want some bloke fantasising about me shagging his missus!'

'Ugh. I didn't even think of that.' Jack recoils.

'You're both idiots,' Tim says. 'They're basically two people that have decided they want to be together, but also acknowledge that they can't be all things to each other. So instead of lying and cheating, they're honest about it and allow each other to fill the gaps elsewhere. It makes sense.'

Jack and I look at each other. We both want to ask.

'You and Em aren't...' Jack beats me to it.

'Crikey no. My dick'd be hanging next to yours.' Tim laughs.

'Ariella's safe then,' Jack quips.

Tim's face reddens. 'What?' he growls.

'Come on, Tim. That fireman's lift out of the kitchen? Look, you're going red,' Jack teases.

I decide to save Tim. 'She's stubborn as hell. That was the only way she was leaving that kitchen.'

'She can't be that stubborn, or that controlling ex-boyfriend wouldn't have got away with half the shit he did. I can't even imagine suggesting a restaurant to Louisa.'

'That's because you're the Ariella in your little situation,' I throw in.

'Only without any redeeming features or discernible talent,' Tim adds, making us laugh. 'How's she doing?' he goes on.

'When I got home this morning, she'd gone to work. She was doing all right before I left. She seems to be enjoying bothering innocents on Swipey.'

'She's not on Swipey? She'll get eaten alive.' Tim shakes his head disapprovingly.

'She's holding her own, actually. Apart from when I stopped her from sending bedtime pictures to some creep.'

'I didn't think she was the type.' Jack gasps.

'No, she isn't. I should've let her send them. Her hair was wet and dripping around her face, she was wearing that ridiculously baggy Elma Fudd onesie she loves and had her toothbrush hanging out of her mouth. Thankfully, he picked the wrong day. She normally sleeps in what I think are Jasper's boxers and a vest. Anyway, I put a stop to it and put a blanket ban on anyone asking for pictures.'

'We should do something nice for her. Maybe cook her dinner or something,' Tim suggests.

Jack and I say nothing.

'What? It got me thinking. We're all like her ex-boyfriend in some way. Em always asks what the boys and I want to eat, and sometimes she cooks four different meals for dinner. I often come in, eat and flop into bed because I'm so tired. So last weekend, I woke up, got her flowers, cooked breakfast, then took the boys off her for the day. When she came back, the boys and I had dinner waiting. It felt nice. I'm going to do it more often.'

'Tim, if you and Jack cooked dinner for another woman, Lou and Em would kill you both and have absolutely no problems framing me for it. Then, they'll take pleasure visiting me in prison to remind me of what they did.' I eye them both.

'What's the big deal?' Tim shrugs.

'After your little day of flowers, cooking and actual parenting, what happened when you put the kids to bed?' I ask Tim pointedly. He can't contain the smile that creeps across his face. 'That's what I thought. Now imagine you telling Em that you did the same for another woman.' The lightbulb comes on.

'Louisa would throw me off the balcony.' Jack laughs.

'Jack, your girlfriend needs serious help.' I shut down the idea and turn our attention to Jack's bachelor party.

'When are we going, guys?'

'Next month sometime. We locked it down with the girls,' Jack announces.

'That was too easy – what's the catch?'

'The girls are coming,' Jack confesses.

'You're having a laugh. That's a couples' weekend, not a stag!'

'They're going to do their own thing. They'll just be in the hotel room with us.' Tim sighs.

'That's the only way we're going.' Jack shrugs.

'Both of you are pathetic. Let me guess, it was Lou's idea.'

'Em saw the itinerary, got excited and called Lou,' Tim admits sheepishly.

'There's no way Lou's letting me out of the country alone with you guys.'

'Honestly, Jack, where are your balls? Are you sure you want to marry this girl? She doesn't trust you to be in France for three nights?'

I'm livid.

'No, she doesn't trust me to be alone in France for three nights, with you.'

'Tim?'

'Whatever makes my wife happy, goes.'

'This is seriously crap, guys; I can't believe you are letting this weekend get hijacked.'

I toss my pint back and make my way back home. I like Em, but Louisa is bad news. I wish Jack would just dump her and start again.

I walk in and find Ariella cross-legged on the couch, surrounded by paperwork, with a massive bouquet of flowers on the coffee table in front of her.

'Hey, how was SF?'

'Revealing. Oh hello. Who are those from?'

She beams at me. 'Tim. He brought them round the other day and stayed for some tea and chat. It was nice. He said he'd swing by again when you're out of town.'

'Ariella, you know Tim is really, *really* married – right?'

'He just checked in to say thanks for dinner.'

It must be innocent, but Tim is playing a dangerous game. I play the flowers down.

'He's too overprotective for his own good. How are things over here?'

'One of your Singaporean clients cancelled a week-long conference, which left a massive ops hole in the event schedule. That's all we talked about at the ten a.m. today. The professor texted, he dumped me. If you're hungry, there's some plum chicken in the fridge – want me to heat it up for you?'

'No thanks, I'll heat it up myself. You don't seem that upset about the professor?'

'I'm happy for him. He's met someone else and he didn't think we were going anywhere, which I fully understand.'

I walk over to the kitchen while digesting the conference cancellation. We will retain our fees and I will keep my bonus, but it's a big hit. I'll be heading to Singapore for damage control, which I am not totally displeased with. I look over to Ariella as she hums to herself and pokes her lips with her pen. She is a funny one. She doesn't even care that she has been dumped.

'Wine?' I ask her.

'Maybe tea?' she suggests.

I pour myself a glass and make her tea, just in time to grab the chicken from the oven. I want to put an end to her working and watch *The Sopranos*, so I deliberately move all her papers away to clear a space next to her, knowing it'll irritate her.

'Caleb!' she groans.

I laugh inside. 'What? Let's watch *The Sopranos*.'

'You're so annoying.' She packs up her papers, stacks them neatly on her laptop and picks up her tea.

I chuckle and nudge her. 'I bet you missed me.'

'No, I didn't.' There's her cute little frown.

'Oh, don't be grumpy. Besides, I bet you're dying to see

Bobby, and your new crush Artie Bucco. Why do you go for the losers?'

'They're not losers. In that environment, it takes strength to be vulnerable.'

'It's survival of the fittest, Ariella. Darwin—'

'Are we going to argue, or watch the episode?'

'I'm on it.'

The intro starts to roll. It feels good to be back home and settled. I'm also pleased to see Ariella seems to be moving on from Jasper.

'Is she here?' Jasper asks, standing in the doorway looking jittery.

It's been raining all day but, even though he is soaked through, I have no intention of letting him in.

'No.'

'Are you sure?' Panic crosses his face.

'She isn't here.'

'Shit.' His desperation comes through in that one word. It is loaded enough for me to change my mind.

'Come in.'

He does so, and immediately starts pacing around the living area.

'When did you last see her?'

'She left a few hours ago for Zachary's party. Didn't she make it?' He's making me nervous.

'No, she was there.'

'Then what's the problem?'

'We had an argument.'

'You're not together any more. It happens. You people and your fairy-tale bullshit need to understand what it means to have broken up.'

'It was bad.'

I feel the anger rise quickly inside me.

'If you touched her, I'll break your neck,' I state calmly, for the record.

'Of course not! She started having a panic attack and I walked away from her. I went back immediately and she was gone. Now I can't find her. I've been calling and she's not picking up.'

'She's probably in a car on the way home.'

He shakes his head and looks like he is about to cry. 'No, this was two hours ago. Shit! I really messed up.'

'Jasper, Ariella is an adult and I'm expecting a friend to come over shortly, so you're going to have to stalk her elsewhere. You broke up, probably because of what you're doing now. Leave your number and I might call you when she gets in...' I say, whispering, *you controlling twat* under my breath.

'Ariella gets attacks that can trigger her asthma, but she refuses to carry an inhaler around.'

The fury hits me. 'You knew this and you walked away from her?' I shove him across the living room, but he doesn't fight back. The self-contempt that radiates from him hits me as he pinches his eyes. I get my phone out and try to call her, but it goes straight to voicemail. I step away, dial Nicole and hope she isn't already on her way. There'd be no stopping her then.

'Nicole, I have to cancel, there's a bit of an emergency.'

'Are you dying? No. You aren't cancelling. I'm coming.'

'Why don't you come round tomorrow?'

'There's work on Monday. I could bring a bag and we can go to work together?'

'Yeah, sure, whatever you need.'

'Great. See you tomorrow.'

I grab my laptop from my room and flip it open on the kitchen counter. I find the company directory.

'What's the name of that redhead she hangs around with?' I ask as he walks over to see what I am doing.

'Lara. Lara Scott.'

I find her company mobile and I dial. Thankfully, it starts to ring.

'You better have my fucking stage lights!'

'Lara?'

'Yes?'

'This is Caleb Black from work. Is Ariella with you?'

'No. What's wrong?'

'I'm here with Jasper. She was with him earlier, then she disappeared. He hasn't seen her for a couple of hours and he's worried.'

'Why should I tell that clotpole—'

'He thinks she may be having a panic attack.'

'Fuck. Okay. I have her on my Find My Friends app. I'll text you her location. I'll let you know if she's moving.'

Lara hangs up quickly. I put on my trainers and coat while we wait for what seems like for ever to get the pin drop from her. As soon as it comes through, I grab my keys, slam the door shut behind us and jump in the black taxi I'd booked in the meantime. Jasper is on the edge of his seat the whole journey there. He should be. If Dahlia finds out, she'd Tracey Emin his insides and proudly submit it to the Tate.

'Relax, she'll be fine,' I offer.

'You don't know that. Oh God.' He puts his face in his hands, distressed. 'I shouldn't have—'

'There! Stop!' I call out.

I see her drenched, cold and shivering at a bus stop.

'Aari!'

Jasper is out of the cab and running across the road before I finish. He almost gets hit. Twice. I give him a couple of minutes with her and send Lara a text and negotiate a return with the driver.

Jasper has wrapped her in his jacket and is trying to coax her away from the bus stop. Ariella is having none of it. She is trying to wriggle out of his grasp while pushing him away. I put my hand on him to stop. He does.

'Ariella, let's go home.'

I touch her hand gently and she stops struggling and looks up. Her face is puffy, covered in a mixture of tears, snot and rain. She sheds Jasper's coat, throws it in his general direction and walks into my arms silently. I take off my jacket, drape it over her and walk her back to the cab. She gets in and hurries into the far corner, burying her head in my coat. I tap her lightly to get her attention.

'We can't leave him out here.'

She nods, mute. I step back into the rain, call him over and position myself between them as we drive silently back to Hampstead. Lara sends a text back.

'Lara says she's going to sneak out of the gig soon and that she'll be over before midnight.'

Ariella nods and I send Lara my address. When we get back home, Jasper doesn't get out. Instead he asks the black cab to take him home. As soon as we get in, I pop Ariella on a bar stool. She is a sorry, wet mess.

'You daft little bird, look at you. I'm going to run you a bath, don't move, okay?' I reprimand her softly.

She nods as she shivers on the stool. I dash to her bathroom, turn on the taps for her bath and return to the living room as quickly as I can.

'The water's running. I'm going to take off as much as I decently can, but you're going to have to do the rest.'

I help her out of my jacket, her jacket, her cardigan, her boots and her socks. I dump them all on the floor next to the stool. I take her in my arms and carry her to her bathroom, placing her on the side of her bath.

'Will you please get in? I'll go and make you some cheese on toast.'

She doesn't move.

'I know you're not okay and we can talk about that later, but please get in the bath and warm up. I'll make you something to eat and Lara will be here soon. I don't know what's going on, but you're not going to... try anything, are you? I just need to know that.'

For the second time that evening, her tears fall. She shakes her head.

'Good. Now get in. I'll check up on you in thirty minutes. If you're not in there, I'm going to undress you myself and toss you in. I don't care about all your no-touchy business. Also, if you're not out, I'm going to drag you out. There's nothing you've got that I haven't seen before, and you know I'll enjoy it because I'm a creep.'

I see a little smile. Good.

'I'll give you a five-minute warning.'

'Thank you for coming to get me, Caleb,' she whispers.

'Well, it was Jasper really. He was worried out of his mind; but I take it all of this is his fault anyway, so you're welcome.' I leave the door of her bathroom open, but shut her bedroom door.

I have no idea what to do. I can deliver cheese on toast, but I don't know how to handle anything like this. Thankfully, Lara the hot redhead is coming over. In the meantime, I'm just going to throw things that make her happy at her. I rush to get out of my wet clothes and have a quick shower. I chop up all the bits I need for the cheese on toast until my five-minute warning. I line up the next episode of *The Sopranos* and make her evening tea. I unfold the blanket on the couch ready for her. When she emerges, I am ready. I lead her to the couch, bring over her cheese on toast with tea and press play. I sit next to her after I cover her with the blanket.

'And I'm going to slo-mo all the bits when Bobby comes on. Give you the true Bacala experience.'

She reaches over, gives me a hug and rests her head on my shoulder. 'Thank you.'

'You're welcome. Feel better, okay, Mason?'

We sit through the episode and, by the end, she is a little chattier, so we watch another one. Halfway through the second, Lara turns up. She blows in, full of raw hostility and energy. I fancy her immediately.

'That bastard, Aari. What did he do? I'm going to kill him. We can set fire to his bloody five-thousand-pound suits. Let's go.'

'Not tonight, Lara.'

Ariella smiles a little more. Lara launches herself at the couch, completely covering Ariella's body with hers.

'What's with all this tea? You. What's your name?'

She snaps her fingers at me. She knows my name. I laugh.

'Servant boy,' I respond, deadpan. Ariella laughs.

'Servant boy. Tequila. Lime. Salt. Lots of it. What's this?' She looks at the screen. '*Sopranos* – perfect. Has Tony's mother ordered the hit on her son yet?'

'Oh come on!' I complain.

She fixes me with her beautiful eyes. 'Shut up... You're so late, this show can drink legally in New Jersey. You deserve the spoilers. You just wait till they get into the whole storyline with Bobby and—'

'Stop!' Ariella shouts and bursts out laughing.

Lara hugs Ariella tighter and they hold on like they need each other to breathe. Lara turns her head to face me, winks and mouths the words 'thank you'. I smile, head to the kitchen and grab some tequila, lime, salt and shot glasses.

'Things are about to get messy,' I announce.

'Yes! Rack them up.' Lara slaps her hands together and rubs them quickly.

Ariella frowns. 'Just one. I'm not meant to be drinking after an attack.'

'Just one,' Lara assures her.

It's enough to make her groggy. She doesn't last half an hour, so Lara puts her to bed and stays with her until she falls asleep.

'She's sleeping. What happened?' Lara tiptoes back and sits opposite me in the lotus position. I can't help noticing how perfectly hourglass-shaped she is. I like a woman who fills her clothes and—

'Pervert! Stop staring at my boobs and pay attention.' She snaps her fingers at me and pushes her wild hair away from her face. She oozes sex.

'Pervert?' I laugh, as I pour her another tequila shot and pass it to her. She knocks it back and beckons for a refill. I happily oblige.

'I know exactly who you are and I'm trying not to get killed by Nicole.'

'Nicole?' I ask, not knowing how to respond.

'Don't try that ignorant shit with me. Yes, Nicole. *Vogue* cover model meets psychotic, narcissistic sociopath. *That* Nicole.'

'We're just friends.'

'Funny, so are we. I'll be sure to tell her you said that. When you're done thinking with your dick, want to tell me what happened with Ariella?'

I like it. I have started in worse positions. She'll take a little time, that's all.

'She and Jasper got into a fight. He walked away from her mid-panic attack. He came back, she was gone, he spent two hours looking for her and eventually ended up here.'

'Dahlia and Hugh are going to kill him.' She smirks.

'You're going to tell them?'

'Of course not. Ariella would murder me. I bet if we ask her what happened in the morning, she'll come out with a version that doesn't completely nail his arse to the cross. It makes me so mad!'

'I can tell. You're cute when you're mad.'

She narrows her eyes at me. Feisty.

'Am I?'

She rolls her eyes and I take my swing.

'And you're much more beautiful up close. I've seen you in the office and you turn my head every time, but up close, you're... wow.'

She moves closer. I move in too. It can't be this easy.

'Listen to me, you syphilis-riddled dickhead. I'm going to do you a favour, save you some time and not twist your nuts off for thinking I'm going to fall for that shite; only because of what you did for Aari tonight. So here goes. I am a LEZZ-BEEE-YAAAN. Your uninspired, outdated lines are wasted on me. It's never gonna happen.'

Wow, I like her even more. Ariella needs someone like Lara in her corner. I can tell that we've come from similar places; dragged up in a hard, harsh world. I pour another shot in her glass.

'Good to know. Tequila?' I offer.

'It's no use trying to get me drunk either, you'll lose.'

'Is that a challenge?'

'No, it's a fucking invitation.'

She looks me in the eye, knocks the shot back, slams the glass on the table, smiles slyly and compels me to bring it.

'Come on, Girl Scout, I've got all night.'

'So have I.' Smiling at her, I refill both our glasses.

FIFTEEN

ARIELLA

As my eyes open the next morning, I feel embarrassed and ashamed about the night before. Jasper is not a bad person. We are both broken and hurt, and I clearly overreacted. It isn't fair to blame him.

I'd been looking forward to Zachary's little party for Isszy's birthday, but I was also looking forward to seeing Jasper. I was hoping to move past the tension between us at Mommy's birthday and return to being friends.

The usual suspects were there: Franco and a whole bunch of guys the boys went to school with, Isszy's family, and her friends from the fashion and editorial world. It was intimidating. They were all nice, but I felt self-conscious and alone in my jeans and shirt, standing next to designers I had never heard of. Thankfully, there was a girl from Isszy's office, Zoe, who didn't know anyone either, so we stuck together. She was in promotions and was interested in some event stuff too. I promised her Caleb would give her a call. She was cute. I just hoped he didn't try to sleep with her.

When Jasper turned up, I didn't notice until Zoe asked who he was. My stomach erupted like a butterfly farm. I immediately felt every breath, every kiss, every smile, every laugh with him. What had I done? Life was awful without him and dating was miserable. If I was being completely honest, I didn't care about the people I was speaking with. They were nice, but if I didn't see or speak with them again it wouldn't bother me. Jasper caught me looking at him, so I smiled, and he walked over. My heart jumped to my throat. He was so beautiful.

'OMG. He's walking over. How do I look?' Zoe fussed with her hair and her outfit.

'You look great. You should know that he's...'

'Ariella.'

I inhaled as much of his familiar smell as I could when he leaned in to give me a kiss on the cheek. He used my full name. What was that about?

'Hey, Jas.' I smiled the warmest smile I could. Everything I was feeling lay behind that smile. *I want you. I'm sorry. I have no idea what I'm doing.*

'Who's your friend?' He extended his hand. 'Hi. I'm Jasper. Do you work at Ivory Bow too?'

'No, I work with Isszy.'

'Fashion. I've never understood it, to be honest.'

'That's surprising. You're wearing Desmond Merrion couture.'

'I tip my hat. You're out – drink refill...?'

'Zoe.'

'Zoe. Gorgeous name...'

Jasper and Zoe walked away from me. I stood there, stunned. Of all the people he could have zeroed in on, he took away the one person I was speaking with.

Normally, I'd be huddled inseparably with Jasper all night, making little jokes and enjoying the company of people we were speaking with together. He and I loved finding the tiniest space to kiss at these things. Now, he was flirting intensely with Zoe. I made my way to my safe place, the kitchen. Someone, surely, would need help there.

'I knew you'd end up in here,' Zachary said, joining me a few minutes later.

'I thought I'd come and help.'

'No. You're hiding from him.'

'Maybe.'

'Why are you doing this to each other?'

'Doing what?'

'He's out there hitting on someone he has no interest in, knowing it's killing you to watch, and you're in here hiding, so he's guaranteed to be worried sick, praying you're not in one of the little spaces you usually disappear into, with another bloke.'

'I'd never do that.'

'It might be better if one of you leaves, and you're kind of the one out of sight. It's just that the room is talking about both of you, rather than Isszy.'

'Zachary!' Isszy appeared, looking furious. 'What's wrong with you?'

'Isz. It's not a good vibe out there.'

'And kicking your sister out is going to fix it?'

'I'm not kicking her out. She's hiding. Jasper is out there, enjoying the party. I'm just suggesting that if she wants to leave because she's having a terrible time, it'd be okay.'

'Did it occur to you that she's in the kitchen because she doesn't want to cause a scene? And that if Jasper did the same instead of snogging the face off Zoe in the middle of the room, people wouldn't be talking?'

'I'm sorry... he's what?' I didn't think I'd heard right.

'Shit. I'm sorry, Aari.'

'Brilliant work, Isszy,' Zachary complained.

I called up my taxi app as I walked through the room with my head down, so that I didn't have to acknowledge anyone calling my name. No cabs. When I safely made it out of the front door, it was pouring with rain, so I stood against it for shelter. I checked the app again. Still no cabs. I quickly ran to the bus stop in front of Zachary and Isszy's home.

Jasper joined me. 'Where are you going?'

'Please leave me alone, Jasper.'

'It's pouring, Scrappy—'

'Don't call me that! Don't you call me that EVER again!' I screamed at him so hard, I knocked the wind out of myself and bent over to catch my breath. I knew then that I was in serious danger of triggering an attack.

He stepped towards me.

'Stay away from me! I don't want to be anywhere near you.' I knew an attack was on its way, but I couldn't stay here. I stepped into the rain and started to walk.

'Ariella, are you having—'

My chest hurt, I was struggling to breathe, I couldn't see where I was going, but I walked as fast as I could, away from him. *I cannot pass out. I cannot pass out. I cannot pass out,* I repeated to myself as I put one foot in front of the other. Thankfully, a small alley whose wall I could lean against presented itself... That was when I felt the Earth start to spin and I let myself fall to the floor.

I don't think I was out for long. I sat up slowly, trying to steady my breathing, then continued walking as far as my legs would take me, until sheer exhaustion forced me to stop. Only then did I allow myself to break down and cry.

I go into the kitchen the next morning ready to apologise, only to find both Caleb and Lara passed out on the couch, surrounded by bottles of spirits. They obviously didn't stop at the tequila. I smile.

Lara pops up first, like a jack-in-the-box. Her bouncy hair is everywhere as she rubs the sleep from her eyes.

'Hey,' I call softly as I catch her out of the corner of my eye.

'Hey. How are you?' she asks.

'Embarrassed, but all right.'

'Embarrassed? If anyone should be embarrassed, it's this fool over here.'

She kicks Caleb hard. He shoots up, startled.

'What happened!?' he asks, and we burst out laughing.

'Why?' I laugh.

'Your room-mate tried to sleep with me last night. I'd been on the couch all of ten seconds before he started hitting on me.'

'She's gay, Caleb,' I fill him in.

'It was worth a shot.' Caleb gets up and stretches. 'She looks even more gorgeous this morning.'

I turn around from the kettle and catch Caleb winking at Lara.

'No!' she shouts, before rushing to the guest bathroom. 'You bastard!'

Caleb's laughter fills the flat.

'What's going on?' I ask him.

'We had a little bet last night. I won.'

When Lara emerges from the bathroom, I notice a pair of curly moustaches that have been drawn on her top lip in single lines. Caleb hadn't been shy with the curls.

'How am I supposed to get this off?'

'Figure it out. I need a shower. Ariella, can I have some coffee?'

'Sure.' I smile and turn to Lara. 'You look cute, though.'

'I'm going to spit in his coffee.' She charges at me.

'No you're not, Inspector Clouseau. You shouldn't be making bets with Caleb. What was it?'

'First person knocked out loses.'

'Looks like you've met your match. Want me to rustle up something fun for breakfast? Do you need a painkiller?'

'Too many questions. I'd love a painkiller, yes to breakfast – loads of it! Are you okay? What happened last night?'

'It was my fault. I didn't mean to scare you. Jasper met someone he liked at Isszy's party, so I left. I had a little attack and he offered to help, but I walked away from him. I was stupid.'

'I'm fairly certain that wasn't what happened, Aari. You're a little emotional, but not irrational.'

I don't want to get into it with Lara, because I need to stay calm. 'What are you up to today?'

'You're trying to get rid of me but I'm not going anywhere. I'm going to hang out here with you all day... and you're going to help me get back at Caleb. How do you live with him?'

'It's quite easy once you get over the women coming in and out. He's terrible...' I laugh. 'But he's actually a good person.'

Lara points at her moustache. 'Would a good person do this?'

She disappears to try to get the moustache off while I cook us a huge breakfast. Caleb returns as I plate up.

'Oh my goodness, yes!' He sits next to Lara at the counter. 'All right?' He beams at her.

Quick as lightning, Lara grabs her fork and starts to bring it down on Caleb's hand. Caleb is quicker, thankfully, and moves it away.

'You're feral!' He laughs at her.

'Best believe it – and if you think that's my last attempt, you're in for a shock.'

'Ariella, will you tell your friend that she's a nutcase?'

'Say that again, and I will fucking lamp you.'

'Breakfast, guys,' I announce.

For a few blissful minutes, there's silence. Caleb and Lara's sparring is pleasing to watch, but if you didn't know either of them you'd probably be a hair's breadth away from calling 999.

After breakfast, the three of us go for a long walk on the Heath, then hit the pub for Sunday lunch. Caleb is expecting Nicole later, so we don't stay out too late and return to watch *The Sopranos*.

'I better go to the bathroom and head out,' Lara declares as soon as the door goes, announcing Nicole's arrival.

I am immediately suspicious.

'Hi,' Nicole says, breezing in. She is overjoyed to see Caleb, who really needs to commit to this girl or let her go. She may be intense, but anyone can see that she is completely in love with him.

'Hey,' he grunts without any real emotion.

No, Caleb. What are you doing?

She spots me, and all her warm, fuzzy feelings evaporate. 'Hello, Ariella.' She looks at me like mud on her shoe.

'That was amazing. I'm out of here.' Lara emerges from Caleb's room, wearing the corset top and shorts she had on last night. She is holding her jacket, *my* bra and her shoes to her chest. 'Hi, Nicole!' She smiles coyly, then tiptoes up and kisses Caleb on the cheek. 'I had the best time, Cay. Maybe again, sometime soon?' She looks at me and waves shyly, whispering: 'Bye, Ariella. Thanks for having me over.'

I had no idea that, all this time, Lara knew how to whisper. She breezes past Nicole and walks out of the door. My first thought is that she had better bring my bra back into work tomorrow. My second is to get out of the way because Nicole is going to blow.

'I'm going to bed, guys. Goodnight.'

Oh, Lara. She got Caleb back in the worst way possible. Nicole starts screaming at him before I've shut my bedroom door.

Today has been a good day. Caleb and Lara really came

through for me. Hanging out all day pointlessly with them has been refreshing and spontaneous – but exhausting. I shower, settle into bed and look at my phone for the first time in over twenty-four hours. Twenty-two missed calls and a whole bunch of texts from Isszy, Zachary and Jasper, asking me to come home.

I turn off my phone. This is home now.

SIXTEEN

CALEB

Lara Scott has a wicked streak. Unfortunately, I loathe and admire her in equal measure for it. Right now, loathing is where my dial is. She is completely nuts, but hides it with raw, wild charm. She served her purpose, though, because Sunday was the most I have seen Ariella laugh. At one point we thought she was having another attack, because she was laughing so hard she was struggling to breathe. I had such a good day with those two.

Just when I thought I was safe, though, Lara pulled that stunt with Nicole. The next forty-eight hours were painful. I resolved to break it off as soon as I got back from my whirlwind trip to Singapore, just to make sure none of Mel's contacts were firing us. They weren't. And I made sure of it, because no one was left disappointed, if you catch my drift. It was nice to leave everything behind for a few days, but I did miss home and was pleased when my car stopped outside my building.

'I'm home!' I chime as I walk into the flat, which is filled with Ariella's usual apple and grapefruit smell. I've always wanted to say that. It sure is nice to come back to a warm home.

Normally, I'd be dreading freezing my bollocks off during the time it takes for the apartment to heat up after a trip. No response from Ariella. It isn't 10 p.m. yet. Surely she isn't in bed already? She usually doesn't start yawning and stretching like a kitten until ten thirty. She's probably in the shower. After five minutes I give up waiting to wash the aeroplane from me. I'll wait for a little bit to scratch her behind the ears. I smile. She's a sweet girl. She needs a bit of looking after, but she's all right, really.

It isn't until I am clean and wander back into the kitchen that I see the sticky note on the fridge.

Your sister called. I tried to reach you. Your mum has been taken to hospital. Have gone up to Liverpool to lend a hand until you get there. Call me when you get this. X

Shit.

I scramble around for my phone and charger. I shouldn't have let it die. It takes a few minutes for it to spring to life with a flurry of texts from Ariella, followed by texts from two unrecognised numbers that turn out to be my sister and father. I call her, but her phone is off, which is highly unusual. I have no choice, and dial the number that belongs to my father.

'Caleb,' comes the greeting.

'Where the fuck is she?'

'She's at the Royal. Kayleigh says it's a nice ward—'

'I'm not talking about your wife. I'm talking about Ariella.'

'Lovely girl. She just left to go back to her hotel. We've had a good day. She's not like them.'

'Them?'

'She's half-caste, isn't she? Fine by me...'

I don't get into how offensive his language is, because I wouldn't expect anything less from the racist bastard.

'Do you know where she's staying? I've been trying to reach her.' I am sincerely hoping the answer is a flat no.

'She was looking for her phone earlier but she said she was staying at the Razzmatazz, Lazpaz or something – it's right in the centre, though.'

I immediately know where he means. Thank God. If she was looking for her phone in that house, though, I know exactly what has happened to it.

'How is she?'

'She's been wonderful. Took us all for a big food shop. Bought the kids some toys, did some laundry and cleaned the front room and kitchen. You know Kayleigh's had to leave the children here, and with my back it's hard—'

'I meant your wife.'

'Doing as well as can be expected. The ambulance came very quickly—'

'I'll be down in the morning.'

'Gracing us with your presence, are you?'

I don't rise to it.

'You can tell Kayleigh's little shits that Ariella's phone better be found by the time I get there tomorrow morning or there'll be hell to pay.'

I don't wait for a response. I hang up, livid. I look up train times. The first one is at 5.30 a.m. I'll be on it.

I try the Andaz and ask to be put through to Ariella's room. It rings out, so I leave a message, trying to sound as calm as possible.

'Ariella, it's Caleb. I'll be on the first train tomorrow, so I'll be at your hotel before nine. Stay there. Don't leave. Don't let anyone in apart from me.'

I hang up and pace the apartment. No one checks their hotel voicemails. So I call back and leave a message with the worried night manager. After alerting work that I won't be in, I try to control my worry. Not for my mother, who was never a mother to me; for Ariella. She's just spent the day in close proximity to a senior National Front member who put his own son in hospital for two weeks when he found out that I had been working on Jerry's stall. I will never forget the sound of my nose breaking, my jaw crushing, my teeth coming loose and my skull cracking as the rings on his massive knuckles connected with the bones in my face. The beating was so bad, I was kept away from school and the hospital, and forced to heal at home until I passed out. My jaw still clicks to this day.

Ariella had just spent a day around this beast, the man who not only inspired me, but made it absolutely necessary for me to learn a martial art, to ensure my survival from his brutal beatings.

I don't hear from Ariella all night. I dash to her hotel room as soon as I get into Liverpool the next morning. She isn't there. Next stop is the house. I make the taxi keep the meter running.

The house still makes me shiver. I remember every dark nook and haunting cranny. The National Front flag still hangs out of the top bedroom window. For the first time I can remember, the curtains in the front room are open. I am shaking as I walk up to the door, and feel like I'm going to vomit when I press the bell.

One of Kayleigh's kids opens the door and lets me into the narrow hallway. Clearly, school is still optional in this hellhole. I am struck by how it all looks exactly the same. Ariella, standing with her back to me, is wearing a Liverpool FC hoodie, cooking. She is chopping her ingredients into her usual little colourful soldiers ready to go into battle on the countertop.

The monster I used to call my father is standing next to her, wearing a matching Liverpool shirt and laughing. Ariella has just smacked him lightly on the arm with a wooden spoon.

He seems to be enjoying it. I feel the anger rush from the base of my spine to the nape of my neck. She points to some carrots with an apologetic smile. I stand there quietly for a little while, watching as he obediently hacks carrots next to her.

He looks clean. His hair is combed. He isn't wearing the dirty white string vest I grew up frightened of seeing every day. Maybe I don't have so much to worry about. Then I see it. That loaded, disgusting smile as he pats Ariella on the bottom and lets his hand linger. Ariella picks up a clean wooden spoon and smacks him, much harder this time.

'I said, don't do that,' she whispers loudly. 'I'll happily leave and head back to London if you don't stop.'

I am between them in a flash, and push him away. 'Ariella.' I keep my voice low and level.

'Caleb!' She smiles. 'I'm so glad you're here.'

'I've been trying to reach you.' I pull her into a hug. She holds on tighter than I expect. It worries me. I'm relieved she's okay. Dahlia would have murdered me, which would have been preferable to whatever Hugh Mason might dream up.

'I'm sorry. I lost my phone yesterday, but the kids went back to the shops we visited and found it this morning! It's charging. I was going to call...'

'Are you okay?' I ask, inspecting her face.

She nods. 'I'm sorry about your—'

'I need you to listen to me right now.' I hold her gently and look directly in her eyes. 'Please stop what you're doing and get your stuff,' I state calmly.

'Hold on, son...' my father starts.

'I'm not your son. I'm here for her and that's it.' I try to stay calm.

'But your mom, Caleb...'

'Ariella, get your stuff right now. We're leaving,' I reassert.

'You can't—' he starts again.

'I can do anything I like. You think wearing matching football tops makes you less of a monster?'

He has the decency to look embarrassed.

'I'm sorry,' Ariella says to my father as she pulls the tea towel from the back pocket of her jeans.

'Don't you *dare* apologise to him.' I realise that I am shouting at her. That's not my intention. I just want to get away from here.

'Please don't yell at me, Caleb,' she shoots back in a tone that is anything but pleading.

She's cross at me? Cross can't even begin to describe what I am feeling towards her, now the worry has abated. She walks past, annoyed. She, I can deal with later. My father starts to follow her, so I stand firmly at the door, blocking the hallway.

'It's been years, Caleb.'

I look at the psychotic, violent, racist, alcoholic bully. He is older, frailer, greyer, weaker and more pathetic than I remember.

'You haven't changed,' I respond.

He turns and makes his way, very slowly, to the dining table to sit.

'Stop making it look harder than it really is. I have no sympathy for you.'

'Things don't work the way they used to.' He smiles at me.

'Years of alcoholism and evil eventually catch up.' I watch carefully just in case the animal surfaces. 'Is the ward looking after her?'

'I haven't been. Someone's got to look after these little fuckers.'

'I thought that was what Ariella was doing.'

'With my help...'

'You're a burden.'

'I'd be a burden to that arse, those tits...' He licks his lips. I punch him before I know what I'm doing.

'Get off!' My father shoves me back and holds his nose. Then laughter erupts from him. 'The apple doesn't fall far, does it?'

Ariella returns. 'Caleb! What's going on?'

'What took so long?'

'I was saying goodbye to the kids.'

'Let's go.'

'Goodbye, Graham. You should have enough food to last for a couple of weeks. Just defrost the stuff we froze last night for dinner. The kids' vitamins are in the top drawer and the curtains just need to be picked up this afternoon. Will you be okay putting them back up?' Her hands are shaking.

'He'll be fine.' I usher her out of the house, maybe a little too roughly.

'Stop it, Caleb,' she snaps through clenched teeth as we make it through the door and climb into the taxi. She is seething silently. She came here, without my permission, and *she's* the one who is angry?

We get back to the hotel and I follow her to her room.

'Pack up, we're leaving.'

'You can stop right now. I understand you're angry at everyone here, but please don't speak to me like that.'

'I'm also angry at you.'

'Why would you be mad at me?'

'You had no right to come up here!'

'For goodness' sake, the landline I didn't know we had started ringing at about five a.m. and didn't stop until I was about to leave for work, so I picked up. It was your sister. She was absolutely hysterical because your mum had had a stroke. She was overwhelmed, Caleb. She really needed you, so I came up because I couldn't reach you. What did you expect me to do? Go to work?'

'I didn't ask you to.'

'No human being should need to be asked, when something like this happens!'

'We're leaving.'

'No, we're not. You need to go and see your mother. I went to see her last night.'

'What else did you do?' It is my turn to seethe.

'I helped out your family, that's all.' She looks at me; not for thanks, but as if she is defending herself. I can't help relenting.

'They're not nice people, Ariella,' I say quietly, sitting on the corner of the bed.

'Maybe not. I saw the flag. I'm not stupid. But your mom is really ill, Caleb. I don't think she's leaving that hospital any time soon.'

She walks over, crouches to my level, takes my hands in hers and looks right at me.

'Caleb. I know things were horrific for you growing up. But please go and see her. Be angry, yell at her, forgive her or don't, but talk to her. Just in case you never get the chance to again. She's extremely frail and she'd love to see you. Please. And when you come back, we'll be on the next train out of here. I promise.'

'I don't understand why you care so much!'

'Because I hope someone would do the same for me if I was in your shoes. Please go. You don't have to be long. I'll come with you, if you want. If you prefer to go alone, I promise I won't return to the house.'

She is not letting this go.

'Don't leave this room,' I command as I leave to make my way to the hospital.

I am faced with a very different woman from the one I last saw four years ago. There is nothing left of the round, red-cheeked woman I remember.

'Ma.' The word feels unfamiliar.

'Caleb?' A small smile spreads across her face. 'I'm so glad you came. I met your friend yesterday... I forget her name.'

'Ariella.'

'Yes. She kept calling me Mrs Black. I kept explaining that Mrs Black was my bitch of a mother-in-law.' She laughs weakly. Even in hospital she still has space for hatred. I ignore her. I don't want to pick a fight right now.

'This isn't just a stroke, is it?'

She shakes her head slowly. 'No, it's not, but I don't want to talk about that yet. Your friend said she lost her phone. Did she find it, and was anything else missing?' she asks knowingly.

'Yes, we found it, along with one of her credit cards.'

'Those little rats.'

'Yup.'

Our eyes meet and we burst out laughing together for the very first time in my life.

'I'm sorry, Caleb.'

It hits me like a punch in the chest. 'Now isn't the time,' I respond, searching for anger that I can't find.

'Now is exactly the time. Sit down.'

She pats the bed and shifts over painfully. I stand where I am.

'I'm sorry. I made every mistake I could ever have made with you. I was meant to protect, nurture and love you. As you can see, I was successful.' She smiles sadly before she continues. 'It's no excuse, but I knew I wouldn't have to worry about you.'

My eyes moisten. 'Why didn't you need to worry?'

'You've always been a fighter.'

'And you know this how?'

She starts to cry and reaches out for my hand. I move both of them into my pockets.

'You made me responsible for the family as a child because you knew I'd be okay?'

'Tell me what I need to do to make things right.'

'I shouldn't have to.' I finally sit down in the chair next to her bed; but not before I make sure it is out of her reach.

'I'm happy you've found such a lovely girl. She's very beautiful, and kind too. You know she stayed with me all night listening and fell asleep in that very chair.'

'I haven't found anything. She's my flatmate and a soft touch, you got lucky.'

'You're not together?'

'No. Decent human beings actually exist. Good luck with your health. Don't catch anything you didn't come in with.' I get up and turn to leave.

'No. Please. Wait. I'm scared this'll be the only chance I'll have to say I'm sorry.'

Against my better judgement, I sit down; and stay there all day and evening, talking to the woman I've hated for so many years. Crying. Releasing my anger. Feeling sorry for her, but never quite reaching the edges of forgiveness. I don't return to Ariella's hotel room until 11 p.m., and she is fast asleep. I am so exhausted that I get into bed with her and, for the first time in years, I don't wake up until after noon. She is up and dressed, working on her laptop at the small desk in the room.

'I extended our stay so you could sleep. We can go back to London today or stay. It's up to you.'

'I want to go back home.' My eyes hurt, my head feels heavy and I have the effects of a stinking hangover without the pleasures of the night before.

'I waited up for you as long as I could. How did it go?'

'I don't want to talk about it.'

'You're sure you don't want to stay?'

Ariella cautiously comes closer and gives me a hug. I bear it for as long as I can, then move away.

'Let's go.'

'Okay. Clean up and I'll call us a car, meet me in the lobby?'

She shuts her laptop, grabs her suitcase and walks out of the bedroom.

We travel back to London in silence. It is exactly what I need.

The next morning, I get a text from my sister.

SEVENTEEN

ARIELLA

It is the second funeral I have been to. My grandfather's was just over four years ago, and I remember feeling a jumble of love and loss during the slowly unfolding week we were out in Louisiana. The funeral was on a lovely sunny day. We mainly spent it eating and speedily forming relationships with new family. I remember missing Jasper terribly and wishing he could be there. Everyone wanted to talk and share memories, but I just wanted to sit in the sun with someone I really knew, and cry quietly. I could have done that with my Gigi, my Granny Grace, but it just seemed unfair to ask her to wipe my tears along with hers.

Today is rainy and grey. It didn't start terribly well, with me forcing myself onto the train with Caleb. The crematorium is full by the time we get there, so we sit in the back. After Caleb's sister and father speak, Caleb is called to say something, but he doesn't move. When I reach for his hand he pulls it away. I feel excruciating pain emanating from him and, when it is over, the coffin is slowly introduced to the furnace.

The reception is at the pub around the corner from their home. Caleb walks in, puts a thousand-pound bar tab on his credit card and makes his way to the pub stage, set up for karaoke. He turns on the microphone and, shockingly, the crowd begins to boo. He just waves it away slowly, like he is lazily dealing with a passing fly.

'There's a thousand pounds behind the bar for you to drink to your hearts' content in honour of my mother.'

The pub cheers. He continues like he doesn't hear them.

'She brought me into this world and contributed to the circumstances that have made me the man I am today. For that, I owe her.' With a scowl, Caleb steps back from the microphone, and grabs my arm as he walks past with a short, sharp, 'We're leaving.'

We get into the waiting taxi and I notice Caleb's sister fighting through the crowd to get to us.

'Lime Street,' he instructs calmly as Kayleigh pushes through the pub doors and we pull away.

Our taxi ride back to the station is as silent as the ride to the crematorium. Caleb only lets out a sigh when we are in our seats on the way back to London. I give him half an hour before I dare to ask the question.

'Are you okay?'

'No. You had no right, Ariella. You had no right to come up here in the first place. You had no right to speak to or meet my family. You had absolutely no right to go and see my mother in the hospital, and you definitely had no right to make me go. You're not meant to be here. I hate that I'm doing this; and I especially hate that I'm doing it with an audience. This is my life, my problem, my family, and you forced your way in. You pushed and pushed and pushed. Right now, I wish you'd just fuck off!' he shouts at me.

'Oi, mate! Don't talk to her like that,' the man sitting across the aisle speaks up.

Caleb gets to his feet. 'And what business of yours is it?'

'Mate, you do *not* want a piece of me.' He joins Caleb on his feet.

'No?' Caleb asks and starts to loosen his tie.

'Will both of you just calm down!' An older lady in front stands up, opens her wallet and shows us all a police badge.

'You.' She points at me. 'Get your things. Come and sit with me.' I swiftly do as I am told.

'You!' She points at Caleb. 'I suggest you take a walk and stay away from this carriage.'

Caleb huffs and leaves the carriage.

She turns to the guy who intervened. 'Thank you, sir, you can take your seat.'

The carriage claps as I sit at her table.

'He's not a very good boyfriend, love.' She shakes her head kindly.

'He's my housemate. We're coming back from his mother's funeral.' I tell her what happened, starting with the call, and she listens quietly.

'It's still no excuse, love, but I can see why he's upset. Maybe mind your business in the future, though. Family's complicated, and his sounds like it's worse than most. He'll thank you for this one day, but for now maybe keep the meddling to a minimum.'

I nod.

As we pull into London, she asks one more time. 'He's not going to give me reason to be concerned about you, is he?'

I shake my head.

She takes her card out and gives it to me. 'That's my mobile. If you ever feel threatened, call me. Put it in your phone.'

She watches me put her number in before we leave the carriage. On the platform I spot Caleb wobbling towards the exit barriers, so I run to catch him. I can smell the alcohol on him. This is going to be difficult.

'Caleb?'

He looks at me vacuously.

'Come on.'

I manage to usher us through the taxi rank and push him into the back of a black cab. My heart pours out for him during our ride home. When we get back to the flat, I help him out of his suit, shirt and tie, then pop him into bed. He looks peaceful. For all his usual bravado, right now he just looks vulnerable and alone.

He has every right to be mad at me. I did push my way in, I did push him to see his mother and I did push myself to go to the funeral. I wanted to be there for him because I know he is alone. Even with the friends that he has adopted as brothers, he has built his life alone, he bought his home alone; he had sacrificed alone and he had grown up alone. I bend over and kiss his forehead.

'I'm sorry, Caleb. I'm sorry I didn't listen. I'm sorry I didn't understand.'

He grunts and moves away from me. He is going to sleep; and, just like he has learned, he would rather do it alone.

'I'm sorry I got out of hand on the train last night. You didn't deserve that. You were just trying to help.' Caleb is standing in the kitchen, fresh in from a run and preparing my grapefruit.

How he does it, I don't know.

'You're not hungover?'

He laughs like he doesn't have a care in the world. 'Please. I've been in much worse states before.'

'How are you feeling?'

'Fine, the run cleared the cobwebs. I slept well. I noticed you undressed me, you little hussy. If you're going to do that again, can we both make sure I'm awake, alert and consenting?'

'You were out cold.' I am suspicious. He has bounced back worryingly quickly.

'Therein lies the problem. Keep your hands to yourself next time, Mason. We both know you're not getting any at the moment and, contrary to what you may believe, I have standards.'

He winks and pops a plate of perfectly prepped grapefruit and my tea in front of me. Oh no. The old Caleb is back. This time he is making me breakfast and apologising while still being insulting.

'Want to head in to work together? I can wait?' I should keep an eye on him.

'No. We've had too many days off together and I don't want the idea that we might be shagging even crossing people's minds. I have an infamous reputation to protect.'

'Oh, you should be so lucky,' I toss back.

'Look at you with the comebacks. Just when I was getting used to you being miserable. Right, shower time.' He laughs as he goes into his room.

I am relieved he is okay, but equally concerned. Yesterday he was a ball of anger. I promise myself not to push it; but, should he ever start to grieve, I'll be there.

'Hey!' Lara slides up to my desk.

'Morning, honey.' Her face instantly makes me happy.

'I know this is ridiculous, but I have to ask...'

'Lara, I'm *always* prepared for your ridiculousness.' She pinches me. 'Ow!'

'Are you shagging Caleb?' She screws up her face in disgust.

'No! Why on earth would you think that?'

'You never take time off, he never takes time off... then you both start taking the same days off, and...' She raises her eyebrows.

'His mom got rushed to hospital a couple of weeks ago and I went to help. She was cremated yesterday, so I went with him.'

'And he's in today?'

'I know; but don't say anything – he's stoic.'

Lara nods in Caleb's direction. He is sitting in Nicole's swivel chair, playing suggestively with the hem of her skirt and throwing her flirtatious looks as she stands over him, giggling and swatting his hand away playfully.

'He's clearly distracting himself,' Lara says sarcastically.

'Maybe that's what he needs. Thankfully he's going away with his friends soon, so that'll do him some good.'

Lara feigns surprise. 'He has friends?'

'He's not that bad,' I defend him.

'I suppose he isn't as appalling as I thought. Still planning on getting him back for that moustache, though.'

'Didn't you get him back with that little stunt you pulled in front of Nicole?'

'Nope. I was hoping she'd set him on fire. Instead, he turns up the next day with no burn marks.'

'Maybe you should—'

'Ariella?'

I turn back to my desk to see Harrison Ivory, one of the company's co-founders, hovering over me.

'Hello, Harry,' Lara sings as she bats her eyelids at him.

'Lara.' Harrison clears his throat nervously and avoids eye contact. I try not to smile. I'll ask Lara later. Actually, I won't. I don't want to know.

'Ariella, can you pop upstairs now to see Chris and me for a couple of minutes?'

'Of course.'

I grab my phone, notepad and pencil before I follow Harrison to the lift. I like Harrison, and Christopher Bow, our founders. They are young, down to earth and always looking to keep the company evolving. I'd been hired by Christopher, the steady, sensible COO, who oversaw operations and delivery, but started reporting to Harrison, the charming and fun sales head, after my second promotion.

When I joined, I didn't think I'd last long, but Harrison and Christopher seemed to like what I was doing. I initially ran local and international events for clients, often travelling from one city to the next to deliver them. Today, I am responsible not just for the entire events team and global delivery, but also for the compliance and safety of every Ivory Bow event worldwide. I am still unsure how I got here, but I have enjoyed the journey and challenge. Each promotion, however, increasingly anchored me to the UK, which relieved Jasper no end.

'I heard your boyfriend broke up with you,' Harrison says gently as we enter the lift.

'Yes.' I don't bother to correct him, and avoid eye contact, because I don't want to go into the details of my personal life with him. I respect both Harrison and Christopher very much, but our relationship has been strictly professional up to this point, and I am not about to let that change.

'He's a complete idiot to let you go. If you need anything, let us know.'

'Thank you.'

Christopher is waiting in the large conference room reserved for client meetings.

'Hi, Ariella. How are things going down there?' Christopher always gets straight to the point.

'Smoothly. Client feedback scores are still in the ninety-fifth percentile for the last quarter. Operationally, I'm putting together the training updates for our global compliance officers, and looking into introducing webinars to cut costs and increase our touch schedules with them. Due diligence is in place for the markets we have gaps in, and we've cut our speed of delivery by seventeen per cent. I think we should grow our network of local partners, to leave positive footprints and continue to speed up delivery deadlines...'

'Ariella? Breathe. You're doing an awesome job. Water?'

Christopher doesn't wait for a response before he grabs a bottle for me.

'You should reconsider moving up here. You're pretty much our number two, and it makes it easier for us to pop into your office. Everyone down there still thinks you're just an event manager.'

It's not the first time we have had this conversation.

'I'm happy downstairs. I still have a lot to learn and I'm only going to learn it in the thick of things.'

'Is that why you haven't changed the job title on your email footer since you started?' Christopher teases gently.

'My job title isn't important to me.'

'Or are you scared of responsibility, Ariella?' Harrison asks with a smile playing on his lips.

'No. Of course not.'

'Good. Because we have a job for you.' Christopher pulls a chair out for me to sit on. 'We've inherited a project in Zambia, and things aren't looking good.'

'There's barely any budget,' Harrison adds.

'Okay. We can deploy health, safety and due diligence from South Africa and, depending on how that goes, I can get this delivered remotely.'

'I'm going to need you to look after this one personally and on location. You can use the South African resources, but I need you there.'

'Why?'

'They've sent invitations out to their clients already. I can send you the brief?' Harrison suggests sheepishly.

'Is that it?' I point at a folder in the middle of the table, and they both nod. 'I'd rather see it now, if that's okay?'

Christopher reaches out and slides it over. It is a self-rated, five-star boutique hotel with thirty bedrooms overlooking Victoria Falls. It is to be a four-day and three-night 'trip of a lifetime' experience with Michelin-star dining every night, European continental breakfasts, and picnic or barbecue lunches. Alarm bells go off in my head.

'Is there a site visit report?' I ask, looking through the folder.

'No,' Harrison responds.

'No one has seen this place?' I catch Christopher rubbing his fingers across his forehead out of the corner of my eye.

'No.'

'Is this the budget?' I ask, pointing to the figure on the front page.

'Yes. It's been approved.'

'You're going to have to get some more, Harrison, or they're going to have to cancel.'

'How much more do you reckon?'

'Double, if they're lucky. Triple, if there's a problem. We also need to prioritise a site visit.'

'When do you want to leave?'

'Monday. You and the client should come along.'

'That's less than a week, Ariella. It's impossible.'

'Okay, Wednesday. We have to deliver this in four months. I'd like to get started right away. What demographic is the clientele?'

'Twenty-five of the top two hundred of Forbes five hundred,' Harrison says casually. 'Get a bucket and a mop, Ariella. You're on shit duty.'

I walk out of the meeting room and allow myself to contemplate what I have just agreed to. It is going to be a heck of a ride, and I'm excited because I know there is no way I am going to fail at this – the challenge is exactly what I need.

When I get home that night, the flat is filled with music and the smell of cooking, and Caleb is watching the microwave intently.

'Hey,' he calls chirpily.

He's ramped up the charm offensive with Nicole tonight. At least, I hope it's Nicole in his bedroom. With old Caleb showing up, it's anyone's guess. Caleb has been spoiling me lately, narrowing his escapades down to only one familiar consenting adult; but I am aware that could change at any moment. I decide to grab a yoghurt and get out of his hair. I spot one of my lasagne experiments next to the microwave.

'Oh, I'm not sure about that one. Try the lamb-based one. It's the safest option. I'm not sure how this one is going to come out.' I dive into the freezer to grab a different frozen lasagne.

He turns to me, concerned. 'You don't like this one?'

'It's not that I don't like it, I just don't know if your "friend" will like it. Best be safe.'

'Eh?' He looks at me quizzically.

I point to his room and he just looks confused.

'Who are you cooking for?'

'You. You were late, so I thought I'd get something ready for you.'

'Really?'

He gives me the strangest look. 'Yeah, but I was hungry too, so I grabbed the first thing in the freezer. I was going to eat half and leave the rest for you, but now you're here, want to eat together?'

'Sure. Do I have time for a quick shower?'

'Yeah.'

By the time I've hopped through the shower, dinner and a glass of wine is on the bar waiting.

'This looks great, Caleb!'

'You made it, I just heated it up. Hurry up, I'm starving.'

We clink our wine glasses and eat in silence until I test the Nicole waters.

'I thought you were cooking for Nicole tonight.'

Caleb looks mortified. 'Why would you think that?'

'Lara and I were watching you both today. I thought you might make it official.'

'Make what official?'

'You know, settle down. Become a one-woman man...'

Caleb erupts with laughter. 'That's never going to happen, Ariella.'

'You seemed pretty close today...'

'I buried my mother yesterday and got blind drunk on a train. I'm certain the police were involved somehow, and I had to be put to bed by you. It's safe to say that my ability to make good decisions can't be trusted at the moment. I'm fine as we are.'

'Is *she* fine as you are? Caleb, this may come as a shock, but you're actually a good person – yet you go out of your way to make people believe you're the worst.'

'Are you done?' Caleb tries to look bored, but I know that he is listening.

'No. You're focused and driven, resilient, astute, and you're so clever. You're warm, you're kind, and empathetic. You're extremely loyal and such a softie. You complain about your pupils, but you pay for the hall hire, their kit and uniforms yourself. You run the marathon for Macmillan every year and you—'

'What the fuck...'

'You shouldn't leave your letters open, strewn all over the kitchen top. I have plenty of time to kill over breakfast in the morning. It was a relief to see that I can share a bathroom with you if I need to. Well done for keeping on top of your sexual health. I see who you are, Caleb, and you're lovely.'

He looks at me like he is about to say something and then stops himself. I continue.

'I'm no angel – I walked away from Jasper in the cruellest way – but you're a much better person than what you're putting Nicole through right now.'

'You think I'm being a bastard to Nicole.'

'I do, and she's addicted to whatever you're doing to her. It needs to be healthier for both of you, or you need to stop.'

'I wasn't expecting this tonight.'

'Me neither,' I concede. 'I was going to come home to ask you if taking on a project in Zambia was a good idea.'

'That motherfucker.' Caleb bursts out laughing. 'Did the project come from Harry?'

'What's going on?'

Caleb laughs harder. 'Harry lost a poker game to a competitor. He's been spitting about it and, when he found out that they won a pitch for a massive company, he swore to nick the account.'

'He's nicked it for sure.'

'That bastard did it.'

'And thanks to him, I'll be out there for most of next week.'

'Why you? No offence, but Christopher should be delivering this.'

I shrug.

'Be careful out there. Work trips with Harrison can be wild, and I know how important your early bedtime is to you.'

'Thanks for the heads-up, but I think I'll be okay.'

'It'll be good to have the flat back to myself for a while. I might have an orgy.' Caleb shrugs as he gets up to clear the counter. He registers the horror that crosses my face and suddenly bursts out laughing.

'I'm joking. Calm down, Ariella. Ice cream?'

I nod as I sigh with relief.

'The flat isn't big enough...'

'Oh get lost, you've never been to an orgy!'

'Not this year.' A mischievous smile makes its way across his face.

'Really? All those body fluids? Ugh!'

Caleb casually makes his way back from the freezer with ice cream and bowls.

'No grosser than you sharing bodily fluids with ol' Jasper. Unless you showered immediately it was over with.' He chuckles.

I look away.

'No!' Caleb exclaims, catching my expression.

'I don't like to go to sleep dirty...'

'Ariella Mason! Every time? Before and after?'

Embarrassment overwhelms me.

'I don't want to discuss this with you,' I state firmly, irritated. The laugh that bubbles from him is explosive. It really hurts my feelings.

'No wonder you're...' He lets the sentence tail off.

'I'm what?'

'Uptight. You need a re-education from someone and that poor bloke's going to have a job on his hands!'

I've had enough. Caleb is having too good a time being cruel.

'I'm going to bed.' I leave my ice cream.

'No *Sopranos*? I suppose not. You might need a shower after Bobby comes on screen!'

He starts laughing all over again. I blink away the tears forming.

'You're the worst.' I point at him and narrow my eyes. I'm looking forward to a break from him.

EIGHTEEN

CALEB

Angry Ariella is fascinating. She makes passive-aggressiveness feel like warm cuddles. It was surprising to see that this, of all the things I had done, was what set her off. Dahlia had warned me about the showering thing, but I didn't expect Ariella to be *that* sensitive about it.

The next day, she seemed to be giving me the silent treatment. She was as pleasant as ever, but she wasn't herself. She moved stiffly, avoided my eyes and refused to share a space with me. We often manoeuvred easily around each other at breakfast, but the next morning she sat at the bar, waiting patiently until I finished and left the kitchen before she entered the space.

We communicated easily, but matter-of-factly, and she stopped laughing. She still cooked for us, but would intentionally eat at a different time. There were no *Sopranos* episodes that week. She declined politely every time I asked. It was a truly odd experience. She was the same. She spoke the same, behaved the same, kept to our normal routine; but she was absent somehow.

She even went on a date with some dude, told me about it

like she was reading from an instruction manual, and went to bed. I made a terrible joke about the barista wanting to roast her, and she just smiled and shook her head like she felt sorry for me. On day one, I thought she'd need the day to get over it. On day two, I decided to let her be; that maybe it was better this way. By day three, it was driving me absolutely mental.

'Mate. You've obviously pissed her off. Apologise,' Jack scolds as we come to the end of our sprint in front of the pub the following Sunday.

'Hello, lads. What took you so long?' Tim shows off, looking at his watch. For a big bloke, he's fast.

'Fuck off, Tim. We're not all Jonah Lomu.' Jack coughs.

'I don't know about you guys, but I'm getting the fry-up.' I walk into the pub and the guys follow.

'Why did you have to piss her off? We could be round yours having something awesome. I hate eating here now. Tim and I can go round. She's not refusing to cook for us; just you,' Jack complains.

'She's not refusing to cook for me. Last night I told her we were coming here instead. She didn't seem bothered.'

'Why on earth would you do that?' Tim asks, exasperated.

'He pissed her off and instead of saying sorry, he's being a dick. As usual,' Jack chips in.

'What did you do now?' Tim looks down his nose at me.

Tim is annoyingly overprotective when it comes to Ariella. He's supposed to be my friend, not hers. I am about to tell them, so they can see how ridiculous she is being, but I stop myself. I usually tell the guys everything, but I know that telling them this would make things with Ariella worse.

'Bloody hell. He slept with her.' Jack puts his face in his palms.

'You are such a swine, Caleb. Can you not—' Tim starts.

'I didn't sleep with her! For the last time, there's no way in hell I'm going near that. She's like a puppy. She's nice to be around and fun to scratch behind the ears, but she does absolutely nothing for me in that sense. I'm not even tempted.'

Jack picks up on this. 'You didn't just call her a puppy. That's terrible.'

I go on the attack. 'Better than living with Louisa the dragon. Set a wedding date yet, Jack?'

Tim tries not to laugh.

'That's out of order, Caleb.' Jack jabs his finger at me.

'When are you going to end it, though? You can't even get your shit together enough to have a proper stag,' I say, poking him.

'No matter how many times you say it, Caleb, it's not going to happen,' Jack says dismissively.

'Of course not, mate. This is true love. What else would make you want to marry Louisa and her multimillion-pound trust fund?' I raise an eyebrow and chuckle at Tim.

'Tim...?' Jack starts to complain.

'I'm staying out of this.' Tim puts his hand up and the waitress acknowledges him.

'Thanks for the support there, Tim. She's only best mates with your wife.'

'Yeah, but she doesn't scream at my wife in public and claw my wife's face in the middle of a restaurant. We love Lou, but you guys have a lot of stuff to work out,' Tim responds quietly.

Louisa has always had a short fuse and the way she sometimes speaks to Jack is deplorable, but physically attacking him is taking the piss.

'She attacked you at dinner? Mate, you can't marry her. I've been saying this for so long.'

Tim turns to the waitress. 'Bacon sandwich and builder's tea please?'

Jack and I order the same.

'Jack. Dump her,' I appeal.

'We're working through it.'

'The only thing you should be working through is a break-up. It's just going to get worse.'

The conversation takes a heavy, silent pause.

'I don't often say this, but Caleb's right. You guys need to see someone. Things can get messy really quickly,' Tim says supportively.

'I'm not a domestic abuse victim.' Jack laughs.

'Well, if you were the one screaming at her and slapping her in public, you'd be in jail by now. You're about to marry her, you're sure to have kids, and those guys see and copy everything. You don't want to start fixing this when they're here. It'll be too late.' Tim puts his hand on Jack's shoulder.

'Unless, of course, that plan is to say nothing, marry her, then dump her a few years in and make away with half the bank? In which case, I can play on that team for a small five per cent kickback.' I smile conspiratorially at Jack. He doesn't smile back.

'You're an idiot, Caleb,' he throws back at me.

'Speaking of kids, Em is throwing Alfie a birthday party in two weeks – Friday, after school. It'll either be dinosaurs or pirates. Jack, you're invited. Caleb, as godfather your attendance is mandatory.'

'There's no way I'm missing it,' I assure Tim.

When we've finished breakfast, I take leisurely strides to delay going back home to Ariella. I walk into her as I let myself in.

'Hi.'

'Hey, Caleb. I'm going home to spend time with Mommy and Daddy till Tuesday. I want to see them before I fly out Wednesday.'

She smiles at me; maybe she's back to her old self again.

'Say hi to Dahlia for me.' I smile back at her.

'I will. Anything in the fridge is fair game and there are many options in the top drawer of the freezer, so please dig in. I'm playing with the bits in the middle drawer, and the bottom drawer is just full of raw ingredients. If you use anything from the bottom, can you make a note so that I can replace it?'

'Sure.' We both know that is not going to happen.

'Have fun.' She waves as she leaves the flat.

I hit the shower and catch up on some work. My sales figures are solid, my regions are performing well and the trip to San Francisco is beginning to shift projects across nicely. There's been a small uptick of projects from Singapore, but not as big as I would like. It's too soon to go back, though. I spend time going through my quieter accounts and putting a contact strategy together for them. When I look up, the sun is setting and the flat is eerily quiet. I reach for my phone.

'*Qu'est-ce que tu veux?!*' she barks down the phone.

'Don't be like that, Nicole.'

'I see you've found my phone number... again!'

'It's a Sunday, let's not fight—'

'Why not?'

'Do you want to come over and fight instead?'

'No. I've entertained that Barbarella enough.'

Nicole knows exactly what her name is. I shouldn't, but one of the things I like about Nicole is that she can be petty. I don't correct her either.

'She's not here for a few days, so I thought we could spend some proper time together. I'll make you dinner and you can really tell me off if you want,' I offer happily.

'I'm glad you're amused. I'm not.'

'Come on, Nicole. I've missed you.'

'I'm not sleeping with you.' She is softening.

'Agreed. Let's hang out, watch some TV. I'll sleep on the couch, you can have my bed.'

'...And you can't do the thing with the finger.' She sounds serious.

'I won't do the thing with the finger.' I am enjoying this.

She goes silent, thinking about it. I go for the clincher.

'There's a lovely Pauillac here waiting for you. I'll decant it before you get here.' It's Ariella's wine, so it's probably expensive, but I'll replace it.

'Why are you being so nice?'

'I told you. I've missed you.'

'Fine. I'll see you in an hour.'

'Don't forget to bring some comfortable pyjamas and an overnight bag!'

She hangs up and I get to work. I go into Ariella's boxes, grab the wine and pour it carefully into the decanter. I swirl it about a bit to let it breathe. Next stop, the fridge. I spot a dish with three duck legs suspended in duck fat. Bingo! She'd already made duck confit. I shoot off a text.

Mind if I cook off the duck legs? If not, how?

Not at all. Pop the dish in the oven at 180 fan, when the legs start bubbling in about 30 mins, remove the dish, lift the legs out and pop them under the grill on a drip tray for 15 mins.

Thanks mate, side suggestions?

There is salad in the fridge. Plate that up when you put the duck legs in so it gets to room temperature. The mash in the fridge will also work well with the leg.

How's home? Tell Dahlia I miss her.

Nicole is coming over. Shouldn't you be focused on her?

How did you know Nicole was coming over?

If you were alone you'd have stabbed a leg with the fork, popped it in the microwave and hoped for the best. We still have her coffee and her pain au chocolat in the freezer. Enjoy.

I set two dinner places the way Ariella does and follow her cooking instructions to the letter. As I place the duck legs under the grill, the doorbell goes.

'Hey.' I open the door to Nicole.

She is wearing more clothes than I have ever seen her wear but she looks irresistible. She is in a chunky jumper with leggings and thigh-high boots. Her silky blond hair is up in a tight bun and her face looks perfect, finished off with her usual red lipstick.

'You look beautiful, Nicole.' I beam at her.

She turns one side of her mouth down. I reach out to take her overnight bag from her. She lets me. Her deep inhale at the food cooking makes me feel good.

'Dinner will be ready soon. Want me to take your coat?'

She nods and I hang it up before I get her a glass of red.

'Delicious.'

'Good. Take a seat, we're almost ready.'

She finally smiles, sits and fixes her eyes on me as I carefully arrange the mash, salad and duck.

'Bon appétit,' I whisper as I take my first mouthful.

As ever, Ariella's cooking doesn't disappoint. The mash is earthy, almost gamey, right next to the salty duck. Nicole moans with pleasure.

'There's no way you made this, Caleb. Where did you order from?'

'A gentleman never tells.' If she finds out Ariella made this, she'll flip her lid.

'So, what *is* all this, Caleb?' She waves her fork around the apartment. 'First you don't talk to me at work, but I come here after. Then you avoid me and I can't come any more. Last week, you were hugging me at work, but you ignored me later. Now you're cooking for me and want to just hang out. What's going on?'

'I realise that I don't know much about you, and I thought maybe that could change. We could be... healthier.'

'I'm not sleeping with you, if this is a new tactic.' Nicole takes another sip of her wine.

'It's not. I know I've been a bit of a bastard, and I thought we could just talk.'

She smirks as she lifts her eyebrows. 'Where's Rubella?'

'At her parents. Why are you so hard on her? She's not bad, you know.'

'She's one of *those* girls, isn't she? She walks around like we're all beneath her, and she gets everything she wants. All you boys are just lining up to help her, like she's some broken bird, especially now that she's single. Even Chris and Harry. She's constantly up there, having meetings and doing whatever else.'

'That's because she's leading the Zambia project.'

'Exactly. Why's she on the Zambia project? Jane has worked in events much longer than she has.'

'Can we not talk about Ariella?'

'This is my point. Why are you defending her?'

'I'm not. I'm trying to spend time with you and not talk about my housemate.'

'Wait. Am I here because she isn't?'

'Yes. I mean no. It's just hard to do this with someone else in the house.'

'I think I will tire of being your rag doll soon, Caleb. Everything you do to me, hurts.'

A silence falls between us, and we barely speak for the rest of the evening. It's an experience I'm not keen to repeat.

. . .

I wake up the next morning to the sound of the coffee grinder and Nicole moving around the kitchen, wrapped in a towel.

'Morning. How did you sleep?' she asks, almost apologetically.

'Good. It's a comfy couch. There's pain au chocolat in the freezer, if you want some.' I grab my phone and see that it's too late to go for a run. 'I'll shower in Ariella's bathroom.'

Nicole laughs. 'You can use your own shower, Caleb. It's not like there are any surprises between us.'

I am rinsing the shampoo out of my hair when I hear Nicole and feel her place her hands on my shoulder blades. I turn to face her.

She perches on her tiptoes to kiss me. I kiss her back and her hands snake round my neck. Her perfect body presses against mine and the familiarity of her skin feels glorious. My hands caress her waist and stay there.

'I'm sorry I was so angry with you yesterday. I was just fed up with the games we've been playing,' she whispers.

'I know. I haven't been very good to you.'

Nicole's hand moves down my back and makes its way round my hips. I know where she is going and I instinctively step back quickly.

'What's wrong?' she asks with confusion flooding her face.

'Things aren't going to get healthier between us if we do this right now, Nicole. Let's try without it?'

I know that I have bruised her as she silently leaves. I turn off the hot water and stand under the ice-cold spray for as long as I can take it. By the time I step out she is gone.

I purposely sit next to Nicole in the 10 a.m. meeting. She is stony-faced until I drape my hand round her shoulders in front of everyone. She relaxes after a while and gives me a smile. I smile back, until I catch Lara scowling at us, a few rows behind.

'You're so cute,' I exaggeratedly mouth at Lara before sending a wink and air-kiss in her direction.

She clenches her fist before flipping me off. Ariella, sitting next to her, catches her mid-offence and puts her hand over Lara's finger to cover it up. She looks up to see who Lara is insulting and gives me an apologetic smile. Nicole chooses that point, of course, to look behind her to see who I am looking at.

Ariella gives her a small smile. The thunderous look Nicole gives me is no laughing matter.

'Settle down, folks, let's get to it!' Harrison walks in, quieting the chatty room. 'Caleb, this isn't secondary school. You and Nicole can PDA elsewhere, and only after you've spoken to HR; though I understand that horse has bolted.' Harrison shoots us a pointed look and the room chuckles. Nicole covers her eyes in embarrassment, even though I can tell she is delighted.

'Right, I'll start. We're definitely going ahead with the Zambia project!'

The whoops and claps come thick and fast from the sales team. 'I know – right?' he follows up, looking pleased with himself. 'But it's a tough one. I'm off to Zambia with Ariella, over there, hiding in the corner, and we need to turn this thing round before the final client inspection in three months.'

Ariella shrinks in her corner as the whole room follows Harrison's nose. I try not to laugh.

'We leave on Wednesday and the client will be coming too. That'll give us an opportunity to potentially expand into the rest of the organisation. I'm going to be working, so you slackers in sales better be doing the same,' he lightly reprimands with a laugh. 'Ariella, wanna tell them what we have ahead of us?'

This is going to be interesting. Ariella never speaks at these things. She looks terrified. I watch Lara put her hand on Ariella's arm to comfort her as she stands.

'Our focus for Zambia is to ensure the venue is compliant to universal standards for the clientele, which it unfortunately isn't at the moment. We're going to source local experiential suppliers with cross-border potential just in case we wander into Zimbabwe, negotiate our way around the vacillating agricultural import bans at a governmental level, introduce and schedule fine dining training for all staff with global certification to give back to the community, hop over to South Africa to interview the Michelin-starred chef and team, arrange fumigation services for the kitchen, redesign, purchase furniture and renovate the bedrooms, vet aviation providers for the Livingstone transfers—'

'And much, much more!' Harrison laughs nervously as he cuts in, saving the room from boredom and terror.

I feel for her.

'Thank you, Ariella.' He clears his throat. The mood in the room changes measurably. The electric high of the sale has just been sucked into an operations black hole by Ariella, and everyone looks worried. The enormity of the project just multiplied. A little smile plays on Nicole's lips. I don't like it.

'Just a second, Harry...' Christopher Ivory, our other co-founder, who has been standing at the back of the room with his hands in his pockets, pipes up casually. 'Ariella, it sounds pretty impossible to pull this off?' he asks with a glint in his eye.

Ariella sighs nervously and reluctantly stands again.

'Most of the work has been done from here. We're already working with the UKTI for government access, we're meeting an aviation expert out there, we have suppliers lined up and the chef will be on-boarded during the day trip. Suppliers and talent are all sourced, with second and third options in place. Approvals for the renovation have already been agreed, and the social responsibility skills transfer programme has already been written and approved on a local and governmental level in order to give us our agricultural exemption. I also have renovation plans under way.'

'Are you saying the execution is already pretty much there, with all the players in place?' Chris smiles.

I see what he is doing.

'Yes.'

'But you've only been on it for five days,' he presses.

He's giving everyone the answer to the question that has been floating around the office. Why they picked her. Ariella, however, doesn't get what he is doing and I can see she's frightened that he doesn't believe her.

'I have all the plans and paperwork filed and categorised on the server. I'm happy to take you through it if you set a couple of hours aside for me today?'

'No. You've done an unbelievable job, Ariella. Thank you.'

She sits down quickly.

'Phew, for a second there I thought it was going to be a shit-show,' Harrison announces as everyone laughs, relieved.

Chris has just used Ariella to stop the rumours and reassure the entire company. That's what I like about Chris. He is practical, intuitive and steady. If Ivory Bow was a rock band, Harrison would be the charismatic frontman and Chris would be the level-headed songwriter.

I feel pride in Ariella rise up in me. You wouldn't think it to look at her, but in her own way she is a badass. I didn't understand half of the things she was talking about, but I know she is on top of it and nothing is going to get past her.

No one wanted to give their progress reports after that. Compared to what Ariella was faced with, all the other updates paled in comparison. With everyone suddenly becoming update-shy, the meeting finishes early. Ariella dashes out of the room quickly, clutching her notebook.

As soon as I make it back to my dome, Piers – a total creep – walks in.

'Caleb, can we talk?' He didn't bother to knock.

'Make it quick.'

I know he wants to be continent sales lead for Africa and needs me out of the way. It would mean an automatic promotion. I can't stand Piers but I hope he gets it. It'll keep him busy and away from my customers.

'I was thinking...'

'You want continent lead.'

'Yeah.'

'I won't stand in your way. I have my hands full with Asia and West Coast USA.'

'How do you think I should pitch it to Harrison?'

Do I look like a guidance counsellor to this idiot? 'Just tell him. Maybe ask to tag along to Zambia, shift your sales commitments and start setting up meetings. Start with Tanzania, Kenya and South Africa. Prepare to bust your balls.'

'You researched the position already?'

He's threatened. Good.

'I looked at Africa last year. All the money is in South Africa and Nigeria, but for this trip you're best staying in the east and south of the continent.'

'Okay, thanks. One last thing... This is a bit embarrassing. Ariella... She lives with you, doesn't she?'

'Yeah.' Oh, hell no.

'Is she seeing anyone?'

'Why?'

'I was thinking of asking her out on a date.'

He has a shy smile on his face. If I wasn't disgusted before, I am now.

'Go for it.'

'Thanks, mate.'

'I'm not your mate,' I respond before he walks out of my office. There is no way Ariella would say yes to Piers. However, he does have enough 'smarmy rich kid' in him that there could be a minute chance, so I call Harrison.

'What's up?'

'I just had Piers in here. He wants continent lead for Africa.'

'What do you think?'

'He'll be good for it.'

'I wasn't expecting that.' Harrison laughs down the phone.

'Heads-up; he's going to ask to come to Zambia.'

'If he's keen...'

'He is, but he's also planning to get into Ariella's knickers on the trip.' I skip the intermediate date he is planning, and get right to his end goal.

'You want me to bench him if he asks to come, don't you?'

'Pretty much.'

'I'll think about it.'

'Thanks, Harrison. I don't think she needs some snake hitting on her. We both know Piers has trouble keeping his hands to himself.'

'I'll hear his pitch and decide. Thanks for the heads-up.'

'No problem.'

I hang up and look over at Ariella's desk. She is typing furiously and staring intently at her screen.

'You're welcome,' I whisper at her with a smile, before I boot up my computer.

NINETEEN

ARIELLA

'How long are you going to be annoyed at me for?' Caleb asks as I take a break from packing for Zambia to grab some water.

He is standing in the kitchen with a bottle of beer in front of him. Home has left me feeling energised and ready to face the world. I want to hold on to that feeling.

'I'm not.'

'Yes, you are. You didn't say hi earlier, we hardly talked last week and you still won't look me in the eye. What's going on?'

I make a point of looking him in the eye.

'Forcing yourself to do it doesn't count,' he says with a laugh as he fetches a bottle of red. He pours a glass, slides it over to me across the counter and makes happy slurping noises with his mouth while nodding at it. I fight the urge to laugh.

Thankfully, he is cut off by my ringing phone. I pick up immediately.

'Hi, Lara. What's up?'

Caleb rolls his eyes and walks away.

'Great, I caught you. I should've done this ages ago, but could you look over the risk assessments for my Shoreditch Carwash gig?'

'Already done. They're on the server and good to go.'

'Thanks, Aari. I swear I'd have been fired by now if it wasn't for you. Ready for Zambia? Sorry I called so late!'

'It's fine. You saved me from a lecture from Caleb.'

'Lecture? Caleb? That's an oxymoron with an emphasis on the moron, isn't it? What was he moaning about?'

'He accused me of freezing him out.'

'Doofus. He called it quickly for someone with semen swimming between his ears. He should be used to it by now.'

'Used to what?'

'Your ice-queen thing. Why's he complaining about it now?'

'What ice-queen thing?'

'You don't realise you freeze people out? It's your thing. Comes with the territory.'

'I've never frozen you out.'

'Of course you have, loads of times. I just don't care because I love you.'

'Are you serious?'

'Yup. When people get close enough to upset you, you stop engaging with them and there's no way back. I simply ignore you and your crap. How did you think you alienated the whole department? I used to think it was just your thing... and in that first month, I may have been trying to sleep with you because I thought it was kind of sexy. I thankfully realised you're just really sensitive and it's how you cope. I concluded that you're probably one of those needy types that wants to cuddle after sex. I went off you quickly after that.'

'I can't believe I've been doing that to people.'

'Yes. It's bloody harsh, but entertaining to watch. The best ones are when people don't know what they've done and realise there is no more getting through to you.'

'I'm sorry if I ever did that to you, Lara.'

'No apologies. I most probably deserved it. Go to sleep. I'll call you before you fly.' She laughs down the phone.

'Goodnight, Lara.'

'Night, Aari. Wait! Before I go, whatever you do, don't go drinking with Harrison. Love him to death and he's pretty harmless, but you won't like him tipsy.' She laughs again and hangs up.

Lara is right. I did alienate Caleb. I find him on the couch, nursing his beer; so I sit next to him.

'Turns out it's a thing I do. I'm sorry,' I apologise.

'I'm sorry too. Can you go back to being annoying now?' He pokes me in the ribs and I can't help laughing. I've missed Caleb talking and distracting me from the mountain of work I have to get through. It's been a lonely few days.

'As long as we don't go back to normal with you. You've made Nicole your girlfriend?' I've been dying to talk to him about it.

'You're obsessed! No.'

'That's not what it looked like yesterday – and you cooked her dinner.' I clap.

'Stop bobbing up and down like a toddler. I'd almost prefer you go back to being quiet,' he says, already irritated.

'Caleb, having a girlfriend is a good thing. Maybe you'll soften each other up.'

'You're actually happy at the idea. That scenario can only end as a true-crime special. One of us is going to wind up dead; and it's not going to be her found choking on her own penis.'

'So why all the public affection?'

'I'll fucking murder you if you repeat this...'

While Caleb looks distressed, I can't help feeling excited.

'I haven't been able to get the excitement going with Nicole for a while.'

'What do you mean?' I am perplexed.

'How are you an adult? I've struggled to meet her needs... sexually.'

'Oh...'

I honestly don't expect the laughter that escapes. Caleb is visibly annoyed.

'I'm sorry, I'm sorry. Did you break it? To be fair, it was bound to happen. You do use it a lot. Is that why you've been avoiding her? Isn't there a tablet you can take for that?'

'It's working, but just not with her. Any more. On Monday morning, the conditions were perfect, but no lift-off...'

'Nothing happened on Sunday night?'

'I slept on the couch.'

'Oh, man.' I reach over and give Caleb a hug.

'It's pretty fucking embarrassing and if I don't handle it right the office is going to hear about it.'

'You can't pretend there's more between you to hide your...' I point quickly at his crotch. 'It's a little cruel.'

'I could sleep with someone else at work. That'll be easy enough.' He shrugs, seriously considering it.

'Caleb! No. That would be terrible.'

'I was doing quite all right until you started infecting me with your conscience.' He takes a swig of his beer, looking sorry for himself. 'You got the energy for a *Sopranos* episode?'

'Yes. How far did you get without me?'

'I didn't.'

I grab the sofa blanket and pull it over us. It is amazing how one conversation brought my friend back. The screen fills with Tony Soprano in his car and we both start singing the theme tune. I'm going to miss him while I'm gone.

The flight was easy. Harrison and the client sat together while I sat directly behind them, next to a late sales team addition, Piers. He was a little flirty, but funny all the same. He gave me his noise-cancelling headphones before I went to sleep and made sure I had some water waiting when I woke up. He promised to take me out to dinner in a cool place he'd found online in Lusaka before we got the plane back home and made a point of telling me it wasn't a date, which relaxed me.

The next few days were magical. With the help of our SA compliance team led by Kangwende, we nailed a lot of our outstanding tasks, leaving us time to enjoy the surrounding beauty. Harrison and the client helped vet the experiences and suppliers, and we decided on a dining experience on the beautifully restored Royal Livingstone Express Locomotive, a Zambezi River small boat excursion, helicopter tours of Victoria Falls and some National Wildlife Park tours.

After a wonderful few days by the Falls, we spent the last two in Lusaka, finalising government paperwork. While Zambians are warm and friendly people, I found it difficult dealing with the strict patriarchal society and customs. Often, I had to stand behind and defer to Harrison and Kangwende to get things done, which was hard, especially as I had to reframe our purposes on the go. Harrison had to imply that we were together so that I would not be touched if I didn't want to be. Those last two days were exhausting, but worth it. We'd done everything that needed to be done, but it had left me so shattered that, when Piers arrived the day before to catch our flight back home from Lusaka, I was too tired to go to dinner.

I spent the entire flight back sleeping, so by the time we landed at Heathrow I was refreshed and looking forward to the weekend. Jasper and I had exchanged a few texts and a couple of calls while I was away; we'd agreed that while we weren't ready to meet, we could handle chatting. I headed to the airport lounge to have a shower and change my clothes, before realising I didn't have my house keys with me.

I texted Caleb and he told me to go to Tim's house, where he was, to get his keys. The first attempt to ring the doorbell was thwarted by two children carrying gifts, followed by a happy-looking mother locking her car and running after them. It seemed one of Tim's children was having a birthday party.

Deciding not to turn up empty-handed, I found and nipped to a small toyshop nearby.

I exhale as I press the bell.

'Hi.'

A small blonde-haired lady with pink cheeks, curly wild hair and a food-covered apron opens the door. She places the tea towel she is holding over her shoulder. Her face, with its easy smile and kind eyes, is open, friendly and welcoming. This has to be Em.

'Hello, erm, Caleb said I could swing by?' It is more a question than a declaration.

'Caleb told you to swing by?' There's a naughty smile playing on her lips.

'Yes... I'm sorry if I'm intruding. He has my keys and I need to go home...' I look at my suitcase.

'Caleb has keys to your house?'

'Well, our apartment... I moved in some months ago—'

Her eyes light instantly. 'What am I doing?' she interrupts. 'I'm Em. Come in!'

She flings the door open, offers to help with my suitcase, but I hand her the gift instead.

'I wasn't sure whose birthday it was.'

'That's very thoughtful. It's huge! Can I get you a drink?'

She leads me past a large living room, where football commentary is blaring loudly. The hallway is long and light-filled, and leads us into a huge kitchen that shares a glass wall with a large, green, lush garden. I see a group of children running around, being chased by a tiny-armed T Rex.

'Louisa, this is...'

'Ariella.' I return my attention to the kitchen and offer a smile and a tiny wave.

'Ariella. She moved in with Caleb *months* ago.'

I hear an inflection at the end of her sentence, but dismiss it. She seems really lovely, so I am probably imagining it.

'Prosecco?' Em offers.

'No thank you. I'd be grateful for some water; I'm hoping to make a yoga class later.' I smile.

'Where do you go?'

The beautiful Louisa approaches us from the kitchen island, lifting her shiny, deep-chestnut hair over a fur gilet-covered shoulder. I immediately feel self-conscious in Jasper's oversized, faded blue Oxford shirt, jeans and my trusted but battered Converse.

'I registered at the small one by Hampstead station?'

'I know that studio.' She flashes impossibly white, straight teeth at me. 'There's a much better one ten minutes away. It's a lot less poky.'

'She likes the one she registered at, Louisa,' Em reprimands jovially and hands me a glass of water.

'I'm just giving her options,' Louisa says, turning to me. 'I know the owner. I can get you a free month's pass.'

'Thank you. It'll be fun to check it out.'

'We can go together.'

She looks excited. I laugh along with her.

'Where are you coming from?' Louisa points to my suitcase.

'Zambia. Sorry. I'm just here to grab my keys and I'm going to head home.'

I catch Louisa's smirk before she brings her face back under control.

'You should stay,' Em calls from the stove.

'What were you doing in Zambia?' Louisa pulls out a stool and sits, facing me.

'Work. I'm trying to deliver a client event out there.'

'Where in Zambia?'

'Livingstone, Victoria Falls.'

'Wow. You should give me your details. My family could use your help.'

'Unfortunately, we don't do private events... but I can share my resources with you?'

'Oh no, it's a company. My family own the House of Gabrielli.'

'That's cool. Is it a venue?'

The laughter from Em is so piercing, it gives me a shock. I turn to see her holding both her hands over her mouth; she has abandoned the carrots she had been chopping. I return my gaze to Louisa. She has a dark, disapproving look. It's obvious I should have heard of the House of Gabrielli.

'It's a fashion house,' Louisa says coldly.

'That's amazing,' I gush. 'That explains a lot. You look like a supermodel.'

That seems to cheer her up and her warmth returns.

'Do you work with your family?'

'Yes. I'm the creative director of the new urban line.'

'That's impressive.'

'You don't have to be nice to her, Ariella,' Em says with a smirk as she puts some potato faces in the oven. Just then, we hear a commotion outside. The T Rex has taken a nasty fall and all the children are now jumping on it. Em rolls her eyes and yells.

'Tim! Garden!'

Tim appears in the kitchen in a flash.

'What's up?' he asks as Em wipes her hands on her apron and points to the garden. They look at each other and chuckle. 'Nah, leave him.'

'It doesn't look good.' Em chuckles.

'He'll get up eventually,' Louisa pitches in with a sly smirk.

One of the kids decides to execute a running jump that ends in a body slam on the dinosaur. We all hear the loud growl. Louisa, Em and Tim burst out laughing.

'Okay, I'll go and rescue him. Oh hey, Ariella,' Tim calls as he jogs towards the garden.

Both Louisa and Em immediately shoot me a look.

'Want a hand, Tim?' I offer, walking towards the garden. I feel both ladies watching me as I walk through.

'You all right, mate?' Tim bends over as he grabs a tiny arm.

I grab the other and pull the T Rex up. 'Want some water?' I ask as we lead the groaning dinosaur into the kitchen.

'You arseholes left me out there!' Caleb whispers, irritated, as Tim lifts the head off him and I move his hair out of his eyes.

I can't help the laugh that escapes. Caleb is far from the party entertainer type.

'Good to see you're back alive.' He shoots me a dirty look. His attempt at cutting sarcasm makes me laugh even harder.

'Jack. You're up next, mate,' Tim calls from the kitchen as we start to unzip Caleb from the suit.

A reluctant-looking Jack turns up, clutching his beer.

'I don't think I can get in the costume, mate, I've been drinking... oh hey, Ariella. How was Zambia? What are you doing here?'

'Keys.' I smile at the guys.

We eventually get a frazzled Caleb out of the suit, as Jack attempts to avoid it by suggesting it's time for the kids to eat. Caleb throws the costume at Jack and marches to the fridge for a beer.

'How long was I out there? It felt like for ever.'

Tim looks at his watch. 'Forty-five minutes?'

'You guys were supposed to tap in fifteen minutes ago,' he complains.

'You know Alfie loves you, why ruin a good thing?' Tim laughs, pulling Em close and planting a kiss on her forehead.

'You *are* his favourite!' Em adds, stroking Caleb's arm.

'That's me done. What's the score?' Caleb heads towards the living room.

'Caleb, can I grab the keys?'

'Stay, Ariella.' Louisa reaches out.

'I'd love to, but—' I try to excuse myself.

'I could use some help with the party food? Louisa's been pretending that her nails haven't dried for the last two hours,' Em says.

I laugh as I unbutton my cuffs and roll up my shirtsleeves.

'How can I help?' I navigate towards the huge hob, tidying the work surfaces nearby.

'How do you know the boys?' Louisa asks.

'We—' Tim begins.

'I believe Louisa asked Ariella, Tim?' Em interjects a little abruptly.

'I'll go and see what Caleb's up to then.' Tim shrugs and leaves.

'Tim and Jack helped Caleb replace our front door. They're good guys.'

It's enough for them. I listen as they change the subject and chat away while I wipe the surfaces, grab dinosaur plates and volcano napkins, and lay the table.

We call the children in shortly after and a relieved Jack walks through the house in the dinosaur costume. It's fun to watch the mess and fun of a children's party unfold. I am on crisp and juice duty and enjoy every minute of it. After cake, more dinosaur time and the kiddie guests are picked up, Em puts the birthday boy in the bath while Louisa and I clean up. Em reappears with Alfie, fresh from the bath, in dinosaur pyjamas, smelling of toothpaste and bubble gum shower gel. His big brown eyes shine under his thick, curly wet hair. He looks sleepy, but is clearly fighting it.

'Where's Caleb?' he asks Louisa.

'Ugh. Goodness knows.'

She shoos him away with her hand. I bend down next to him. He is a beautiful little boy, at that stage all kids go through when their two front teeth are humongous next to the rest of their milk teeth.

'I think he's with Daddy in the living room. Would you like me to take you?'

'S'okay.'

'Okay.' I smile at him and stand.

'He won't go to bed when Caleb's around.' Em follows her son with her eyes.

'Only because he gives them ice cream for dinner.' Louisa rolls her eyes. 'Children are cheap dates.'

'Thanks for today, Ariella,' Em says, finally sitting down and plonking some bubbly and fresh glasses on the kitchen island.

'It was so much fun. I've never been to a children's party.'

'So, what's the deal with you and Caleb?' Louisa drains her drink.

'Ignore her, she's tipsy,' Em reprimands. Louisa turns to Em like I am not there.

'Moving her in is new, but he's going to dump her, like everyone else.' Louisa turns to me. 'If I were you, I'd run; leave your bags if you have to.'

'Louisa! I'm so sorry about this, Ariella.' Em shakes her head exasperatedly as she snatches Louisa's drink.

'We're just flatmates.' I laugh.

'There's nothing going on between you two?' Em clarifies, curiously.

'No. We're friends, that's it.'

'How can you be friends with *that*?' Louisa points in the direction of the living room.

I feel the need to defend Caleb. He isn't perfect, but he is my friend. 'I think he's a great person, Louisa,' I disagree gently as I sip my drink.

'Are we talking about the same Caleb?' Louisa spits.

'Yes.' I nod. 'He takes a bit of getting used to, I know.'

'She's sleeping with him.' Louisa addresses Em, for the third time that evening, like I am not there.

'I'm not. He's kind to me. We've had the usual teething problems, but that's to be expected.' I shrug.

'Did those teeth belong to different women?' Louisa cackles.

'If you want to know about Caleb's private life, it might be best to ask Caleb,' I say, beginning to feel quite uncomfortable.

'Why are you defending him? *Surely* you've seen what he does?'

'I understand that your relationship with Caleb may be different, Louisa,' I say, pushing back. Maybe we aren't going to be friends after all.

'Lou, leave it.' Em tries to rein her in.

'Why should I?' she challenges Em. Her voice is getting louder.

'Because even though he says he's fine, I think he's still grieving, and could still use some support.'

'Grieving?' Em suddenly sits up.

Crumbs. They don't know. 'Maybe I should let Caleb...'

Em reaches out to touch my hand. 'Ariella, Caleb is part of my family. We can't support him if we don't know what's going on.'

I look into her pleading eyes. I like Em. More importantly, I trust her.

'Caleb's mom died about three weeks ago.' I tell them how it unfolded, but skip my involvement and the train journey.

'Em?' Caleb whispers as he pokes his head round the kitchen door, and we stop talking immediately. He is carrying little Alfie, who has fallen asleep on his chest with his thumb in his mouth. His other hand is wrapped tightly round Caleb's neck.

'His bed or yours?' Celeb asks quietly.

'His. Thank you, Caleb,' Em answers with a crack in her voice.

'Come on, little man,' he whispers to the sleeping Alfie as he turns around to leave. Moments later, we hear his footsteps on the stairs.

'Tim and I don't know anything about his family. How is he?'

'Dealing with it in his own way. He's tough, though. Maybe sometimes too tough.'

'It's still no excuse for the way he treats women.' Louisa is back on track, albeit taking a gentler tone.

'As far as I know, he's always honest. Is it the healthiest type of relationship? Absolutely not. But I left my fiancé, the most wonderful man I know, by clearing out all my clothes while he was at work, and leaving him nine words on a Post-it stuck to the fridge. So, I'm in no position to judge him.'

'Noooo. You didn't!' Em fills my glass up.

'It wasn't my proudest moment.' I feel the tears well and I blink them away quickly.

'You have to spill,' Em beckons, so I tell them the whole, sorry mess.

TWENTY

CALEB

'Caleb,' Em calls softly as she puts a steaming mug of tea down next to the couch. I search for Jack. He's already awake, with his mug in hand.

'Tim's gone to work and I have to take the boys swimming. I'll be back in an hour. Can you stay with Jack till then?' She smiles sadly and tiptoes out of the room.

No one expected last night to end the way it did. I knew Ariella's acceptance by Em and Lou had been too easy and was fairly certain that, if her awkwardness around people didn't get her, Louisa would. Instead, the girls joined us in the living room with some wine after the kids went to bed. She joined in easily with the chatter and it felt good to have a sixth person join our usual five. I think everyone appreciated it too. However, the minute she popped to the bathroom, an inaccurate assessment was made.

'She's beautiful, decent and clever. Bit of a departure for you, Caleb,' Em commented suggestively, raising an eyebrow at me.

'Her rent is all I'm interested in,' I said dismissively.

'Thank God for that, because you have zero chance. She

told us about her ex-boyfriend. It'll be like going from Michelin-star restaurant to a kebab van,' Louisa declared from Jack's lap.

They all chuckled quietly. Seriously, guys?

'Why are we having this conversation? She's my lodger. That's it.'

'Any particular reason why you had your hand on your lodger's thigh?' Em nodded at my hand.

'She's also my friend.' They all laughed, just as Ariella walked back in, so I changed the topic quickly.

'Lou, how's that creative guy from Milan working out? Still think he's after your job?'

Em, Tim and even Jack shot me hateful looks. Lou was going to make the next few hours about her, so I got comfortable and tuned her out. Em wasn't done, and kept sneaking me suggestive glances and winking whenever Ariella wasn't looking. I retaliated with stern looks and telepathic messages to *stop*.

Em was slyly mouthing something to me when Ariella's voice interrupted my lip-reading.

'That's abhorrent, Louisa,' Ariella said, sounding intensely disappointed.

The smile disappeared from Em's face. Oh. Shit.

'Excuse me?' Louisa questioned with venom. Jack shifted uncomfortably in his seat.

'I said, that's abhorrent, Louisa. It's totally unacceptable.' Ariella spoke calmly, as if she was dealing with a toddler. If Louisa's blazing stare was having any effect, she didn't show it.

'How dare you?' Louisa's voice rose. 'Don't lecture me on what's acceptable!'

'Putting your hands on someone like that *is* unacceptable, Louisa. Jack, are you okay?'

Louisa held Ariella's gaze as she smacked the side of Jack's head with the back of her palm. We all heard the thwack. So that's what happened. Tim, Em and I froze.

'It's fine. She's just playing around,' Jack said.

'It really doesn't seem like it,' Ariella responded softly. 'She shouldn't be hitting you.'

Louisa started to get off Jack. It was escalating. Fuck.

'Ariella, Louisa's always doing that. It's not a big deal.' I tried to laugh it off.

'If Jack hit Louisa like that, would it be a big deal then?'

'He'd never do that,' I replied, trying to minimise the fallout. Truthfully, I desperately wanted to cheer Ariella on and call Louisa a monster to her face.

'Then she shouldn't either, Caleb. It's violent, it's abusive and it's wrong.'

'Don't talk to him. Talk to *me*, bitch!' Lou got to her feet.

'Lou!' we all roared at the same time.

Ariella turned to her slowly and calmly delivered the lines that shook us all.

'I would, if I thought I could get through to you, but I can't, so I'm talking to the people who love you and Jack instead. They owe it to both of you to intervene.'

'Jack. We're going home,' Louisa demanded.

'You're welcome at ours, if you don't want to go,' Ariella said reassuringly to Jack, as if Louisa wasn't screaming the place down.

Jack forced a laugh. 'It'll only be worse in the morning.'

'That's frightening, Jack. If you don't want to come home with us, maybe you can crash here? Give yourself some time?' She looked pleadingly at Em and Tim.

'Who does this bitch think she is?'

'Okay, calm down, Louisa,' Em finally came in. 'Maybe it's best for you and Jack to have some space, for things to calm down a bit.'

'Things were calm before *that* opened its mouth.' Louisa jabbed her finger at Ariella.

'Hey!' I interjected.

Ariella stood calmly and walked past Louisa, into the hallway.

'We've talked about this, Louisa.' Em seethed quietly. 'I love you, but she's right.'

Louisa's madness has become normal to us, so we've messed up and let it slide. Jack had occasionally shown up with scratches or a bruise, but he dismissed it too quickly; and we moved on, too quickly. He often talked about how Louisa lost her temper, but we'd dismissed it, because he is a bloke. We were complicit, and the realisation made me feel sick to my stomach.

Ariella reappeared in the doorway with her suitcase. 'Caleb, can I have the keys please?'

'Ariella, don't leave like this. Stay, let's talk it through,' Em pleaded.

'I'm sorry, Em, I can't. I'm intruding. It's obvious that you all love each other very much, so you're going to need some privacy to work through it together.'

'I'll come home with you,' I said, standing up and placing myself between her and Louisa.

'Jack's going to need you here, Caleb. This doesn't get better if they don't have your support.'

'Oh fuck off!'

'LOUISA!' Tim and Em shouted in unison.

'Goodnight, Em and Tim. Thank you for having me. I had a lovely time. Jack, look after yourself, please?' Ariella turned to me with a small smile. 'I'll see you in the morning.'

With that, she walked out of the front door, rolling her suitcase behind her.

'Good riddance!' Louisa shouted after her.

The room fell into silent shock. What just happened?

Jack spoke first.

'Is it okay if I crash here tonight?'

The first blow from Louisa landed on the side of his head. It took me a second to react, because I couldn't believe what I was seeing. I had no idea it was *this* bad. When Tim and I eventually pulled Louisa off Jack, the room was stunned into silence. What were we going to do now? As much as I wanted to, we weren't going to call the police on her.

'Go home, Louisa,' Em pleaded.

'Come with me now,' she screamed at a silent Jack.

'Just go home, Lou,' he responded, looking away from her.

Em was now crying. That was Tim's final straw. You did not mess with his wife.

'Let's get your stuff, Lou.' He gently ushered her out, while I grabbed her bag and phone. 'We'll talk in the morning, yeah.' It wasn't a question.

After he shut the front door behind her, we stared at each other.

'Fuck!' he whispered at me in disbelief.

That word contained everything we could possibly say. We returned to the living room, where Jack was glued to his chair.

'Mate, we had no idea it was *that* bad!' I started as I sat opposite him.

'It wasn't always. I don't know how we got here.'

The four of us sat there silently, wondering how we let this happen.

'Is Jack all right?' says Ariella, walking into the kitchen just as I come in through the door. She's showered, judging by her damp hair and that familiar apple and grapefruit smell. It makes me smile. She's such a creature of habit. It feels good to have her back.

'Yeah. He's still there.'

'How's Louisa?'

'No idea. She left shortly after you.'

She looks relieved.

'Hungry?' That's all she says. I'd personally be all over the juicy, gossipy details.

'Ooooh, yes! I'll make us some tea.'

I pull out a couple of mugs and pop the different tea bags in, then fill them with hot water.

'Eggs okay? I'm thinking scrambled, with smoked salmon, on some avocado, and sesame spinach?'

'Sounds perfect. So how was Zambia?' I sip my tea and sit at the island.

'It was busy, but so, so beautiful.'

'Sounds like you had a challenging time with the guys.'

'Oh, that. They seemed to talk to Harrison, or they talked to me through Harrison. He may not be the best at operations, but is an exceptional communicator,' she adds.

I watch her move around the kitchen gracefully. I've missed this. I notice she has come back with a lovely golden glow.

'You caught the sun,' I observe. What did I say that for?

'Hard not to, there.'

'Did you manage to get a break?'

'I had a couple of quiet evenings, when Harrison was entertaining. I had a lot on my mind going out and I got time to declutter it a little.'

She places two plates down in front of me before sitting next to me. I take a bite. Heavenly, as usual.

'What was cluttering up your mind?'

'Lots of things, but mostly discovering that I've treated people badly.' Her mouth turns down slightly at the edges.

'Rubbish. You disappear into yourself when you feel threatened, that's all. There are worse ways to handle it.'

'I treated Jasper badly,' she admits sorrowfully.

Why are we still talking about Jasper? I bet he stalked her while she was away.

'I think he was reacting to my behaviour. I didn't share my

feelings, so he wasn't responding, and we eventually stopped talking.'

'Maybe reach out to him. Have a chat.'

That's the last thing I want her to do. I want Ariella to be happy, but getting back in touch with Jasper isn't a good idea. The guy controlled her every move in their relationship, embarrassed her in public when they were over, and left her alone on the streets of London in the middle of a panic attack.

'I was thinking of giving us another shot and maybe trying to do things differently this time.' She looks at me, embarrassed and unsure. 'We spoke a little while I was away... he's not a bad person.'

My appetite disappears.

'I'm down for a Jasper and Ariella reunion if that makes you happy...' I so am *not*. 'But aren't you jumping into this? Have you come to terms with why you left? You weren't happy, Ariella. It sounds like you went away, blamed yourself for everything, and decided you're the bad guy.'

'What if I *am* the bad guy?' She looks at me, distressed, like it is actually a possibility.

'Ariella Mason, you're not, and never could be, the bad guy. Jasper can wait a bit, you just started talking again. Give yourself time to feel things out.'

She nods. Phew. She is not going back to Jasper. Not on my watch.

'Besides, what happened to all the hunky guys on your dating app?' I tease.

'Andrew, the oil rig guy, is the only one left. He's coming in on Wednesday and wants to have dinner.'

'The roughneck is the last man standing. You're terrible at this, Ariella,' I tease her.

'I'm trying to take your advice.'

'What advice is that? You need to start ignoring me. I take all my own advice and I'm hardly winning here.'

'Getting under someone to get over Jasper?'

'Whoa! Slow your roll, Speedy Gonzalez, you have to let them stand next to you first. Seriously though, why don't you start by committing to kiss your next date? If you can't, maybe Jasper is your best choice, because at the rate you're going it sure as hell isn't going to be anyone else.' Only, there is no way I am going to let her go back to Jasper. I need her rent.

'I can try.'

'Don't try, just do. Put mouthwash in your bag for afterwards if you have to. He won't resist. He's been on a rig for months. I won't be surprised if he tries to sink his teeth into you, as a starter.'

Her disgust is obvious. Nothing much has changed there then. I try not to laugh.

'He's a gentleman,' she defends him vigorously.

'Fine, maybe he'll wait until dessert.' This is fun.

'What if I can't?'

'Then I'll bloody well shag you myself so, at the very least, you don't go back to Jasper in the same state!'

The shock on her face is comical. The laughter I've been holding on to breaks through.

'I'm joking, Ariella. Don't look so scared.' I laugh, and she joins me. The girl has no hope.

'Speaking of shagging... How are things going with Nicole?'

'Shitty. I cancelled a date, she backed off and I've done nothing about it.'

'We're both all talk and no follow-through.' She sighs.

She is right. I need to man up and end things with Nicole.

'Chin up, you're back. Let's celebrate.' I nudge her gently with my shoulder as I grab our plates.

It is nice to have my weekend back to normal. I run, do some work and emerge later to help Ariella take some food to the shelter. She has more than usual, because her food delivery came while she was in Zambia. They are going to eat well tonight. We return, watch a couple of *Sopranos* episodes and hit the hay. I'm invited to Sunday lunch with her family, but decline because I've asked Nicole out to brunch.

She walks into the busy restaurant on the Strand looking spectacular, turning the heads of most of the diners. She sits, offers a dazzling smile to the waiter and is immediately handed a menu when she orders her coffee. Nicole Bonnaire is made of the stuff of every man's fantasy, so I regret what I'm about to do.

'I think we should call it quits, Nicole.'

'*Excuse-moi?*' She leans in.

'Work is killing me, I have a ton of stuff to deal with. I can't do this right now.'

'You're saying I am less important than stuff? *Who* is the stuff you *are* dealing with?'

'I'm not dealing with anyone. We're not having the fun we used to—'

'You selfish bastard. I knew this was coming when you asked us to get to know each other. You don't get to know anyone. I should have stayed away from you after the Christmas party. I knew we made a mistake, but you wouldn't stop texting, calling and flirting all the time. All I heard was, "It'll be fun, Nicole. I really like you, Nicole. Why don't you come over, Nicole?"' She mimics me while contorting her face with disgust.

Surely I wasn't that bad?

'When you told me you were going to get a housemate, I wasn't worried, but then *she* moved in. I thought it might be good to have a girl around you. Instead, it got worse. One minute, I can't come to your flat and you won't pick up my calls; the next you're keeping my favourite coffee at home, hugging me in the office and asking to get to know me. I know she is behind this. She sees you every day and is influencing you. When you called me, I rushed over like your fool; but you didn't call me because you wanted to see me, did you? You called me because she wasn't there. You couldn't even get it up!'

All the people at least two tables deep around us have stopped eating and are staring at us. They might as well enjoy the show. I deserve this. Nicole isn't done.

'I tell myself I'm sick of it, but here I am, because you called. I wish you'd just left me alone when I asked but now, you've made me fall in love with you, Caleb. I know you hear me when I tell you, but you ignore it anyway. *Je t'aime*. I'm so in love with you, I will take you any way you will let me have you; but she's poisoning you against me and I can't tolerate that.'

An American woman next to us pipes up as she passes Nicole a tissue while throwing me a dirty look, encouraging her to, 'Tell him, honey!'

Bloody Americans. I ignore it.

'She's doing something to you. You're always protecting or defending her. We've been together for almost a year now and you've never defended me. In fact, whenever I've needed you, you've just rolled your eyes and said, "That's just Nicole". It's not "just Nicole". I'm a human being too! I cry. I hurt. I bleed, and I expect my boyfriend to defend me!'

I look at her, shocked. 'Nicole, I'm not your boyfriend. We were never dating. We just hooked up once in a while.'

The collective 'Oooooh!' that comes from the immediate tables around us now has the whole restaurant paying attention. I hear a 'what a dickhead,' and 'bastard' from somewhere nearby. Londoners are so nosy.

Nicole suddenly tips her cappuccino over towards me and stands. The hot coffee burns my thigh and drenches my jeans, leaving me glued to my seat. The restaurant seems to come to a standstill.

'Don't look so surprised, Caleb. How do you English say it? Your chickens are roosting at home.'

She walks out with more attention than she got when she

walked in. Only this time, the busybodies at the tables surrounding us are clapping so loudly, the whole restaurant joins in. It's followed by boos when I leave. I know I've treated her badly. She's better off without me.

The fallout is quick and effective. It's only Monday, Nicole isn't even in the office but new rumours about us are already spreading. Lara bursts into my office, unannounced, after lunch.

'Why are you such a fucking liability?' she says, slamming the door behind her.

'Hello, Lara,' I respond, deadpan. 'What brings your delightful self in here?'

'Listen, nitwit. Nicole seems to have told everyone in extremely graphic terms that you've been screwing Ariella for months. She's now making a big song and dance about getting herself tested for a myriad of diseases.'

I look across the floor at Ariella. She has her headphones on and is blissfully typing away at her computer.

'People believe it?'

'Of course not. It's Nicole, she's nuts. No one believes Ariella would touch you with a bargepole.'

'What's the problem, then?'

'The problem, you sociopath, is that if Ariella finds out it'll devastate her. I already spent most of the morning talking her off the Jasper ledge. Jasperella is over and it needs to stay that way.'

This is news. She isn't a Jasperella fan either. I cringe at using the term, even just in my head.

'She must know what this place is like. It'll die down.'

'No, she doesn't! This isn't the first ugly rumour that has popped up about her. Think her promotions came without the usual misogynistic, "sleeping with the boss" rubbish? Who do you think has been keeping the fucking wolves at bay?'

'Then do the same again.'

'It wouldn't be a problem if she didn't live with a thicko who lands her in Nicole's cross-hairs. Wanna tell me what you did?'

'I finished with Nicole yesterday.'

'You finished with that crazy bitch and you wandered into work today like nothing happened? Please say you've told Ariella?'

'She wasn't around—'

'Do you have a death wish?'

I don't know how to respond to that. Lara grabs the door handle.

'For all his faults, Jasper would've never made her the butt of some psychopath's drama. Put your ex on a leash!'

I go over to see Jack at Tim's after work.

'Hey, Caleb, fancy some dinner?' Em offers at the door.

'Sorry, can't stay. I'll take a beer, though.' Just a quick one before I tell Ariella that she is the subject of some nefarious gossip. Jack looks surprisingly well for someone who has been crashing on a couch for three days.

'How are you doing? Where's Tim?'

'I'm good. Tim's running late, and no word from Lou.'

'Is that good or bad?'

'I don't know, but I can't live on this couch for ever.'

'Want to stay with Ariella and me for a bit? We can get your stuff.'

'How is she? I've been meaning to apologise for Lou.'

'Lou can apologise for Lou; if we ever see her again.'

'We will. Em's been on the phone with her quite a bit.'

'Ugh. Anyway, the offer's there if you want to get away from the kids.'

'Who would want to get away from my angelic kids?' Em

appears with my beer, smiling. 'So, tell us. What's the story with you and Ariella, Caleb?' she says, getting comfortable.

'I had a spare room. She found my advert. She pays twenty per cent more rent than I requested.' Not this again.

'Caleb, are you blushing?' Jack laughs.

'It's warm in here! Can someone crack a window?'

'You're very gentle with her,' Em continues. 'The way you speak to her, the way you touch her and smile when you say her name. It's very sweet. You like her.'

'Of course I like her. I don't want to piss her off and lose her rent, do I?' This is getting irritating.

'No, as in you have feelings for her.'

'Shit. Yes!' Jack sits up, mouth agape.

'I don't have feelings for Ariella. Besides, when this idiot and your husband found out a girl moved in, they made me swear not to touch her, because they thought she was some fragile little thing that I'd take advantage of. Turns out she's a Rottweiler presenting as a teddy bear. You saw her handle Louisa.'

'"Rottweiler presenting as a teddy bear"!' Em repeats, laughing. 'You *definitely* have feelings for her. And you know what, I think she might like you too. She's affectionate with you and she trusts you. The way she ran her fingers through your hair when Tim took off the dinosaur head was almost... loving.'

Suddenly, I feel everything shift.

'Men.' Em stands to leave the room. 'We have no hope, besides flashing billboards and shouting "Look here!" through a megaphone.'

I immediately follow Em into the kitchen. 'She's still in love with her ex-boyfriend,' I whisper, making sure Jack can't hear me.

Em smiles so widely her eyes turn into slits. 'I'm so happy,' she whispers back. 'She's lovely. Don't fuck it up, Caleb.'

'Stop being happy. She's *way* out of my league. She told you about her ex-boyfriend. I can't give her all that.'

'But she left him. She's looking for something else.'

'I don't know, Em. She's bloody perfect and... I'm me, aren't I?' I sigh.

Em is jumping and clapping excitedly. I put the brakes on.

'Listen, Skippy, nothing may happen – and not a word to Tim or Jack,' I threaten, before I leave the kitchen and head out of the front door.

Ariella is cooking when I get back.

'You're early. I'm playing with some polenta and this one's unpredictable. I'm wishing both of us luck,' she says with a laugh as she pulls a frightened face at me. 'Everything okay?'

The thoughts unfold quickly. Goodness, she's stunning. She turns her back to me with her hair messily piled on her head, exposing her long, elegant neck. Her T-shirt is gathered slightly at the base of her spine, arching over the leggings that cover her cute bottom, giving way to her long, lean legs. The image of her in that white dress pops up. I clear it quickly. I'm supposed to be responding to her question.

'Yeah. Went to see Jack.'

'How's he doing?'

'He'll live. We might need to give up the study.'

'Of course!' She turns around and smiles as she wipes her brow with the back of her hand. 'Hi,' she greets, looking happy to see me.

If we were together, that 'hi' would have ended with a quick welcome kiss on the lips. It's like I am seeing her for the first time. She is gorgeous.

'Hi.' I want to get the matter at hand out of the way, so I sit at the kitchen island. 'I have some news...'

Ariella slings a tea towel over her shoulder to attention.

'What's up?'

'Nicole and I ended things yesterday.'

'Poor Nicole. Is she okay?'

Poor Nicole?!

'Ariella, Nicole can be a little spiteful.'

'I did immediately wonder how you're not missing a limb.' She chuckles.

'And she might say things to people that aren't true. She'll definitely come after me, but she may come after you too, so just don't worry – okay?' I chicken out. I don't want tonight ruined.

'Okay.' She smiles, turning back to the stove.

That's it?

'Thanks, Caleb,' she calls back.

That was the start to a torturous week. I often wished I hadn't had the conversation with Em, because I basically started stalking Ariella at home and indulged in every smile, frown, walk, stray hair strand and movement she made. I found myself touching her even when I didn't need to, and standing closer than normal. If she noticed, she didn't let on.

I did, however, note that, for someone who didn't like being touched by others, we touched each other an awful lot. She was always moving my hips out of the way in the kitchen, so I placed myself in her way regularly. She'd also smack my hand away if I tried to steal stuff from the pan while she was cooking. I made sure those incidents went up in frequency too.

Even when we watched *The Sopranos*, she'd lean into me on the couch, letting our shoulders touch. I tested the waters, put my arm over her shoulders and prepared to get a questioning look. Instead, she snuggled into me as she kept her eyes on the TV. Not that it lasted; she was asleep in seconds. She even rubbed some fake pain I made up in my right shoulder when I asked her to, one night after I'd been training those rats I call students. The fact that I had missed all of this, all this time, was unbelievable to me. Armed with this newfound information, I consulted the great oracle, Em.

How do I tell her I like her?

Make dinner. Dim the lights. Light candles. Buy flowers.

That crap works for you?

Rude.

What does Tim do to get some action?

Empty the dishwasher. I'm easy pickings. Are you trying to get some action or tell her you like her?

Both?

Try telling her you like her first and maybe some action might happen in a couple of months.

I have to wait that long???

You were right. She's out of your league. You don't deserve her.

Fine. So I cook and just make it all nice. How do I tell her?

I think I might be attracted to you but I understand if you don't feel the same way. I just thought I'd put it out there and be honest. If you don't, it's okay, I'll deal with it, but if you do, maybe we could go out on a date sometime?

I just threw up.

I just stopped giving you advice. You're on your own.

Hahahahaha!

Em?

Em's plan seems a bit dated, but Ariella is hardly up with the times. I ditch the candles, flowers and all that nonsense. I am just going to cook on Saturday night, after we've delivered to the shelter. I just need to make sure she isn't going home, and figure out what to say if it all goes wrong.

I ask as soon as we sit down to eat on Thursday, before I lose my nerve.

'What are you up to on Saturday night?'

'Just the shelter run, as usual. Why?'

'You're not going home?'

'Only Sunday lunch – I think you're invited actually.'

'Cool.' I might delay my RSVP, just in case Saturday is a disaster. 'So no plans for Saturday night then?'

'No... actually, wait. Excuse me.'

I like the way she excuses herself to check her phone at dinner.

'Nope. Piers is definitely tomorrow night.'

Piers? She kept that quiet! 'Piers?' I try to keep my voice even.

'Piers from work. We sat together on the plane out to Zambia, we couldn't have dinner in Lusaka so we made dinner plans for this Friday. I think I like him, so there might be that kiss we talked about.'

Why is she taking my advice now?

'That's great.' Yeah. Really bloody great, Ariella.

'Do you need the flat on Saturday night? You going to try to break the Nicole curse?' She looks too invested and excited for me. There is no way I am having this conversation.

'I might; I have a date on Friday, too.' Be jealous. Come on.

'You have a date?' She's excited.

'Oh yeah. With a lovely girl I've been chatting with on the app.' Too much, Caleb.

'That's amazing. We can have a Saturday-morning debrief after she's left. Curse be gone!' Ariella raises her glass.

'I'm thinking I might take it slow. Maybe get to know her?'

Ariella lowers her glass and blinks twice. Come on, say something catty.

'Good for you, Caleb.'

She raises her glass again and I meet it this time. I secretly clink to Piers choking on the bread basket and no one knowing the Heimlich manoeuvre.

TWENTY-ONE

ARIELLA

I leave the house feeling confident. Piers and I got to know each other a little on the flight and he's been sending me little funny memes and jokes over email since we returned. He's lovely when we meet in the bar of the restaurant. We get along so well that we push our dinner reservation back twice, because we are having such a good time with the cocktail menu. He is gracious and sweet, with bright eyes and an easy smile.

We've been honest with each other, so he knows dinner could easily end in a big, fat nothing. Thankfully he's confessed that he has a proper date tomorrow as well.

As the evening carries on, I grow convinced that I could kiss him. I definitely am not 'getting under' him, but kissing I could do. I mentally schedule it for after dinner, outside the restaurant, before I catch a car home.

'You keep looking at my mouth,' he teases. 'Want to tell me what's on your mind?'

'Sorry. Am I?'

'It's okay, I like you. In fact, I have a bit of a confession.' He looks a bit embarrassed.

'What's that?'

'I cancelled my date tomorrow. I think we have a connection, and maybe if we see how...'

The ringing in my ears starts and everything becomes muffled. I watch the waiter silently serve our starters. This. Is. Not. The. Plan.

'Ariella?' Piers interrupts my internal meltdown.

Just breathe, Aari. 'Sorry, Piers. Why aren't you going on your date?'

'You sound like you want me to.'

'It's your choice, but we agreed this isn't a date...'

'Don't worry about that for now.'

He reaches across the table for my hand. I pull it away too quickly. We both notice.

'I'm sorry.' I look at my lap.

'Hey, it's fine. You told me on the flight you don't always like being touched, remember? Why don't we have dinner and you can go back to staring at my mouth while we pretend I'm going on my date tomorrow?'

I barely taste my food after that. Piers tries, he really does, but it is too late. I have to accept that I am just broken. This was a stupid idea.

'I've lost you again.' Piers smiles his dashing smile.

'Sorry.'

'Want to tell me what's on your mind?'

'I'm still in love with my ex-boyfriend.' There. I said it.

'I could've told you that ten minutes into the flight. We all have baggage. Truthfully, this "dinner" is Phase One of my master plan to sweep you off your feet. Let's just enjoy tonight, maybe have a cheeky kiss after and see how you feel about a Phase Two?'

Did he just ask for a kiss? Is he expecting one? If it had been anyone else, I would have politely declined, but this is Piers. I work with him. Whatever happens, I am going to have to see him every day at work. If this ends badly, HR might get involved. This is a nightmare. I feel my chest tighten with panic as our main course turns up. Dessert is next. He wants his kiss after that.

When I excuse myself, I plan to collect myself in the bathroom to get through the rest of the dinner. Instead, I stop at reception, anticipate what the meal will cost plus service, pay the bill and hop into a passing taxi. I am not proud of myself. I am still considering going back to the restaurant to apologise as I let myself into the empty apartment. Relieved Caleb is still out, I strip off, jump into the shower and stand motionless under the spray, allowing it to wash away the anxiety.

I feel better after a good scrub down, and put on a vest, underwear and a head towel. I hesitantly check my phone. Nine missed calls and text alerts fill the screen. Crumbs. I want a gin and tonic. Actually, I am going to have two. I pull my bathrobe on just in case Caleb comes tumbling in. Wherever he is, I know he is having an awesome time.

I put on some music and am filling two glasses with crushed ice in the dark when Caleb pops his head out of his bedroom door, giving me a fright.

'Sorry,' I whisper. I've obviously interrupted something. I turn the music down.

He looks confused.

'Why are you creeping around in the dark, whispering?' he asks loudly. Realisation takes over his face as he points to the two glasses on the side.

'No!' he also whispers. 'You brought Piers back home?'

He looks hilarious, jabbing his finger towards my room in exaggerated shock, with wide eyes and high eyebrows.

'No!' I chuckle quietly, shooing him back into his room. I'm not going to burden him with my rubbish while he has company.

'Then why are we whispering and pointing at each other's rooms for no reason?' he asks, joining me in the kitchen. 'How did it go? I had high hopes. You were out quite late for once.' He sits at the bar and helps himself to one of my drinks. Typical.

'He was lovely, but I did something really awful...' I cringe.

'What did you do, Ariella?'

'I was going to pee... but I sort of hopped in a black cab to come home after paying for dinner?'

'You didn't.'

'I did, a little bit. I feel awful, but I don't know what happened. I was feeling quite positive, then he asked for a kiss and I panicked. I didn't know how to say no. Then I started thinking – why should I have to kiss someone? I should kiss someone because I want to.'

'Well done, Ariella,' he says, mimicking my mother's voice.

'Is that supposed to be my mom?' I laugh. He is such a twit.

'Good, isn't it?'

'Don't quit Ivory Bow just yet. That reminds me – are you coming to Sunday lunch? Mommy called to check.'

'Of course!'

'What happened to your date? I half-expected to return to find an obscure item of clothing hanging off the speakers. Is the Nicole effect still active?' I take a sip of my drink and point my free little finger at his crotch.

'Of course not. I wouldn't have told you if I knew you were going to start paying close attention. She was nice, but my head was elsewhere, so we called it a night after a couple of drinks.'

'You need to get over it quickly; people might start talking.' I try not to smile. He looks like a lost puppy.

'They already are. It's been six weeks...'

'*Six weeks?* You only broke up a week ago. You were stringing her along for five weeks?'

'She did keep sending me... let's call them provocative selfies for a while.'

'You do like daring and challenging women...'

'Not always.'

'Always! You see a danger sign and can't help going for it.'

'That *is* true. You girls like the excitement though.'

'I don't think that's true for me. After tonight, I think I'm just going to take some "me" time instead and then probably get back with Jasper.'

'Ariella, you and Jasper are over. You're just feeling defeated at the moment.'

'You don't know that.'

'I do. You're only going back because it's safe and easy. You're going to face the same problems and you'll never fully explore...'

'What?'

'Any kind of sex life. If you go back, it's curtains for you.'

'It's curtains now. I can never do what you do.'

'And what's that?'

'Make people sleep with you.'

'Correction. I don't *make* anyone sleep with me. They want to. I only make sure that I'm available, they have a good time and they don't feel shitty about it in the morning.'

'With absolutely no feelings.'

'None whatsoever. If you're serious about running back to Jasper to live miserably ever after, I'd shag you myself for your memory library. And perhaps mine.' He laughs and pokes me in the ribs. I roll my eyes. How are we even friends?

'The chances of that happening are zero. I'm not your type.'

'*I* don't have a type. I'm not *your* type, Ariella.'

'There's no point debating this. It'll never happen, because your morning glow guarantee might actually be put to the test by someone you can't hide from, Caleb.'

'Want to put it to the test?'

Caleb's energy changes completely as he puts his finished drink down and walks towards me. He seems taller, broader, darker. For the first time, I see what I assume a lot of women see. Dangerous, imposing, playful and demanding surrender. I shift slightly. It makes me uncomfortable.

'Caleb, I don't think drinking super-strong gin and tonics in the dark, talking about our sex lives, is a good idea.' I back away. The energy that radiates from him is making me nervous. 'I'm going to bed.'

I grab both our empty glasses to rinse them in the sink. It isn't until I finish washing them that I realise he hasn't said a word.

'Don't go. Stay a little bit. I'll stop threatening to shag you.' He laughs.

'I'm only staying up for cheese on toast. I skipped my main course.'

'Make us another drink and you have a deal!'

I make them quickly and hand him a glass after I hoist myself up to sit on the island. He takes a sip as he starts hunting for the bread.

'Final thought. I know you say he's a nice guy, but Jasper really did a number on you.'

'In what way?'

'You don't think a lot of yourself.'

'That's not true. I know that I'm smart and capable. I'm just not courageous, exciting or the best with people. I also don't always say the right thing, but I'm learning.'

'You don't think you're courageous?'

'No. I hide a lot.'

Caleb stops his bread-buttering.

'You walked away from someone your whole family loved, unprepared, because it didn't feel right. You jumped on a train and helped people with a National Front flag hanging in front of their house. You visited someone you didn't know in hospital, even though you'd heard some horrific stories about them. You challenged me about seeing my mother for what I didn't know was going to be the last time. You confronted Louisa and stood up for Jack when no one else did. You're probably the most courageous person I know, Aari.'

It is the first time Caleb has called me Aari. I like it. He deserves to. He is my friend.

'Some would call it stupidity.' I try to dispel some of the intensity around his words with laughter.

'You're not stupid. You're pretty amazing.'

I don't know how to respond. Receiving compliments graciously is not my forte.

'Okay.' I roll my eyes.

'Please promise me you won't go back to Jasper until you find who you are and you're absolutely certain that Jasper is the one you want.' Caleb is serious.

'If this is about the rent, I'll pay up...' I laugh.

'This isn't about the bloody rent, Aari!' Caleb snaps.

'Caleb? What's up?' Concerned, I reach out for his arm.

'Nothing.' He steps away from the cheese and toast ingredients on the island. 'Maybe going to bed is a good idea.'

He starts to walk off, so I pull him back.

'Caleb, I don't want to fight with you.'

'Then let Jasper go. You were unhappy, he kept you caged and you lost yourself. Why can't you see that?'

'I'm trying.'

I don't expect a tear to roll down my cheek. I wipe it away quickly, but Caleb has spotted it.

'Don't cry, Aari.'

He wipes a second tear with his thumb, running it down my face and across my bottom lip. Something in my tummy lurches. Caleb steps back and I reach for his hand.

'Don't go.' I'm startled at my own words.

'I need you to let go of me, Aari,' he asks softly.

'Wait...'

'I'm going to kiss you if you don't.' He is serious.

'I'm not totally opposed to the idea of kissing you.' It may be the cocktails and gin, but I feel bold. The idea hadn't occurred to me, but it strangely makes sense. I trust Caleb. Also, this won't mean anything to him. We'll be able to move on. He'll make fun of it from time to time, but he'll be kind because he knows why I need to do this.

I pull a surprised-looking Caleb closer by the neck of his white T-shirt. I know he will be gentle with me.

'Let's do it,' I suggest.

'No. I'm not doing anything with you,' he argues weakly, looking at me like I have gone mad.

'Let's kiss and get it over with. You'll probably really hate it.'

I pull his T-shirt the rest of the way, close my eyes and kiss Caleb. Caleb kisses me back with some resistance, initially, until we slowly settle into a rhythm. The kiss slowly increases in intensity until it feels like we are consuming each other. I breathe in every breath he exhales as he somehow finds ways to bring our bodies closer.

Caleb's kiss goes straight up my neck and down to my groin, making my body a jumble of nerve endings. The kiss is lustful, tender and urgent all at the same time. His hands pin mine down to the cold surface of the island, in stark contrast to the heat my body is feeling. When Caleb pulls away, I feel like we have started something that perhaps can't be stopped. Caleb moves his lips and trails sensual kisses from the side of my mouth, across my cheek, and settles on my neck.

'Ask me to stop, Aari,' he whispers, kissing my neck so intensely I feel a pull between my legs, getting more urgent.

'Don't...' I plead. What is happening right now?

Caleb smiles that dark smile I caught earlier as he holds my gaze. He lifts his hand to release my hair from the towel wrapped round it. He tenderly moves my fallen curls from my face as he inspects my eyes.

'Are you sure? You've been drinking,' he whispers, with sincere concern.

I nod. I'm not drunk. I am very aware that we may regret this in the morning, but right now I don't care.

He slowly pulls one side of my dressing gown aside, exposing my white vest underneath. He keeps my gaze as he runs his hand over my left breast. He finds my nipple pretty easily, straining against the cotton, and strokes it lightly. I inhale sharply, taken aback by the pleasure I feel, enjoying the friction between his finger and the vest's cotton. The minute I exhale with desire, Caleb stops, closes his eyes and rests his forehead against mine. His juniper-scented breath is panting lightly.

'Tell me to leave you alone and go to bed, Aari,' he asks again, breathlessly.

'I don't want you to. I feel safe with you,' I sigh into his mouth as I cover it with mine. I don't want him to stop. That is all he needs.

Caleb pushes the space he made in my dressing gown wide apart, and rips my vest in two right down the middle, exposing me. He covers my left nipple with his mouth, sucking hard while teasing my right with his fingers. He lets out a groan and asks if I am okay as he releases the left to get acquainted with the right. All I can do is swallow and nod, keep my balance with my hands, and ignore what's going on in my underwear. Caleb returns his lips to mine.

'Aari, you taste so good...'

I can't respond, I am too busy trying to breathe. I open my eyes and they meet his and everything stops. Breathe, Aari, breathe.

'Look at me, Aari. I want you to remember this. I want you to remember me. When you think about this later, I want you to see me, my face, my mouth, doing this to you.'

Looking straight into my eyes, he traces both his thumbs up each of my inner thighs, making them meet right between my legs. Keeping one thumb gently rubbing on me, he brings the other up to his mouth. He closes his eyes and lets out a deep moan.

'You're fucking delicious, Aari,' he shares with his eyes still closed.

Before I can respond, Caleb slides my underwear off and tips my hips so far forward that I end up lying backwards on the kitchen island, supporting my upper body with my elbows. He moves my legs apart and over each shoulder. His mouth traces the same path his fingers wandered to earlier, and his tongue is now exploring where they met. His tongue dips into me and circles my centre slowly with his mouth between kisses. He eventually settles where he wants, and I surrender. The sensation and the thought of him down there with his mouth on me makes me shudder.

'I'm going to make you come, Aari. You're close, I can feel it. Just go with it, okay? Let yourself go.'

He is right. The feeling of him against me is too much. First my mouth goes dry, I find it even more difficult to regulate my breathing, and there is a tightening in my stomach. The feeling rips through me so hard that my elbows give way and my back slams against the countertop. I let out a throaty, unfamiliar moan as Caleb's mouth stays busy between my legs. His groans alone are enough to bring me to the edge again. Just when I think it is over, he moves his mouth and a new wave of pleasure hits me. Eventually, when my legs begin to tremble uncontrollably, I feel him stop and rub his hand over my thighs to soothe them. He then removes my legs from his shoulders, stands up and holds my hands to help me sit up.

'How are you feeling?' he asks, smiling victoriously.

'Shaky. I think I've just had an orgasm?' I laugh, feeling embarrassed and drained.

'I think you may have had more than one.' He smirks.

'I'm not sure I'll ever look at your mouth the same way again,' I say, smiling and pulling him in for another kiss. Having his tongue in my mouth feels carnal, and the surprise of tasting myself on him is strange.

'I got a bit carried away, you were so...'

He closes his eyes, puts his mouth on mine, parts my legs again and slides one of his fingers into me effortlessly. He moves carefully, confidently and possessively. Like he owns me. I feel myself start on the wave again, so I hold his hand gently to stop. I'm not sure I can take any more. He opens his eyes and smiles at me.

'Shower? We've made a bit of a mess.'

He chuckles gently, and I want to kiss him again.

'Yes please, but we aren't done yet. We need to take care of you as well.' I have no idea who this person is, talking to Caleb, but I like her. She is confident and unashamed.

'Aari, we don't need to,' he says, looking worried.

'I think we do.' I look right at him. *Yes. We are doing this, Caleb, while I still have my nerve.*

'Let's get in my shower; it's much bigger than yours.'

He isn't asking. He lifts my semi-naked body, half-draped in my ripped vest and dressing gown, up from the kitchen island and over his shoulder. He carries me into his bedroom, slamming the door shut behind us with his foot.

TWENTY-TWO

CALEB

I have no idea what just happened. I am even more baffled that I am standing here, naked in my shower, watching Ariella playfully soaping us up and rinsing us off, while making me guess what silly pictures she's drawing on my back. All I was supposed to do tonight was make sure she'd be present when I cook her dinner tomorrow.

Instead, I'm here silently panicking about her plans to 'take care of me' as I watch her talking, laughing and complaining about how she is going to deal with her hair tomorrow. If we do this, I want her to enjoy it and I want her to want to do it again. But only with me. Jasper was an idiot to shackle her. I have no idea how to keep a girlfriend but, based on what I've observed, the idea is you let them fly as far and high as they want. You're just there to catch them if they fall and help preen their wings when needed. Seems pretty simple to me.

I pull her out of the shower, unfold my biggest towel and put it over her head. I wrap the smaller one round my waist quickly and toss her over my shoulder. She seemed to like it the first time. When we get to the bedroom, I plop her on the bed and dry her. When I am done, she wraps the towel round herself, dries me and pops her wet curly hair into her usual twisted pigtails as she sits on the edge of the bed. I squat in front of her so our faces are level. *Tell me you're genuinely okay with this*, I appeal silently. Uncharacteristically, I feel the need to slow things down.

'Are you sure you want to do this, Aari?'

She nods, but I can see that she's nervous.

'Want to talk for a bit?'

She shakes her head. 'No. Come here,' she whispers gently as she pulls me in.

I kiss her gently and slowly, the way I wanted to earlier. The way I'd played it in my mind a hundred times during the week. I pull away after a little while.

'Tell me what's going on in here,' I say, stroking her temple. I want her to let me in.

'I feel self-conscious, which is stupid, considering, y'know – earlier,' she admits.

I don't think I have ever felt such relief.

'Why don't I give you a shirt and some shorts, we do our teeth, and we just sleep?' As I say it, I realise it's all I want.

'I'm only next door.' She smiles.

'It's too dangerous to send you out there at this time of night. I'll drop you off in the morning.' I laugh, and we both relax. I toss her a white T-shirt and some new shorts. 'If you get dressed, I'll grab your toothbrush.' I chuck a shirt and some pyjama bottoms on and grab her toothbrush.

When I return, she is dressed. We do our teeth together quietly and get into bed. I let her have my arm and as she puts her head on my shoulder, I pull her close.

'Thanks for tonight, Caleb.'

'You know me, tart with a heart.'

'Please don't do that,' she says solemnly. 'You didn't have to make sure I... well, you know – and you didn't have to let me stay.'

'You're soft and warm and comfy. I'm only keeping you here for selfish reasons. Now go to sleep.' I wrap tighter around her to hopefully put an end to her 'take care of you' plans. I think I've succeeded for about a minute.

'But I'm not sleepy,' she whispers.

Shit.

Ariella Mason is a messy sleeper. I tend to wake up in the same position I fell asleep in. During the night, she has managed to tangle herself in the blankets and splay her limbs everywhere, which means I wake up cold and perched at the edge of the bed. Her hand has somehow found a comfy spot across my face and her foot is placed behind my calf, as if she is actually kicking me out of bed. Her mouth is dry and ajar, with her face half-buried in the pillow. One of her pigtails has completely come apart during the night, with the other halfway there, leaving a mass of brown curly hair all over the pillow.

My tummy flips. I want to wake up like this every morning. I get up carefully so I don't wake her, and head into the kitchen. A full playback of last night starts as I spot her discarded knickers on the island top. I catch myself smiling and hardening. As I brew some coffee and prepare her grapefruit, I replay her grabbing and kissing me first, and I have to stop myself smiling like an idiot. She is awake when I return.

Goodness, she is beautiful. Even with one eye closed and that morning squint. I want to kiss her, but hold myself back. We don't know what this is yet.

'Hi,' she croaks, pushing her wild hair away from her face.

'You okay? Sleep well?'

'Yeah, thanks.'

'You should've. You grabbed all the sheets and made yourself at home by taking over the bed. I spent the night teetering on the edge, freezing my bollocks off.' I laugh in an attempt to make sure she knows we are still friends.

She gives me that adorable smile of hers.

'Is this you kicking me out?'

'Pretty much.' I nod. No, it's not. Please. Stay.

'I know when I've fulfilled my duties.' She chuckles as she roots around for her dressing gown and now-ripped top.

She dangles the top in front of me and shakes her head, reprimanding me comically.

'It takes two.' I arch my eyebrow in defence.

'It certainly does. Thank you, Caleb.' She kisses my cheek, takes her grapefruit from me and leaves.

I assess the damage. It is like a tornado has been in my bed. I'm still going to cook her dinner tonight. I've flipped the process, but I want to tell her still. I can smell her gloriously distracting scent on me. I can't wipe the stupid grin off my face. Getting out of the house for my run will do me some good. That is the intention, until I find myself knocking on her bedroom door.

'Come in!' she calls from the other side.

I find her sitting on her bed in a towel, drying her hair with another.

'So, I wouldn't say you fulfilled ALL your duties,' I declare.

She studies me with a laugh playing on her lips.

'Really? "Ariella! Shit! Fuck! Stay there! Don't move! No! Wait! Aaaaaarrggh! Hmmpfftgbhvvvmmmmuuughhhh!" sounded pretty duty-fulfilling to me, Caleb.'

I forgot she can be rude when she wants to be. She actually crossed her eyes when she said 'Aaaaaarrggh!'; but I can't help laughing. I take a step forward. I'll show her rude. She shakes her head with playful fear on her face.

'Caleb, no! This is the third time I've washed my hair without putting a comb through it since last night, thanks to you. I'm going to have to shave it off if I keep doing that.'

'We can put a comb through it later.'

'This is a bad idea.'

'I know, right? Welcome to your sex life upgrade.'

'I wouldn't call it an upgrade...?'

She has got to be joking. 'Rubbish. You got an orgasm masterclass last night!'

'There's no doubt you're technically proficient, and I get why you're "popular", but...'

Unbelievable. I delivered four squeals and two shudders in less than two hours. I'm a badass at this.

'I'm intrigued as to how you think I could've fallen short of any expectations,' I challenge her.

'You're a little like a race-car driver. You know all the twists and turns and you're constantly calculating how to take the car, me in this case, across the finish line. Which you did beautifully, repeatedly.' She smiles.

I'm not sure whether I should feel insulted.

'What's the problem with that?'

She looks a bit embarrassed.

'I really wanted you to enjoy the drive. Not just at the finish line, but all of it. You seemed a little preoccupied.'

'You don't think I enjoyed it?'

'For sure the end, but I'm not sure about the rest of it?'

What has Jasper been doing to her?

'I enjoyed every single second.'

'You seemed like you wanted us to stop a couple of times.'

I lift her face to look at mine.

'That's because I didn't want you to feel that you had to see it through. I enjoyed everything we did last night. A lot.' More than I have ever done with anyone else, Ariella, but you don't need to know that. 'So much so, I'd very much like to do it again.' I pull her towards me using the edge of the towel. 'Last night took me by surprise, that's all,' I whisper, bringing my mouth slowly down on hers.

She kisses me back softly. When she pulls away, I see desire in her eyes. Yes.

'Spend the day in bed with me. Don't do anything, don't go anywhere, just stay here, in bed with me,' I ask.

'I'd love to, but I can't. I have to go to the dry-cleaners, cook for the shelter, and I'm making tomorrow's dessert.' She sounds apologetic.

'We can cook for the shelter together and we'll get it dropped off.'

'*You're* going to help me cook for the shelter?'

That cheeky look of suspicion is already one of my favourites.

'Yes. And I'll get the cleaning picked up. Don't move, I'll get my phone.'

I run to my room. When I return I jump into her soft and pillowy bed emanating that delicious smell of her. I find a local taxi firm and do as I promised as I watch her do her teeth. When I lean over to get rid of my phone, I spot a frame holding an image of Ariella and Jasper looking at each other laughing. I flip it face down just as she comes in.

She finds it funny. 'Feeling guilty?'

'Nope, feeling victorious. No need to rub it in his face.'

'Victorious?'

'He took his eye off the ball and now you're here with me. Maybe not tomorrow, or a week from today, but I have you here, now.'

She finally discards her towel and climbs into her bed completely naked. She looks so happy, I swear my heart skips a beat.

'Right, you have just over twenty-four hours to show me what you've got hidden away in that box of tricks of yours.'

'You're nowhere near ready for the box of tricks, Mason; let's just keep it simple and explore what your body responds to. That way, I can use it to my advantage.'

'You make it sound like I'm about to be weaponised for your use.'

'Oh, you will be.' I pinch her nipple gently. She yelps, smacks my hand lightly and laughs.

'Shall we find out what else that button does, and if it works in combination with anything else?' I smirk.

'Caleb Black, you are a very bad boy. I might weaponise you for my use too.'

She leans into my mouth with her lips already parted. What she doesn't know is, it's too late to make those threats. I've surrendered. I'm already hers.

TWENTY-THREE

ARIELLA

'Honey, I'm not sure sleeping with Caleb is the best idea you've had.'

'What?' I splutter my tea, and start coughing because it goes down the wrong way.

Caleb shows up instantly at the kitchen door. 'Aari, you okay?'

He looks worried. My mother bats her eyelashes at me pointedly. I nod at Caleb as I continue coughing, then give my mother a scathing look.

'*Aari* is fine, Caleb,' my mother says with a smirk, emphasising his use of my shortened name.

'What are you girls up to?' He looks unsure.

'Nothing, just cooking,' my mother responds sweetly.

He is doubtful, but leaves. It takes me a minute to catch my breath.

'What makes you think that?'

My mother gives me the look she reserves for those she thinks are particularly dense.

'The last time he turned up you elbowed him in the stomach, he avoided you all evening and he went home with that

Katherine. Now, he's whispering in your ear, even though there's no one around who can possibly overhear, and you're giggling right along. Yes, I caught that at the station. He's opening your doors, checking you're okay, stroking your arm and playing with your fingers in the back seat of the car when he thinks no one is looking, and he smells like you.

'And not your perfume; he smells of your body cream. When he gave me a kiss, I smelled you on his neck. There are only two ways it could get there and, as we have just seen, he hasn't been strangled. I can't say the same for you, though – what are those purple things on your neck? I assume that's why you're wearing your hair down today?'

She points to my neck with an inquisitive look on her face. She knows exactly what they are. Caleb swore he couldn't see them. Great. I rearrange my hair in front of my shoulders.

'Just a bruise.'

'Vampires living in Hampstead now, are they?'

Now she's enjoying herself. I am not going to admit that Caleb and I have been intimate. Mommy has been dying to have this conversation with me but I'm not ready to have it with her. She was as subtle as an elephant on the London Underground when Jasper and I were together. I don't want to discuss it, but I'm not going to lie.

'Mommy, please don't say anything,' I plead.

'Are you kidding? Say anything? Daddy will murder Caleb. He loves Jasper, and it's best to keep shtum, especially as they now go running together once a week.'

My mother knows how to drop a bombshell but make it sound like she is talking about laundry.

'They what?'

'Ariella, you really must work on your vocabulary. Jasper and Daddy have been going running weekly for the last couple of months. They went this morning, regular as clockwork. Don't you think Daddy's looking great?'

'Mommy! Why didn't you tell me?'

'Because it has nothing to do with you. Well, I hope not. It's good for your dad and he really misses Jasper. Did I mention Jasper might be coming to lunch today? Darling, what's wrong?'

She knows what's wrong. I can't breathe. This is not happening.

'Mommy! What else? Just give it to me straight.'

She stops what she is doing and looks at me. Here it comes.

'Jasper's coming to lunch with Katherine.' Mommy rolls her eyes for dramatic effect before she continues. 'Margaret invited her. She still hates you, by the way. I think we're here because your father may have brainwashed Jasper into giving your relationship another shot. Margaret, most certainly, is dragging Katherine along to put a stop to it, so don't expect an easy ride.

'Purely as a recommendation, maybe keep your hands to yourself – and Caleb needs to stop making puppy eyes at you. I might shove Zachary and Isszy between Caleb and Jasper just in case. I don't want to mop up any blood tonight. They'll be here in half an hour. So, if you need to tell Caleb, go now.'

I bolt from the kitchen, run up the stairs and call Caleb up to my room. He bounds up after me. He looks slightly frantic when he arrives, shutting the door behind him.

'Aari, we can't do this now. Your father keeps looking at me. I think something's up. I've just helped him set the table for ten! I thought it was just the six of us?'

'Jasper, Katherine, his mother Margaret, and stepfather Phil are coming.'

'Why would he bring Katherine? Everyone thinks I shagged her – which, again, I didn't.'

'I think Daddy is trying to get Jasper and me back together, and Margaret has probably invited Katherine to be antagonistic.'

Caleb relaxes visibly, then mischief sweeps across his face.

'If that's all, while we're up here...'

He grabs my waist and pulls me towards him.

'That's not going to happen,' I protest, but let myself be pulled anyway.

'It happened yesterday, repeatedly, if I recall.' He laughs into my ear as he nibbles my earlobe. Good grief, he's a quick study. 'Please don't ask me to stop,' he whispers.

'You've changed your tune.' I chuckle, meeting his mouth with mine. Ugh. This is the opposite of what I am supposed to be doing right now.

'Changed my tune? The whole album's in the bin and is currently being rewritten.'

'Caleb, maybe we shouldn't...' His mouth travels to my neck and kills my sentence.

'Maybe we should, a little bit. Now, where's that sneaky little...' he whispers, with his lips brushing against my collar-bone and his hand travelling up my dress. I am hardly clamping my thighs together.

'Cal—' His name is interrupted by a sharp intake of breath. He's found it.

'Aha. There it is. Good to know it's still in working order after all the use it got yesterday... and this morning,' he adds for effect, smiling as his mouth finds mine again.

I could kiss Caleb all day but I have to do something.

'Mommy knows we've been intimate.'

He stops immediately.

'Aari! I thought we weren't going to say anything. Your father's going to make whatever he does to me look like an accident and people will believe it.'

'I didn't. She caught you stroking my arm in the car, apparently you smell of me – and then are these!' I point accusingly to the hickies he gave me. 'You said you couldn't see them!'

'Firstly, I'm quite proud of those. Secondly, it was dark and I was half-asleep this morning when you asked me. They do seem to have flourished quite a bit since then.' He grins, impressed with himself. I want to kill him. Finally, he gets serious. 'Dahlia isn't going to tell your father, is she?'

'No, but she's now plotting to run interference with the seating arrangements.'

'Yes, I love your mother. Okay, we can get through this. I just need to ignore you, make sure I'm silent and not be a dick.' He runs his hand through his hair like it's going to be a challenge.

'Sorry, Caleb.' He didn't sign up for this. I feel bad.

'Don't worry about it. When do they get here?'

'Half twelve.'

I start to leave and he pulls me back.

'Come here. I've been struggling to keep my hands off you since we left home.' He looks at his watch. 'We have twenty minutes. I'll have you trembling in five.'

It's a promise I know he'll keep and I'm embarrassed at how quickly I give in. I don't even argue.

'Put your hands where I can see them, Aari,' he breathes into the back of my neck, placing my palms flat against my wardrobe.

I can feel him behind me. His hands travel up my thighs to my bottom, lifting my dress as he goes along. When he gets to the top, he hooks his fingers into both sides of my underwear and teases it down my legs so slowly, I feel impatient for him. He lifts my feet out one by one, placing them further apart than they were. His breathing matches mine. Standing back up, he tilts my hips back with his hands. I hear his buckle and his zip. My body arches in anticipation. How on earth did I end up here? Caleb leans forward and whispers in my ear.

'Goodness, Ariella, I so badly want to f—'

'Ariella! I need you now please!' my mother barks from downstairs.

'Shit!' Caleb laughs.

'Coming!' I yell back.

'If only.' He smirks.

I give him a dirty look as I pull my underwear back on and lift a box of old photos from the top of my cupboard, shoving it in Caleb's hands.

'Go,' I beg, pointing towards the door.

Caleb is confused. 'What am I supposed to do with these?'

'We can say we found them. Go.'

Caleb and I walk downstairs together. My mother looks outwardly stern, but I see her fighting to contain a smile.

'I see you found some photos. Ariella, kitchen. And Caleb, you might want to pop to the bathroom.'

I look at Caleb. His previously neatly tucked shirt is rumpled and partly untucked at the bottom. I am overwhelmed with embarrassment. At least his fly isn't open... Nope. It is. I want to die. He notices too.

'Dahlia, it's not what you—' he starts.

'Caleb. Bathroom.' I help him out.

He hands me the box and walks to the bathroom sheepishly. In the kitchen, Mommy lowers her voice to scold me.

'Ariella, I'm not intervening when your father starts wondering where his shotgun is and tapping his foot for hollow spaces under the patio. What's up with you?'

'I don't know! On Friday night, we just... I feel alive around him. I'm not so... preoccupied. It's freeing. I've never felt like this before. It's not even emotional.' I've said too much and it is too late to take it back.

'Maybe not for you.'

'It's Caleb, Mommy. It's not like that.' I wave the suggestion away.

'We'll see. Let's talk later. Potatoes. They'll be here any minute.'

I take the potatoes off the boil, brush them with duck fat and start putting them in the baking tray. A few minutes later, the doorbell goes.

'I'll get it!' I volunteer.

'No, you won't!' my mother interjects. 'You need to go upstairs and grab any one of my scarves. The bruises on your neck have acquired a new friend.'

Lunch is tense. Our normally chatty, happy table is exceptionally quiet, and it's winding Zachary up. I can feel his frustration steadily increase as the conversations he starts keep coming to an abrupt end. Everyone seems to be consumed with their thoughts, and have no problems showing it on their faces. Jasper's mom keeps shooting me death stares, alongside loving glances to her son. Daddy is giving Jasper approving looks, occasionally nodding subtly in my direction. I can see you, Daddy. He also manages to throw a permanent look of deep disapproval in Caleb's direction. Mommy is trying her best to keep the peace by being especially nice to Caleb and Margaret. Caleb, thankfully, is ignoring me, but keeps inching further away from Katherine. At one point, he is almost off the table; not that Katherine notices. Her focus is fixed on him, giving Margaret another target for her hostility.

Jasper tries to help keep Zachary's conversations alive while having an exceptionally polite discussion with me about work. It is a precarious situation, but it is beginning to look as if we will all make it out alive; until Isszy drops the line, 'It's so good to see that, even after everything, Jas and Aari can still remain friends.'

Zachary bursts out laughing.

Jasper's mom takes the bait. 'What's so funny, Zachary?' Oh no.

I pray that, for once, Zachary will say nothing, but today is not the day for that prayer to be answered. My mother deflates and shuts her eyes. She knows her son.

'They're not friends. Not even in the loosest definition of the word.'

Oh no. He lifts his fork and starts pointing the potato at the end of it at each of us.

'Can we just talk about this and get it over with? The passive-aggressiveness at this table squarely places this lunch in the fifth circle of hell.'

'Zachary!' Mommy scolds, but it is too late. She knows it too.

'Aari walked out on Jasper for some secret reason that we're all trying to figure out because, let's face it, Jasper is the man we all want to be, but are too flawed to come close. Love you, bro, I don't get it either. Then, Jasper becomes so macho and hostile, even I don't recognise him. So, congratulations, Aari. You broke Jasper. Anyway, he lets Aari go, totally convinced she's going to come back, but it's been almost seven months and there's still no sign of her returning. Five months in, realising he'll need the big guns, Jasper recruits Daddy and they start jogging weekly to invent some dodgy strategy to get her back. What Mom doesn't know, though, is half an hour of that ninety minutes is spent having a fry-up at the Harbour Hotel.'

'Hugh?' Mommy asks, and Daddy looks elsewhere.

Zachary continues, 'Jasper, between jogs, spends most of his time avoiding Katherine, who, may or may not have, shagged Caleb. Instead, he spends most nights alone, drinking, and pining irritatingly about Ariella over the phone to me. Sorry, mate, she needs to know. Now, Scraps, who started this whole thing off, because she wanted to "go and find herself" or whatever—'

'That's enough now, Zachary,' my mother interrupts, giving him a stern look.

'Mom, we need to stop pretending. It's ridiculous. I love these lunches, but this one really sucks. We're all sitting here being nice to each other, but we all know Margaret wants to kill

Aari, Daddy wants Jasper back, and Phil and I just wish Jasper would grow some balls and either talk to Aari or leave her the hell alone. Though making her come back might no longer be an option, because a few things are off.

'Caleb, for some strange reason, isn't his usual self, and hasn't cracked on to anyone or flirted with Mommy yet. In fact, he's pretty much running away from Katherine's advances under the table. He could be having an off-day, but he hasn't looked at Aari once during lunch. Aari, by the way, just happens to be wearing her hair down like she never does, ever, and is covering up what look like bruises on the side of her neck with a scarf. Seriously, Scraps? A flashing neon sign pointing to your neck would've been less obvious. If I were to take an educated man's guess on how they got there—'

'That's enough!' Mommy gets up, banging her hand on the table.

I can't remember the last time I saw Mommy so upset. Everyone looks at me. I look at my plate. I cannot look at Daddy. Yup. They all seem to have come to the same educated guess Zachary was about to share. Jasper gets up.

'A word outside please, Caleb,' he demands, walking into the garden without waiting for a reply.

Caleb gets up and sighs. 'Well done, Zachary. You just threw your dad, your sister and your best friend under the bus. I hope you're thrilled. For the record, nothing happened with Katherine. Anyone wants me, I'll be outside, being Jasper's punchbag.'

He follows Jasper, closing the sliding door behind him. There is silence at the table.

Zachary says, 'I just thought we—'

Mommy holds her hand up. She is livid.

'Aari, Katherine, would you help clear the table please? I suspect we've all lost our appetites.' She starts stacking plates of half-eaten food.

'We'd better go home,' Phil announces as he and Margaret stand.

'I'm so sorry. I forget these kids can be so young and so *exceptionally* stupid,' she says, staring at Zachary.

Daddy gets up next, silently heading into the living room to turn on the TV, leaving Zachary and Isszy at the dining table, talking. Well, Zachary is talking to Isszy. An infuriated Isszy has her back turned to him and is shoving Zachary's hands off whenever he touches her. When I finish ferrying our plates and bowls to the kitchen, I join Daddy to face his disappointment. It is safest there.

I sit on the sofa and lay my head on his shoulder.

'Aari, do you want to come back home for a while?' he asks quietly, stroking my hair. Big, fat tears start uncontrollably rolling down my face.

'No, Daddy, I'm okay.'

'I love you, chicken, whatever happens. Your mom and I will always be here for you; even if I never see the light of day again, thanks to Zachary.' He laughs softly.

I laugh too. 'I love you, Daddy.'

After a while, Isszy comes into the room. Her eyes are red and angry.

'Aari, have you had much to drink? Would you mind running me to the station?'

'Of course, Isszy. Are you okay?'

'Yes. I just need to head back.'

'Where's Zachary?'

'It's just me.'

'Oh, okay. I'll grab the keys.'

As I am leaving with Isszy, Caleb comes back in.

'Hey, I'm just running Isszy to the station. Want to come?'

Caleb walks straight to the front door and grabs his coat without looking at me.

'I'm coming with you, Isszy.'

He speaks directly to her. I tug his arm so he'll look at me.

'But we're meant to go back together.'

'Plans change.' He won't meet my eyes.

Mommy yelling at Zachary and slamming a door filters downstairs and ends my protest.

The car-run to the station happens in total silence. Isszy sits in front, focused on her hands, while Caleb sits behind, staring outside his window. He only speaks when he gets out of the car.

'Just so you know what you're walking into, Jasper wants a word when you get back.' With that, he slams the door, and jogs to catch up with Isszy.

The ground floor is eerily quiet and empty, apart from Jasper sitting at the dining table, when I return. Even the kitchen and garden are deserted. Everyone knows this talk is happening and they've made themselves scarce.

'Where is everyone?'

'Hugh's upstairs having a nap, and Dahlia's probably trying to figure out a way to hide Zachary's body. She's been yelling at him the entire time you were gone. It just went quiet. I'm pretty certain she's killed him.'

He makes me smile. He always knew how to do that. *I love you. I miss you, but I can't.* I clear my head.

'Can we talk?' he asks.

'Sure. What did you say to Caleb, Jas?' I sit at the dining table, next to him.

'Who gave you the love bites?'

He is in the perfect position to appreciate their full glory. I don't want to tell him, but I don't want to lie either.

'You said you wanted to talk, Jas, not interrogate me.'

'You've been quiet.'

'I called you the night I came back from Zambia, like I promised I would. I believe you were busy.'

'I had a friend over.'

'A female friend. At two a.m.'

'We're not together, Scrappy.' The way he says my nickname makes my heart lunge for him. 'This is enormously challenging for me. When you left—'

'Yes, I left and I hate that I did that to you. But I wasn't happy and it wasn't your job to make me happy. I have to do that myself. I wanted to be a better person not just for me, but maybe for you. Eventually.'

'It *is* my job to make you happy, and I can't bear that you weren't. Do you know why?'

'I don't know. We worked all the time. Weekends were the same; dinner and family. Our holidays were first-class, five-star, hyper-sanitised luxury, where you worked and I stayed on the beautifully paved track. Our sex life was scheduled once a week, on Sunday night at nine thirty after a shower. Everything was rigidly planned. I wasn't ready to live like that.'

'Aari, we could've discussed this, cut back on work and changed things.'

'Jasper, work is not my issue, it's yours; I just got the shrapnel. Remember when you almost broke your neck trying to get phone reception when we went skiing? I spent most of that week on my own. I remember thinking I'd much rather be alone with you in a run-down shack in the middle of nowhere, with awful weather outside, but at least we'd be laughing.'

'We had beautiful morning walks and lovely meals together that holiday. You had a chef giving that private cooking course. I had that teacher doing yoga with you every day. We made it work.'

'Because you put me on a schedule. I was a daily entry in your diary, Jas. I would've followed you anywhere because I wanted to be with you. Somewhere along the way, I lost myself. I'm not sure I even bothered to find that out in the first place.'

'You're hardly on your own figuring stuff out. What's going on with Caleb?' he questions. I know what he's asking, but ignore it because answering it would be cruel. He doesn't need to know.

'What did you say to him?'

'I explained that I have much more in common with you than he does. I don't know what's going on with both of you, but he's not good enough for you and he isn't going to stick around once he finds out that he has zero chance of bedding you. Look how quickly he went off Katherine for turning him down.'

'No. *He* turned *her* down. Caleb's no angel, but she was drunk and he's not a rapist.'

'Even so. He didn't stick around, did he?'

'Actually, he did. Until morning, on the couch. To make sure she was okay.'

'Do you love him? Please, Scraps, I can handle anyone else. Just not him. Please.'

'Haven't you heard a word I've said? I'm still in love with you. You still own me. Here.' I stab my chest with my finger. 'I just wish you hadn't played the class card.'

'What?'

'Jasper, come on. We're more similar than Caleb and I are? What else could you have meant?'

'I meant our values.'

'Do you know anything about Caleb's values?'

He looks away. I whip out my phone and dial his number. It goes straight to voicemail. I leave a message.

'Caleb, I'm sorry. Jasper's not the classist ignoramus he just pretended to be. Call me please?' I say, hanging up.

'Ariella, that's ridiculous.'

'Is it? The more time I spend away from you, Jas, the more I realise that we're quite different people, and I have so much to learn. I've met people about to disprove one of Einstein's theories who've walked me through East London telling me its history, and got me into Korean food. I'm changing and I can feel it. I don't always come home in a straight line. I'm not as scared as I used to be of everything and am learning so much more about myself.'

'Would you like me to wait for you?' he asks solemnly.

'I don't think you should. I deeply regret treating you so appallingly and I'll never be able to apologise enough. I hate myself for doing that to you. All you did was love me and I threw it back in your face. I'm so sorry, but we have to let each other go. I'm sorry.'

'I can't, Aari, you're the centre of everything I am.' His voice cracks.

'And I feel the same about you; but you know who you are. I have no idea who I am.'

'Please, Scrappy. Just come back to me,' he whispers, and he lifts my head to kiss me.

I don't pull away; in fact, I lean in and surrender to my heart. Kissing Jasper is home. It's safe, secure, enveloping and warm. I kiss Jasper and, with no doubt in my mind, I know this is what love feels like.

I pull away. It's not fair to either of us.

'Jas, I can't.'

He nods, resigned, and we hold on to each other silently for a few more minutes.

'It's getting late. Can I give you a ride back to Hampstead?' he asks finally, kissing my forehead.

Mommy and Daddy, who have clearly been eavesdropping, descend the stairs to say goodbye. They hold on to Jas and me so tightly, I am reminded everyone caught in the middle of this is hurting too.

When I've strapped on my seatbelt in the car, Jasper looks at me with uncertainty and opens his palm. I put my palm on top of his and he transfers both our hands onto the gearstick, with his hand covering mine, like he always did when we went anywhere in the car together. We shift into first gear and our hands stay together, shifting and staying on the gearstick all the way to Hampstead. Neither of us utters a word until we get there.

'Thank you, Jasper,' I say as we pull up.

'Goodnight, Aari. I love you.'

'Goodnight. I love you too, Jasper.'

'Come here.'

He gently pulls my face towards his and we settle into a long and comfortable kiss. If this had been any day last week, I would have left everything at Caleb's and gone back home with my soulmate. But things are different now. I slept with Caleb this weekend. A lot. Most recently today. And enjoyed it much more than I should have.

'Can we keep talking? I know we're not together, but it doesn't mean that I don't want to share things with you.'

'Really?'

'Of course. You're my best friend.'

He raises an eyebrow and smiles. My heart skips several beats. Goodness. We look at each other for longer than we should, saying nothing, before I exit the car and enter my building.

'Caleb, are you home?' I call as I walk into the kitchen to get some water. I'm relieved when he emerges from his room.

'Caleb, I'm so sorry about this afternoon.'

'It's okay. We can talk tomorrow.'

'No, it's not okay. Zachary and Jasper weren't at their best today. Zachary was being Zachary, but Jasper didn't mean it. He really didn't.'

'We have work tomorrow. Let's just sleep today off.'

Caleb is obviously still annoyed and doesn't want to talk about it, but I don't want him to go to bed angry.

'You should know that I had a long chat with Jasper and he

knows he shouldn't have said what he did. He's not a bad person, it's just that—'

'Caleb, are you coming or shall I just head out?'

A gorgeous girl with rainbow-coloured hair walks out of his room, pulling a thin cream jumper over a beautiful silk bra and sharply carved six-pack. She is wearing a short skirt and black biker boots. I can't help feeling inferior.

'Hi, sorry, please stay. I'm just the housemate.' I wave at her and duck into my room quickly.

'Aari, wait—' Caleb calls after me.

I shut my door gently behind me.

'I asked you to give me a minute,' I hear him complain to the girl.

'I did! Are you coming?'

I walk into my bathroom and have just turned on the shower when he starts knocking.

'Aari! Open up. Please.'

I shut the bathroom door, step under the water and stay in there. All of today's emotions catch up with me and I let the tears fall. I'm exhausted. Caleb doesn't owe me anything, it was just physical. This just confirms what I already know. I am probably feeling this way because it was fun, but now it is over.

I wanted real life, and here it is. I need to grow up.

I step out of the shower and the knocking is still going. This time it is softer and less urgent.

'Come on, Aari, open up.'

I'm too tired to respond, so I lie there listening to it until I fall asleep.

TWENTY-FOUR

CALEB

I didn't sleep with Dash. The circumstances that led to Dash and me being slightly unclothed in my room are relatively innocent. I didn't touch her. Much. Aari's not going to buy it, is she? To be honest, what did she expect? Lunch was excruciating. It was basically the Ariella and Jasper emergency summit. As messed up as Zachary's actions were, he did us all a bloody favour. The bomb was there in the middle of the table, ticking away. He just slammed down on the detonator. The minute Jasper asked to meet me outside, I knew I had to tell him how I felt. I ducked the questions about the hickies on her neck. I wasn't going to admit to them and, if asked whether we were sleeping together, I would have flat out lied. He didn't even consider the possibility. It filled me with relief, but it also pissed me off. So I hit him where it hurts.

'If I touch Ariella, it'll be because she really, *really* wants me to.'

I was so busy enjoying the emphasis I put on that second 'really' that I didn't see the right hook coming. I took it because, deep down, I felt sorry for him. Zachary was right. She'd broken him. Although he had also, very clearly, broken her.

'Stay away from her.'

'Can't, mate. You fucked up and that's the only reason she's living with me.'

'What did you just say?'

'I said you fucked up. You caged her and then you ignored her, mate. Her life was going to work, coming home and waiting for you. Sometimes till midnight. She wouldn't eat alone or go to bed until you told her to. That's downright abusive.'

'She told you I was abusive?'

'Of course not. She thinks the sun shines out of your bloody arse.'

He stood there quietly, digesting what I just told him.

'I always called to make sure she'd eaten and that she wasn't waiting up for me.'

His tone wasn't one of defence, but of self-criticism. I did my best to hold him against the ropes, but anyone could see that he wasn't a bad bloke; which made it hard to dislike him.

'Maybe if you'd got home straight after work, like you demanded of her, you would've seen it.' Take that. You are not my friend.

'Ariella's panic attacks are exacerbated by alcohol. She used to get them all the time. Sometimes they'd grip her so hard, she'd pass out. They were terrifying. I wanted her home so I could look after her.'

'Yet you let her walk away mid-attack from a party and regularly worked until midnight?'

'I apologised for that. I was annoyed. I didn't make good decisions that day. Also, I didn't work till midnight all the time; I was usually home by ten.'

'Any other woman would think you had a bit on the side.'

'I most certainly did *not* cheat on her. I never would.'

'Whatever. The choice is Ariella's. If she ultimately decides to go back to you, I won't stand in the way.'

'Why would you stand in the way?'

Time to let him know he has some competition.

'I'm falling for her.'

The last thing I expected Jasper to do was laugh.

'You're a good guy, Caleb, and it's obvious you care about Ariella, but you can't give her what she needs. She's used to a level of access that is beyond your reach. You just don't have the same values or opportunities. You'll always feel like you're catching up, and you never will, because she's two hundred miles in front of you, and that gap is only going to get wider, because she's in a sports car and you're on a bicycle.'

I would have ignored him if there was the slightest hint of malice in his voice. But even my friends saw the gap. Everyone believed I'd never be enough for Ariella and she'd never let me near her; but she had let me touch her. She'd kissed me. I checked almost obsessively to make sure she wanted to, because a large part of me couldn't believe it either. It was very clear that she was still in love with Jasper. Only then did it hit me. She'd called my bluff. She got under *me* to try to get over Jasper. I was just her means to their end.

I'd watched them hold each other's gaze and communicate silently during lunch while everyone at the table was rooting for them. Only Dahlia checked in with me, mouthing, 'Are you okay?' whenever she caught my eye. Even she knew. Only Jasper could give her what she needed. I was just the entertainment. Em got it wrong. She didn't see what I had seen. I felt the fury rise.

'I'm going home.' I didn't need this.

'Just hold on—'

'No. Talk to your girlfriend. If you handle it right, she'll be back at home with you tonight.'

I wanted to get out of the house as quickly as possible. I wasn't expecting to see her by the door. I was so angry, I couldn't look at her. The sooner she moved out, the better.

. . .

The first pint I sank by myself reminded me of how much I'd missed being in the pub alone. I didn't notice Dash until she nudged me.

'Hello, stranger.' She placed her hands on my shoulders.

I liked Dash and her new rainbow-coloured hair, and since I'd missed the last few quizzes I hadn't seen her around for a while. She was always fun to have a post-quiz chat with, so I bought her a drink. After a couple of hours drinking, we were starving, so I invited her over to raid the fridge. We were kissing by the time we got out of the lift and we were in our underwear before I found the strength to stop myself.

'You're gorgeous, Dash, but I'm sorry, I can't.'

'Is it me?'

'Definitely not. It's me... There's someone.'

She immediately understood.

'Wanna still grab a bite? The chip shop closes soon but we can make it if we hurry. Then I want to know more about this "someone".'

We were almost dressed when I heard Ariella call my name.

'Sixty seconds,' I instructed, leaving Dash in my bedroom.

If I felt bad before, I felt even worse as she stood there apologising. She looked tearful and exhausted. The day had been tough for her too, and it made me want to crawl into bed and hold her until she fell asleep.

Dash was going to have to go for chips on her own, but first I had to get her out of the flat without Ariella knowing. I'd never been so grateful for her compulsive showering. I could sneak Dash out then. Unfortunately, Dash didn't receive any of the telepathic messages I'd been sending her to stay put. Ariella's wall went up in an instant. She shut down and put me on the outside again. When it comes to Ariella, it's the worst place to be. I spent the night asking her to let me in, until I fell asleep on the floor outside her bedroom door to nothing but silence.

. . .

I wake up at a few minutes to six the next morning, shower quickly and get dressed for work. At 7 a.m. I'm sitting at the bar, waiting for Ariella to emerge for breakfast, but she's late. After knocking for ten minutes, I open her door, and she's gone. Her wardrobe is ajar and I spot her clothes in there. At least she hasn't moved out.

Ariella eventually walks into work at nine thirty, with shopping bags. I go to her desk immediately.

'Hi—'

I stop in my tracks. She's wearing make-up. She looks beautiful, but nothing like Ariella. Her eyes are defined, her lips are a deep chocolate and she has a slight golden shimmer to her cheeks. Her hair is pulled up into a much neater bun than normal. She is wearing a black turtleneck instead of her usual open-collared Oxford shirt.

'Hi.' She gives me a closed-lipped smile. 'What's up?'

That smile doesn't touch her eyes. Great. Icy-Ariella has come out to play. She has the same voice and smile, but this isn't the Ariella I spent the weekend with. That Ariella was warm, vibrant and present. This Ariella is anything but.

'I was hoping to catch you this morning. Can we pop into my office for a minute?'

'Sorry. I have to prepare for the ten a.m.'

'Are you coming home straight after work?'

'I'm going to the office drinks.'

She smiles that dead smile at me again. We both know the office drinks are torture for her. She doesn't want to come home to me.

'Ariella Mason! I approve.'

Lara rushes to her desk, shoving me out of the way purposely and then standing in front of me. The smile Lara gets is wildly different from mine.

'Really? I don't feel like me.' She pulls at the turtleneck uncomfortably.

'Darling, no one ever looks or feels like themselves. Loving the face. Make-up counter get you, did they? Oooh! Did you see Jasper yesterday?'

She casts a quick glance at me and Lara notices.

'Oi. Move it, creep. Don't you have someone to sexually harass?'

She jerks her thumb behind her twice as she sits down on Ariella's desk. I'll have to wait. I get to my office, only for Nicole to join me as soon as I sit down. Like I don't have enough problems.

'What do you want, Nicole?'

'You're different. Is it because of her?'

'No. It's because of you. If you'll excuse me, I have work to do.'

'You're sleeping with her. I know it.'

She doesn't wait for a response. I steal a glance at Ariella. Her head is down as she concentrates on what she is writing. She tugs at the top of the turtleneck again. I smile. My hickies are hidden under there. I bet they're still tender to touch. I am still with her. I remember giving her the first one, and shut it down quickly, before I dive too deeply into the memory of her smell and that breathy sigh she emits. We need to talk. I just have to wait till tonight.

'Ariella, it's almost three a.m.'

'Isszzz it?' she slurs. Oh boy.

'You're plastered.'

She laughs, loses her balance, then puts her index finger to her lips.

'Shhhhhhhhhh... Oop!' She stumbles again.

'I wanted to talk to you tonight.'

'Ooooookaaaaayy, Caleb. Let'ssss talk.'

'Not when you're like this.'

'I am puuuurrrfectly fiiiiinee...' She waves her hand around and falls on the sofa.

I grab some water. I laugh to myself. I've never seen my little pisshead drunk.

I stop. She isn't mine.

'I need to get back to yoga.'

She pushes out her bottom lip and reaches both her hands out to grab the glass from me.

'I'm sure yoga will do you a world of good. Right now, let's get you into bed.'

'You take your hands off me.'

She smacks me away. The words hurt much more. She shakes an angry finger at me, then notices it like she is seeing it for the first time.

'I don't even know why I'm mad at you.' She laughs.

'You're mad at me?' I close the distance between us. I catch my disgusting behaviour. She is drunk and I am trying to pump her for info like an absolute coward. I force myself to step away and wait until she's sober. 'Don't answer that. Want me to turn your shower on for you?'

I run to check the boiler and boost the hot water just in case. I return to find her playing with her fingers mid-air.

'Those colours are so pretty. I love the popping sound the yellow one is making,' she remarks, pointing to a blank wall. Real fear grips me.

'Ariella, did you take anything?'

'No!' Her eyebrows form a cute v.

'How much have you had to drink?' There is no way she is seeing pretty colours and hearing them pop on just alcohol.

'Dunno. Not much, but enough,' she responds with child-like stubbornness. 'Nicole was buying. She is reeeeaaally niii-ice.' Her expression threatens to change, stops for a second, then does. 'Oh, wait. I might need to throw up. Don't go anywhere.'

She gets up, only to fall back on the couch. I offer my hand for her to steady herself. Once she's on her feet, I steer her into my bathroom and, just as she predicted, she is sick. I hold her steady, admiring her aim. When she is done I run to the kitchen, grab some more water and make her drink, despite her protestations.

'Caleb?'

My name emerges from her in a way that hits and melts me, right in my chest. 'I'm right here, Aari.' I rub her back.

'I don't think I can stand. The room is spinning.'

I carry her off the floor and deposit her in my bed. I open my bedroom windows and undress her quickly, while trying not to look. Once I have her down to her vest and knickers, I place her under my duvet. She almost instantly pushes it off, complaining that she is too hot. My shower. I make the temperature of the spray a little cooler than normal, and place her, still in her underwear, on the floor of my walkthrough.

'Stay?' she asks, holding on to my hand.

I strip down to my boxers and sit next to her. With the water beating down on us both, I fold her into my arms until it starts to run really cold. When she starts shivering, I turn it off and get us some towels.

'I'm going to have to take off your vest and knickers, okay? I won't look. I just need to put you in some dry clothes. Is that okay?'

She nods as I do my best to focus on the task at hand. I put her in a clean T-shirt from my drawer and my boxers. I know I am an arsehole. I should have grabbed her clothes, but didn't because I told myself I shouldn't be rifling through her knicker drawer. But truthfully, I love seeing her in my clothes. I put her in my bed and arrange the covers around her. I pull her into me and lie there next to her, until she starts her cute little teddy bear snores; then I place a double-lined bin next to her before I head back into the living room.

I call Nicole. I don't give a shit how late it is.

'What the fuck are you playing at?'

'Ha! Ariella? She's fun.'

'What did you do, Nicole?'

'You weren't talking, so I decided to ask her instead. The drink wasn't working, so I added a little something to it. She just became incoherent and kept saying that she wanted to go to yoga. Booooring.'

'I'm reporting you to HR.'

'Go ahead. Did I mention that I got that "something" from Lara?'

'You need to stop this shit, tout-fucking-suite, because—'

She hangs up and I feel powerless. She plans to take Lara down with her. When I return to the bedroom to check on Ariella, she has discarded all the covers, so I replace the duvet with a light blanket.

'I'm going to look after you, I promise,' I say. I've disappointed her with Dash. I've disappointed myself with the way things ended on Friday night. I should have done things properly, like I'd planned. I should have resisted and kept walking. If I had done that, though, I wouldn't have a piece of her with me. I felt like I was flying before Zachary's little intervention.

I email work and say we have food poisoning. If Nicole gave her what I think she did, she'll need a good twenty-four hours until she is back to normal, so I'll wait it out with her. I really want to get into bed with her but now she's asleep, I'd be getting in purely for my benefit. I grab the pillow she's somehow tossed off the bed and the discarded duvet. I make a bed on the floor beside her and I fall asleep easily, listening to her breathing.

I check on her before I go for a quick run the next morning. I have some breakfast while I prepare her grapefruit, knowing that when she gets up I'll be in the firing line.

She eventually surfaces, pissed off, at almost noon.

'What did you do, Caleb?'

'I didn't do anything. You came home drunk and on something last night, declared your love for Nicole, threw up in my bathroom and passed out. I put you in bed and told work we had food poisoning, because I have no idea what Nicole put in your drink.'

'Nicole spiked my drink?'

'Yes, and it scared the shit out of me.'

'I'm calling HR and then I'm calling the police,' she starts, walking to her bag on the sofa.

'You can't. She got it from Lara.'

Ariella stops. Yup. Nicole 1, Human Decency 0.

'Want some water?'

'I'm calling Lara.'

'That's not a good idea. Let's just deal with one crime at a time?'

Lara is downright feral. There will be no polite conversation with Nicole.

'Everything's such a mess. I want to do my job, come home, cook and just be normal.' Her eyes start to pool with tears. I want to hold her and tell her I am here for her, but I am aware that I am also part of the mess. Although, I can't help hoping that her idea of normal is being here with me.

'I might be able to help with that. Can we talk about Sunday?'

'Caleb, what Jasper said to you was shameful and offensive; and I'm sorry. I put you in a situation that you didn't deserve to be in.'

'I actually wanted to talk to you about Dash being here when you came back.'

'Nothing to explain. I overreacted. I knew what I was getting myself into.' That infuriating tight smile returns.

'Ariella, stop it. I messed up – okay? Nothing happened.

I've known her for years and she came round for food because the pub stopped serving. She made a pass and I stupidly didn't say no, but I stopped it before I did something I really regretted. When you came in, I felt sick to my stomach.'

'I'm no better, I kissed Jasper on Sunday. I couldn't help it. Maybe we both let ourselves down.'

She shrugs like it is no big deal, but I know that's total bollocks. I play along.

'So, are you and Jasper going to try again?'

'No. Not now anyway. We're working on being friends and this time, no judgement or strings attached.'

'But he wants you back.'

'Yes. I want him back too, and think I always will. But I'm also aware that we may never make it back.'

'Where does that leave us?'

'Caleb, we're friends.'

'We took it somewhere else this weekend, though.'

'Yes. It was fun and I don't have any regrets. I also completely understand that it has run its course.'

'Has it?'

'Caleb, come on. Your friend on Sunday may have been a mistake, but you're going to be out there again soon and I can't go on your list. I live here. I'll have front-row seats to your shenanigans.'

'That's not—'

'Caleb, I'm sorry, I need to shower and do my teeth. I feel, to put it bluntly, foul.'

She runs away to hide in her shower. I let her. I know this has all been a little much. She went from zero to a five-person emotional pile-up in two days. She needs time to sort through it.

While she's in there my phone pings. It's Nicole.

How's the food poisoning? Lol.

You could have killed her.

I don't know what you're talking about.

My phone starts to ring. Nicole. I switch it to silent and return to work.

'My head hurts.' Ariella emerges in a full grandpa-pyjamas set I haven't seen before. I've only ever seen her in the bottoms with a vest. She clearly feels she needs the baggy button-down top to ensure she doesn't give me any ideas. I inspect her carefully as she hops on the island top to eat her grapefruit. It's the exact spot where we... She catches me looking and climbs down. She just had the same thought.

I grab some painkillers from the drawer, throw them at her, fill a glass with water and make her drink it. I stand opposite, in silence.

'Why are you being weird?' I ask straight out. I am going for it.

'Weird?'

'Yes. Weird. You're hiding. I know this weekend meant something to you. I know you're pissed off with me. Contrary to my stupidity on Sunday night, it meant something to me too.'

'Caleb, I can't be one of your friends with benefits,' she says, pointing her spoon at me.

'Maybe I don't want to go back to having friends with benefits. Dash was a bit of a lapse in judgement.'

'"Dashes" are par for the course. Honestly, I'm not mad at you. I was a little hurt, I guess, but not surprised.' She shrugs. This is not the intended result.

'I don't want "Dashes" to be par for the course.'

'Caleb, stop.'

'Why?'

'Because part of me feels like I'm cheating on Jasper.'

'But you're not together.'

'I know, but he's constantly here.' She taps her index finger to her temple.

'Let's clear your head then.' I pass her a page ripped out of my notebook, setting my plan to dislodge Jasper in motion.

She takes it curiously. 'What's this?'

'I got you a month's pass to the yoga studio near the station. Here's the activation code. It has a great write-up, so I booked you into a class today, because sweating out whatever's in your system might help. There's another one near work where celebrities go to realign their chakras or whatever. They have private shower pods and smoothie bars with fresh grapefruit too, so you can grab breakfast there if you want. I got you a month's pass for that one too, so you can decide which you prefer.'

A smile spreads across her face, lighting up her eyes.

'Thank you. You didn't have to.'

'You're welcome. It seemed pretty important to you. Anyway, you should go, a class starts in an hour.'

'Will you come with me?'

'It's supposed to give you space from everything, me included.'

'Please? Just this once?' she pleads.

'Okay. Just this once.'

I grab some swim shorts and we make our way to what looks like a yoga shop. Ariella walks in, finds an assistant and dispatches her to find two sets of yoga wear in a medium. We leave with clothes, mats and towels in under ten minutes. She is childlike in her excitement and chatters as we walk to the studio. I like her like this.

But the next ninety minutes are a nightmare. Normally, being surrounded by women in tiny bits of Lycra, making suggestive body shapes, would be heaven; but throw in a room the temperature of the Sahara and encouragement for me to make the same body shapes, and it becomes hell. Of course, Ariella sails through. For me, it is torture. I have the flexibility of a brick.

I reward us on the way home with a huge, loaded pizza from the local takeaway. Ariella whispers that she has just seen a mouse as I order. She's minimising. It is a bloody rat the size of a squirrel. I don't care. I carry the pizza home and inhale a slice in the kitchen before I get in the shower. It's late afternoon by the time I get out, weak with exhaustion. I carry the pizza to the living room, place it on the coffee table and flop onto the couch. Everywhere hurts. Ariella emerges shortly afterwards in the ridiculous pyjamas she was wearing earlier, and I swear that top has even more buttons than it did before.

'*The Wire*?' she says, suggesting the new series we are working through now we've finished *The Sopranos*.

'Two conditions.'

She smiles at me and nods eagerly.

'First. You're sharing this pizza with me. No cooking for you tonight. Secondly. Try and contain yourself when Omar comes on screen.'

'He's lovely, though.'

'I'll never understand it. Everyone else in the world has a crush on Stringer Bell and you're all about low-level criminal Omar? You're not even his type!'

'He never swears and he loves his granny,' she defends him happily.

I have my Ariella back.

'Okay...'

I flip on the TV and Ariella grabs a slice of pizza before she cuddles up to me. She's asleep by the end of the second episode and I watch a third, enjoying the weight of her body asleep against mine. At some point, I too fall asleep for a short while, waking up to a dark apartment lit only by the TV screen. It's only nine thirty. Today has been a good day and I am not going to push it. We can be like this for a while and take it slowly. All I need to do is be all the things Jasper wasn't. I'll be present, I'll encourage her to do anything she wants, and I'll be here to help her face the world. I kiss her head before I wake her.

'Hey. Time for bed.' I stroke her arm. She stirs and yawns.

'What time is it?'

'Quarter to ten.'

She sits up slowly as she stretches.

'I'm sorry. I wasn't a very nice person to you earlier, Caleb.'

'I'm just glad you're okay. Nicole isn't going to get away with what she did, I promise.'

'Please don't do anything. I'll speak to Lara about it.'

'You know Lara's handling of the situation will be much worse than mine, don't you?'

We both laugh.

'I have no choice. Nicole has involved her. Y'know, Lara and Jasper—'

'I'd rather not talk about Jasper, Ariella.' I'm tired of hearing his name.

I move her off me and, as I start to stand, she gently puts her hand on my arm to stop me.

'I was just going to say—'

'Were you thinking about him this weekend? When we were... together?' I interrupt accusingly.

'Caleb, I could barely string a rational thought together, let alone think about anyone else. I was completely consumed by you and everything else disappeared – that's a little scary. You leave very little room for anything other than yourself. Unfortunately, it's left us here.'

'Here doesn't seem like such a bad place to be. Does it?' I ask, ready to lay my cards on the table. I am going to tell her.

'No, but this isn't just about me.'

'Shouldn't it be, though?' I stroke her hair and she wells up.

Yup, I am going to have to deal with Jasper whether I like it or not. He isn't going anywhere. Damn it.

'Also, I really hate wearing turtlenecks.' She sighs. 'They're so uncomfortable. Lara said I looked like Steve Jobs.'

The laugh I produce explodes out of me; she joins in and we can't seem to stop. It feels good, releasing the tension that has built up over the last few days. Her eyes are gleaming with laughter as she absent-mindedly touches her neck. I stay my hand.

'Thank you for looking after me today, and for the yoga. It means more than you know.' She's sincere. I'm on the right track.

'I just want you to be happy. If that's yoga, tolerating Lara, finding you comfortable turtlenecks, making Jasper disappear, even if it's only for a while...'

'Thanks, but for the last bit I'm good.'

'You sure? Because I heard I'm all-consuming.' I raise an eyebrow and throw her a smirk.

'Go consume elsewhere. You have plenty of options.'

'I don't want plenty of options.' I meet her eyes.

'Caleb...'

'While we're being brutally honest, you pretty much consume me too.' I let my hand travel up her pyjama-covered thigh. I like that Ariella is watching it move and doesn't stop me. This is not the plan. I'm supposed to be keeping my hands to myself. It's bloody difficult, but I remove my hand. 'Sorry.' I look away.

'I like the way you touch me,' she admits under her breath.

'Then let me.' I meet her eyes.

Her mouth is on mine; open, letting me in. I waste no time pulling her onto my lap. She holds my face as she kisses and straddles me. I open the button at the top of her pyjama shirt and she immediately stops. I search her eyes as I undo the next button slowly. When it pops open, she closes her eyes. She doesn't want to do this. I stop myself.

'We don't have to.'

Ariella lifts her pyjama top over her head to reveal her vest.

'We have layers.' I laugh, trying to put a smile on her face. It works.

'We do,' she whispers back as she comes back in with her mouth.

I have free hands and an invitation, so I hook my fingers under the vest's shoulder straps and pull them down to reveal her breasts. I hear her exhale as I close my mouth over one. I find the other with my hand and caress the tip with the surface of my palm. She needs to know that I don't want anyone else but her. I look up to see her mouth ajar, lips wet and parted, with her eyes closed.

'Look at me,' I whisper, and her thick eyelashes part to do as I ask. 'Whatever this is, there's no one else. It's just you.'

I lean in and kiss her. She pulls away a little.

'I'm a big girl, you don't have to say that.'

'Aari, you don't leave a lot of room either.'

I re-engage our kiss, finding her tongue with lustful intent as I carry her to my bedroom. Laying her on her back, with one swift move I pull off her pyjama bottoms, leaving her with just her vest and knickers on. Her eyes are on me, watching, wanting and waiting.

'Just being near you does the craziest things to me, Aari.'

'You're not alone,' she whispers.

'I want you to put your hands over your head, your feet on the bed and open up for me.'

She splays herself open in the diamond shape I request and I can see every bit of her. Her chest is rising and falling in anticipation. Her belly is smooth and soft, waiting to be touched. I undress as she watches me, grab a condom, roll it on swiftly and lie on top of her as I enter her. I feel her stretch and close around me. As I thrust, she counters my movement and comes up to meet me. I need to be close to her. Still inside her, I put my hands behind her back and hold her close. Her chest is now crushed against mine and I can hear every breath she takes as I thrust into her. She wraps her legs round me and offers me a slow moan. Then, with one swift move, she flips me on my back and assumes her position on top.

'Fuck, Ariella,' I gasp as she adjusts her body.

Is that a dirty smile? I reach my hands up her belly, waist and chest before I get where I am going. She's speeding up.

'Come for me,' I demand quietly.

I squeeze her breasts tighter and arch my torso up to meet hers. Ariella's hands suddenly land on my chest as she steadies herself. She's pushing me deeper by grinding down. It feels sensational.

'Caleb, I'm...' she whispers, with pleasure, anguish and helplessness all over her face.

That undoes me. She lets out a low moan as she begins to stiffen, which, it now seems, has become my trigger. I try to hold off my climax, but I can't. The feeling of her quivering only accelerates me joining her. I am surprised at the howl I emit when I explode inside her, as she also reaches her climax. We hold each other's eyes right until the point where she collapses on top of me. I can't stop the smile that spreads across my face.

'You look thrilled,' she observes, also smiling.

'That's because you're thrilling.'

She sweetly hides her face from mine as I run my fingers up and down her back.

'You know what I enjoyed the most this weekend?' I ask.

'I know this one. You had me on my knees, holding on to the headboard, and you—'

'No. Though that was one of my favourites.'

'No? I was convinced. I can usually tell, because your vocabulary for a few minutes consists purely of my name, preceded by an obscenity of your choice. Shit, Ariella. Fuck, Ariella. Damn, Ariella, and so on... Then you get into the Holys. Holy shit. Holy fuck. Holy Mother...' She counts them off on her fingers as she chuckles to herself.

'You're such a cheeky cow.' I pretend to be offended but, truthfully, I love it when she takes the piss out of me.

'Anyway, tell me, which one was it? I was pretty certain that was it. You swore the most, by far, when you were doing that.'

She isn't wrong. That's going to be repeated. I make a note. She enjoyed it too.

'I think I enjoyed Sunday morning the most.'

I pull her close to breathe her in. We lie there silently, embracing each other for a few minutes. I don't want to let her go.

'Caleb,' she starts. 'I really enjoyed Sunday morning too, but it blurred a lot of lines for me. I don't know if I can give that to you.'

I nod, even though the lines are very clear to me. Last Sunday morning was bliss. We woke up entangled in each other's arms after a day of sexual exploration and chasing each other around the apartment. If the shelter knew how many times Ariella and I came close to burning various body parts while cooking for them, they would have had me arrested. She did look cute in nothing but an apron. We were up to greet the sun, talking and kissing all morning, then eventually got into the shower together. She washed me all over and I helped wash, condition and detangle her hair while chattering away. We needed a second shower that morning because we got a little carried away. She made me baked salmon and caviar eggs for breakfast while I prepped her grapefruit, stealing kisses with our bodies rarely disconnecting. After breakfast, we watched a couple of news shows under a blanket with wandering hands, kissing, arguing and laughing, before we got dressed and walked to the tube station holding hands. I wanted to lock our front door and never leave. I wouldn't have cared if we never had sex again. We were so connected; it felt like we had blended into one.

'Snippets of Saturday then?'

'I'd like that.' She looks away smiling, embarrassed.

It's not what I want, but it will do for now. However, I'm going to throw everything I have at her, to get Jasper out of her system.

'That's such good news...'

I break our embrace and get on top of her, kissing my way down her body as she giggles. I slide her knickers back off slowly, then plant kisses up her perfect leg until my mouth finds her delicate space. I raise an eyebrow and throw her a wink before I bury myself in it. It doesn't take long for her moans to take over.

TWENTY-FIVE

ARIELLA

I am seized by an intense panic as my eyes open. I remind myself to breathe deeply and slowly. The bedside clock flashes 05:12 at me as my ears tune in to Caleb's breathing. I am waking up in Caleb's bed. Naked. Again. What am I doing? I roll out of bed quietly on to my knees, then scramble through a crumpled pile of clothes on the floor, searching for my underwear. The humiliation settles in. I need to make my escape with whatever little dignity I have left.

I eventually find my underwear and tiptoe silently to the door.

It seems like for ever since I deserted my date on Friday. In reality, it has only been four days. Oh no. Piers. This is turning into a nightmare. Friday was completely unexpected. I had dismissively toyed with the idea of getting under someone, but hadn't expected to; and I certainly hadn't expected it to happen with Caleb. In my imagination, it was going to be awkward, embarrassing, silent and inconvenient, so I nixed the idea.

However, Saturday was hands down the best twenty-four hours I have spent with another person, ever. I had a lot of fun. We talked and laughed a lot. It was easy and comfortable. I felt seen, safe and in control. I want more. I catch myself smiling. Oh boy.

The kettle boils, so I fill my cup and watch the tea steep as I sit at the bar.

'Morning...' Caleb sneaks up, kissing me behind my ear. 'We missed you in bed.'

He presses his hips against me, just in case I am wondering who 'we' is. Oh dear. I should do it now. End it, Ariella.

'I needed some tea and didn't want to wake you.'

When he swivels the stool round I'm met by shining, mischievous eyes, framed by messy dark hair and a naughty grin. I am surprised at how happy I am to see him. Stop it, Ariella.

'I wish you had...'

He traces a finger along my chin and kisses the top of my head before he tilts my face up and kisses me on my mouth. My body immediately responds. In what seems like a flash, my legs are apart, Caleb is standing between them and his hand is right at the top of my thigh, teasing a destination we both know will end any resistance. I should end this now. I can't help kissing him back; his hand shifts and his fingers make their way behind my underwear. I let him stroke me.

'You feel so good,' he sighs in my mouth.

He makes me feel desired. Caleb watches me with a sexy smirk as he brings me close to the edge.

'Give me your hand.'

He guides my hand where he has just been, and together we bring me over.

'Bloody hell, you're beautiful when you come. Good morning, Ariella.'

He kisses me, then brings my fingers to his mouth. I need to stop. I push him away gently.

'Caleb, I need to get to work; and super early, so we don't walk in at the same...'

'Why?'

'We were both off sick together. We should stick with keeping a lid on this.'

He starts kissing me again.

'We live together. No one is going to think there's anything sketchy about us getting to work together. Besides, we have a bit of time.'

'Only, we never arrive or leave together, ever.'

'I don't think anyone cares.'

His kiss deepens. I am falling into him. I can't afford to do that. I pull away, catching my breath.

'They do. I didn't want to tell you this, but people are betting on whether you'll get into my pants, and when.'

'I know; I started it,' he dismisses and comes back in for another kiss.

'You what?'

'I started the pool. It was a joke.' He shrugs.

I get up. As far as wake-up calls go, I can't imagine I'd need a bigger one. I cross my arms and stare at him.

'A joke?' I challenge. He looks confused.

'Yeah. Just a bit of fun. I don't think anyone took it seriously.'

I leave my tea and start walking to my room.

'Aari! Come on.' I ignore him and keep walking. 'Does it help that I lost?'

I stop and turn round. The only way this has a positive outcome is if he bet against any success with me.

'Tell me you bet that you weren't going to sleep with me?'

'Not really...'

'What did you bet, Caleb?'

'Two weeks?' He winces.

I stare at him in disbelief, turn round, walk into my room and slam the door. What a jerk.

. . .

I was a bundle of nerves mixed with anger, going in. Of course Caleb started a pool. He keeps showing me who he is and I keep ignoring it. I steel myself to face questioning glances as people pour in, and summon even more courage when I make my way to the 10 a.m.

'Hi, darling, are you okay? I called you a couple of times yesterday. It just kept ringing out.' Lara hugs me, concerned.

'Yeah, I feel better.'

'I heard you had a bad tummy. I'm suspicious.' She laughs.

'That's my story and I'm sticking to it.' I smile. I want to ask her about Nicole but decide it's best left until lunch.

She smirks.

'Why did Caleb have a bad tummy too? A bunch of us know exactly where you were on Monday night, and it was nowhere near him – or eating, for that matter.'

'Are people talking about why we weren't here yesterday?' I try to change the focus.

'A few of the girls touched on it at lunch. Nicole, of all people, she stamped it right out and asked us all to have some compassion. Compassion. From Nicole.' She guffaws a little too loudly, turning a couple of heads.

'Wait... did you say "us"?'

'Yeah! I was there running interference. They like me; it's you they're still trying to figure out. The one thing they do know is that there's no way anything is going on between you and Caleb. Ugh, gross.' She shudders for effect.

'Thank goodness,' I respond, knowing that I have just lied to Lara.

'I've got your back, girl. You should still watch out for Nicole, though. I know you buried the hatchet, the way you were hugging on Monday night.'

Lara rolls her eyes. It's out before I can control it.

'We were hugging because Nicole spiked my drink, Lara. I can't call the police and I can't report her to HR, because she's going to make sure they know that she got it from you. Please tell me you're not some drug dealer?'

Lara's shock silences her, but only temporarily.

'That bitch! I'm going to—'

'Shhh!' I try to silence her.

'Don't shush me, Aari. This is serious! Seriously, like, what the fuck?'

'Lara!'

The entire room is now looking at us and Christopher is giving her a look that would freeze a meeker person. I disappear behind my notebook as Lara mouths a quick sorry.

'Right,' Christopher begins. 'Good to have Caleb and Ariella back from a ferocious bout of food poisoning yesterday that rendered them both, weirdly enough, incapacitated at the same time.'

There are a few chuckles and I don't look up. If Christopher is commenting, it's bad news. He tends to stay above the fray. It's one of the reasons I like him.

'Let's kick off.'

I sink further into my chair and focus on following the events team's updates, making sure they don't miss anything, until the meeting is over. Now all I have to do is make it to the safety of my desk. I wait for the room to empty. When Lara and I get up to leave, I see Nicole standing by the open door to our main workspace. She waits for Lara to walk past before she steps out in front of me.

'Aari,' she coos, with fake concern dripping from her voice. I want to ask her to use my full name, but I decide that it is easier to get this over and done with. 'How are you feeling?'

'Fine,' I answer quickly, trying to get past her.

She moves to obstruct my path out of the room. She wants the whole office to have eyes on us without being able to hear what we are saying.

'You know it was just a little joke on Monday? No big deal.' She shrugs.

'Drugging a person without their knowledge is a crime. I believe it's also grounds for immediate dismissal, but I'd have to ask HR,' I deliver matter-of-factly. She knows I'm not going to do that without hurting Lara, but plays along anyway.

'It doesn't need to go that far, Aari. It was just a silly joke. *Je suis désolée.*' She smiles sheepishly, tips down her head and looks through her eyelashes at me.

I see Lara fuming behind her and choose not to dignify her insincere apology with a response. When she doesn't get a reaction from me, she turns to exit and the next thing I see is Nicole, almost in slow motion, hurtling through the air, to the ground as a high heel is sent flying. Her head narrowly misses the corner of a desk before she lands on her hands to protect her face. The gasp from the whole floor is almost deafening. I catch Lara quickly tucking an angled, outstretched foot back in. I give her a disapproving look before I drop to my knees to help Nicole. Lara just shrugs a shoulder silently, then steps over Nicole to get to her desk.

'Get off me.' Nicole pulls away as a couple of the guys join me. 'Lara!' she screams. 'You tripped me on purpose.'

Lara, almost at her desk now, turns round, calmly clutching her notepad to her chest. She looks more bored than remorseful.

'Did I? *Je suis désolée.*'

Lara doesn't try to pretend it was an accident and just continues to walk to her desk. She's livid. I understand why, but it all needs to stop. Everything, everywhere needs to stop imploding.

'I need you to stop, Lara,' I request as we sit in our favourite Japanese lunch spot.

'I haven't finished with her, Aari. She could get me fired.'

'Then maybe you should stop supplying drugs to people,' I snap quietly. 'Nicole would be cleaning out her desk right now if you weren't her source.'

'What happened was—'

'I don't care what happened, Lara. If I can show restraint, you can try not to kill her in the middle of the office.'

Lara leans back, averts her eyes, crosses her arms over her chest and sticks out her bottom lip.

'Are you sulking?'

'Yes. You're telling me off and I didn't do anything. I've had that molly for ages. CrimeSpree came to office drinks and was handing it out like sweets. He insisted I have one, so I palmed it and tossed it in my bag. Fast-forward to Monday evening, Nicole asked if I still had it, so I gave it to her.'

'That's it?'

'That's it! And she knows I'm not going to drop CrimeSpree in it.'

'I need you to let it go.'

'I can't. She's got me pinned in and I want to beat her face in for it.'

'You're going to have to. I don't want to have to deal with this too.' I deliver that last line a little more painfully than I intended to. Lara's expression changes.

'Babe, what's going on? It's obviously not just Nicole.'

I swallow the tears that threaten to erupt. Thankfully, our food arrives, giving me time to compose myself.

'Things are just hard at the moment, especially with Zambia.'

'Ariella Mason, don't lie to me. You can deliver Zambia in your sleep. It's Jasper, isn't it? Ariella, you can't go back to Jasper.'

'So I keep hearing.'

'Ooooh, I thought I was a lone voice out here in these streets.'

I pop a rock shrimp in my mouth to avoid answering. I don't trust myself to stop short of telling her everything.

'It's not Dahlia. She's the most likely to have reservations, but she loves him... Oh, yuck. Caleb. I feel like vomiting for actually holding the same position as him, but in this specific scenario it must be done.'

'Caleb was very sweet and looked after me yesterday.'

'Ew. Just make sure everything in your underwear drawer is still there and your new bestie hasn't been rummaging, because that's the closest he's going to get.'

'He'd never do that.' I defend him automatically. Lara's eyes narrow at me.

'Ariella, Caleb may be good in a crisis, but he's intrinsically selfish and I'm sure he's a walking vaccine for some STD that none of us have heard of yet. All these days you've been taking off together are obviously messing with your sense of judgement.'

'He's not a bad person, even though he does some childish things like run a pool about sleeping with me.'

'I know. I had fifty quid on "never", but he pulled it this morning. I assumed he realised he doesn't stand a chance and doesn't want to pay up, so is pulling a fast one. Who told you?'

I feel sick to my stomach. 'You knew? Thanks, Lara. I had the pleasure of hearing it from Piers.'

'That wanker? I bet he told you just before he tried to stick his tongue down your throat.'

'He told me when I shared that I live with Caleb. Although, I would have preferred to hear it from you.'

'That stalker has known you live with Caleb for weeks. In fact, I have it on good authority that he told Caleb he was going to crack on to you in Zambia.'

'Piers's behaviour isn't my grievance. You not telling me about the pool is, Lara. You're supposed to be my friend.' I unfairly feel more annoyed with Lara than I am with Caleb and Piers.

'I didn't tell you because it was just another stupid thing tossed around at the office drinks that you didn't need to know about and were guaranteed to miss anyway, because you refuse to engage in any universe you're not the centre of. Maybe you would've found out earlier if you'd told me you moved in with Caleb. Any particular reason why you didn't tell me, your supposed friend? I suppose it's just another thing you hide.' Lara raises her voice accusingly. 'I assumed Caleb started the pool because he was bored and found out you'd broken up with Jasper. Of all the fucking people you could've moved in with, Ariella, and then you don't tell me for weeks! Even Nicole found out before me. Fucking *Nicole*!'

Lara and I are having our first fight and I don't need it. Right now, I am in an uncomfortable place with Jasper, Zachary, Nicole, Piers, Caleb... and now Lara. The bodies keep piling up.

'I'm full.' I stand, leaving four ten-pound notes on the table.

'Ariella Mason, if you walk away from me right now, our friendship is over,' she threatens.

'I believe you just made a case for an absence of friendship, Lara.'

The energy of my fight with Lara stays with me until I reach the safety of my desk, where I compose myself by tapping into my breathing exercises to refocus. When I'm finally calm, I open my eyes to see Piers standing over me, smiling. This is not going to end well.

Thankfully, because it's Wednesday Caleb will be home late, so I get the flat to myself for a few hours. I indulge in a long shower, followed by an ice-cold glass of Chablis while I finish cooking a creamy truffle tagliatelle. Caleb, however, unexpectedly turns up early, just as I am grating some truffle on my pasta.

'Aren't you meant to be at Muay Thai?' I sound more abrasive than I intend to.

'Hello to you too. I cancelled the class. I needed to talk to you.'

He approaches for a hug. Oh no. I duck under his arm and walk to the other side of the island. I clock the surprise on his face out of the corner of my eye. I know I've just been hurtful, but I am hurt too.

'Any of that going?' He nods at my food.

'In the oven. I made yours with cavatappi and truffle butter, because I thought you'd be back late.'

He makes his way to the oven to find his pasta bubbling away. He grabs a bowl, scoops some in, and takes the stool next to mine. I am contemplating taking my food into my room when he speaks.

'I'm sorry about the pool. It was a ridiculous conversation at the drinks with a couple of guys from the team. Maybe five people knew about it. I honestly didn't take it seriously. People mentioned a few quid in bets and timelines, but nothing was written down. To be honest, I'd forgotten about it by my third pint. It was a shitty thing to do.'

I'm just going to come out with it.

'Caleb, I don't think we should sleep together any more. We should put this weekend down to, I don't know, getting it out of our systems. Now it's done, it's done, y'know?'

A response comes back quicker than I thought it would.

'If that's what you want, consider it done.'

'I'm sorry.'

'Don't be. We had fun.' Caleb just carries on eating, unbothered.

'Thank you for ending the pool.'

'It was stupid.'

We eat in silence and I feel a great loss because this isn't what our evenings look like; they're normally chatty and fun. I make the effort to lighten things up a little.

'I ended my *friendship* with Piers today.'

This will, for sure, have him pressing for the details. Caleb likes a good gossipy story. I wait for it. But all I get is, 'He'll get over it. Are you done?'

I look at my bowl of half-eaten pasta and nod. He clears it from in front of me, then starts washing up. The emptiness I feel quietly watching him is hard to bear, but we need to do this. When he's finished, he grabs his gym bag and heads into his room.

All of a sudden, I feel alone. I'm used to being by myself, but this is different; everything feels out of kilter. I step into my bathroom and have my second shower of the evening. I feel better, and I know what to do now. While the feeling is still there, I get dressed and knock on Caleb's bedroom door.

'Yup?'

He's sitting on his bed with his laptop open.

'Can we talk some more?'

He nods before he puts his laptop aside and gestures for me to sit on the bed.

'I was awful to Lara today.'

I unexpectedly burst into tears. Caleb is beside me in an instant. When he puts his arms round me, my sobs become uncontrollable.

'What happened?'

'I just got angry. She knew about the pool and she didn't tell me.'

'She probably thought you didn't need to know, because it was such a throwaway conversation; not that it excuses the pool. I remember her putting fifty quid on never *very* loudly, if that helps?' He smiles warmly as he defends her.

'She could've hurt Nicole really badly. Her head was

centimetres from a desk corner when she fell.'

'I saw that. It was brutal, but Nicole is threatening everything Lara loves. You, her job, her clients, her reputation, and even, potentially, her ability to make a living, ever again.'

'Then she wouldn't stop digging around about this weekend—'

'Aari, I don't mean to downplay how you feel, but these aren't massive infractions, compared to the shit Lara gets up to normally. Just tell her you're sorry and everything will go back to normal.'

'It won't.'

'Why?'

'Because I lied to her.'

'About what?'

I look away and shake my head.

'Aaaah. She asked if something happened between us, and you denied it.'

I nod. I feel Caleb's body deflate with a heavy sigh as silence descends.

'Tell her,' he says quietly after a while. 'She's all you've got. If you need her to know, to make you okay again, just tell her.'

'But we promised each other...'

'Ariella. She's your best friend and this is new territory for you. You need her. Tell her.'

Perhaps it is his kindness, or him giving me permission to do the one thing he made me repeatedly promise not to do, but I kiss him. It is meant to be a short, friendly kiss, until he kisses me back. Then I can't bring myself to stop and, it seems, neither can he. I wrap my arms round his neck as the kiss intensifies, with our tongues moving in a perfect, familiar rhythm. With no warning, he breaks it, shaking his head.

'No, Ariella. We handled this earlier. You're right. We shouldn't be doing this. It's confusing for both of us at the moment.'

I feel embarrassed. 'I'm sorry, Caleb.'

We hold each other's gaze for a couple of seconds before he continues.

'We should sleep on it and try to keep it platonic.'

I nod. He's right. He leans in to kiss my forehead, then stretches out his hand. I take it and let him lead me outside of his bedroom door. He offers me a small smile.

'Goodnight.'

With that, he returns into his bedroom, and quietly closes the door inches from my face, leaving me standing alone in the cold, dark living room. I leave the lights off, return to my room and sit on the bed for a couple of minutes, before I reach for my phone and text Lara.

I'm sorry.

I wait. Nothing. I resign to do this face to face tomorrow, so I retreat to do my teeth. I hear the ping from the bathroom and run to get it.

Oh babe. I'm sorry too. I've been such a shitty friend. I should have told you about the bet and warned you about Piers. And because you're my favourite person in the whole world I'll try to leave Nicole alone. I love you and you should tell me off more often. I deserve it much more than you realise.

I wipe my tears.

Lunch tomorrow? I'm buying.

You are. The manager gave us lunch for free today, thanks to you being distressed. Steak, lobster and some cheeky lunchtime bubbles?

Yes please.

TWENTY-SIX

CALEB

I was useless all day yesterday. All I could think about was her smell, the softness of her body, the sound of her laugh. I especially couldn't shake the memory of her face, invaded by pleasure. My stupidity was going to rob me of that, so I needed to right some wrongs. I sent a message to everyone I could think of to reconfirm that there was no pool.

There. Done. I run my hands through my hair, which is getting long and beginning to flop in my face. A memory of Ariella noticing how long it has become while washing my hair and then drying it on Sunday morning, jumps in. She was gentle, even tender, and it opens the floodgates. The images unfold rapidly. Joining her, already naked, in the shower. Her smiling through the shower water running down her face. Me attacking her with the hand attachment. The way her eyes turned into slits when she laughed, the softness of her lips when she tried to distract me and make a grab for it. Her flipping the shower to the coldest setting, just as she jumped out.

Today, nothing has changed. She's dancing through my mind and I can't focus on anything. I thought the last nail was well and truly in the coffin at dinner last night. But then she came into my room. If I hadn't found the strength to escort her out – and trust me, I had to dig deep – we'd definitely be over. I want her to trust me. She'd had a shitty day and was feeling vulnerable. She needed Lara, not me; and I wasn't going to step into that place just because it was vacant. I want her to need *me*.

Unfortunately, the chances of that are now hair thin, because she is going to tell Lara. I wanted some privacy to just see where this might go, but I know a full-on anti-Caleb propaganda campaign, with Lara firmly situated at mission control, will kill any possibility of that. Lara confirms my fears by text after lunch.

> Seriously though, what is wrong with you? Do you put crack at the end of that thing?

I howl. Lara has just unintentionally let slip that not only did Aari admit to enjoying the time she spent with me, but she's not sure if she is done with us. I take a jab.

> You offering? Nicole recommends you highly.

> Funny. Ariella is going to be surrounded by so much available, charming Viking dick when she comes to Norway with me tomorrow, you'll be lucky if she returns on Sunday.

Of course Lara would cripple me at the kneecaps and target the weekends. It won't surprise me if she has a plan in motion for every weekend from this point on. Thankfully, I enjoy Ariella most during the week; chatting in the kitchen, eating, watching *The Wire* together on the couch with her soft body pressed against mine and polishing off wine and affogatos. It's heavenly.

But if Ariella is going away with Lara this weekend, I want

her to remember me. I decide to skip the office drinks and head straight home to lay grounds for a counterattack.

'Hey,' I call out.

She's already out of the shower, and rummaging in the fridge. She stops what she is doing and looks embarrassed.

'I'm sorry about last night.'

I dismiss it lightly. 'You were in a shitty place.'

'I shouldn't have blurred the lines.'

Bless her. She has no idea what I have in store, especially now that Lara is involved. I intend on making sure that she finds it impossible *not* to blur those lines. It's just going to take a little time and patience.

'You've had a lot to deal with in a really short space of time. Remember what life looked like this time last week?'

'It was all so simple.' She smiles.

'Let's just go back to that. Wine. Food. *The Wire*. Omar.' I raise my eyebrows twice when I mention her favourite character's name. She laughs.

'Okay,' she agrees and turns back to the fridge. 'How does Thai sound?'

'It sounds great!'

I walk into the kitchen and shake her bun. I intentionally lightly graze the back of her neck when I drop my hand. She stops. I pretend I have done nothing.

'I'll go and get changed.'

I smile inside as I walk into my bedroom and hop in the shower. I plan on keeping her focus squarely on me. There will be no Viking dick for her, not that she would consider going there; but I am dealing with Lara here, so I am not taking any chances. I know every inch of Ariella's body and I am going to use it.

She's still in the kitchen when I emerge. I decide we should have beers, for no other reason than to move her away from the front of the fridge. I place my hands lightly on her hips and shift her like I have done hundreds of times before, with a gruff, 'Move over, Mason.' I make sure I stroke the base of her back in the process. She stops again and I ignore her like nothing out of the ordinary is happening.

'Caleb, Lara's invited me to Oslo this weekend for a couple of gigs. I thought it would be good to get away from everything.'

I can tell she is nervous, anticipating my reaction.

'Great idea. You haven't stopped since Zambia fell in your lap, and this sounds like fun. I think it'll also be good to get some distance from everyone, including me.'

'It's nothing to do with you...'

'Ariella, we decided to go back to last week, remember? Let's be honest. Yes, you need a break, and one of the things you need a break from is me.' I put my hand softly under her chin and lift her eyes to mine. 'Please make sure you enjoy yourself?' I let go. 'Wanna eat at the bar or in front of the TV?'

'I don't mind. I can pop dinner in bowls if you want to eat and watch.'

'I'll get the blanket. Let's do the TV.'

By the time I return, she has set the coffee table up with our bowls and is grabbing the beers from the counter. I park myself in my space on the couch and, when she joins, she sits at the furthest end of it, practically perched on the arm. I give her a questioning look, nodding at the distance on the couch between us.

'Come here.'

I reach over, grab her by the waist and pull her towards me. She allows herself to be dragged close.

'Don't make this awkward, just because we're no longer sleeping together, Ariella. I'm not going to bite you. We'll be all right. I promise.'

'Okay.' She nods, trusting me completely.

I feel like shit, but that doesn't last long. She is leaning comfortably against me in five minutes, and asleep in my arms just as the second episode starts. It's the best feeling in the world. I am not letting this go without a fight. Normally, I'd wake her up when I drag myself to bed, but this time I get comfortable and leave us on the couch for the rest of the night.

'Caleb, it's twenty past five,' she whispers, stroking my hand awake.

I know this already, because I have had a terrible night's sleep; but it was worth it, listening to her breathe and feeling her body rise and fall all night. We get off the couch and I ferry our bowls and beers to the kitchen, while she folds the blanket, then follows me with the napkins and cutlery.

'Did you let the shelter know you won't be coming this weekend? It's getting really cold outside.'

The look on her face tells me no.

'If you put all the fresh stuff together in a box, I'll run it over in the morning, then they can use it,' I offer. I may be point-scoring right now but I actually do care about the shelter. It's impossible not to, after doing so many Saturday runs with her.

'Brilliant! Thank you, Caleb.'

She takes a couple of steps towards me and stops. I pretend I don't notice, but I am doing air punches inside.

'No worries.' I turn around and head towards my bedroom, leaving her in the kitchen.

'What are you doing in my house on a Friday night?' Em asks, opening the door.

'Caleb!' Alfie runs past her and flies into my arms. I lift him up.

'Alfie!' I match his excitement.

That's my boy. I drop Alfie's head so he is dangling upside down. Em gives up and lets me and her giggling son in.

'Please don't kill my son.'

I follow her into the unusually quiet house. 'Where is everybody?'

'Seb and Leo are sleeping over at friends', Tim should be back soon and Jack spent the night at Lou's last night.'

'Jack went home?'

'Yes, he's going to spend the weekend, to see how it goes.'

'He's going back. It's all been for nothing.'

'I wouldn't say that. She's been putting in some work. She admits she has a problem.'

'Whatever problem Louisa has isn't going to be fixed in two weeks.'

'Louisa has a problem! Louisa has a problem!' Alfie is now swinging on my arms and singing. I join the chorus two more times.

'I don't have the strength to deal with both of you right now,' Em sighs, while giving me a dirty look. 'Beer?'

'No thanks. Apple juice, straight up, on the rocks please. Apple on the rocks, Alfie?'

'Yeah.'

I sit on the stool and put Alfie on my lap.

'Bartender, make it snappy please,' I demand.

'Yes, bartender! Snappy!' Alfie echoes.

'I hate you,' Em mouths at me.

'What was that, bartender? Hope you're not expecting a tip! Should we tip her?' I laugh and Alfie laughs along with me.

'No tip!' he says, still laughing.

'No tip it is,' I agree.

Em serves up two pretty decent apple juices on the rocks with decorative apple wedges and cocktail umbrellas.

'Want to tell me why are you really here? It's Friday night. We know not to even think about you on a Friday night,' Em interrogates.

'Apart from coming to hang out with my buddy here...' I

hold my palm up and Alfie meets my high five, '... I wanted to check on Jack and maybe take him and your husband out for a beer. Now I know why he's been ghosting me.'

I notice Alfie is keenly following the conversation.

'Alfie, if you let Mum run you a bath and you play in it like a good boy until she comes to get you, I'll get her to pack a bag with your homework, so you can stay with me this weekend. I'll even drop you off at school on Monday morning.'

He is off my lap like a shot, screaming, 'MUM!' as he rushes up the stairs.

'Are you serious?' Em asks, looking delighted.

'Yup. I'll take him. Let's give Tim something to come home for.'

'Tim? I'm just looking forward to being drunk in an hour.'

She runs up the stairs as fast as her son and, within minutes, she's back downstairs with a video monitor, so she can keep an eye on Alfie in the bath.

'Tell me everything,' she demands as she grabs a bottle of wine and glass before sitting down opposite me. 'Did you take my advice?'

'I really wanted to. In fact, I had a plan in motion, but other circumstances came up, things changed rapidly, and...'

'You didn't cook her dinner, did you?' Em has her judgy face on.

'No.'

'But you slept with her, didn't you?'

'Yes.'

'Let me guess – now she doesn't want to sleep with you any more and things are awkward.'

'A little.'

'In fact, you're round here tonight because she's moved out, and willing to take Alfie because you're going to be home alone this weekend.'

'She's in Norway until Sunday, but that's not why I'm

taking Alfie. I'm taking him because you and Tim might want to get up to no good this weekend. I know you still want a girl.'

'Tim doesn't want the additional debt. Wait. Hold on. You're not moving on to the next available thing? Why?'

'I'll kill you if you repeat this, but I'm done. I don't want anyone else. She's it for me.'

'Caleb. You're smitten?'

'Yeah, and it's bloody annoying.'

Em clasps both her hands over her mouth before she flings herself on me. It feels nice. 'How does she feel about you?'

'Not the same. She thinks she's just a shag.'

'Have you told her any different?'

'No. She's still hung up on Jasper.'

'The super-hot and loaded fiancé? Louisa and I may have drunk-Googled him,' she titters.

'You may have drunk-Googled who?' Tim says, walking into the kitchen.

'Ariella's fiancé,' Em responds jovially.

He looks knackered. 'Move away from Caleb, Em. Goodness knows what contractible diseases he's got.' Tim grabs his wife and kisses her, then pats me on the back.

'Caleb's taking Alfie for the weekend. Are you really concerned?'

Tim's eyebrows shoot up.

'Where's Alfie now?'

'In the bath. I've packed for him already. He's just—'

Tim is gone. Em and I watch on the monitor as Tim coaxes and then lifts Alfie, who gladly complies, out of the bath. Within five minutes, Tim is back downstairs, carrying the weekend bag Em packed and with a pyjama-clad Alfie in tow.

'I've called you boys a car. Two minutes,' he announces as he all but shoves Alfie and me into the hall.

He taps his foot impatiently while we wait for the car. Em

has the grace to look embarrassed. Tim doesn't care. When the car arrives, we get hustled outside the door.

'There.' Tim points vaguely to five random cars sitting in front of the house, before he disappears back inside and slams the door shut.

We hear a particularly loud and delightful yelp from Em as we try to identify the right car. I smile to myself and, for the first time, I realise that is what I want.

TWENTY-SEVEN

ARIELLA

I'm exhausted by the time I return on Sunday night. Lara made sure Norway was busy and loud, but bags of fun. On the jet out with CrimeSpree and his entourage, she rebranded the weekend 'Viking Dick Fest', with the intent to scrub my body of any sexual memories related to Caleb. As soon as we landed, she kept dragging random Norwegians in front of me, and, by Saturday afternoon, I'd gone into hiding with the set-up crew and even volunteered to go jewellery-shopping with Crime-Spree, even though I knew I was leaving Lara unsupervised with a supposedly napping Bamidele.

Surprisingly, I didn't think about London until Jasper reached out on Sunday morning. It was comforting to hear from him, so we ended up talking for most of the morning and made plans to have dinner somewhere fun and categorically unromantic the following Friday.

I return to the flat on Sunday evening to a loud television, messy kitchen, untidy living room and Caleb asleep on the couch, with Alfie, thumb in mouth, asleep on his chest. I laugh at a trail of tiny chocolate-covered fingerprints on the counter, next to big ones. I can't help the smile that spreads across my face. Judging by the pan and bowl, they managed to successfully melt chocolate, but whatever they were doing with the ice cream was an absolute disaster.

The mess is sweet but those two, now with matching haircuts, asleep on the couch, warms my heart. I tiptoe into my room to drop my case, and return to the kitchen to clean up as quietly as I can. When I am done, I pick up the jumpers and shoes around them so the apartment looks tidy again. Only then do I wake Caleb.

'Hi.' I smile at him, stroking his hand.

'Hey! When did you get back?'

'About half an hour ago. I see you got yourself a little guest and you've been attempting home-made Magnums.' I smile at the still-sleeping Alfie and run my hand through his hair.

'Yeah. Kids, chocolate.' He laughs quietly. 'He looks good in a crew cut and low fade, doesn't he? Em is going to lose her shit when she picks him up from school tomorrow.'

'It's sweet. They even flicked it up and to the side like yours.' I laugh. It feels good to be back home.

'What time is it?'

'Eight-ish. Why?'

'I need to put him to bed; gimme a minute.'

Caleb holds on to Alfie tightly as he lifts him off the couch and carries him to his bedroom. He returns a few seconds later with a pillow and a blanket, and tosses them on the couch.

'He is so adorable.'

'I know! Do you know how many women cracked on to me this weekend? That little chick magnet is my wingman for life. Single dads and active godfathers are doing okay out there. Who knew?'

'What did you guys get up to? Want a drink?' I ask, going to pop the kettle on.

'Just some water. He's kept me on my toes. I grabbed him on Friday and we just played video games and hung out here. We delivered your stuff on Saturday, got our haircuts, hit the winter market at the Southbank, did the aquarium and popped into the Royal Festival Hall for some children's festival. We got back pretty late, so today we just went up to the Heath, ran around and played frisbee, went to the urban farm, did our homework, had a bath and put a film on. It's been fun.' Caleb yawns. 'How did the gigs go?'

'I've never done so much walking in such a tiny space. The soles of my feet are killing—'

'These are new.'

Caleb reaches out, puts my hair behind my ear and strokes my earlobe softly. My body fires up. Jeeze! When I finally got to know him, I became comfortable with him touching me. Since things got intimate, every time he touches me, brushes against me or simply moves me out of the way, my body responds in ways that are alien to me. Norway has done nothing to diminish the effect of Caleb's touch.

'Ariella?'

I snap out of it. 'Sorry?'

'I said these are new. Are those diamonds?'

Thankfully, he doesn't touch me again.

'Yes. They're little Viking shields. CrimeSpree gave them to me this morning as a thank-you gift.'

'They suit you. How did the rest of it go?'

'Amazing. Oslo was really busy, but Tromsø was indescribable. We played on a massive boat between glaciers. Lara did a fantastic job with the concert and still found time to parade the male population of Norway in front of me like a buffet. Impressive, but unsettling.'

He smiles that smile at me.

'Did you pick one?'

'No. I've had enough sexual partners for one lifetime. I'm cooling off. Besides, Jasper and I are talking again. He called me on Sunday morning and we're going to meet up as friends.'

'Lucky Jasper.'

I don't like the way that sounds but I ignore it. 'Do you think you could be nice to him if I invite him over?' It isn't really a question.

'Sure. He's your guest. Knock yourself out.'

Caleb makes a show of plumping his pillow and spreading his blanket. I know it's code for 'Get lost, Ariella.'

'Are you still aggravated by what he said at lunch? He didn't mean it.'

'Ariella. I need some sleep now.'

'We should talk about it, Caleb. I don't want you to be uncomfortable when—'

'You just got back from getting away from all of this. You've been home for an hour and we're straight into it. Can we give it a couple of days before we dive back into Jasper?'

'Okay,' I concede.

'Thanks. Night.'

'Goodnight, Caleb.'

He is right. I've been back an hour and things are already tense. I leave it and hop into the shower. I stand under it and enjoy the spray washing away the tenseness of the exchange; leaving it there, for the rest of the week.

I can barely walk, with all the nerves in my tummy and the heels Lara put me in, when I arrive at the restaurant. The soles of my feet are still painful from Norway, but Lara was on such a crazy high from taking me shopping that I didn't argue. Plus, I do like them. I always feel small next to Jasper, and the additional height makes me feel a little more equal to him.

Lara had, according to her, taken pity on me and gone for a short but beautifully tailored black skirt, paired with a black V-neck top, sharply cut wool winter coat and, thankfully, nice thick black tights. The financial pity stopped short when she added the plain black Louboutin heels. I felt like the entire office had eyes on me all day. Thankfully, I left the house in my yoga wear, so I escaped Caleb making fun of me. He did, however, text his feedback around lunchtime.

> You look lovely today. Stop walking around like you stole something and are expecting to be caught any minute. It looks awkward AF. Have fun tonight.

Before I left the office, Lara draped a long, thin gold pendant over my head, shoved some plain gold hoops in my ears, and slipped on a couple of chunky gold bangles.

'You look amazing,' Jasper says with a smile as I walk towards the table.

All my discomfort disappears and I relax immediately. I'm home, because he's here. I shake my head and gesture at the simple but pretty distinct outfit. It isn't too bad, but I still immediately try to justify my appearance to Jasper.

'Lara made me. Emotional blackmail. Long story. How are you?'

He laughs as I slide into the corner booth and sit at a ninety-degree angle, facing him.

'Lara made you, did she? What are you, in primary school?'

'You'd think I'd be over peer pressure by now.'

'She did a great job. Was she responsible for the dress you wore to Dahlia's birthday?'

'Yup.' I nod, laughing.

'I'm sending her flowers. That dress was... diverting.'

Tonight is off to a great start. He seems happy, light and playful; which is exactly what I need him to be.

'You didn't answer; how are you?'

'I'm great. Work is busy, but I'm cutting back my hours.

Also, it's Friday night and you're here. I have nowhere to be tomorrow and I'm a little nervous, but happy we're doing this. I've missed hanging out with you.'

'Me too.'

'In between flying everywhere?' he teases.

'Of course. Zambia and Norway are hardly everywhere. Plus, I haven't fake-laughed at your unfunny jokes in a while.'

'Let's get the booze rolling then. Monkey 47 and tonic?'

'Yes please.'

We order our food shortly after. It's obvious that while we are both trying to figure out how this 'new us' is going to work, we've really missed each other. Why did I think it would be so difficult? I watch his gorgeous face move animatedly while listening to him talk, and he looks like the boy next door again. I miss his face, his kind eyes, his smile; I just want to reach out and touch him.

'So, honestly, how has dating been for you?'

I was expecting it, but the question still catches me by surprise. I really want to tell him, but he is happy and smiling. I decide to be vague.

'It's a jungle out there.' I make a joke of it.

'I know! What happened? One used to start a relationship and, eventually, you got into bed with each other. Now, it seems everyone is ready to hop into bed with you that night. In the morning, you end up on your knees, searching for whatever's left to build into a relationship. It's odd, it makes me feel very old, and scares me a little.'

He has fun in his eyes. I try to play down the jealousy and surprise I'm feeling. I didn't expect him to be celibate, but I didn't expect him to come out with this either.

'And how many times have you found yourself on your knees the last few months?' I ask, before I realise my mouth is open.

He stops eating and raises an eyebrow at me. I pretend to be concentrating on my food and wait for the sledgehammer he is about to take to my chest.

'Twice. After that, I gave up scrambling and just went along for the ride, if you'll forgive the pun. I just ended up feeling worse each time. It's not how I want to feel, so I'm in limbo at the moment and not forcing anything; just living day to day. How about you?'

I am still digesting the fact that Jasper has just admitted to sleeping with at least three women in the last few months. I need to tell him. I want to be honest, but I'm petrified. Here goes.

'I haven't had anywhere near your level of success, Mr Reluctant Playboy, but I did, at one point, get it into my head somehow...' I remind myself not to mention Caleb's name under any circumstances, '...that to get over you, it might be helpful to get under someone else.' I see him pause and swallow hard. 'Are you sure you want to hear this?'

I watch him smile with great difficulty.

'Sure. Keep going. We're friends. You can tell me anything.'

'So, I went on a lot of dates. Like, a lot. But I couldn't get to a place where I was comfortable with someone other than you touching me.' I see relief flood Jasper's face. Oh no Jas, wait for it.

'They'd try to kiss me goodnight on the cheek and I'd duck. I literally ended up pushing one guy's face away with the palm of my hand. It was mortifying. Eventually, I plucked up the courage to go through with it with this one guy and, while it was fun, it was a little dangerous, but I now know that "getting under" someone else doesn't work. The hard way. Pardon the pun.' I start praying that he doesn't ask me who it is. Instead, thankfully, he looks concerned.

'Did they hurt you? What do you mean by dangerous?'

Phew.

'Oh no. It's just that I can see how having meaningless sex

often might begin to feel normal and maybe, eventually, one might start to require that all their partners remain nameless and faceless.'

'I see what you mean. They definitely weren't nameless and faceless to me at the time, but that's probably how I'd want them to end up; especially when things return to normal.'

I ignore the 'return to normal' and I raise my glass quickly.

'To namelessness and facelessness. May you remain so.'

He laughs and clinks his glass. Now there is no way he can ask who I slept with. After that hurdle, we navigate safer territory and I have so much fun, the restaurant around us disappears.

We skip dessert, I pay the bill – much to his annoyance – and we walk out into the cold air, both with more booze in our systems than we intended.

'That was fabulous. Thank you so much for this, Jas.' I go in for a hug.

'We should do it again, it was nice. I can take you home?'

'You live round the corner, you don't need a round trip to Hampstead.' I laugh.

'It's not about the trip, Scraps...' He looks at his shoes. I understand. I don't want the evening to end either. I flag down a black cab.

'Come on. I'll make you an affogato and show you my place.'

'Ariella Mason, are you coming on to me?' He feigns shock and offence.

'Goldsmith, trust me, all you're getting is dessert. You coming?'

'You know, dessert is a fairly common colloquialism for—'

'Forget it.' I shove his shoulder jokingly.

'I'm coming!' He laughs, joining me in the taxi and interlacing his fingers through mine.

. . .

As soon as we get in I take off my heels, get some ice cream out of the freezer, flip on the kettle and grab the coffee from the cupboard. Jasper makes his way to our sound system, connects his phone and, soon, Jill Scott and Daley are singing about pain softly through the living room.

'Is it naff that I made you a playlist?' he says with a laugh as he joins me in the kitchen.

'You'll be asking to see my bedroom next.' I smirk.

'I was planning to, but purely out of curiosity.'

'Come on then.'

I lead Jasper to my room and let him in while I stand in the doorway. Tonight is going well. I don't want to send any unclear messages.

'Nice. I see you learned to pick up your clothes after yourself.'

Cheeky boy. 'You'll be amazed at my list of achievements when you're not around.'

Jas picks up the single photo frame on my bedside table, containing a picture of him and me grinning cheesily towards the camera, looking extremely happy.

'You've still got this?'

He puts the photo frame down gently and walks round to sit at the foot of my bed, opposite the doorway.

'Come, sit with me.' He pats the bed.

'No.' I smile.

'Why?'

'The distance helps my resolve and any signals I may be sending unintentionally.'

Jasper walks towards me quietly and my heart starts beating hard. He stops with his face inches away from mine. He's so beautiful.

'What signals should I be receiving?'

I can't breathe. I know he might kiss me, depending on what I say next.

'That space is a good thing and—'

I don't get to finish. Jasper gently places his lips on mine. He is slow, but intent. He bites my bottom lip and slowly entwines his tongue with mine. He interlaces my fingers with his, then slips his other hand under my top and up my back. He pulls me so close to him, I can feel his heart thumping too. The longer we kiss, the more I want to pack up my things and go back home. Our home. He gently pulls away and reality comes rushing back. We still have a lot to deal with.

'Come home, Aari. We can fix it.'

It's my turn to lean in and kiss him gently, but quickly.

'I need us to fix it first.'

'So, you're in? You want to fix it?'

'I do.' I nod and his face lights up.

'I don't care how hard I'm going to have to work. I'm ready.'

'You're going to have to work harder than telling me that you want to "Teach me a lesson". You know that song is about sexual domination – right?' I point to the speakers, where Robin Thicke's voice is softly issuing sexual threats.

'What? No.'

We both crack up.

I pull him, fingers still intertwined, into the kitchen, where I make the coffee, check on the softened ice cream and start making our affogatos. Just as I finish, the front door crashes open and a very drunk Caleb stumbles in loudly.

'That was fast. Heeeelllooo, Jasper.' Caleb raises a hand, waves hello and sits on a stool at the far end of the island. 'Mmmm, affogatos. Can I join? It's not like I'm a third wheel. You guys are just friends, aren't you?'

I know what he's doing and I don't like it.

'Caleb, come on.'

Before Jasper can pat him on the shoulder, Caleb blocks it with the back of his hand.

'Ariella, you don't mind, do you? Shall we assume our

normal positions?' he asks me before diverting his attention to Jasper.

'I normally sit here.' He points to his seat. 'Ariella usually sits on the counter – here.' Caleb slaps his hand down on the workspace to the side of him and runs his fingers over it. 'Your ex-girlfriend... girlfriend? No? Okay, yes, ex-girlfriend is not a fan of the stool.'

He narrows his eyes at me and I pray that I am mistaken about what is coming next.

'The one thing, however, that she can sit on, quite successfully, come to think of it—'

'Caleb, you're drunk.' I interrupt sharply, terrified that he might finish.

'I'm thinking more clearly than you are. What's he doing here? The last time I checked, you'd broken up, and now it's all nicey-nicey?'

'It's none of your business.' I clear my throat.

Caleb tilts his body in my direction and whispers, 'You deserve each other.'

'There's no need to whisper, everyone can hear you,' Jasper says, irritated. Caleb looks around, as if perplexed at where 'everyone' is.

'Great. So, let's all share our news with everyone.'

'You should get some sleep, Caleb.' I beg him with my eyes.

'No chance. There's sooooo much to catch *everyone* up on.'

'Please, Caleb?' I hear my voice shake as I beg again. That gets through to him.

'Weeeellll, I suppose it is late. Keep your hands to yourself, Jasper!' He points at Jasper before he stumbles into his room.

Jasper and I watch him as he shuts the door.

'Wow! Does that happen often?' Jasper asks, still staring at Caleb's shut bedroom door.

'Not as much nowadays. It was almost daily when I first

moved in. He'll wake up tomorrow morning as bright as a button and knock out five miles in thirty minutes.'

'I don't know what on earth made me think you could ever be with him.'

I say nothing and put a spoonful of dessert in my mouth. I encourage Jasper to do the same. I want to defend Caleb, but his behaviour tonight has deeply upset me.

'So...' Jasper continues. 'Do you want to bum around Notting Hill Market tomorrow? I can come and get you.'

'Exciting! What are you trying to buy?'

'I'm asking you out on a date, Scraps. Taking it back to square one. I've had a lot of time to think about what you said and you're right. We skipped a lot the first time round. If we're going to try again, let's try properly.'

I'm not ready to leave the friend zone yet. I know we kissed and it was nice, but I don't want to be attached to Jasper again. I need to keep things clear; but I can see he's nervously holding his breath. He knew it was a leap, but he took it anyway.

'Sure. How about I come to you instead and not call it a date, so there's no pressure?'

I actually hear him exhale.

'Great. Noon?'

'Perfect. If that's the case, let's get you a cab. I better get some sleep.'

We finish our desserts just as the car arrives, and I walk him to the door.

'I'm glad we did this, Aari. I made so many mistakes, I couldn't see a path back. I thought I'd really messed up and we were done.'

'I've done some pretty unforgivable things to you, too.'

'I'd forgive you for anything.' He plants a soft, full kiss on me one more time before he leaves.

I close the door, put my back against it and stare at the space Caleb slapped on the kitchen island. Jasper is wrong. He won't forgive me for Caleb; he said as much at lunch, and I just lied to him. I look at my watch. 00:45. This time only a couple of weeks ago, I was on that counter with Caleb's head between my thighs.

I run into my bathroom and throw up tonight's meal.

I can't carry this.

TWENTY-EIGHT

CALEB

The last week has been shit, but the last forty-eight hours were a firefighting nightmare and, in one particular instance, a fire-lighting extravaganza. I'm still getting contracts cancelling out of Singapore. We are getting paid, but the bottom seems to be falling out of the actual projects. So much so, that I broke my own rules and got in touch with Mel, asking if everything was all right. Mel, of course, told me everything was fine, but said I'd have to fly out to see to the finer details.

I scheduled a Monday-to-Friday trip in two weeks. Work authorised it in a flash, with Piers happily offering to accompany me. For someone who is supposed to be growing an entire continent, his workload seems surprisingly light. He's probably fuming. Ariella was gracious when she told me she'd ended her friendship with him. Rumour has it, she told him to sling his hook right in the middle of the office and everyone heard. Since then he's been cosying up to Nicole. That'll be fun to watch. Nicole is a beast and she'll eat Piers up like an amuse-bouche.

Home hasn't been great either. Ever since Ariella announced that Jasper could be back in the picture, I've wanted to smash everything in sight. The worst I thought I had to deal with last weekend was some horny Norwegian being more suggestive than Ariella was comfortable with, not Jasper wooing her by text.

I swear he does it on purpose. He waits for her to go away and then slides into her inbox. Of course, he managed to destroy his chances after Zambia with his behaviour at that lunch, so it's only a matter of time before he screws up again. I even toyed with having him and Zachary over for dinner to hurry it along, because Ariella is unbearable at the moment.

She was so bloody happy about exchanging texts with Jasper that, every time I touched her and she responded to me, unbearable guilt invaded her face. By Monday evening I'd grown a conscience, and stopped playing with her trigger points. Instead, I focused on trying to get Singapore to stop the cancellations, training myself, training the boys, avoiding Nicole and staying away from Ariella.

Lara, however, has been unintentionally entertaining. She started sending me nudes, asking me to guess who Ariella would prefer. When she got bored with that, she moved on to pictures of what she thought my junk looked like, with running commentary. It was actually quite funny. I won't admit it publicly, but being trolled by Lara is one of the more surprisingly fun things to have happened this week.

When I saw her name pop up on my phone on Friday with a picture attached, I was expecting more of the same, so I ignored it. Just as I was about to leave for the day, I finally turned my phone over to open it. Surprisingly, it was a bottle of Glenfiddich.

> You need to drink with me tonight. I don't want to be seen in public with you so I have found somewhere hidden. Flirt with me once, I'm leaving. 10 Lower Ground, Candover Street. Text when you get there. Don't press the bell.

I was curious. Jack wasn't returning my texts and Tim was working. I had no plans, other than to go home and drive myself crazy thinking about what Ariella and Jasper were up to at their dinner. Ugh. Lara it is.

The residential-looking door is tucked tightly under a small stairwell. Lara emerges when I text and leads me through a small, dark room, softly lit like a Prohibition-era drinking den. There is a burlesque act on a tiny stage moving to some slow music.

'She's not a stripper, lechy-eyes,' Lara informs me as she parks herself in one of two armchairs next to a small round table. She has already started on the bottle. A bald guy in braces silently drops off an additional glass and an ice bucket at our table.

'This place is amaz—'

'Shut up. You're not allowed to come back here or say anything about it. Members only and it's not exactly legal.'

Lara pours a neat whisky and hands it to me.

'Cheers.'

She knocks hers back and pours another one. I take a sip. There is no way I'm getting drunk with Lara. I cut to the chase.

'Why am I here?'

She ignores my dig, while making her disdain obvious.

'What's going on with you?' she asks, leaning forward.

'What do you mean?'

'You're acting... neutered. You're less grabby, haven't been your usual slimy self and aren't even acknowledging the low-hanging fruit.'

'Maybe if I didn't have to deal with all those dick pics you've been sending me all week...'

'Bollocks. I gave what's-her-chops from the lads' mag downstairs fifty quid to take you out for a drink.'

'I've no idea who you're talking about.'

'The one with the boobs that giggles, says "seen" at everything and won't stop jumping up and down when she claps.'

'Nope.'

'This is my point. She said she asked you, but you gave her some lame excuse and didn't bite.'

'You mean Di?'

'That's it. Di. She said you've been after her for a while. Now she's game, you're thanking her for the invite, but declining? I want to know what's going on.'

'Nothing.' Lara is the last person I want to talk to about this.

'That's what I thought. You've caught feelings. Serves you right. That's what you get when you stick your bits in places they don't belong. How bad is it?'

'Lara, find somebody else to play with.' I put my glass down and get ready to leave.

'Don't make me say it, I might vomit.'

'Say what?'

'Ariella can't go back to Jasper.'

'Why not?' I ask.

'Because, much to my disgust, I'm fairly sure she has feelings for you too. Yuck. I *am* going to throw up.' Lara balls up a fist and puts it to her closed mouth.

Everything stops; this is Lara I am talking to.

'She told you that, did she?' I get ready to catch her in a lie.

'Of course not. I'm not even sure she knows, but it's jumbled up in there somewhere. She won't shut up about you. She hardly ever spoke about Jasper, but with you she's a right bloody canary. It's annoying, but I love her, so I put up with it. Stop smiling. It's painfully depressing.'

She's still talking to Lara about me. My heart wants to burst out of my chest but I do my best to keep an indifferent exterior.

'Why are you telling me?'

'She's changing. She's alive and actually happy. She's taking risks, making the effort to come out, and is open to doing stuff that she may not be completely comfortable with – something that you've clearly taken advantage of.' Lara accuses. 'If she goes back to Jasper, all of that goes away. I like the new Ariella. It feels like the real Ariella; and, if that means I have to deal with you to keep her, then so be it.'

Lara is basically heavily hinting that we need to team up to kill Ariella and Jasper's relationship.

'Am I here to help you make this Jasper break-up permanent?'

'Bingo.'

I know for sure that, if I agree to this, we'll succeed.

'No. I'm not going to manipulate her into picking me. It has to be her choice.'

'Is it her choice that she tingles every time you touch her? To be fair, it seems Ariella has the terrible habit of falling in love with her kidnappers, so it's not all on you.' Shit. Lara sussed it.

'I may be flirting, but I'm not going to outright interfere with her relationship with Jasper. She needs to decide if she wants to be with him, by herself. I need her to choose me, freely. You're a feminist, Lara. Surely you know how consent works. Besides, any plan you've already cooked up can't be good.'

'You can drop the bullshit morality, Caleb. You have no idea what you're up against. Here.'

Lara grabs her phone and texts me the website of a restaurant walking distance away.

'They're having dinner there right now. You should go and see for yourself. Maybe you'll change your mind.'

That's why she picked this place. Bloody Lara.

'I'm not going to spy on her.'

'Suit yourself, but you're going to have to hop it. I have a date.'

. . .

I am filled with self-loathing as I order a drink in the restaurant's busy bar twenty minutes later, with a clear line of sight to Ariella and Jasper. Their eyes are trained on each other like there is no one else in the room, but there is a good, healthy distance between them in the corner booth they occupy. I should finish my drink and go home, but I don't. I find myself ordering another and then another. By the time their dinner is over, they are sitting so close together she is practically on his lap, with their arms closely intertwined.

I watch him hold her close as they make their way outside and get into a taxi together, no doubt going back to his. I double down on the drinks until I am eventually cut off by the barman, and stumble home, thinking the torment is over.

When I walk in on Ariella making them dessert and him looking like he owns my place, with slow music playing throughout the flat, I lose it. I only manage to regain control when I see how frightened I'm making her.

I don't want to see Ariella the next morning for all sorts of reasons, so I jump out of bed early, go for a run and end up at Tim's.

'You're round here a lot these days,' Em says, not looking pleased, when she opens the door.

'Good morning to you too, Em. Is Tim in?'

'We both know he's not the one you've come to see. You look a mess. Everyone's still asleep, so be quiet.'

I feel a mess.

'Any chance of a coffee?'

'Make your own bloody coffee. You're lucky I let you in after you all but shaved Alfie's beautiful hair and turned him into you.'

'He wouldn't stop asking at the barbers'. It's just hair. It'll grow back.'

'And that's the problem with you.'

'What?'

'It's not *just* hair. You do whatever you like and expect everyone else to just deal with it. Does it occur to you that, maybe, they have enough on their plate and don't want to have to deal with your shit too? Or that maybe, instead of making life harder, they might appreciate it if you made it easier?'

'Shit, Em. I didn't think it'd be a big deal. I'm sorry.'

'Don't apologise, just stop being a dick.'

'Too late for that, I'm afraid...' Last night comes flooding back and I try to hold myself together.

'I know that! How about you commit to— Caleb, what's wrong?'

'I'm such a shithead, Em.'

'It's Ariella, isn't it?'

Em pulls up a chair and sits opposite me, giving me her full attention. This is one of the things I like about Em. One minute she is ripping the shit out of you, and the next she's there for you, regardless of how pissed off she is. Tim is a lucky guy.

'I met up with her friend last night.'

'Caleb, you didn't sleep with her friend, did you?'

'Of course not.'

'Just asking... old habits et cetera. What happened?'

'She said Ariella had feelings for me and wanted to launch some counter-attack to remove Jasper from the picture. I said no.'

'She sounds awful.'

'She's actually all right.'

'Either way, you're winning morally there.'

'Not really. She gave me the details of the restaurant where they were having dinner...'

'Caleb, you *did not* spy on Ariella.'

'I did, and I got plastered. Then they were there when I got home, and I was an absolute arsehole.'

'Please tell me you didn't tell him you'd slept together.' Em has her face in her hands.

'No, not that it absolves me of anything. I threatened to tell him in front of her and she had to ask me to stop. Twice. I know I behaved deplorably, but I was so angry. She was in my house, looking happy with him, like I didn't even exist.'

'Have you apologised?'

'The way I behaved was so disgusting, an apology isn't going to come close.'

'Caleb, when we first spoke about Ariella you were supposed to tell her how you feel. Did you?'

'No.'

'You can't expect her to act on something she doesn't know.'

'I need to tell her.'

'You need to tell her,' Em repeats, leaning back.

'How the hell do I do that? I'm not going to be cooking and lighting candles after the crap I just pulled, am I? It won't surprise me if she's moved out by the time I get home.'

'You're going to have to try. How about I get rid of the kids and invite you both to dinner, along with Lou and Jack, one night? I promised I would, and Lou has some apologies to make. Maybe try to have a nice evening together, so it's not just you?'

'Are you kidding? With Lou?'

'She's working really hard and could use some forgiveness. Ariella strikes me as someone that would come if you told her Lou wanted to apologise and needs some support.'

'I don't like it.'

'Then you can do it on your own. If you change your mind, let me know.' She stands before she continues, 'Stay for breakfast. You shouldn't go home while you're feeling like this.'

Ariella doesn't return from her day out with Jasper until midnight, and I can't help my relief when I see that she's alone.

'Hi.' She stops when she spots me at the island.

'Hi. How was it?'

'Okay.'

She looks at me with uncertainty. I deserve it, so I try to reconnect.

'You don't have to be so awkward. Seriously, how did it go?'

'I don't want to fight, Caleb.'

'I don't want to fight either. I'm just asking how it went.'

'It was fine. I shouldn't be talking about Jasper with you anyway.'

'Why not?'

I know, I am an idiot, but I have nothing else. She maintains a neutral expression and ignores the question.

'I'm sorry for bringing Jasper home without telling you yesterday. I know that you're still infuriated about what he said at lunch, I won't ask him over again.' Wait, she's apologising?

'You did nothing wrong, Aari. My behaviour last night was appalling, and I should be apologising.'

'It's okay,' she responds automatically and turns towards her room.

Her wall is up. I reach out, grab her hand and pull her back.

'You're not going to do that. Tell me it's not okay.'

'It's fine, seriously.'

Her eyes don't meet mine.

'It's not fine, Aari. Tell me that I scared you. That I threatened you. That I betrayed you. That you don't trust me any more.'

A single tear falls and I pull her in to me.

'The way I behaved last night was inexcusable and you didn't deserve it. I know you're not going to believe this, but I promise I'll never do that to you again. I'll even be nice about Jasper.'

The first sob escapes, then she breaks down in my arms and I hold her while she cries. I don't think I can feel any worse. I hold her until she's got it all out and gently extracts herself from me.

'Can I make you some tea?'

She nods. 'I'll just go and wash my face.'

I pop the kettle on as I wait for her, praying I don't screw this up. By the time she returns, her tea is ready and steaming next to my coffee.

'I won't be an arsehole. How did it go?'

'I had a good day.' She smiles but looks unsure.

'But...' I ask gently, trying not to rock the boat.

'Something's missing.'

'Do you know what it is?'

'No, but we're going for a walk tomorrow. That might help.'

They're out again tomorrow? I swallow my irritation and make a light joke. 'What are you guys doing next weekend?' I chuckle.

'We're going to this Lebanese place he discovered and I'm going to show him some of the places in Shoreditch and Hackney that Seth took me. On Sunday, we're going to a lunchtime concert. We're doing stuff together to try to become friends again.'

For someone I genuinely believe is smarter than most of the general population, Ariella is as thick as bricks when it comes to Jasper. I listen as she excitedly tells me about her and Jasper's plans. From one dinner, he has just sewn up every Friday, Saturday and Sunday, three weekends in a row; and she thinks all of this a good idea. Lara was right. I had no idea what I was up against.

'Why are you asking about next weekend?'

'Next Saturday, Em's having a dinner party. Jack and Lou will be there. You're invited. Lou has been working on whatever's wrong with her and she needs to own up, ask forgiveness and be reassured that she has our support as she continues to heal and so on... I'll let Em know you have plans, and she'll reschedule.'

'I'll come. I'd like to support Louisa and Jack. I'll move things with Jas when I see him tomorrow. I'm seeing him on Friday and Sunday anyway, so he'll be fine.'

I didn't expect it to be this easy. Now all I have to do is tell Em that she has to find a way to kick her kids out, get Lou and Jack over, and throw a dinner party on Saturday night.

TWENTY-NINE

ARIELLA

I think I am finally finding some equilibrium. Since Caleb's intervention, I'm attending my 6 a.m. yoga class every Monday, Wednesday and Friday. It's making a difference. I feel centred and happy. I've inherited an Arctic Circle project everyone in my team was hesitant to touch; but I'm hungry for the challenge as Zambia is ticking along nicely and all it requires is regular check-ins. Save for any fires that erupt, we are three weeks ahead of schedule.

Rebuilding my friendship with Jasper has also helped. He convinced me to change my weekend patterns, which made sense. When we were together, I spent most of my weekends at home; now that we are apart, he suggested that I should be doing stuff with my weekends, so we put some activities in to get me started.

So far, they have been fun. Togetherness with him is so easy, we've had to adopt a no-kissing rule so that we don't blur the lines. We do, however, spend most of the time holding hands, and there is lots of hugging. I've missed his hugs.

Even Caleb, since our chat on Saturday, has been quietly neutral. We've returned to being comfortable around each other, and day-to-day life is back to being easy this week. We have restarted our *Wire* marathon and it's good to have my friend back there as well. I know he doesn't like Jasper, but he has been free of judgement and a good listener. Which is much more than I can say for Lara.

'The route to getting over Jasper isn't handing over all your free time. You do realise he has managed to monopolise all your weekends, and you've gleefully consented to this?'

Lara is in a foul mood as she moves salad leaves around on her plate. She has imposed a diet on herself and has grumbled all week. It's day three and it is only getting worse.

'Lara, why are you on a diet? Your body is amazing. You're not going to sustain eating salad three times a day, and it's making you really grumpy.'

'I know I'm gorgeous, but I can't fit into my favourite skirt! It cost an arm and a leg, and I have at least two million more wears left.'

'But you're miserable. I'm considering force-feeding you pasta to make you happy!'

'Nope. Must be done. Besides, you wouldn't understand. You're toned and glowing. Are you secretly still playing with Caleb's magic stick?' She waves her fork accusingly at me. I burst out laughing.

'No. I'm back at yoga. You should come.'

'Sweaty people in a hot, still room, shoving their bums in the air, trying not to fart? No thanks! Is it helping with your foot?'

'Sadly not. It still hurts. You should come to yoga, though.'

'I'd rather have salad for the foreseeable future.'

'Caleb came, and he was fine.'

'Still pretending to be supportive, is he?'

'He's not pretending. He's trying not to be so hard on Jasper.'

'Have you asked yourself why Caleb's being so nice?'

'We're friends.'

'Does your friend still make your body tingle?' She raises an eyebrow.

'No, actually. We haven't touched each other much since I got back from Norway.' I hear the disappointment in my voice.

Lara drops her fork. 'You *miss* the tingles. Ariella Mason, you dirty ho.'

'I do, a little,' I admit, embarrassed.

'Just ask him to make you tingle again. He won't mind.'

'Goodness no. That ruins things.'

'No, *you* ruined it last time with all your drama. I'm sure Caleb will gladly oblige. It's not like he's obliging anyone else at the moment.'

'It's not fair to Jasper, he said anyone but Caleb.'

'For the billionth time, Jasper is your ex-boyfriend. Everything you do right now is your decision only. You're single for a reason. That reason is Jasper. If you continue to behave like you are tied to Jasper, you're wasting everyone's and, most importantly, your time. Aaaarararrgghh!'

Lara shoves her plate away and puts her hand in the air and the waiter comes straight over.

'Sirloin and chips please, with the macaroni cheese. Please can you take this away?' She hands her plate over to the chuckling waiter.

'Of course, madam.'

'You'll feel much better in a minute,' I reassure her.

'Oh, I know I will. It's you I'm worried about. Fuck, I love that skirt!'

The chicken pie I make for dinner keeps me moving around the kitchen, and should be ready just after Caleb gets home. As predicted, he walks in just as I pop it in the oven. He's developed the habit of getting straight into the shower when he gets in from training, which I am immensely thankful for. When he emerges, he flops on the sofa.

'Hard day?' I smile at him.

'Absolute nightmare. Singapore is a shitshow and the team are driving me round the bend.' He looks beaten.

'Are you heading out there?'

'Yeah, Monday.'

I open a bottle of red I know he likes and pour us a glass each. He watches me quizzically as I bring them over to the couch, while we wait for the pie to do its thing in the oven.

'Why are you walking weird? It's funny, but it's super odd.' He chuckles for the first time.

'I think I did something to my foot arches in Norway, and they still hurt. I've been trying a couple of poses that might help.'

'Show me.'

I start to lift my foot arches to sit in chair pose, while still holding on to the wine glasses, and he immediately stops me.

'Now, that's a grimace.' He laughs.

'I'm glad you find it funny,' I say, rolling my eyes.

'I had the same problem about a year ago. I'll find my arch roller for you. If you come here, I think I can remember the exercises and pressure points the physio used.'

I sit on the couch and put my feet on his lap.

'Not so fast, Cleopatra. Sit up straight with your feet flat on the floor. Now, put your left foot on your right thigh. Good, pull your toes up, toward the ankle. Wait, hold it for ten seconds.'

I watch his serious face as he looks at his watch, timing my holds.

'Okay, good. Now the other foot. You'll be able to do this during the day, or when there's no one around to help you.'

He makes me repeat it five times on each foot, then gestures for me to put my feet back on his lap. When his warm hands grip my outer foot, I feel a tug between my legs, and I shift. Caleb shoots me a concerned look.

'Did that hurt? You okay?'

I manage a breathy 'Yes', before asking him to continue. He looks unconvinced, but turns his attention back to my feet. He applies gentle pressure on points that get to the areas of pain, but also other areas that connect to places that have nothing to do with my feet. He is focused and serious, which makes me thankful, because he can't see how I am reacting to his touch.

'I need to do some toe stretches, so they may hurt a little, but I'll make it fun.'

I nod, because anything else will give the way I am feeling away. He holds my left foot.

'This little piggy went to Norway with Lara...'

I laugh as he manipulates my pinkie toe gently.

'This little piggy had a date with Piers...'

I scrunch up my face and shake my head in regret, making him smile.

'This little piggy went to Zambia with clients...'

'Yay!' I cheer myself on, and he joins in.

'Which means, this little piggy is bravely conquering all her little fears!'

He gives me a warm smile that makes me feel proud of myself.

'And this little piggy cried wee-wee-wee I love Jasper, he's so amazing and wonderful and perfect, but I need to find myself.'

He laughs and I join him.

'Is that what I sound like?'

'Any similarities to any persons living or dead, represented in this arch-relieving exercise, are purely coincidental.'

I relax as he releases my foot. The second he takes hold of

the other, I let out a gasp so loud there is no way he didn't hear it. To cover my tracks, I ask him to please be careful. He raises an eyebrow at me, turns his attention back to my foot and continues.

'This little piggy likes Caleb's foot rub... This little piggy likes a little naughty sex...'

I hide my eyes behind my arm and giggle.

'This little piggy is getting horny...'

He's noticed. I want to die of embarrassment, so I avoid his eyes.

'But this little piggy thinks she'll be compromising her self-respect.'

I sneak a peek at him, but he is still concentrating on my toes. As I am about to look away, he looks right at me to deliver his last line.

'And this little piggy cried wee-wee-wee, I want you to kiss me, Caleb, but I can't deal with the eventual guilt that I'll feel when I see Jasper.'

I am straddling him and my mouth is on his before I can form my next thought.

'Aari,' is all Caleb says before he carries me into his bedroom and throws me on his bed.

'Take off your clothes,' he instructs.

There is so much desire coursing through me that I do as I am told, removing my vest and leggings. His eyes meet mine and we hold each other's gaze. He makes me feel confident and powerful.

'*All* your clothes.'

He nods at my underwear. I step out of them, feeling a little more self-conscious.

'You're so fucking perfect. Want to try an old favourite?' He inhales, as if to regain some control.

I nod slowly.

'Kneel on the bed, grab the headboard and separate your knees.'

I celebrate inside. I know what is coming. We did this that first weekend and it was sensational. I assume the position, eagerly waiting for Caleb's touch.

He makes me wait for what seems like for ever before his head appears between my knees, then guides my hips down to him and places me on his mouth. It doesn't take long for me to start to oscillate and pant, as my hips take over. I feel a bead of sweat make its way between my breasts and down my belly as I start building to an explosion. Caleb abruptly lifts my hip from his mouth and disappears.

'Put your hands on the bed,' he asks gruffly.

I comply as my build starts to ebb.

'Are you okay?' he asks, holding my hips from behind.

'Yes,' I whisper. With that, Caleb sinks into me from behind.

'Does this feel good?' he whispers, pausing.

'Yes.' I can barely get a breath out.

He starts off slowly, but his pace quickly builds, taking me with him. There is just no denying that Caleb and I have an uncanny ability to move in sync. It doesn't take long for me to tremble with him inside me. It grips me hard and fast, getting more intense with every stroke. As I ride my wave, I lift my body, knowing from experience that he enjoys the extra constriction it brings. Caleb moves even quicker and harder, almost out of control, pulling me towards him, increasingly tighter, before he releases a loud groan between clenched teeth. I love that sound. It makes me feel everything. Caleb collapses on his back and I snuggle up to him.

'I could do that with you all day, every day,' he sighs, smiling at me. Just then, the smoke alarm goes off.

'Pie!' I exclaim and we both rush out of the bedroom. Caleb grabs me and stops me from entering the living room.

'Wait here,' he commands.

The kitchen is full of smoke, slowly making its way across the ceiling to the living room. I rush to the windows to open them completely, letting the freezing winter air rush into the flat while Caleb takes the battery out of the smoke alarm. I dash to the oven Caleb turned off and gently open the door to let the rest of the smoke out. It takes a little while to get the house under control, by which point we are freezing.

'Shower?' Caleb suggests.

I follow him with no complaints. We wash the cold and the smoke off us, helping each other reach the places the other can't. When we emerge, we are squeaky clean.

'Can I stay?' I ask nervously, unsure of the answer. The last time I was in here, I was escorted out.

'Are you going to be weird in the morning?' He looks worried.

'No.'

'We can't mention the J-word.'

'Okay.'

A huge smile breaks across Caleb's face as he tugs the corner of my towel to unwrap me. 'Get in.'

I scramble into his bed, wet hair and all.

'Please don't move.'

He leaves the room and returns with my toothbrush, a blanket, our open bottle of wine, some cheese, crackers, ham from the fridge and a jug of water.

'Picnic?' he asks, laying it all on the table at the side of his bed.

I don't know why it touches me so much that he brought some dinner in for us, but it does. I lift up the duvet and encourage him in, then dive immediately on top of him to place my mouth on his. We spend the rest of the night snacking, having too much wine, laughing, talking and doing naughty things, until the sun comes up. We slip, almost too easily, back into the intense, indescribable intimacy we share when we are together and I relish the feeling.

I end up living in Caleb's room for the rest of the week, and he is right: on Friday morning, I feel so riddled with guilt, that I want to cancel seeing Jasper.

THIRTY

CALEB

'Are you okay? You seem a little tense,' Ariella asks as the taxi takes a turn.

I nod, but I'm more than a little fucking tense. I am downright pissed off. She didn't get back until just before 2 a.m., because she was out with Jasper.

I was in bed when I heard the front door open. A soft knock on my bedroom door followed shortly afterwards, so I pretended to be asleep, willing her to go to her room. If she had come in, I would have been screwed, because it would have left me with only two choices. The first was to let her stay, basically reinforcing my approval of her hanging out with Jasper until 2 a.m., which I am obviously vehemently opposed to. The second was to kick her out and deal with a very messy fallout, essentially taking us back to square one. Thankfully, she left.

I genuinely thought she was going to cancel dinner with Jasper. The last couple of days had left her covered in covertly placed hickies, which I proudly counted from bed as I watched her get into her yoga kit on Friday morning. I didn't come away unscathed. My shoulders and back are covered with fingernail scratches, which I happily wear as a badge of achievement, as she likes to keep her nails trimmed short. I like the way they feel, especially when I have forgotten they are there and am reminded when I reach for something.

I saw the guilt infiltrate her whole body when we talked about Jasper on Thursday night, and I would have put good money on her cancelling. By Friday evening, I would have lost all my cash.

I woke up dreading tonight, a feeling intensified by the news that dinner was going to be at Lou's because she wanted to cook to make amends, apparently. I went for a hard run to expend as much energy as I could.

When Ariella and I met in the living room to leave, she looked beautiful in the evening light. Her hair was swept into a loose bun from her make-up-free face and, even in her simple white V-neck tee, blue jeans and ballet flats, she looked regal.

Ariella interlaces her fingers in mine when we step out of the cab. 'Are you sure you're okay?'

The minute our hands entwine, I feel every negative feeling fall away.

'Yes, I'm fine. Just tired, that's all.'

She rubs my hand between hers. 'We have booze if all else fails.'

We walk into Lou's Knightsbridge apartment building and announce ourselves to the concierge, who promptly calls up to confirm we are expected. He quickly hangs up the phone, escorts us to the lift and selects the appropriate floor once the lift cabin opens.

We step out of the lift on the top floor and see Lou standing in her open doorway, with Em beside her. They are all smiles as we walk towards them.

'Hello, Ariella.'

'Hi, Louisa.' She smiles politely.

'Caleb.' Lou's smile disappears.

'Lou.' I beam back at her. A scowl starts to form, but she keeps control of it.

'Hi, Ariella.' Em shoves her way past Lou and wraps herself round Ariella.

'Hi, Em,' she responds with the same enthusiasm.

I'm next for a hug. Em will help out tonight. As she hugs me, she quickly whispers that Lou's sister and best friend will be joining us for dinner. Shit. There is no way the weekend that I slept with both of them isn't going to come up. When Em releases me, Lou steps aside to let us in.

During the walk to the living room, I calculate that Lou's apartment is about three times the size of mine. Well done, Jack. I smile to myself.

'Hey, Caleb,' Jack and Tim call just before we reach the living room.

They are both standing in a huge kitchen, next to a massive worktop, gesturing for me to join them. I hold up an index finger and follow the girls into the living room, which is framed by a huge terrace.

'Ariella, can I talk to you?' I ask, and she approaches me. 'Lou, can I use your terrace?'

'Sure, but shut the door – it's freezing out there.'

I lead Ariella outside. 'Things might get a little awkward tonight.'

'How come?' she says, reaching for my hand.

'Lou's sister, Luciana, and best friend, Genevieve, are going to join us tonight and they aren't very happy with me.'

'Why?'

'We've been intimate.'

She giggles. She's taking this a lot better than I thought she would.

'Caleb Black! Which one?'

'Both of them.'

'Do they know?' She now looks concerned.

'Yes. It was at the same—'

'At the same time? Caleb!'

'No, McJudgy. Separately, but at the same weekend away. Come on, it's cold out here.' I pull her coat round her. 'Let's get you warmed up.'

I open the sliding door and let us back into the luxurious living room. I take Ariella's coat from her, add mine to it, put them on the coat stand and head to the kitchen to meet the boys.

'Hey, guys. Got one of those for me?'

Jack opens the door to a hidden fridge, liberates a beer and hands one to me.

'Nice flat, Jack,' I say, raising an eyebrow.

'Please don't start? She's trying to make amends, Caleb.'

'Is she? Is that why Luci and Gen are on the guest list?'

'Both of you stop. Caleb, if it helps, be here to support Jack. And apart from giving you a hard time about Lou's birthday, Luci and Gen are pretty harmless,' Tim referees.

I want to list all the harm they could do, but I keep my mouth shut. All I need to do tonight is be on my best behaviour with Ariella.

'Fair enough. So, what's for dinner?'

'Soup, pasta, fish, meat and tiramisu.'

'Bloody hell, Lou's been busy.'

Jack smiles conspiratorially. 'She had it all delivered. The chef, sommelier and waitress just popped out; they should be back soon.'

'At least she put in the effort,' Tim adds.

Luciana and Genevieve arrive with the kitchen team, so we are called to dinner shortly afterwards. I take the seat in between Ariella and Em, with Louisa at the head of the table and Luciana at the other end.

Louisa stands up just before the first course is served.

'Thank you all for coming. I know I have a lot of apologies to make and some hard truths to hear, but for now I just wanted to share how grateful I am for you all. The team from Porto Sicilia are here and the chef would like to introduce tonight's menu.'

We all clap. As soon as the chef steps in, he stops.

'Ariella!' He walks straight to her, pronouncing her name in a thick Italian accent.

'Chef!' She smiles as she stands up, with her head respectfully bowed, but he gives her a big hug.

'It's been a long time. How are you?'

'I'm fine.' She beams. 'You?'

'Very well. You have to come by very soon.'

I catch the scowl on Louisa's face before she sees me looking at her and hides it.

Ariella nods as she sits, then looks at her hands, embarrassed. I interlace my fingers with hers under the table, where no one can see. The look she gives me makes everything in my chest warm.

After the chef describes the menu, he affectionately squeezes Ariella's shoulder as he leaves the room.

'So how do you know the chef, Ariella?' Genevieve asks.

It is the worst question anyone could've asked at that moment. I see Lou shoot her a look that could kill.

'Work.' She smiles, giving nothing else away. 'It's amazing to have him tonight, Lou. It's almost impossible to coax him out of his kitchen. Thank you.'

You wouldn't think she was calling Lou out for domestic abuse a month ago. Lou perks up at the conversation being directed her way, and takes over. It's the last we hear of Ariella and the chef's relationship for the rest of the night.

Dinner is fun, with incredible food and what seems like unlimited, amazing wine. Ariella spends most of it quietly absorbing and occasionally participating in the conversational flow between Luciana to her left and Genevieve opposite. I can't help listening, in between the conversations I am having with Em, Lou, Tim and Jack. Luciana and Genevieve are doing all the talking and Ariella is just asking leading questions. After the palate-cleanser that follows the osso buco, Louisa gently introduces her dessert spoon to the side of her wine glass.

'Thank you very much for coming, guys. I wanted to say thank you to Em and Tim, for being wonderful friends and sticking by me. I'm sorry. I'm doing my best to be better and I will never put you in such an awful position again.'

Em gives her a hug.

'Luci and Gen, thank you for being the best friends a girl could have. I'm sorry for my horrifying behaviour and I appreciate your understanding, but I'm relying on you to keep me in check. I'm only able to keep getting better with your help.'

'We love you, Lou!' they say in unison, blowing kisses at her from the other end of the table.

'Ariella, I'm sorry for the way I behaved that night, and I want to thank you for drawing my attention to it. Without you, I may still be that same person. Thank you for coming tonight and giving me another chance.'

I'm not buying any of it, but I say nothing and squeeze Ariella's hand.

'I'm humbled by the invitation, Louisa – thank you.'

I am next.

'Caleb, erm, thank you for being there for Jack.'

That's it for me. The whole table, including myself, laugh. Ariella manages a slight smile and squeezes my hand.

Finally, Louisa turns to Jack. 'Jack, I'm so, so sorry.' And she starts to cry, hard. Even I don't doubt that she means it.

Jack kneels by her chair and holds her. 'It's okay, we've done this already, Lou. We can get through this,' he consoles her.

'I've come to realise, that it's those you know will hold on to you in the dark, that matter the most. I know that we're not there yet, but...' Louisa stands up and gets on one knee, next to Jack. 'Do you think you would reconsider wanting to marry me?'

She was kicking the shit out of him a few weeks ago, and now she wants to be re-engaged? I spend all my energy trying to telepathically convince Jack to say no. I catch Tim's face. He looks like he's doing the same.

'Baby—' Jack starts.

No Jack, no. It's not a yes, but it's not a no either.

'I have something for you,' Louisa interrupts.

She takes a small box out from under the table. She opens it and Jack's face makes me want to jump over the table to have a look. He lifts what looks like a fob up to show everyone. The curved T is unmistakable. The whole table gasps. Lou only went and got Jack a Tesla. I even start to feel guilty, because I'd pushed for this dinner.

'Lou! This is too generous,' he gushes.

Tim darts a look at Em, who has a rictus smile frozen on her face. Good. I am not the only person who thinks this shit is weird. Jack, on the other hand, is kissing Lou and repeating, 'I love you' like a dedicated puppy that's pleased its owner hasn't kicked it in a few weeks. There will be no reaching him tonight. Lou, of course, is delighted as she settles back into her chair.

'It feels good to have this back on, baby.' She smiles, showing everyone the rock Jack spent the equivalent of close to a year's salary on. He's going to be paying that loan off for ever if he doesn't quickly clarify that 'Baby' didn't mean 'Let's get re-engaged'. I suppose, if it all goes pear-shaped, he can sell the Tesla. If it's in his name, that is. I chuckle – to myself, but Louisa catches it.

'What's so funny, Caleb?' She rounds on me to attack, before calming herself down mid-sentence. At least she is self-policing now.

'Nothing. Nice Tesla, Jack.'

I see Tim shut his eyes and Jack's knuckles go white. I really want to egg her on and dismantle the whole contrite show, but Luciana decides to have a go instead.

'Caleb, what Lou has just done tonight is the bravest thing I've ever seen anyone do,' she says, venom dripping from her words. 'We could fill this building with people you've treated like crap without any apologies.'

The last person I expect to speak up, just because she'd maintained a neutral position on everything up to this point, pitches in.

'Louisa is so lucky to have you ladies in her corner. How long have you been friends with Luciana and Louisa, Genevieve?' Ariella asks.

Luciana points an index finger at me. 'Long enough for *you* to have had zero impact.'

'Was that since you were kids, or—' Ariella tries again.

'You're such a scumbag, Caleb. Why would you laugh?' Genevieve piles on.

'Whoa!' Tim intervenes. 'Tonight isn't about Caleb, ladies. It's about Lou. I know you've had your grievances, but this isn't appropriate.'

They both pipe down.

'I'm sorry,' Ariella whispers, offering a sympathetic smile.

Luciana instantly cackles and turns to her. 'Wait until this emotionally desolate arsehole turns you into his plaything. You'll really be sorry then.'

Ariella smiles and nods quietly at Luciana, like she has just given her the best advice. It stings a little.

'Actually, Luciana,' Ariella starts as she adjusts herself, 'I'm a proud, card-carrying member of the Caleb plaything club, and I'm not sorry or ashamed. In fact, as a fully consenting single and unattached adult, I not only trust Caleb, but respect him too. When it ends and he moves on, I'll have nothing but gratitude and affection left for him.'

Yup. Ariella just told the whole table we are sleeping together. I can feel the anger rising from Tim, Jack has his 'holy shitballs' look, Louisa's mouth is open so wide something is bound to fly in there. Luci and Gen are quickly trying to work out a retort.

I hear Em mutter, 'Shit, you're on your own' under her breath before she shifts her chair away. Thanks, Em. Louisa is the next to speak.

'You're sleeping with Caleb.'

'Yes. I am.' Ariella smiles sweetly at Lou.

'And you're okay with him being completely devoid of feeling?'

Ariella laughs. Her reaction makes me feel like I have been stabbed in the chest.

'I'm more than okay with it. I'm learning a lot. No complaints here.' She smiles at me. The silence that settles in the room is deafening.

As if on cue, the waitress enters the room with dessert. We eat in complete silence through to coffee. Em tries to restart the conversation, but no one is biting, apart from Ariella. I catch Jack mouthing, 'You bastard' at me, and Tim's anger is nowhere near subsiding. At the end of the meal, the chef reappears and thanks us all, and the sommelier returns with rocks glasses and pours us all a cognac. Tim grabs his glass and is the first to get up. He walks over to Em and gives her a kiss on her head.

'I need air. Caleb, you coming?'

He doesn't need air at all; the air in the room is just fine. Jack also gets up. 'I'll join you guys.'

'I might just chill out here with Ariella...' I start.

'It's okay. I'm going to catch up with Chef.'

Ariella heads towards the kitchen. Of course she is. Shit. I get up with my glass and lead the way to the terrace. Jack quickly shuts the sliding door behind me and turns to lean against it.

'Guys. Help. How do I keep the Tesla, but tell Lou I don't want to get re-engage—'

'You just can't help yourself, can you?' Tim shouts at me, cutting Jack off.

'Look—'

'We're doing this first? Fine. You did say "she's like a puppy",' Jack adds.

'Things have changed.'

'No, they haven't!' Tim erupts.

'Nope,' Jack agrees. 'It'll be the same story when—' he tries to continue, but I just want him to stop.

'It's different this time, all right?'

'That's the best you've got?' Tim seethes.

'That's all I've got.'

'Then why is she referring to herself as your plaything?' Jack says, stirring.

'She doesn't know things are different; and she's only gone and started seeing bloody Jasper again. It's all a bit of a clusterfuck.'

'There's a bloody surprise. We told you to leave her alone, Caleb. You just couldn't, could you?' Tim challenges.

'I wasn't the married one, visiting her for cups of tea and bringing her flowers when she was on her own. Why would you even do that?' I spit back.

'Wait. What?' Jack stares at Tim.

'Don't make it sound like I was doing something wrong!' Tim points his finger in my face.

'You told Em, did you?' I fire back.

'Fuck you, Caleb!'

Tim is raging. I know I'm out of line and there is a chance I might end up over the balcony, but I am raging too. Tim and I square up to each other. I am almost hoping he throws the first punch.

'What the fuck is happening?!' Jack tries to step between us.

'Tim, it's Caleb. We knew this was going to happen. He always does this—'

'No. I don't always do this. I think I'm in love with her!'

'Shit,' Tim says, immediately backing down.

'He's not...' Jack tries to laugh it off.

Tim ignores him and reaches out his hand. 'I didn't know it was like that, mate.'

I take it and he pulls me in for a hug and a pat on the back.

'It is. Painfully. Fucking. So,' I respond.

'You going to tell her then? Because "I'm learning a lot" sounds more like a job placement than an epic romance,' Jack says.

'It doesn't help that Jasper's bloody hovering. I need to find a way to—' I start.

'Just tell her, mate. Let the chips fall,' Tim advises.

'What if she says it's all just physical for her?'

'Like you've said to every single female that has wandered across your path unassumingly up till now?' Jack chuckles.

I watch the street lights illuminate her face one by one as we head back to North London in the cab, and I feel uneasy. Ariella's admission felt good, but was soul-destroying at the same time. She stood up to take my punches by placing herself in the firing line, which thrilled me; but was it really just about the sex? Is that all it's ever going to be?

THIRTY-ONE

ARIELLA

'Drink?' I ask when we get home.

'Whisky,' he responds sharply.

'I was thinking more coffee for you and tea for me, but I'll join you.'

He looks at me quizzically for a couple of seconds, then just grunts and shrugs. He grabs two glasses, fills them both with whisky and slides one over the counter to me as he throws the contents of his glass down his throat. He is refilling his glass before I take my first sip. I've seen this Caleb before and I know what is coming. I try to get ahead of it.

'I'm sorry you were attacked tonight, Caleb. You didn't deserve it.' I reach out to rub his back, but he shifts away to get more whisky.

'Did you mean it?' he whispers.

'Mean what?'

'Forget it,' he says through clenched teeth. He tosses his third whisky back, slams the glass down and turns to his room.

'Did I miss something? I'm confused.'

'You seem to miss plenty of things, Ariella,' he says dismissively.

'What are you talking about?'

'You really pissed me off tonight, Aari,' he states softly, looking down at the floor. 'I get what you were trying to do, but for you to laugh when they called me emotionally desolate and devoid of feeling was just... gutting.'

'Caleb, you brag about your superhero-like ability to remain emotionally detached. You challenged me to ask any of the girls who stride through here, for goodness' sake.'

'And when was the last time you saw any girls stride through here?' he challenges, looking squarely at me.

'I know it's been a while...'

'And yet, for you, nothing has changed.' I hear Caleb try to control the volume of his voice.

'I don't understand.'

He takes two steps towards me before planting his feet.

'And another thing, you've never been my plaything, Ariella. Ever. I, on the other hand, am yours. You've always called the shots.'

It hits me all at once. That first night, I kissed him, then invited myself back to his room. I initiated things again that night after our shower. The next morning, he made me breakfast and kicked me out. Although he came to find me a few minutes after that, I had been the one to jump on him again. I'd climbed all over him after yoga. He put a stop to our kiss and ejected me from his room. I straddled him when he helped me with my foot. Even after the smoke alarm, after I'd asked to stay over, he'd brought us dinner and I'd pulled him right back into bed. I've been the initiator this entire time.

'I'm sorry, Caleb.' I feel predatory, even though Caleb was hardly pushing me away.

He sighs and hangs his head for a couple of seconds, before reaching out to pull me into him.

'Don't do it again. I'm fragile.' He smiles, letting me know our disagreement is over.

A feeling of immense relief floods through me.

I wake up early the next morning to find Caleb contorted around me, still dressed in last night's clothes, holding me tight, with his breath softly hitting the back of my neck. I feel happy, even as I start to replay last night's row in my head. I'm not a fighter. Caleb dragged the fight out of me last night and I did not enjoy it at all. Hopefully this will be the last time...

'Stop fidgeting, Ariella.' Caleb's groggy voice comes through as he kisses the back of my neck softly and shifts around me, making himself comfortable.

'Sorry. Morning.'

'Morning. Come here.' He pulls me in even tighter. 'Close your eyes. Go back to sleep.'

I look at the time. Jasper is going to be here in an hour to give me a ride home for lunch. I feel sick at the thought of telling Caleb, but I have to. I start quietly. 'Caleb? I need to get up. Jasper—'

'For goodness' sake!' he announces abruptly, untangling himself and snatching his shoes and jacket, before storming out. The door to his room slams so hard, it reverberates around the flat. I follow and barge into his room.

'Why are you angry now?'

'I just want to get some sleep, Ariella. I don't want to hear about you, Jasper and the sneaky shit you're getting up to!'

'There's no "sneaky shit". He's my friend!'

'The way *I'm* your friend?' he spits back.

'What's *that* supposed to mean?'

'Nothing. I'm trying to sleep.' He shuts his eyes and turns away.

'What do you mean?' I am not letting this go. His mood swings are getting unbearable.

'Are you doing more than friendly things with Jasper, Ariella?'

'No! We're just hanging out.'

'You do know tonguing each other's faces off isn't just hanging out, don't you?'

'For the last time, I'm not kissing Jasper. And even if I was, who cares? It's not like it matters!' I yell at him.

'Of course it matters!' he yells back.

'Why? Why the hell should it matter?' I shout at the top of my voice, raising my hands and my eyes to the sky in frustration.

He shouts louder and harder at me. 'Because I'm not running a sexual training course here. For the love of everyone's fucking sanity, how can you not see that I have feelings for you?'

Neither one of us moves. Caleb looks just as shocked as I am. He springs up, grabs his jacket, shoes and keys, then shoots to the front door barefoot.

'Caleb, wait!'

He makes it out of the flat and slams the door behind him. I am shaking when I call Jasper and make my excuses. The next call is going to be harder. I decide on a strategy as I return to my room and sit on the bed. I am going to keep it short. I lie back and make the call.

'Hello, Mommy.'

'Aari. We can't wait to see you later!'

'I'm really sorry, Mommy, I can't come today.'

'Oh no. Are you okay?'

'Yes. Can I come up for dinner during the week maybe?'

'You don't sound great, baby. I'm sure Daddy will be happy to come and pick you up. Honey, what's wrong? Please tell me, I'm worried... You sound like you're about to cry.'

I burst into tears. It's times like this that I know I need my mother. It isn't until I start to talk that I realise how much I needed to tell her everything. So I spill it all. I recount every last detail, including those that are inappropriate for a mother to hear, while she sits silently over the phone with me. When I finish, the phone is so hot against my ear, I put my earpods in, and as I do so I notice the clock. I have been talking solidly for nearly an hour. I check that my mother is still there.

'Mommy?'

'He finally told you.'

'You knew?'

'I wasn't sure at my birthday, but I was certain at lunch. From what you've said, my suspicion is he was trying to give you some space to decide whether it'd be him or Jasper. I guess he found out that he wasn't even in the running when you announced it merrily to the entire table at dinner last night. I imagine it would have been hard to hear that there was nothing deeper going on with you, other than...' Mommy is never at a loss for words.

'But there isn't anything deeper.'

'Oh honey, you're either lying to me or, even worse, you're lying to yourself.'

I am silent.

'For the last few months, all you've done is talk about Caleb. How proud you are of him, how hard he's working, how he got you a blanket; how you watched *The Sopranos* together, his Muay Thai class and students, how funny he is, some silly little thing he did. And you're happy or laughing the entire time. Jasper hasn't had a look-in. Have you considered the possibility that you might be a little more attached to Caleb than you'd like to admit, and that you might have feelings for him too?'

'I can't have feelings for Caleb!'

'Why not?'

'He's *Caleb*. And everyone will kill me.'

'I actually quite like Caleb.'

'I know. Why?'

'I have a hunch about him. Your father wasn't exactly an angel, y'know.'

'You said you and Daddy were meant to be.'

'Maybe, but it wasn't easy. He was some white army guy and I was an upper-class black girl with a "good name", so I really couldn't do any worse. He borderline stalked me until I agreed to a picnic with him. We had many more picnics after that. Then he showed up in my dorm one night with a bag that he said contained everything precious to him in the world. He asked me to hold on to it and wait for him because he was coming back, so I did. Within a year, your grandparents had disowned me, we were living in England, I was knocked up and we were planning a wedding. So, there were challenges. Anyway, the point I'm trying to make is, as long as you're honest with yourself and you follow your heart, it doesn't matter what anyone thinks. It'll be all right in the end.'

'I still don't know what to do.'

'Reaching out to him from a place of honesty might be a good place to start. It doesn't have to fit into a neat little box, it just has to be honest.'

I hear the front door shut and my heart stops.

'I think he's home.'

'Then I better let you go. No time like the present. I'll call for an update later.'

My mother hangs up without saying goodbye, removing any opportunity to delay.

I jump in the shower to stall for time. I stand under the water until it goes cold and I have to get out. I take my time moisturising, getting dressed, tidying my room and clipping my nails, but hunger eventually forces me out of my room to face him. The music in the living room is deafening. He's out of yesterday's clothes, in a T-shirt and tracksuit bottoms. I approach as he moves his shower-wet hair from his forehead and eats cereal at the island with his back to me. I startle him when I put my hand on his shoulder.

'I thought you'd gone,' he shouts over the music.

'Can you turn it down please? I want to talk to you.'

He moves his bowl out of the way to put his head down on the cold counter. After a few seconds, he gets up to turn the music down, but remains next to the speakers with his arms folded.

'Go,' he challenges.

'You're wonderful, Caleb...' I catch myself fidgeting.

'But...' he interrupts. I ignore him.

'...And I think the world of you...'

'But...' he repeats.

'Will you stop? This is hard for me,' I snap. He keeps quiet. 'Sorry, this can't be easy for you either, but I'm trying to find the right words to be honest with you.'

'Save it. I know what's coming. I've given this speech a million times.'

'Caleb, I can't live here if you don't let me try to work this out, so please let me say what I have to say.'

He walks to the couch and sits. I approach cautiously and join him.

'Okay. Talk.'

'When I first moved in, I couldn't imagine a day when we could become friends, but we have; and being friends with you has been instrumental in redefining a lot of things for me. Home used to be a place where I happily shut myself away, but with you here it's a place where I feel safe to open up. I definitely make more dangerous and challenging decisions with you around.' I smile at him. He returns a small one.

'I really look forward to being home with you. It doesn't matter if you're being silly, or you're annoyed, or you're tired – even if we're just on the couch watching TV. After I kissed you, I didn't think I'd care if you started seeing other people again. I thought we'd just end this and you could simply carry on, but that may have changed a little bit. I like waking up next to you and thinking of you waking up next to someone else hurts a little.

'I don't know what I'm trying to say, Caleb, but please will you forgive me and tell me you're not mad at me any more?'

Caleb bites a corner of his bottom lip as his eyebrows furrow, before he shakes his head.

'No. I think you know what you're trying to say, but you're afraid to say it.' He fixes me with an unforgiving stare and continues. 'I'm not going to let you sidestep it. I want you to tell me why the thought of me waking up next to someone else hurts.'

'I think of you as more than a friend.' I exhale.

'Do better.' Caleb sits back and re-folds his arms.

I clear my throat and avert my eyes. 'I think I've fallen for you.'

I feel a tear roll down my cheek, and then Caleb's palm on my face as he tilts my head so that my eyes meet his. He pulls me into a hug and I fit perfectly into him. I lie there quietly in his arms, listening to his heartbeat while we rise and fall with his breath.

'Should we select a picture and start drafting my missing person's flyer, for when we tell your dad?'

We both start laughing. It's nice to do that together again.

'Is that what happens now?' I ask, and Caleb erupts again.

'Ariella, don't freak out. Nothing happens now. I'm just happy that I'm not alone in this. I was a little nervous that it was just me.'

I lift my head and move up slowly to put my lips onto his. Caleb responds carefully, taking his time. It feels different. Kissing Caleb has always been exciting, but this feels somehow whole. I climb on to his lap to sit on his legs, and, as our kiss deepens, I pull him closer. He keeps his hands firmly on my waist and, when I realise they aren't going anywhere, I make the first move and start to tug on his T-shirt. He stops my hands.

'No, Aari.'

'No?' I repeat, disappointed.

'No. We know something's going on here, but I think we should give it some time before we jump in. Too many people are going to be hurt at your end of things. Your dad will kill me. I think Dahlia will be all right. Zachary probably wouldn't care, but Jasper...' Caleb shuts his eyes and lets his head drop back with a heavy sigh. 'This is going to destroy Jasper. I know I've been a bit adversarial, but I actually like the guy. He's uptight, but he's just trying to get his girlfriend back.'

Caleb lifts me off him. I am not happy about it.

'Stop sulking. If we are doing this, we should do this properly, which means I need to tell him. He can't hear it from anywhere else.'

'I'll tell Jasper,' I say. It can't come from Caleb.

'Let's tell him together. I don't know how he'll react.'

'I need to tell him alone. He won't appreciate the audience.'

'Understood, but we don't need to rush this. I leave for Singapore tomorrow. Maybe we should use the time apart to make sure we're not just high off the fumes of last week? We can make some solid decisions when I get back. In the meantime, let's keep things as they are?'

He strokes my face gently.

'I'm a little sad you're going away tomorrow.'

'Yeah. It's going to suck.' Caleb sighs. Then he lifts my hand, presses my palm against his mouth and sighs heavily into it. We just sit there for a while in silence, listening to each other breathe.

'Want to go for a walk?' I suggest after a while.

Caleb looks genuinely elated. 'I'd love to.'

THIRTY-TWO

CALEB

Thoughts of Ariella invade my thirteen-hour flight to Singapore. Even when I shut my eyes to get some sleep, she's right there. Yesterday almost didn't happen. I'd showered, packed my bags and reserved a hotel room near Heathrow. If I hadn't decided to eat at home, I'd be on this flight, relieved to be going away. Now I have a delicate stomach and an ache in my chest. There is no point pretending that it's not as bad as it is; I know I am in love with her.

The feelings thing was a bit of a cop-out, but I am glad I blurted that out instead of a massive declaration. I'll never forget the look on her face when she admitted she'd fallen for me. I wanted to make love to her there and then, but she looked so sad, I couldn't. I'm not someone you would normally associate with romance, but our walk through London yesterday, holding hands and kissing without a care in the world, felt pretty close to it.

Walking through arrivals in a daze, I feel someone tug the back of my jacket.

'Caleb!'

I come face to face with Melissa, joyfully glowing, her arms open wide and ready for a hug. I oblige quickly and put on my brightest smile. Crap.

'Melissa! What are you doing here?'

'Melissa? That's a bit formal,' she said.

She interlaces her arm with mine while I walk alongside her attempting to look happy. I can feel the sweat rolling down my neck and back. What is she doing shouting my name in public places and happily holding hands?

When we get to the car, her driver opens the Bentley's doors and I barely have my belt on before Mel closes in. Something huge has changed.

We check into our suite, but I have kept my reservation at the Hyatt just in case. I feel nauseous when we are greeted with familiarity by the same butler as last time.

'Welcome back, Mr Black.'

I have to end it, and quickly. When I do, all this will be gone and, surprisingly, I'm okay with that. My only worry is how it will affect work.

'I've cleared everything so I can spend the week with you,' she says, and giggles naughtily.

'Fantastic!' I walk to the window and stare out over the city. *Shit. Shit. Shit.*

'Maybe you could get rid of some of your meetings?'

'I can't, Mel, we agreed last time.'

'We'll see. Now, tell me – how much have you missed me?'

She wraps her arms round my waist from behind. I feel like I might vomit. I have to tell her, but I don't. Instead I turn to face her, lift her chin and kiss her chastely.

'Mel, I'm disgusting, starving and kind of wiped. How about I take a shower and we get some room service?'

She releases me.

'Sure. We're going to need all our energy. I've been so excited, I almost forgot to get the lawyers to insert another ridiculous clause into the prenup.'

I have to handle this carefully. I spend as long as I can get away with in the shower. When I emerge, room service has arrived, and we eat in bed. When we have almost finished eating, I give an exaggerated yawn and lie on my back. I pretend to fall asleep, but soon afterwards it's pretence no more.

Mel's in her dressing gown and glasses in bed, reading the paper, when I wake up.

'You must've been exhausted. It's eleven and you've missed your first two appointments. Lydia cancelled for you. You got the business anyway.'

'I need to tell you something, Mel,' I start quietly.

'You've met someone,' she delivers drily.

There is no point trying to hide it. We promised. No bullshit.

'Yes.'

'Can we survive alongside it?'

'We could, but I don't want to. I'm already nowhere near good enough for her.'

'Wow. Look who's made of boyfriend material after all.'

I note her irritation and try to temper it.

'I don't know. It's painful, keeping my hands to myself right now. The only way to do that is to come clean.'

It works, and she smiles. 'Farewell tour?'

'I don't think that's a good idea.'

'Who is she?'

'It's Ariella.'

She looks put out. 'You're dumping me for the annoying, spoilt black girl that moved in with you?'

'I'm asking you to let me go, Mel...'

'I thought I'd be the one ending this. Are you going to tell her about us?'

'Yes. Eventually. You changed my life, Mel.'

'And you're "asking me to let you go" because you know I have the power to change it again.'

It is a thinly veiled threat, masked behind what looks like a smile. I feel sick.

'I know you do.' This is getting uncomfortable.

'Stay with me this week and give me a chance to change your mind.'

'My mind is made up, Mel. I want you to know that you've been the closest thing I've ever had to a girlfriend; it wasn't just about the work.'

'Are you getting emotional, Caleb?' Mel grabs a pillow and hits me.

'Shut up!' I grab a pillow and retaliate and it descends into a pillow fight. Danger over. Phew.

I knew it was wrong, but I stayed with Melissa that week. I kept my hands to myself even though she made it almost impossible to do so. She stripped, got dressed and paraded her beautiful naked body in front of me. She slept next to me in various states of undress, constantly touching and cuddling me. If I wasn't so stupid, I would have known she was circling.

Thankfully, Ariella never rang, her texts were always short and they arrived at the same time each day. The limited contact made me crave her presence more, but I kept my focus on getting through the next few days.

I was positively gleeful on my last night in Singapore. Mel arranged for us to have a champagne-fuelled Michelin-star dinner in our suite to celebrate our last night together. She looked beautiful and, with every movement she made and look she gave me, I felt myself getting hard. I'd battled with keeping myself in check all week and won, but tonight there was nothing I could do to control it. I spent the meal keeping my groin covered.

After dinner, we sat on the balcony, drinking and chatting. I held on to my napkin for as long as I could.

When the food and staff are gone, Mel leads me by the hand to the bedroom before turning her back to me.

'Zip, please,' she asks softly.

I cover my anxiety with laughter. 'When did you get polite?'

'Since I'm about to ask you to make love to me. One last time.'

She drops her dress, then to her knees to undo my trousers.

'Mel, I can't.'

I try to grab her hands but my belt is gone and my fly is already open. She looks up at me from the floor with her big brown eyes.

'You're definitely ready now... I popped a little help in your cocktail earlier.'

She pulls down my trousers and my hard-on springs free. I am not only furious, I'm disgusted. I want to shove her away, leave and never see her again, but I swallow it all and plaster a smile on my face. I cannot lose Singapore's sales. She will take it all from me. They are already panicking about the cancelled projects and, if I fuck this up, I'm getting sacked.

She takes her time stroking me and then closes her mouth around me. Revulsion and loathing invade me, but I am trapped.

'Good boy,' she says, giggling, like she is talking to a pet.

It's degrading. I close my eyes so that I don't see her sickeningly take her time with me, pulling me into her mouth and out again. When she has had enough, she undresses me as I stand powerless and fearful of what pushing her away might unleash.

I've seen people who end up on the wrong side of Melissa. She delights in their destruction. After she peels away my shirt, she sits me down on the bed before she pushes me onto my back.

'I want you to make love to me, Caleb. Just one last time,' she demands. I try again.

'Mel, I'd rather we didn't.'

'Caleb, I made you. I just want this little thing. We're still friends, aren't we? You can keep it all, but I want this. You want your cancellations to stop, don't you? I can make that happen. Do this for me and you have my permission. I'll let you go and *she* will never know about tonight.'

She delivers her words so softly and calmly, while kissing me, that she could be telling me all the things she loves about me. I could shut this out. It would just be this last time. Ariella and I haven't made anything formal, we are still figuring it out, so this really isn't cheating, I try to convince myself, when I know otherwise. I shut my eyes as Mel kisses my chest and strokes my torso softly. She doesn't wait for my response.

'Stay still,' she instructs, impatiently.

She climbs on top and manoeuvres me inside her, as I lie as still as I possibly can underneath. She pulls my hands to her breasts, encouraging me to grab them, but I just want this to be over. She finally finds her stride as I try to block out the feeling of her body rocking back and forth on top of me. She grinds down deeper into herself, oscillating her hips and getting what she needs from me, eventually bringing herself to a climax and collapsing on top of me. At the very same time, I feel debased. She looks pleased with herself as she crawls up next to me, then wraps my arms round her.

'I just wanted to say goodbye, Caleb. Are you angry with me?' Mel has never cared what I think, so I tell her whatever vile thing she wants to hear.

'No. I understand,' I lie.

'I'll look after you, I promise. Are we still friends?'

'Of course we are.'

I lie there repulsed at myself, trying not to move, until she falls asleep. When she does, I stare at the ceiling in the dark room, trying to justify what has just happened. This is the last time with Mel. She knows we are done. It's good closure to have an encore. I know it's all bollocks. That's why I had my hands above my head the minute she let go, and kept my eyes shut, begging silently for it to stop. I check if she's sleeping deeply. When I'm satisfied she is, I quietly pack my things and write her a note.

Hey Mel,

Ridiculously early meeting. As usual it was an absolute pleasure. I still like you.

Your friend,

Caleb

I leave it on my side of the bed for her to find and take a car to my Hyatt room. I head straight into the shower to scrub every inch of me free of Melissa. It's not until I sit on the untouched bed in the dark, wrapped in nothing but a towel, that I feel like I can finally breathe. Then, for the very first time since that first night in a police cell, a wave of regret, fear and uncertainty hits me. Without any warning, I put my head in my hands and cry. All the tension, thoughts, turmoil and trappings of the last few weeks rush out.

When I've composed myself, I turn off my phone, get dressed, leave the clothes I was wearing that night on the floor of the hotel room, check out and head to the airport. I never want to come back here again.

THIRTY-THREE

ARIELLA

'Hi,' I say when Jasper opens the door excitedly. His hair is messy and his eyes are bright with mischief. He is barefoot, in his most worn jeans and an old Indiana Jones T-shirt I bought him from a French street market. The butterflies in my stomach jolt awake.

'Hi.' He puts out his hand. 'Come on in.'

I am not sure I want to. Jasper is supposed to be in his suit, fresh from work and a little stressed. The person I have just come face to face with looks like the boy I once knew.

Jasper helps me out of my coat and calls out for me to follow him as he half-jogs down the hallway. His excitement is infectious and I find myself hurrying after him. He stops in front of the living room, encouraging me to go in. Right in the middle of the room, where our furniture used to be, is our old tent, complete with wonky and taped-up poles. It is still covered in old stickers, holes we poked through and paint, pens and glitter.

Jasper has lit up the inside with fairy lights, added two cushions and laid snacks out in the middle.

'Back in a minute – get in!' he says with a laugh, heading to the kitchen.

I take off my shoes and jumper, get in and sit on a cushion. Jasper has been to Partridges. The snacks are a mixture of our favourite childhood British and American snacks.

The tent seems bigger than I remember. Zachary, Jasper and I used to spend hours in it reading my favourite childhood book *Chicken Licken*, telling stories, stashing food and sleeping over.

'Hey,' Jasper announces as he joins me, carrying a jug of water and another of red liquid.

'That's not Cherry Kool-Aid?' I screech.

'Yes, it is!' He laughs and nods.

'This is amazing, Jasper!'

'Remember this?' he says, pointing to a cluster of sparkly stickers I loved as a child.

We reminisce about how easy growing up together was as we work through the snacks, before he disappears again and returns with two supermarket pizzas from the oven, plus packet ham, Marmite and honey. He opens the cold ham, rips it up and drops it all over the pizza, and hands me a slice with honey slathered all over it. I make a face.

'Don't knock it till you've tried it. It tastes exactly like the ones Hugh made when Dahlia was away.'

He's right. Even the Marmite smell from his slice takes me back. For dessert, we, very dangerously, blowtorch some marsh-mallows to make s'mores. I insist on clearing up and refuse any offers of help. I feel safe and settled with Jasper. My Jasper. The boy I adored and the man I am in love with. I fell in love with that smile, that laugh, the crinkles at the corners of his eyes and that tiny scar on his temple. I love him all the more for that scar, because I know exactly how he got it, and all his others too. He knows everything about me; we have no secrets to discover, and our lives are so intricately woven they can't be separated. I am enough and I feel complete with him.

When I return to the living room, all the lights are off and the soft glow of a torch is emanating from the tent. I approach and find Jasper sitting on his cushion.

'Come in. Don't look so scared!' He smiles kindly.

As I do so, he clears his throat and temporarily blinds me with the torch as he adjusts it to point to his lap.

'Jasper—'

'Shhhh!' he interrupts. 'As Chicken Licken was going one day to the wood, "whack!" an acorn fell from a tree onto his head. "Gracious goodness me!" said Chicken Licken, "The sky must have fallen; I must go and tell the King."'

It is too much. I crawl over to him and put my palm over the page.

'Stop, please.'

'I'm sorry I got distracted and out of touch, Aari. Please don't leave me.'

I find his eyes. Jasper is and will always be part of my soul. 'Make love to me, Jasper,' I whisper. 'In here.'

His surprise is unmistakable.

'Scraps, I don't think we should until we figure out what's going on...' he starts.

'I don't care.'

For the first time ever, I can see that Jasper doesn't know what to do. I grab the bottom of his shirt and pull. His familiar, natural smell, our detergent and the warmth of his body envelop me as I take it off over his head. Jasper's eyes meet mine with a bewildered curiosity, like he is observing a creature he has never seen before.

'You're different,' he whispers.

'I am.'

I unbutton my shirt and dump it on top of his, then move closer to place my lips on his. It seems to wake him from his temporary paralysis. He gently transfers me onto my back before slowly peeling my jeans off. He plants a gentle kiss on my foot, and follows with kisses in a little trail up my body, eventually finishing at my lips. I undo his jeans and help him out of them as he hovers over me. Once he discards them he lets himself lie on top of me.

He separates my legs with his knees slowly, sits back and carefully slides my underwear towards him. He does it so softly that his touch makes my heart flutter. He then helps me into a sitting position to unclasp my bra. We sit there for a few seconds, looking at each other. I wait for desire to take hold of me as he takes his time savouring the moment between us. Maybe I just need to get back in tune with his body.

I lean forward to kiss him and carefully push him backwards until he is lying on his back. I make quick work of his boxers, travel to his hips and close my mouth around him. I hear his deep groan as I take as much of him as I can into my mouth. The love I feel for him in my heart is unconditional and immense, but I am really hoping for the magic, the lust and the need to turn up. I love him, trust him, adore him – but right now, I really need to want him.

It dawns on me that I've never seen Jasper like this. His total sexual submission to me is completely new. He'd always been the more dominant partner and I was always happy to do whatever he wanted. Jasper lets out another deep grunt and I hope that I am ready. Maybe if I just surrender to him, instead of trying to find a physical connection, it might change things. I push my body over him and kiss his lips. Moving my legs over, I straddle him without warning, guiding him into me. His eyes fly open as he lets out a long gasp as I dig deep for my desire.

'Aari...' he whispers as he meets me with a thrust.

I pull away from him and adjust myself to deepen his reach. With every thrust, Jasper sinks deeper, and I shut my eyes; wishing for any kind of sign that might be the beginnings of... anything. Supporting himself by holding on to my waist, Jasper suddenly sits up and wraps my legs round his hips. He presses our chests together as he holds on to the back of my head with his hand.

'Hold on, Scraps,' he whispers lovingly as he shifts his weight forward and lays me, gently, on my back.

As soon as he's checked I'm comfortable, Jasper pushes faster and harder into me. I meet his hips with mine and dig my hands into his bum to push him further in. I continue to try to summon a response – any kind of response – from myself. This is Jasper. I have loved him for as long as I can remember. Today has been wonderful. There is no reason why I shouldn't be in this moment, right along with him. Suddenly, Jasper's hands tighten around me, quickening.

'Shit!' He exhales, hard.

His climax quickly follows. He pushes hard, right through me, and I feel him empty himself into me just before he collapses on top of me.

'What was that, Aari?' Jasper laughs with laboured breath as he rolls over and pulls me into him. 'Are you okay? Was I too rough?'

'I'm fine, Jas. You were lovely.' I shake my head as a tear rolls down my cheek. Another tear follows and, soon, I can't stop the flow.

'I feel it too, Scraps,' Jasper says quietly, kissing my forehead as he holds me tighter.

When he looks at me, I see the years we've loved each other swimming in his eyes. Jasper pulls his boxers on, then picks up his T-shirt and pulls it over my head, before getting out of the tent to extend his hand.

'Shower?' he asks.

I let him lead me out of the tent and up the stairs into our bedroom's bathroom. He turns the shower on and helps me out of his shirt as the water warms.

'Together?' he asks.

I stand still as Jasper soaps my body and quietly starts to speak.

'When you left, you took everything, Scraps. Right down to your half-used toothpaste. I understood why you'd left the moment I stepped in here the next morning and realised that I could see your stuff was missing, but I couldn't tell what was missing. At some point, I'd stopped paying attention.

'I wasn't expecting us to be intimate today. I lugged that horrendous tent back on Sunday because I wanted to show you that our relationship is bigger than what we're going through now. My world is empty without you and I feel like I'm walking around with this massive hole in my chest. I want you to come back, Scraps; but, if you choose not to, I can find a way to move on. I'll find something to fill that hole. It'll be the wrong piece because I'll always be in love with you, but I'll make it work. Do you want me to wash your hair?'

I nod through my tears. He washes my hair in silence, putting in the conditioner and rinsing it out. He gives himself a quick wash and steps out of the shower to grab us some towels. When we re-enter the bedroom, I summon all my courage as I sit on the bed. Jasper, concerned, takes a squat in front of me.

'Scrappy, talk to me.'

I look at him and wipe the tears from my eyes.

'I slept with Caleb.'

Jasper lets out a deep sigh.

'I know, Aari. Well, I wasn't sure until now. I thought it might be him, but then he behaved so terribly that night after dinner that I didn't think it could be. It later occurred to me that he could've been behaving like that because he was reacting to seeing me.' Jasper shrugs.

'You're not mad at me?'

'I'm devastated, but maybe you needed to. It's a relief, to be honest. I can't begin to count the number of nights I lay awake, with my heart wondering who you were with that night.' He reaches out and holds my face. 'I can find a way to handle it, if you come back, Aari.'

'I'm sorry.'

'I know and I'm sorry too. I behaved badly at lunch. He came out of nowhere and suddenly he's at Sunday lunch with my family? I lost it a little when he told me he was falling for you and had the audacity to try to shake my hand on the promise that he wouldn't tell you until he thought you might feel the same. All I could imagine was him giving you those love bites. What happened before, what happened after. And I lost it. That was when I knew that I didn't deserve you in that state. I needed to zero out and build myself, and hopefully us, from the ground up again.'

'He told me he had feelings for me.'

'When?'

'Sunday.'

Jasper catches my eyes and holds my gaze.

'Do you have feelings for him?'

'I think so.'

Jasper stands silently and starts getting dressed.

'I'm sorry, Jasper.'

'Get dressed, Aari. I need to take you back home.'

'Can I just stay for a little bit?'

'No. I'm sorry. I'd love for you to stay but, if you think you have feelings for Caleb, it means you don't belong to me any more. There are some clothes in your cupboard. I couldn't help buying you stuff that I thought you might like. I'll drive you back.'

'What if I don't know what I want?'

'I love you, Aari, and I'll always be here if you need me, but sharing you will drive me mad.' He crosses the room, kisses my forehead and strokes my cheek, before looking away.

'Get dressed, Scraps, okay?'

I feel my heart break. 'I can't believe we're here,' I say, starting to cry.

'I can, and we're here because of me. I was so busy chasing a life I told myself we wanted that I completely forgot to be present. I wish I'd taken the time to be with you when I had you. I failed us.'

With that, Jasper leaves the room. I walk into the wardrobe and find some underwear, socks, jeans and a shirt. I feel so drained, I dress slowly. When I emerge, Jasper is dressed and sitting on the bed, car keys in hand and with his shoes on. He smiles through tear-filled eyes.

'Come on.'

Jasper drives sensibly through late-night London. I sit quietly with his hand over mine, fingers interlaced, shifting gears through the quiet streets. We get to Hampstead too quickly.

'I can't believe this is it.' I choke up.

'Don't be mistaken, Aari. This isn't it. I want him to rip your heart to pieces so that I can put you back together again, because I'll be waiting. I'll always be waiting. I won't ever stop waiting for you.'

THIRTY-FOUR

CALEB

I watched planes take off and land, chasing one Guatemalan rum with another, for the five hours it took for my flight to be called.

By boarding time, I was so drunk my ability to fly was questioned. I managed to successfully talk myself on by promising to be a good boy, and woke up when the wheels hit the tarmac at Heathrow. I navigated the arrivals process in a haze, and found my driver while carrying the world's loudest drummer going at full speed in my head. I switched on my phone and cleared all the call and text notifications from Mel.

I get home to find Ariella, buried in her duvet, asleep on the couch surrounded by that morning's newspapers, a mug of tea, half a packet of biscuits and all our remote controls. She looks so peaceful, revulsion at myself resurfaces. We have taken a while to get here but, now that it seems like we've made it, the first thing I do is mess it up.

I retreat quietly into my room and jump in the shower. It feels empty without her, but I accidentally wash my hair with her shampoo, which makes me chuckle, immediately making me feel that we'll be okay. I have to tell her about Singapore. She'll understand. If she doesn't, I'll make her. I return to the kitchen and pop the kettle on and my phone starts to vibrate, causing her to stir. I decline the call.

'Hi.' Her sleepy voice is hoarse.

'Hey.' I stop myself from rushing to her side. 'You look like you had a rough night.'

'I feel like it. How was Singapore?'

'Okay.' I swallow hard. Fuck. I can't. 'Anything been going on round here?'

She looks at me with furrowed brows. She knows.

'A little bit. Please can we catch up after I shower? You should know, woman from the hotel you stayed called a couple of times. She said they found a document on the pillow after you checked out. She said they will hold on to it until you call.'

She doesn't look at me once.

'Did she say anything else?'

'No. Just that you should call.'

She disappears into her room. Maybe Mel said something when she called. Maybe she's giving me the chance to admit it. I distract myself by making breakfast for both of us and she emerges just as I take some bacon from the grill for myself, after cutting up her grapefruit.

'Can I have one of those please?' she asks, pointing at my bacon sandwich. She still isn't looking at me. I cut it in two and hand her half.

'You okay?' I try to feel her out.

'Hungover,' she murmurs, so quietly I barely hear her.

The space between us is so tense, she has to know. When she picks up her grapefruit and returns it to the fridge, she stops in front of me and looks me right in the eye. I open my mouth and nothing emerges. I can't do this. I am a coward. I can't bring myself to tell her.

She suddenly shuts her eyes, clenches her fists and takes a deep breath.

'I slept with Jasper.'

It feels like someone has punched me in my gut so hard, it knocks the wind out of me. At the same time, relief washes over me. She doesn't know about Melissa. But she slept with Jasper? He must have done... something. Then again, this is Ariella. It's almost impossible to make her do anything she doesn't want to. They are back together. They have to be. That's the only explanation. I've been feeling like shit for nothing.

'What happened?' I am surprised at the anger in my voice, considering I am the undiscovered pot to her kettle.

She keeps her eyes closed, ashamed to look at me.

'I went over there to tell him and it just...' She claps her hands softly and then rubs them together slightly.

'I don't need a visual, Ariella.' I am fucking livid.

'It was me. It was my fault.'

They are definitely back together. I'm getting dumped.

'Did you bother to tell him why you were there?'

'Yes.'

'Was that before or after you screwed him?' I spit. It's rhetorical, dispatched to make her feel like shit.

'After.'

She ignores my venom. There's no use delaying the inevitable. I want her out of this flat now. If she thinks she's going to be kissing Jasper in the kitchen or I'll be bumping into him at breakfast, she has another thing coming.

'Let me guess. You're now back together, all is forgiven and you'll both be riding off into the sunset.'

'No. He made me get dressed and drove me home.'

'So, he kicked you out.'

'Yes.'

'Don't try too hard to make it sound like you want to be here, Ariella.'

'I *do* want to be here, but I knew what I was doing. At the time, I just didn't know what I wanted. I'm sorry.'

'Do you know what you want now?'

'I think I want you.'

She finally opens her eyes and I don't doubt it for a second. She's choosing me. I try to control my anger, but I can't. The train has already left the station.

'You *think* you want me? I need you to get away from me, Ariella. I can't look at you right now.'

She escapes to her room and I let her. I should have stuck with Mel. She was brutal, ravenous and demanding, but she came with some serious perks and knew what she wanted, with none of this emotional bullshit. Instead, I am here holding a heart that I don't particularly care to have in my hands, because some spoilt rich girl I burned it all to the ground for only *thinks* she wants me. I see Mel's name pop up again on my ringing phone, so I switch it off.

After a hot shower, I spend the rest of the day in my room. At seven, I order some dinner for us to show some civility, and knock gently on her bedroom door when it arrives. No response. I try a couple of times and am met with silence, so I open the door, to find Ariella and some of her stuff gone. I walk quickly to where my phone is charging, turn it on, clear more call and text notifications from Mel and call Lara. I'm adamant, as it rings, that if she is there I don't want to speak to her.

'Dick for brains,' Lara answers cheerily, laughing heartily at her insult.

I know immediately that Ariella isn't with her. I try anyway, just in case.

'Hello, Lara. Is Ariella there with you?'

'Ooooh! Has she taken my advice and is finally clawing back some of the dignity she lost rolling around in the mud with you?'

'Lara, I just need to know if she's there.' I hear my voice crack.

'Caleb. What did you do?!'

'What did *I* do? Have you talked to your friend lately?'

'That stupid girl. I told her not to tell you.'

'You knew? Well, there's a surprise.'

'Of course I knew. She's been self-flagellating since she got home last night. I was all for telling you, so she could rub it in your face and dump you, as part of my whole "pick neither one of those arseholes" agenda. She, however, chose to tell you everything because she wanted to have total honesty, which we both know you're incapable of. I completely forgot about your superhero-like ability to fuck everything up!'

She laughs to the point where she is struggling to breathe. I quietly hope she suffocates. I am not calling an ambulance. I have no idea where she lives. That's my excuse. Someone will find her in a few days. Maybe.

'I don't know why I was worried!' She sighs happily, finally gaining control of herself.

'Have you finished enjoying yourself?'

'Actually, no. Wait. Is that a tear? This is such an emotional phone call for me... Do you think she might be back at Jasper's right now? Livin' la vida horizontal loca?'

Bloody hell, Lara is irritating. I hang up. While I am ruminating over whether or not I should just call her, a text comes through from her.

> Hey dipshit. Try her parents. ANY idiot knows that's probably her most likely location. Oh, and if she isn't there, can you call me and let me know how they reacted to you losing their daughter? Pleeeaaaassseee...

I weigh up calling Ariella versus calling her parents. I dial the lesser of the two ego-crushing choices. Please let it be Dahlia.

'Hugh Mason.'

Shit.

'Evening, Mr Mason. It's Caleb.'

'Caleb who?'

Hugh Mason knows exactly who I am.

'Caleb Black? Ariella's flatmate?'

'Oh, you. What do you want?'

'I was just wondering if Ariella is there?'

'Why?'

I scramble. 'I got home and she wasn't here, so I just wanted to make sure she was with you.'

'Why the concern?'

'No concern. I mean, of course I'm concerned. I'm just making sure everything is okay.'

'Is it usual for you to call around, tracking my daughter?'

In the back I hear Ariella call out.

'Daddy, I need you! Mommy is using American words again.'

I immediately relax. She's safe. She's home and not with Jasper. I hear Dahlia respond.

'You're such a cry-baby. It's a valid word. Your father isn't going to help you. Can you calculate my triple word score please?'

A loud sigh comes from the other end of the phone and Hugh Mason hangs up. Just then, I notice a Post-it note on the floor by the fridge.

I'm really sorry about what happened. I know you're angry. I'm moving home for a while to give you some space. I'll move out if you want me to. I am so, so sorry Caleb. I really am. Aari xxx

Before I can help myself, I am calling her. I know I am going to ask her to come home. I don't care if she slept with Jasper. She made a mistake, and so did I. When it hits her voicemail, I hang up. I'm going to come clean about Melissa. We both messed up. We can start again.

'Can we talk?' I know she won't like me doing this at her desk, in the middle of the day at work, but she has left me no choice.

She pauses, before nodding.

'Not here, though. Is that okay?'

'Will you please come home tonight?' I like the way 'come home' sounds.

'Okay,' she acquiesces, giving me an embarrassed 'please, not here?' look.

It gives me the steam I need to power through the day. Just before I leave, Lara quickly sneaks into my dome.

'What do you want?' I complain.

'Shut up, she's gone to the loo,' she whispers. She's looking behind herself every five seconds.

'I don't know what you're—'

'Shut up, thicko, and listen. For some inexplicable reason, she's bought your bullshit. Be nice. She's blowing up everything by choosing you. Drag yourself up from the gutter in which you dwell, and prove her twenty-five per cent right. That's your high score. It doesn't get any higher because we both know you don't deserve her. I was never fucking here. Bloody hell! I hate you so much! Why you?!' And with that, Lara is gone.

THIRTY-FIVE

ARIELLA

'Hi.' I enter the flat, embarrassed and ashamed.

'Cheese on toast?' Caleb's smile from the kitchen is warm and forgiving. It hurts because I know I don't deserve it.

'Yes, please.'

He pops a couple of loaded slices under the grill and pours us some wine.

'I know you love him...' Caleb's phone starts to vibrate loudly against the kitchen counter before he sends it to voice-mail. 'But why did you do it?'

I wipe away the tear rolling down my cheek.

'I intended to say goodbye, but then I had a wobble. I am so sorry, Caleb.'

'I should have listened.' His phone starts buzzing again and he silences it swiftly.

'I hurt you. I understand why you didn't want me around.'

'I do want you around, but only if you want to be.'

I smell the toast burning just as Caleb grabs the grill pan and tosses it on the top quickly with bare fingers. I dart round the counter, flick on the tap and hold his fingers under cold running water. Unexpectedly, Caleb puts his free arm round me to pull me close. I close my eyes and breathe him in.

'Tell me you want only me,' he asks solemnly.

'I want only you.' And I mean it.

Just as he shuts off the tap, his phone starts vibrating again. He sends it to voicemail.

'Want to get that? It seems important,' I say, happy to wait.

'No. Nothing is more important than you, here with me, right now.' We silently enter a space, dammed by our emotions, where I feel no one can touch us and, in that moment, I know that I'm exactly where I want to be.

A LETTER FROM THE AUTHOR

It's an absolute privilege to share *Roommates* with you and I hope you enjoyed your journey with Ariella and Caleb. If you would like to join my reader community to have exclusive access to new releases, bonus content and other little surprises, please sign up for my newsletter!

www.stormpublishing.co/ola-tundun

For a debut author, a short review can make all the difference in encouraging a reader to discover my book for the first time. If you enjoyed my book and can spare a few moments to leave a review, I'd be immensely grateful. Thank you so much!

I'm drawn to exploring characters who the reader recognises and finds hard to judge, and who are rarely truly guilty or innocent of their less-than-honourable acts. I enjoy finding the beauty in the messiness of life, encouraging the reader to reconsider where they stand on a series of modern issues while enjoying a fast and fun read.

Thank you once again for being part of this unbelievable journey with me and I hope we can stay in touch – there is so much more to come!

Ola x

ACKNOWLEDGEMENTS

This is a dream I never dared to have until Emily Glenister made a home for me at DHH Literary Agency. My dear Fairy God Agent, thank you for letting me in, nurturing my hopes and helping to realise my dreams.

To Emily Gowers and everyone at Storm Publishing – thank you for welcoming me to a community that I am honoured to be a part of. To be included in this exciting journey Storm is embarking on is an absolute privilege and I am immensely grateful to be part of it.

For all the people who gave me the strength to dare:

Myriam, thank you for being my fear-buster. Ashley, thank you for being my cheerleader. Oriton, thank you for harassing me for more pages and for the long nights you spent helping to make sense of my indecision. Debola, thank you for being my ride or die FOR LYFE. Your worrying enthusiasm and sheer determination to fight people on social media for these characters is one of the millions of reasons why my love for you is unshakable. Nataliya, thank you for your dependable honesty; your perspective during this process was essential. Diana, thank you for your generosity with your experience and the naughty foodie trips. Els, thank you for your softness and empathy. Lola, thank you for encouraging me past my boundaries. Natalie and Mon, thank you for pushing doors open and shoving me through them when you had to. Saskia, thank you for your enthusiasm for this book, it came through when I needed it the most. Iwona, thank you for helping to create balance when I am incapable. Josie, thank you for those early giggles, two chapters in.

Seun, Huma, Mr J., Ayomi, Jeannette, Nicky, Neema, Yael, Beejal, Kay, Zainab, Sara, Bisola, Matthew, Sarveen, Esther, Dave and Segun – I repeatedly told you this could be a hot mess; but you cheered me on anyway. I know you have quietly built a trampoline to catch me if I fall. The commitment with which you have consistently, and sometimes aggressively, tried to convince me that it won't be needed, fires my belief in myself. Let's just keep it close though.

To my extended family who find out about this book from 'other' sources, the author of this book only looks like me. All similarities are purely coincidental, so please feel free to purchase this at full price and enjoy it, knowing it had absolutely nothing to do with me.

To the men who helped keep me honest – Spencer, your kindness and unique perspective gave me the confidence to keep going. Thank you for meeting and seeing these characters exactly as they are. Dominic, I wouldn't be here without your gentle, honest guidance and ruthless chopping suggestions. You inspire me to keep getting better.

To the loves of my life, my husband and daughter. The space, patience, encouragement, pride and love that I am showered with daily, feeds everything that I am.

Most of all, to God, my creator, keeper and protector. I am humbled by your blessings and grace.